"DON'T SCREAM," The voice warned her as a hand cupped her mouth, and another slid around her waist.

Tory stood stock still. She knew who it was; there was no mistaking that compelling voice, or that accent.

As if he read her mind, he whispered against her ear, "I've come to collect my wager."

"Are you mad?" she demanded.

"No, just determined."

He pulled her even closer, so close that Tory could feel the warmth of him through the thin silk drawers that she wore. His hand splayed across her waist, fingers extending. Then, abruptly, he released her. "Turn around," he said, his voice a growl.

Tory did so, slowly. "Just what is it that you want if it's not money?"

How naive she sounded, Rhys thought. He detected no fear, just confusion on her part. "A kiss."

Other *Leisure* Books By Gail Link:

WOLF'S EMBRACE

GAIL LINK

LEISURE BOOKS NEW YORK CITY

A LEISURE BOOK®

November, 1991

Published by

Dorchester Publishing Co., Inc.
276 Fifth Avenue
New York, NY 10001

This book is gratefully dedicated to Joan Hohl, sister of my soul, to say thank you for all the words of encouragement and support; for your keen sense of humor; for your intelligence—which always cuts deep and runs true and isn't afraid to ask what if?; and especially for sharing the myth and the music.

Gracias, amiga!

Acknowledgments

My gratitude to two ladies who believed in me and my work: my agent, MaryAnne Colas, and my editor, Alicia Condon, who both saw the possibilities and were willing to take a chance.

To Kathie Seidick for your cool wit and your caring warmth.

To Rita Clay Estrada for showing me Texas and giving me a sense of place. "Old times, good times, all times."

Much thanks to the people I'm proud to call friends!

And, most especially, to my parents: for my Mom—the wind beneath my wings—and to my Dad—the first man I'll remember, the last man I'll forget.

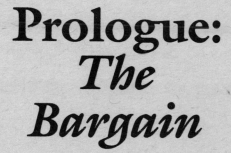

Prologue: *The* *Bargain*

Texas 1877

"Papa, you can't be serious!"

"I assure you that I am." Sam Reitenauer poured himself a splash of whiskey and turned to face his daughter. "Very." He drank the whiskey in one large swallow.

"But why?" she demanded, coming to stand beside his desk.

"Because you wouldn't decide," came Sam's firm reply.

"I can't believe that you'd do this to me," was her incredulous response.

"Believe it," her father stated emphatically. "I cannot allow this situation to go on any longer. The years are going by too fast; I'll not be here forever, you know." If his child didn't think about that fact, Sam did—more so since the passing of his wife, Christina, the previous year. "I want to see you settled."

"To someone I've never seen, never met? It's ridiculous!" the feminine voice snapped as she began to pace back and forth.

"Ridiculous or not, it's done."

"I'll refuse."

"Do that," he said, "and you risk losing the ranch." It was his trump card and he had no hesitation in playing it.

"You wouldn't disinherit me?" she asked, slapping her hands down on the polished wood of the desk, scattering some papers lying there. She could read the answer in his pale blue eyes. No words were needed between them. He would.

"I don't want to hurt you, *Liebchen*, but you need a man."

"There are plenty of men on the ranch," she countered.

"Damn it, you're deliberately misunderstanding me," he shouted. "You need a *husband*. Someone to be here for you when I'm gone."

"Then I shall choose my own," she responded frostily.

"If I allow you to do that, I'll wait another lifetime. You're too exacting, my girl. No. I have chosen for you."

"And just *whom* have you chosen? Where's he from?" She straightened; her feet, clad in soft, knee-high moccasins, made no sound as she crossed the room and sank onto an oaken settle.

Absently she fingered the blue-and-cream quilt that lay across the back rails, rubbing the pattern of raised stars.

"Why would any self-respecting man allow himself to have a wife chosen for him?"

Her father smiled with the thought of how very American his child was. In the old country, the choosing of a mate was always the concern of the parents. "He answered my advertisement in the paper."

"A notice . . . in a newspaper?" she asked, not quite believing her ears.

"Yes, an advertisement. You'll be pleased to know that I received numerous replies."

Her tone bitter, she replied, "No doubt. Who wouldn't want to get their hands on one of the largest ranches in Texas?"

Her father smiled strangely. "The ranch wasn't mentioned."

"It wasn't?" his daughter questioned. "Just what did you say in this notice?"

From the pocket of his plain brown vest Sam produced a folded piece of paper. He got up from his desk and went to his daughter, giving it to her.

Taking the ad in her slim, leather-gloved hand, she read the contents swiftly:

Husband needed. Must be in good health, strong. No older than forty. Fee paid.
Send replies to Samuel Reitenauer,
Menger Hotel, San Antonio, Texas.

"Fee paid?" was the acid query. "Just how much was I worth?" she paused, clenching her fingers into her palm. "Or should I ask how much you paid for this stud?"

"Now *Liebchen*, don't be like that," he coaxed.

"Like what, Papa?" She stood, facing him. "What's a husband worth on the open market? What is the price that a man will sell himself for? I hope that it wasn't too cheap," she commented bitterly. "I'd hate to think I was getting someone who didn't value himself."

"That's none of your affair."

It was hard to believe that the young woman could be further incensed, but she was. "Of course it is. How much?"

"He is worth it, whatever I had to pay."

"I'll just bet. Now tell me. How much?"

"Whatever I paid for him wasn't near what I would pay to see you happy, to see you settled."

"Papa, I am happy; I am settled. The ranch is my life."

"I know," her father replied, a trace of sadness creeping into his tone. "It's too much for you to handle by yourself." He didn't doubt his daughter's iron will, nor her ability. Having had the benefit of someone to share his life with, Sam wanted that, especially now, for his child. A day didn't go by that he didn't miss the gentle calm Christina had brought to their union. He savored the memory of that love and believed that it was his duty to provide for the future, both for his daughter and for the ranch.

"You need a man—if for no other reason than

14

to present me with the grandchildren I've always wanted."

"There's time for that," she protested.

"You are twenty-three, Victoria. All the women your age have been married for years. They all have families. There is no use talking about it any longer. It's been decided."

"You won't change your mind?" she asked.

"No, I won't change my mind. Plans are being made for his arrival."

Sam's gnarled hand reached out and stroked the contour of her cheek. "It's for the best. Trust me, *Liebchen*."

She had always trusted him, she thought. But marriage to a stranger? It wasn't fair. She'd refuse. She'd . . . do what?

Tory had spoken the truth. The ranch was her life. She'd been exiled once before, when she was a child, because of the danger of having a Union sympathizer father in Confederate-held territory. While the conflict raged, she was forced to live with a cousin of her mother's in Philadelphia. It was a nice place, but it wasn't home. It wasn't the softly rolling hills, the blended colors of bluebonnet and Indian paintbrush. It was regulation and decorum, remembering one's place in society. It wasn't laughter and freedom, racing one's mount across acres of open ground, hearing the sound of voices, at ease with the combination of German, English, and Spanish.

If she denied her father's request—nay, command—Tory would have to turn her back on the land and the heritage that she loved. She couldn't permit that to happen. Never again. This land was too much a part of her.

Victoria resigned herself to her fate.

Her softly spoken "Yes" brought a grin to the old man's features. He placed a swift kiss on her forehead and left the study.

A sudden hard smile curved her full mouth.

She might have to marry, but she didn't have to be a *wife*. This man would find that his bride had a mind of her own.

LONDON

"Please take a seat inside, sir, and I shall see if his lordship is receiving just yet."

"I believe he *will* see me when you show him my card," the portly man pronounced as he removed his hat and coat and gave them to another waiting footman while the first he'd addressed carried his card on a silver salver towards the back of the elegant townhouse in Berkeley Square.

Jason Beaudré eased himself into one of the leather chairs and let his keen gaze survey the room. Gone were quite a few of the paintings that had hung on the walls; missing also were several *objets d'art*, as well as the gold and silver Georgian clock which he knew to have been given to one of the daughters of the house by her French lover, a vicomte, before he met his death at the hands of an ugly, angry mob in Paris. Truth be told, Jason acknowledged, there wasn't much about this man and his family that he didn't know. It was his business to be informed, and he was. He could easily enlighten his lordship, should he wish to know, about just how much he was worth, down to the last Farthing, though Jason had a hunch that this man already possessed that information. Why else would he have answered the advertisement in the London *Times*?

He was well aware that Samuel Reitenauer had hundreds of applicants for the position he wished filled. His job, as Sam's man of business in England, was to vet the numerous respondents who were willing, for whatever reason, to become a husband. He'd been tempted to dismiss the earl's request as soon as it had crossed his desk. He knew the reputation both the man's father and his older wastrel brother had enjoyed. However, his promise to help Sam superseded his own reluctance. Surprisingly, the earl turned out to be the best candidate among the applicants for the job, and he'd said so to Sam.

Sam Reitenauer obviously agreed, for of all the many responses he'd received personally, he'd sent notice to Jason to seek out the earl and procure his services.

"I understand you wish to see me, Mr. Beaudré?"

Jason stood as quickly as he could. There was no ignoring the tone of authority in that polished voice. Even though this man had been raised the younger son, he still had the unmistakable arrogance of the aristocrat.

Jason smiled. He'd heard that same timbre in Sam's voice.

Rhys Alexander Fitzgerald Buchanan, the Earl of Derran, walked into the room and extended his hand.

"Good of you to see me so early in the day, my lord."

"I appreciate your coming to my home instead of insisting that this meeting be held in your office." Rhys motioned for Jason to re-seat himself as Rhys pulled a bell cord, then sat opposite Jason.

"I have brought the necessary papers for you to sign. Of course you'll wish for your solicitor to look them over." Jason opened his leather portfolio and withdrew several documents and handed them to the earl.

"Yes, my lord?" spoke the butler, Kinsenning, from the doorway.

Rhys turned his head and said, "Bring coffee for two."

"Very good, my lord," was the butler's response before he left as silently as he had come.

Rhys quickly scanned the top copy, flipping through the pages until he came to the agreed-upon sum. His hand tightened on the page. It was enough to cover the huge debts incurred by his father and his elder brother, with enough left over to see that no further rape of the remaining estates would be necessary. His mother and his younger sister would be provided for, not left to the whims of the creditors.

"Your Mr. Reitenauer appears more than generous."

"It wasn't in either his interest or yours to haggle, my lord." Beaudré looked the earl square in the eye. "You could have asked for much more."

"I think not," was the clipped reply.

At that moment, a knock sounded on the door and a footman arrived with a silver coffee service.

While the man, attired in the earl's livery, poured their coffee, Jason kept his eyes trained on the younger man opposite. He could see that he'd struck a nerve when he mentioned money. The cold arrogance in those wintery gray eyes was unlike the greedy, profligate look the earl's late older brother had possessed. Jason's judgment was proving correct.

"I can't understand it, Rhys. Were you really almost penniless?"

Rhys smiled, a cynical twist to his fine mouth. "Not yet in Queer Street, but almost there. What father didn't gamble away, Tony managed to squander." He pulled the woman closer into his embrace, adjusting the blankets over their nude bodies. "Christ, when I think of the way mother looked when the will was read and the creditors came out of the air, all dunning her for their share." Bitterness edged his deep voice. "It seems hard to believe that between them they succeeded in destroying a fortune that it took generations to build."

"I'm sure the countess was devastated."

"No, surprisingly, Mother was a good deal stronger than I expected."

Lady Beckworth-Bridge slipped from his arms and left the warmth of the bed to get more champagne.

Rhys watched her pouring the bubbly liquid, admiring the trim figure she possessed. No one would guess that she'd borne three children. Anne was a handsome woman in her late thirties, older than Rhys, a widow, and his mistress for the past three years. Theirs was an easy relationship, founded on mutual pleasure and friendship.

"Why didn't you let me know?" she asked, returning to the wide bed.

"Because it wasn't your worry," he said.

Anne handed him his glass, her mouth curving into a delighted grin as he threw back the covers, revealing his own lean body. Her heart beat faster as her eyes beheld him in all his grace. She drained the contents of her glass before joining him. "What will you do?" she questioned softly, snuggling against him, running her hand caressingly across the soft black hair on his broad chest.

"Whatever I have to do to keep my inheritance secure."

Anne thought about the many generous gifts Rhys had given her over the years. She lifted her hand. In the gaslight the diamonds sparkled. There was a necklace to match, as well as earrings. And there was the pearl collar, the one with the huge ruby catch. They could be sold, she thought, and would fetch a handsome sum.

"I could lend you . . ."

Rhys silenced her with a swift kiss. "No, Anne." he said with finality.

Anne heard the note of steely pride in his tone. Still, she felt that she owed it to him to try again. "Are you sure?"

"Yes."

"What about a bank loan?"

"They're a bit tricky to obtain with no collateral, my dear. The manor is mortgaged, and what treasures I could part with have already been sold. No, I'm afraid it wouldn't do and I won't ask."

"If only there was something else," she said, bringing his hand to her lips.

"I'm the only asset I have left, my dear."

"What do you mean?" she questioned, abruptly sitting up.

"Just what I said." This time it was Rhys who left the sanctuary of the bed. He grabbed the black velvet dressing gown that lay on the floor where it had been carelessly tossed earlier that afternoon. "Do you think I'd allow what's been in my family for generations to slip through my fingers?" Rhys' voice hardened. "I shall do whatever I have to to hold on to what's mine." His hands clentched into fists as he pulled tight the gold cord around his slim waist. He knew that it was time to tell Anne that this would be the last time for them. Regret weighed heavily on his mind as he formulated the words.

"Anne, I want you to know that I'm getting married."

A look of blank shock came over her face. "Married? When? To whom?"

He refilled his glass. "Within the next few months."

A bittersweet smile traced her lips. "An heiress?"

"Yes."

"Who?"

"Victoria Reitenauer."

"Who?" Anne searched her memory for a face to put to the name.

Rhys smiled at the sound of her question. "You don't know her."

"Where did you meet her?"

"I haven't," he replied.

"Rhys, are you joking?"

"No, I'm not joking." The look of intensity on his features told her that he was in deadly earnest.

"Then how did this come about?"

"Quite simply," he answered, "I responded to a job advertisement in the *Times*. Wanted: one husband."

Anne's eyes widened in shock. "Husband? A job?"

"Correct."

"That's absurd."

"It's the truth."

"You can't be serious, Rhys. It's utter madness!" she protested.

Rhys merely smiled. "It was an expedient measure, my sweet. Only that and nothing more."

"But to marry someone you've never met, someone you don't know."

"Dear Anne," Rhys spoke in a calm, even tone, "it is the fashionable thing to do, is it not?" And it wasn't as if it hadn't happened in his very family before. An ancestor, one Cameron Alistair Buchanan, had left Scotland at the insistence of his king, Charles II, to accept Charles's gracious gift of a wealthy bride, Marissa Fitzgerald.

An understanding gleam lit Anne's dark eyes. "She's an American?"

"Yes."

"Will you be married in London or at your country seat?"

"Neither," he responded. "I'm leaving England in a few weeks time."

"You're to be married in America then?"

Rhys nodded his head. "It would appear so."

"New York? Philadelphia? Boston?" she asked.

"Texas."

"*Texas*. Oh, Rhys." She sighed. "That's so far away." She shuddered. "Such a savage place, I've heard, filled with red Indians."

He shrugged his shoulders.

Anne left the bed, pulling on her own dressing gown. "When will you return?"

"As soon as I possibly can," he replied.

23

"You came to say good-bye then?" She asked the question, although she already knew his answer.

Rhys bent his head and placed a sweet kiss on her lips. "I couldn't leave without seeing you once more. I owed you an explanation."

"How sweet of you to think so, my darling, but you didn't, really." Anne cupped his face in her hands, tracing the contours of his mouth with hers. "And, since this is to be our last time together, let's not waste any more of it talking." She dropped her robe to the floor; her hands were busy loosening the tie that bound his dressing gown closed.

Rhys threw back his head, banishing thoughts of his wife-to-be, enjoying the feel of her mouth on his heated skin as Anne sank to her knees in front of him, paying homage to his masculine glory.

"Kinsenning, when is my son expected home?" asked the Countess of Derran, pouring herself a cup of strong tea and helping herself to one of the many biscuits Mrs. Butler, the cook, had heaped onto a fine china plate, part of the set especially commissioned by the Buchanans from the firm of Wedgewood. She was exceedingly glad that this set hadn't been sold along with some of the others that they'd been forced to part with.

"I'm not sure, my lady. He left several hours ago. The earl indicated he had an appointment."

"With the beautiful Lady Beckworth-Bridge,

I've no doubt?'' she inquired politely.

Kinsenning kept his face impassive. "His lordship did not inform me, my lady."

"Indeed," the countess said, smiling. "When he returns, please tell my son that I wish to have some words with him. That will be all, Kinsenning."

"Very good, my lady," the butler said as he backed out of the room, shutting the door firmly.

Agatha Hart Fitzgerald Buchanan, Countess of Derran, sipped her hot tea slowly. She was well aware of the high regard that the earl's household had for him and knew that should it be in his interest, they wouldn't hesitate to lie for him if they thought it best. It was a welcome change of pace from her other son, the former heir to her late husband's title. Tony hadn't inspired much of anything in the servants' quarters except fear and loathing. Tony had shared her husband's weakness for cards, but where her husband had been merely unlucky, her elder son had combined that with a penchant for strong drink, much as her own older brother had done.

Her gaze drifted upwards to the portrait that hung in her bedroom. It was Agatha, flanked by her sons; Tony had been twenty-one and Rhys fifteen then. The dissolute set of the mouth and the influence of drink were already recorded in Tony's face. In Rhys's eyes she saw life and, more important, strength.

So wrapped up in her thoughts was she that

she hadn't heard Rhys enter the room. Her face beamed when she beheld her son.

He bent and placed a kiss on her cheek. "What brings you to London, Mother?" he asked politely, seating himself opposite her.

"The Duchess of Dorwell's ball is tomorrow evening. Are you attending?"

"I'd thought to."

"Perfect. Shall I ring for another cup?"

He shook his head no. "Did you bring Gillian with you?"

Agatha Buchanan's mouth curved in a wry smile. "No, I thought it best to leave your sister in the country." The countess produced a letter from the reticule at her feet. "She wanted me to give you this."

Rhys took the note from his mother's hand, ripping open the wax seal. He quickly read the contents. "It appears that she loves the pony."

"You spoil her, Rhys."

"It's an older brother's privilege," he said.

"One you can't afford to indulge," his mother reminded him.

"Now that's where you're wrong, mother."

"Since when?"

"That doesn't matter."

"I beg to differ with you, my son," the countess protested. "Where did you obtain the money for the pony? And for the hiring of a groom?"

Rhys stood up. "From my wife's dowry."

"Your what?" The countess's composure cracked with that revelation.

"I am to be married."

She had been about to rise; with that remark she sank back into the cushions of the chair. "Lady Beckworth-Bridge?"

"No."

Relief flooded the countess's face. "Thank God."

Rhys's voice hardened. "Anne is a fine woman, mother."

"You needn't defend your mistress to me, Rhys. I've met the woman. I even like her. She's just not the wife for you."

Casting caution aside, the countess demanded, "Are you in love with her?"

Rhys answered honestly. "No. However, I do hold Anne in high regard, mother. She's been a good friend to me. We have similar interests."

"She's also nine years older than you and already a mother, and, if what I hear about that wild daughter of hers is true, soon to become a grandmother."

"The points are moot, mother."

She waved her hand. "Who then is to be your bride?"

"An American."

The countess absorbed this piece of news with a benumbed calm. The Americans had capital aplenty. She knew that the Prince of Wales was fond enough of them, most especially the ladies, and that they were welcomed at court. Still, an *American*. A woman of uncertain heritage. Silently she cursed the memory of her husband and other son—and fate for putting Rhys in this damnable position. He couldn't afford to wed with just anyone; the woman must be wealthy. And young enough to be malleable. She shrugged her shoulders.

"When am I to meet her?"

Rhys cocked his head. "You won't."

The countess shot her son a perplexed look. "What do you mean? Do you intend to shun your family?"

Rhys cast a glance in her direction, thinking that even in clothes that had seen a few seasons, his mother still possessed all the grandeur of her station. "I shan't be married here, mother."

"If not here," she said, misunderstanding him, "then where?" A horrible thought fogged her brain. "Is there something wrong with her? Is she mad?" she demanded. The countess would rather her son marry his mistress than be saddled with a wife lost to all reason, no matter how much money she brought to the family coffers.

"As far as I know she is quite sane."

Her eyes narrowed. "As far as you know?" she echoed.

"This is an arranged union. I leave for the States to wed her."

"*You* are to go to *her?*" The countess demanded in an imperious tone, "Who is she, this colonial, to make terms?"

"They are her father's terms, Mother, and he is the man holding the strings to the purse," Rhys said truthfully.

"Rhys, she will be *your* wife, and as such it will be her duty to live where *you* live, to

28

become part of *your* world."

"It would seem that is not to be."

"How can you follow this scheme so willingly? Aren't they aware of the singular honor that you bestow on their family?"

Rhys's gray eyes were cool. "When it comes to honor, mother, father and Tony succeeded in blackening ours thoroughly."

"Nonsense," the countess said, "no one was aware . . ."

Rhys snapped, "Christ, Mother, can you still be that naive? Your friends knew all about it. They chose to protect you, to keep up appearances." Rhys could see the effect his words were having on his mother. She shrank back in her seat, her face draining of color with the thought that what she believed secret was common knowledge.

"God, do you think that I want this marriage? And to a stranger?" he demanded. "I've never been such a fool as to expect that when I wed I would love the woman; I had thought only that she would be from the same world as I, have the same interests. Our circumstances have precluded that." He reached out and squeezed his mother's shoulder. "It's not as if there haven't been offers made to me, either, from a few fathers eager to wed me to their daughters."

"You found none acceptable?"

"On the contrary, I considered several." And Rhys had, poring over prospective financial settlements, perusing photographs and portraits. "However, none possessed the amount of capital I needed in their marriage portion. Simply put, the American did."

As the bedside clock chimed four, Rhys pulled the thick, faded velvet curtain from the window of his bedroom and looked out to the starless night sky. Beneath him, he saw the lights of London. What, he wondered, would he see from the room that he would occupy in Texas? An emptiness to equal that which gripped him now?

Rhys allowed himself that momentary lapse. He let go of the curtain and it fell back into place, as did his thoughts.

He was no wide-eyed child, innocent and eager. He knew what he was about, what he had to do to keep the remainder of his heritage inviolate, his family secure.

He'd made the bargain. Now he would see it through.

Part One:
A Lie of the Heart

Chapter One

Samuel Reitenauer strode into the lobby of the Menger Hotel in San Antonio. He pulled a gold watch from the pocket of his vest, popped it open, and checked the time. Staring back at him from inside the casing was a portrait of his daughter, Victoria, the reason he was here to meet his guest. Sam snapped the watch shut. He was aware that he was late; he knew that it was sure to get their first meeting off to a bad start.

Well, Sam thought, shrugging his large shoulders, that was just too bad. His lordship might be something in England, Sam mused, but in Texas he was just another foreigner. Here Sam wielded the power, and he never let anyone forget it. Not that anyone could. Sam owned one of the biggest cattle ranches in Texas. On the

Encantadora, he was as near to a palatine prince as anyone in this country could get. It was *his* empire, and now he was ready to meet the man he'd handpicked to share the throne with his child.

Sam approached the desk. He smiled as the clerk recognized him and anticipated his question.

"Your guest is waiting for you in the dining room, sir."

"Good. Was everything in his suite as requested?" Sam demanded.

The clerk bobbed his head quickly. "Just as you ord—requested, Mr. Reitenauer," he said, beginning to shuffle papers so that his nervous hands would have something to do.

"And my own suite?"

"Ready for you."

"See that hot water for a bath is brought to my rooms in two hours, along with a bottle of your best brandy."

"As you wish, sir." The clerk dipped a pen into the inkwell and made a note to himself to check on Samuel Reitenauer's bath personally. One couldn't afford to displease a man of Reitenauer's ilk. The consequences were too terrible to contemplate.

Sam thanked the clerk and walked into the dining room, slowly scanning the company for the man he'd come to meet.

He wasn't disappointed.

The room was crowded; it contained some of San Antonio's finest, along with ordinary cowboys. The style was relaxed; customers dressed with the ease of the West.

All except one.

He was a tall man; Sam could see that, even though the stranger was seated. The soft light of the room gave his black hair a rich, warm glow. His clothes hadn't come from a general store; they were obviously hand-tailored and very expensive.

Sam made his way to the elegantly appointed table.

"Mr. Rhys Buchanan?"

With that question Rhys's head turned slightly. Plain Mr. Buchanan wasn't the form of address that Rhys was used to. It seemed as though nothing in this place so far was as he was used to.

Slowly, Rhys stood, topping the older man by several inches. In a voice cool and deliberate, he said, "Yes, I am Rhys Alexander Fitzgerald Buchanan, Earl of Derran. And you, I presume, are the tardy *Mr.* Reitenauer?"

Good, Sam thought, a hint of a smile sketching his wide mouth. He gives as good as he gets. He may look like a fancy man, but he's got something.

Sam held out his large hand. Rhys took it in a strong handshake. Again, Sam was measuring the make of the man. The grip was solid, assured. And the hand wasn't the soft, pallid appendage that Sam expected. There was evidence of an iron will in the man's powerful grip.

"Business detained me, couldn't be helped.

Glad to see that you didn't wait supper for me,"
Sam said in a gruff voice; it was as close to an
apology as he would make.

He could see the slight thinning of Rhys's full
lips. However, not a hint of censure passed
them. Good breeding showed, Sam thought.

Both men sat down and Sam lit up a thick
cigar, inhaling deeply. "Best to get this business
over with now, boy."

Rhys raised an arching black brow at being
called "boy." His relaxed manner after retaking
his seat abruptly left him; he sat straighter in his
chair, fixing Sam with a cool, appraising look
from eyes the color of a frozen winter sky.

Sam Reitenauer was a force to be reckoned
with. Rhys guessed he was an inch or so short of
six foot. Square jawed and blunt featured, his
was a face that radiated strength and purpose.
Rhys kept a check on his rising irritation by
calmly and perfunctorily lighting his own cigar,
extracted from a silver case stamped with the
emblem of the Prince of Wales's Marlborough
Club. Along with the engraved snuff box each
member received from the Prince, Rhys had
been given the cigar case as a present for his
recent twenty-ninth birthday. It was a sign of
royal favor and friendship, and Rhys carried it
proudly.

"When am I to meet my betrothed?" Rhys
asked politely. "I had thought that she would be
here."

"My daughter is awaiting your arrival at the
ranch. We will leave at first light tomorrow and

should be there in two days time."

"And the wedding?"

Sam motioned for a waiter, ordered a bourbon, and sat back in his chair. "You'll be married within two weeks."

Rhys's eyes narrowed. "So soon?"

"Why not?" Sam questioned. "That's what you're here for, isn't it?" He took the large glass of straight bourbon and drank a healthy swallow. "There will be an engagement party, followed by the wedding the next day."

"Why bother to have the party?" Rhys asked.

Sam looked him square in the eye. "Because it's expected. Besides, my friends will be coming, for the most part, from a distance. This way they can celebrate both events at once."

Rhys observed the older man through hooded lids. Practical and tough. His daughter would probably be afraid of her own shadow with him for a father. She would be submissive and obedient. He blew out a large circle of smoke. Good. She won't be expecting too much. Perhaps a few kind words would suffice, a gesture or two of comfort. All the better.

"Does your daughter approve?"

"Victoria is my affair."

Rhys observed with wry humor, "She'll soon be *my* affair."

Sam laughed, nodding his gray head. "That she will, boy." And won't that just prove interesting? Sam pondered. His Tory and this dandified gent.

Rhys asked in a polite tone, "Won't there be

talk about this hasty ceremony?"

Sam finished the rest of his bourbon, savoring the taste of good Kentucky whiskey. "People are used to arranged marriages. I've given the story around that it was settled years ago, by me and your late father, whom I met while on a business trip to England. No one need know the truth of the matter. My girl's pride will be protected."

"That's fine with me," Rhys agreed. The notion of his being "hired" was anathema to him. *His* pride was important to him.

Sam reached into the pocket of his coat and produced an envelope. He laid it on the table in front of Rhys.

"What's this?"

"I've taken the liberty of opening an account for you at the bank here in San Antonio. You'll be paid a discreet amount each month for your lifetime."

Rhys took the envelope in his hand, his long fingers pushing open the flap to scan the contents.

While Rhys quickly fanned the bills, Sam observed him. This man's looks couldn't fail to please his daughter. The man seated opposite him was polished, with the strong facial features of the aristocrat. The bones of his face displayed the perfection of years of breeding. Sam beamed. What handsome children this union would produce. Beauty would beget beauty.

He lit another cigar. He felt that he'd gotten his money's worth.

Rhys was surprised by the generous monthly

allowance. Surprised—and disgusted. His lips twisted in a sneer. He'd sold his services as a husband; he'd be damned before he sold his honor. It might have meant nothing to his father and brother, but it was not expendable to him. No doubt the practical Mr. Reitenauer thought he was being fair. A monthly stipend as if he were a kept man, a *macreau*. His thin nostrils flared in anger.

Sam read the angry look that altered the face of the man before him from controlled to turbulent. That change surprised Sam. He hadn't thought that the man would be capable of such strong feelings. It didn't jibe with the image Sam had of Rhys Buchanan as a foppish aristocrat.

"The amount that we agreed upon initially, and that Mr. Beaudré already gave me, is satisfactory," Rhys said coldly. "I didn't expect or want anything else."

"Consider it a bonus. You'll need some ready cash."

Rhys enunciated each word carefully, his voice crisp. "I don't want it."

Now it was Sam's turn to get tough. "My boy, I don't give a damn. It's up to you whether or not you use it. But," he pointed out "you're used to having money, that's easy enough to see. All I'm doing is making sure that you continue to have what you're used to. Understand?"

Rhys understood only too well. His future father-in-law saw him as an empty-headed trinket who, tossed a generous economic bone, would prove tractable. He found the thought both amusing and insulting. He wasn't used to being so blatantly patronized.

"Now," Sam continued, "I suggest that we both retire. We've got a long ride ahead of us in the morning. We'll be leaving here around five-thirty." Sam concluded his speech and rose from the table, indicating that to him, the meeting was over. "Oh, by the way," he asked as an afterthought, "do you ride?"

"Of course," Rhys answered.

"No of course about it, my boy. Known lots of people who can't sit a horse, much less ride one. Out here it's important. I didn't know if you could, so I had a carriage brought from the ranch. But of course, you can ride if you prefer."

In a cool tone, Rhys said, "I think I can handle whatever mount you have for me. In England I was known as a fairly good rider."

Sam chuckled. "Texas isn't England. We do things a bit differently here."

"So I noticed," Rhys added dryly. "My man can occupy the carriage."

"Your man?" asked Sam.

"I brought my valet along."

Sam should have thought of that. God, what a long time ago it was that he also had had one. The thought made him momentarily nostalgic for his family's *schloss* in the Schwarzwald. He sighed. That had been a lifetime ago, when he was a child, before he'd discovered his real home.

"That will be no problem," Sam remarked. "See you in the morning."

Rhys watched Sam leave the room, saw that at the door to the dining room he was met by two men, cowboys Rhys believed they were called. He'd observed them standing in the doorway earlier, one at each side of the entrance. They were rough looking and sported weapons.

"Would you like anything else this evening, sir?" the waiter said as he approached the table.

"No, thank you. I shall take the check now."

"Oh, no need, sir; that's already been handled by Herr Reitenauer," he said with a trace of awe in his voice. Satisfied that the gentleman needed nothing further, the waiter departed.

Rhys checked the watch he wore attached to a gold chain looped across the front of his silk brocade waistcoat. A sardonic smile etched his mouth. He would show Samuel Reitenauer just what it meant to be a Buchanan. Perhaps his father and older brother hadn't lived up to the responsibilities of the name, but he would. Before he left this place called Texas, the name Buchanan would be spoken with the same respect that he'd heard when people mentioned Reitenauer.

Rhys opened the door to his luxurious suite in the Menger and was greeted by his valet, Twinnings, who helped him off with his jacket.

"Would you care for anything to drink, my lord?" he asked as he hung the jacket in the armoire.

Rhys, removing the sapphire cufflinks from his shirt, said, "No." He pulled the white shirt free from his trousers and slowly unbuttoned it. Walking to the window, he opened it wide, breathing deeply of the fragrant night air. His rooms overlooked the busy street. The sights and sounds were very different from his London window.

"Will there be anything else this evening, my lord?"

Rhys turned from his inspection. "No, Twinnings, that will be all. We are to leave early tomorrow. Are my things ready?"

Twinnings, who prided himself on his job, said, "But of course, my lord. Not knowing how long we'd be in this place"—the last word carefully expressed his sentiments—"I only unpacked what I deemed necessary."

"Did you bring along my riding breeches?"

"Just as you instructed, my lord."

"Good. I will wear them tomorrow."

"Will we arrive at our final destination then?"

Rhys smiled at his manservant's obvious lack of enthusiasm for travel. "After another day or so."

Twinnings's mouth pursed. "Just how big is this bloody country anyway?" he mumbled as he left Rhys alone.

Tossing aside the rest of his clothes, Rhys walked naked to the bed. Too restless to sleep right away, he lay awake thinking about the journey he'd made. After docking in Philadelphia, he'd been met by another of Herr Reitenauer's business associates and shown to the railroad car that was awaiting him. In London he'd been told that transport to Texas would be in the form of a train, but instead of sharing space with others across the thousands of miles, he was escorted to a private car, hooked to a regular train. This was a further example of the power and money behind Sam Reitenauer. The coach was magnificent. Paneled in rich mahogany, it was filled with furnishings that would have been correct in any established London home. On board was a chef, a well-stocked larder, bottles of wine and spirits, even a library. To alleviate the boredom of so long a journey, Rhys rediscovered the joys of literature. His adult life hadn't afforded him much time for reading, except for the newspapers, and recently, documents that dealt with his estates. He recalled scanning the shelves, surprised at the range. There were volumes in German, English, Spanish, and French—novels, plays, poetry, even essays. He had picked up the thick volume that lay on the small pine table by his bed. It was a copy of *Les Misérables*, in French. Rhys opened the book and read the inscription inside.

To my darling Victoria: May you abide by the lessons herein, your loving mother.

His betrothed would appear to be a bluestocking, judging from the notes scribbled throughout the text. He'd never seen any book marked as she had marked this one, with random thoughts about characters and ideas, jotted across any available space.

Now turning down the gas light on the wall, Rhys considered his wife-to-be's character. She would be prim, very proper, he was sure.

Just before sleep claimed him, Rhys wondered what this Victoria would look like. Tolerable enough to bed, he hoped, though he knew it was of no real consequence.

The loud pounding on the door awoke Rhys.

Struggling to sit up, he saw that the curtain of night had yet to be lifted outside. He grabed the silk robe that lay on the elegant chair beside the bed and threw it on.

"Twinnings!" he said loudly in the direction of the adjoining room and, receiving no answer, went to see to the door himself.

"Who's there?"

"Mr. Reitenauer said you was to be gotten up if you were going with us—uh, sir," the voice from the other side of the suite door spoke.

Rhys, incredulous at the early hour, opened the door and found one of the cowboys that had been Sam Reitenauer's escort the previous evening. Obviously the young man was at home with the early morning hour, Rhys judged by the smiling face before him.

"What the bloody hell time is it?"

"Just after four, sir," the cowboy answered.

"Christ," Rhys muttered, turning his back on the man. "Is Reitenauer ready to leave now?"

"He will be when he's done breakfast, sir. He said to tell you that if you want to get some grub—uh, food, before we hit the trail, you'd better get yourself ready and meet him in his suite."

"Please convey my thanks to Mr. Reitenauer for the invitation to breakfast, but I can wait till later in the day."

"Begging your pardon, sir, but there ain't gonna be any later for breakfast. Once we leave, there'll be hard riding to the ranch. Don't expect we'll be stopping till nightfall, or thereabouts."

Rhys tilted his head. "Nightfall?"

"Yes, sir. Shall I tell Mr. Reitenauer that you'll be joining him for breakfast after all?"

The slight smile on the cowboy's face did not go unnoticed by Rhys.

"Inform Mr. Reitenauer that I will be happy to join him for breakfast." With that, Rhys closed the door.

"Who was that, my lord?"

"A summons, Twinnings." Rhys walked over to the stand that held a pitcher and bowl. Splashing water into the basin from the enameled pitcher, he reached for his razor. "It appears," he said, soaping his jaw, "that we had better get what nourishment we can now, for I've been warned that once on the trail, as it were, we may not be stopping for a meal until much later in the day."

Twinnings laid out his master's clothes and tidied the room while Rhys finished shaving. "Shall I ring for a bath, my lord?"

"No time for that now." Rhys rinsed the lather from his lean jaw. "I suggest that you get yourself down to the dining room and enjoy a hearty meal. Then arrange for my things to be taken to the lobby."

"Yes, my lord." As Twinnings started to leave, he changed his mind and turned and faced the earl. "Will I have to ride a horse, my lord?" he asked in a panic-stricken voice.

Rhys, knowing his valet's dislike of the four-footed creatures, smiled and said, "No, Twinnings, you are to ride in a carriage."

Twinnings exhaled in relief. It would have been just like these colonials to have forced upon him their preferred mode of transport. He knew that the earl wouldn't mind sitting a horse, being as he was a "neck or nothing" rider.

A heavy sigh escaped his thin chest. How very far away civilization seemed. And to think that his lordship had contemplated leaving him in England. Twinnings had insisted that these colonials should be reminded just whom they were entertaining. When the earl replied that he was going to Texas not to be entertained, but to be married, Twinnings countered that that was even more reason for him to be there.

He snapped the closings on his lordship's portmanteau, wondering if an establishment such as this could possibly have kidneys on its menu.

"I swear, the only thing he had on was a fancy robe like the ladies at the Mermaid House wear. You know the kind, real soft and expensive-like."

Sam Reitenauer chuckled. Obviously his hand

was surprised that the English gentleman wasn't wearing the standard homespun long johns that were the regulation clothing under the denim pants his men wore. A man who sported a silk robe was someone to be wary of. By God, it was going to be fascinating with this Rhys Buchanan around, Sam decided. If only Tory were more . . .

Sam's errant thoughts were interrupted by Rhys's appearance.

He inquired in a smooth, silky voice, "Am I still in time for breakfast?"

"Just sit yourself right down here, my boy," Sam instructed. "I took the liberty of ordering something for you when Ace said that you'd be joining us."

Rhys joined Sam and his two hands at the small pine table. In seconds a plate was set before him by an obsequious waiter. It contained a large cut of beefsteak, eggs, and tomatoes; two heaping platters of biscuits were added to the table, along with crystal pots of honey, jam, and butter.

"Dig in," Sam urged, pouring Rhys a cup of the steaming coffee that the hotel was famous for.

Rhys hadn't realized just how hungry he was until he started in on the huge breakfast, devouring the steak and eggs.

Watching him butter his fourth fluffy biscuit before loading it with blackberry preserves, Sam wondered how the man seated next to him kept his lean frame.

"Do you always appreciate your morning meal so much?" Sam asked.

Helping himself to another cup of the coffee, Rhys sat back in his chair. "To tell you the truth, I'm usually on my way to bed at this hour, not awakening." Rhys saw the way the two cowboys reacted to this news. To say that they were stunned would have been an understatement. Their puzzled looks gave Rhys a moment of satisfaction. This appeared to be a game of one-upmanship that he was engaged in. A thin smile crossed his mouth as he set his lips to the china cup and drank.

He was surprised that the two hired hands were at the table to begin with. Surely Samuel Reitenauer didn't eat with his help at his own dinner table? Rhys was glad that Twinnings wasn't here to witness such a serious breach of etiquette.

Sam consulted his pocket watch. "It's getting late. We'd better be moving on." Sam stood up, putting on the jacket which was slung over his chair. "Ace here is going to take your things and put them in the carriage. John," Sam said, indicating the other cowboy with long, wheat-colored hair, "will be following behind with the carriage and the supply wagon."

"And Twinnings," Rhys added.

"Twinnings?"

"My valet," Rhys stated.

The cowboys exchanged looks again.

"Yes, of course," Sam said. "Still up to that

ride?" he asked, a wicked gleam of amusement in his blue eyes.

Rhys wiped his mouth on the thick linen napkin the hotel provided and answered, "Anytime that you are."

Sam nodded his approval. "Then let's go."

What awaited Rhys when the men stepped outside the hotel was something of a surprise. He'd told Samuel that he was an excellent rider. Many of his trophies graced the library of his home. He had practically been raised in the saddle. An English saddle. On an English horse.

In the courtyard were several men on horseback or in the process of mounting. One man, Rhys noted in surprise, was black. In his gloved hands he held the reins of a magnificent animal that stood, Rhys estimated, at seventeen hands. The mane and tail, which swept the ground, were black; the rest of the horse's body was a blending of black and white, with three black socks.

Upon the back of the animal was a saddle.

An American saddle.

Rhys's eyes narrowed dangerously. He was sure that Samuel Reitenauer knew he had heretofore never ridden on a Western saddle. He looked up, scanning the faces. It was another test.

Rhys didn't back down from the challenge.

Rhys made another observation. The clothes that the men wore were all casual, working garments. His were riding clothes tailored for an

Gail Link

English countryside. Clothes worn for a brisk canter in one of London's parks, certainly not for a long, hard ride.

He knew instinctively that they were all waiting for him to tell them he had changed his mind, that he would gladly follow in the carriage. His formal frock coat wouldn't wear well; the equipment wasn't familiar; the horse practically unbroken. These were the excuses that remained unspoken.

Rhys took the reins from the hands of the black man, swinging his lithe body into the strange saddle.

He turned his head so that he was looking directly into Sam's face. "Are we ready then?" he asked, his tone icy.

Sam smiled. "Let's ride."

That's just what I intend to do, Rhys thought as he felt the power of the beast beneath him, allowing the horse to set his own pace. *I'll ride your damned horse the same way I'll ride your damned daughter. I'll show them both who's master.*

Chapter Two

Encantadora.

The Enchantress.

Tory sat atop her favorite horse, a spirited mare of dark gray, and surveyed her land. She patted the mare's neck, allowing them both to catch their breath after a long run. Hooking one leg over the pommel of her custom-made saddle, she breathed deeply of the cool, crisp morning air, watching the dew-covered bluebonnets and Indian paintbrushes catch the first rays of the Texas sun.

This was her birthright, her home, her blood.

She narrowed her eyes, watching the signs of life around the ranch. Several of the hands were heading for a line cabin on the western perimeter of the property to check on the cattle there. Others were riding out to check fences; some were going about their chores in the corrals. MacTavish, the burly Scots blacksmith, was already at work at his forge making a new pair of shoes for a horse tied to a hitching post.

Activity was the byword at the Encantadora. It was a heritage of pride and industry. And it was Tory's. She was the custodian of the lives and fortunes of all who worked and lived at the ranch.

For her land, her people, for the responsibility that bound together all who were part of the ranch, she would honor her father's wishes, like them or not.

Tory sat alone in the empty dining room, the table having been cleared of the remnants of her supper, and poured herself another glass of wine. She had decided that she would not wait to eat, even though she knew that her father and the stranger were expected later that evening and it would have been polite to wait until their arrival before she ate.

Politeness be damned, she thought as she drank in solitary contentment.

Tory brushed a hand along her thighs. She was dressed in her everyday clothes: rough work pants of the same denim material that most of the hands on her ranch wore; a shirt of indigo-blue cotton; knee-high soft moccasins. Around her slim waist was a belt of hammered silver, upon which hung a knife sheath. Inside was a smaller version of the knife made famous by Jim Bowie, and which bore his name. MacTavish had made it for her sixteenth birthday, and Tory was quite skilled in its uses.

She knew her father would expect her to dress for dinner. Perversely, Tory chose not to. It was important for her to be seen for what she was.

She smiled. It would certainly put the man in his place, show him that she did not consider their first meeting a significant event. Tory knew it would upset her father that she wasn't acting, and dressing, the part of the proper hostess.

Tonight that didn't matter. She was still too angry at him to care about his expectations this night.

Damn this marriage!

The sounds of approaching hoofbeats and excited shouts interrupted Tory's musings.

They were here.

He was here.

Should she stay inside and wait? Should she greet them at the door?

Damn convention, Tory thought. This was *her* ranch and no stranger was going to intimidate her. She touched the heavy weight of the gold signet ring she wore, skimming a finger over the raised R. Drawing strength from it, she strode from the room.

The men were leading their horses into the barn, eager to head for the large bunkhouse and a hot meal. They had been riding hard these two days and were glad to be home.

A stablehand came running from the direction of the barn to take Samuel Reitenauer's horse.

Tory stood on the wide stone steps, watching her father dismount. Behind him she saw a flash of black and white and observed a tall man lift himself carefully from the horse's back. He stood stiffly, his muscles, she surmised, not used to such a rigorous journey. Her lips twisted in a wicked grin. He looked hot, dirty, disheveled, with a tracing of dark stubble across his jaw.

"Papa," Tory said, breaking the sudden silence.

"Come here, Victoria. I want you to meet someone," he said formally, and in a tone which Tory knew was meant to convey his displeasure at the way she had dressed.

Tory slowly descended the three steps, kissing her father warmly on his stubbled cheek.

She narrowed her eyes and gave the stranger a fast, dismissing glance.

"Tory, I want to present to you his lordship, the Earl of Derran, Rhys Fitzgerald Buchanan, your fiance."

My God, she thought. He's going to wed me to a pretty fashion doll come to life.

Tory's face was controlled; she was icily polite. Only the blue of her eyes betrayed the emotions she was trying to keep hidden: they were cold, proud.

Who the hell did he think he was?

Who the hell did she think she was?

Rhys straightened his shoulders and looked at the young woman who stood before him. Was this the American princess he'd come to wed?

54

His nostrils flared in anger and distaste. This creature was to be *his* wife? Sweet Jesus, had he really come so low?

His cold gray eyes swept over her figure in dismay. She was wearing trousers. Bloody *trousers*, he thought. They were made of the same material that her father's men wore.

Her hair, Rhys thought, was . . . unseemly. That was the best word he could come up with. No woman of his acquaintance would have greeted a guest coiffed as she was, her long tresses in two thick braids tied with thin pieces of worn leather.

And what where those items she wore to cover her feet?

Rhys then took note of the silver belt at her waist, the sheath attached. By God, he realized, she actually carried a knife.

The entire effect was rough. Savage.

Rhys's gaze clashed with hers. He'd expected a quiet-looking maid, shy and bookish; instead, before him was a tall, proud blonde amazon, with stubborn eyes the color of pale blue crystal.

Sam's voice interrupted Rhys's musings. "I'd like you to meet my daughter, Victoria."

Inbred manners forced Rhys to take the hand that Tory reluctantly offered him. He lifted it to his lips and felt her immediate withdrawl.

Tory addressed her father as they walked up the steps of the house, pointedly ignoring Rhys. "Papa, I'm sure that you're tired and would like something to eat."

"I would," Sam said in a strong tone, then

added, "as would our guest, I'm sure."

Tory blinked with feigned innocence. "Of course you're welcome to eat too, *Mr.* Buchanan," Tory added sweetly.

Too sweetly, Sam thought. He saw through Tory's apparent pose of sudden concern.

"I would prefer a bath first," Rhys informed her. "Please be good enough to have someone show me to my rooms. Then you may send one of your servants to me and I will tell them what I wish to eat."

They all stood in the hallway of the house, before the staircase. Tory turned to her guest and fixed him with a cold stare.

"I am sorry, your *lordship*"—the last word was forced out through gritted teeth—"but our cook has retired for the evening, as has the housekeeper. If you want to eat tonight, you'll have to have your meal in the kitchen."

Sam sensed the angry vibrations emanating from the two younger people. It was a tangible, potent force that crackled the air around them. He had to break the tension—and he would have to talk later with his daughter.

"I think we can make an exception this time and see that something is available for the earl after he bathes, *Liebchen*. Now I want you to show him to the room I instructed be made ready for him. Afterwards I wish to speak to you."

Tory's face was impassive. "As you wish, Papa." She mounted the stairs, turning her head slightly. "If you would be so kind as to follow me, Lord Derran."

His voice icily polite, Rhys replied, "Of course, Miss Reitenauer."

Tory marched up the oaken steps unaware of the view she afforded the earl of her shapely posterior, hugged gently by the well-worn denim. She guided him to a large room, dominated by a huge walnut bed and wardrobe. Several of the windows were open and the fresh evening air, tinged with a sweet fragrance, wafted through the interior.

"There's a bathroom through this door," Tory said, indicating a smaller room, fully appointed. "To save you asking," she stated, "it's totally functional."

"What about quarters for my man?"

She was standing in front of a rolltop desk on which rested a silver framed daguerreotype of a smiling blond man. Her left hand touched the picture reverently. "Man?"

Rhys joined her. "My valet. He'll be arriving shortly in the carriage."

"There are several rooms below that he may choose from."

"Who is he?" Rhys asked, standing close to Tory and catching her scent. *Roses*. Suddenly, he was reminded of an English garden. Wild roses, protected by thorns.

Her voice was soft, tender. "My brother, Travis."

"Is this his room?"

"It was," she replied tersely, moving away from his proximity.

He noted another door. "Where does that lead?"

"To my room."

She waited for a comment. None came. An enigmatic expression crossed his face when she chanced to look his way as he lit the oil lamp beside his bed.

"If you'll excuse me," he said, turning his back on her.

She was being dismissed as if she were a servant who was beginning to bore him.

As she made her way to the door, his voice floated to her, commandingly clear.

"Don't forget that I require food, if you please."

Or if I don't please, Tory thought as she shut the door with a resounding snap. Presumptuous ass! How dare he?

Tory's hot temper flared higher as she hurried down the back stairs leading to the kitchen.

"Kristen," Tory said in surprise as she entered the room, blinking in the light, "what are you doing?"

"Fixing Herr Baron's supper, *natürlich*," Kristen explained as she set about slicing thick slabs of still-warm ham. She added three different types of cheese to the platter she was preparing. A loaf of fresh black bread and two small stoneware crocks containing butter and a hearty mustard completed the meal.

"I could have . . ."

"Baroness," Kristen affectionately pointed out, "while I live, I serve."

Tory knew better than to admonish Kristen further. Her family had worked for the Reitenauers for close to two hundred years. She was the last remaining servant who'd been born in the old country, and consequently, she refused to ignore the family's hereditary titles. Tory understood and accepted the symbiotic relationship that existed between them.

Tory watched as Kristen made up a second tray identical to the first.

Her father strode into the room.

Tory observed the tight set of his handsome face.

"Victoria, I want you to take this other tray to the earl; then I want to see you in my office."

"Must I?"

"I should like it."

"As you wish, Papa," Tory said, picking up the hefty silver tray as Kristen added a few blueberry muffins.

"Do you wish anything further, Herr Baron?"

"No. *Danke*, Kristen."

"*Gute Nacht*, Herr Baron."

"*Gute Nacht*, Kristen." He inclined his head towards his daughter. "Remember, Tory."

Balancing the tray on her knee, she bent and knocked on *his* door. Tory waited a full minute before turning the handle and letting herself in.

She'd considered just leaving the tray outside the door on the floor. The notion of her fetching and carrying his meal irked her pride.

The room was empty. She supposed he was still washing the dirt of the trail from his body. Good. She wouldn't have to contend with his unmitigated arrogance.

Tory placed her burden down on a small table and spun around, ready to leave.

At that moment, the door to the bathroom opened and Rhys emerged.

Tory's eyes widened. In the place of the travel-worn aristocrat was a man stripped of all trappings, save for a natural masculine confidence and a short white towel wrapped around his slim hips. She refused to hurry from the room like some silly schoolgirl caught unawares. Boldly, she took her time assessing his physical attributes. His tall frame was lean, his shoulders wide. A pelt of black hair feathered across his chest and dusted his legs.

Rhys was man enough to know when a woman found him attractive, when he was being assessed for his potential as a lover. A sly glance, a seemingly demure appraisal, or a prolonged, intense look indicated willingness to oblige in the timeless rituals of nature. None of these, however, was apparent in her cool crystal eyes. She calmly evaluated; there was no hint of the maidenly modesty one would expect.

It occurred to Rhys to wonder if she were indeed a maiden. A woman of his class, carefully sheltered, would have quickly dropped her eyes and hurried from the room.

Not Victoria.

No, she stayed, and in so doing called into question her innocence. By rights he should expect his bride to come to him a virgin. And he would have banked on that fact if his wife was an Englishwoman.

However, he wasn't in a position to make the same demands of this woman.

Rhys returned her frank gaze before he turned away, casually dropping the towel. He shrugged into a robe that he'd found hanging in the wardrobe, tied the belt, and selected a chunk of cheese. "English cheddar," he said aloud.

"Papa has a fondness for it," Tory replied stiffly.

"And you don't?"

"I can take it or leave it."

"Indeed?" he responded, a sardonic gleam in his gray eyes.

Politeness forced her to ask, "Is there anything else you require?"

Rhys wondered what she would do if he said, "a warm, willing woman." She looked the type to tell him to go straight to hell. "No."

Without another word Tory left the room, closing the door softly instead of slamming it as she wished to do. *Ausländer!* she thought. Outsider! This was the man her father had betrothed her to—a pale, slender English aristocrat. An utterly useless fop. She'd seen the scorn in his eyes, and she was sure he'd marked the same in hers.

"Tory!" Her father's voice bellowed up the stairs. "Come down here, now."

She descended the stairs to find her father waiting for her. Silently she followed him as he lead her to the vacant library.

"Just what the hell did you think you were doing?"

Feigning innocence, Tory asked, "Whatever do you mean, Papa?"

"Tory, don't pretend ignorance. Just what did you hope to accomplish?" Sam thundered. "Did you think that by dressing like this and being rude, he would change his mind and go away?" Sam loosened his string tie and sat down in the oversized leather chair. "Well, it won't work. He's bought and paid for, my girl. Here to stay. You'd do well to remember that."

"Unfortunately, I can't forget it," she admitted.

"See that you don't." Sam watched the play of emotions that flickered across Tory's face. His daughter was proud; hell, he reflected, she had every right to be. Nevertheless, he wanted her to be happy, wanted her settled, protected. It was his duty to see that she was, whether she liked it or not.

It was too late for self-recriminations about his child's upbringing. Perhaps he shouldn't have let her run so wild, treating her as if she were another son. With the death of his boy had come the knowledge that Tory was the sole heir. As such, she had to know everything possible about the ranch. She had to be aware of what it took to hold a place like this together. She was brave, smart, resourceful—every inch the educated aristocrat.

But . . . and there was always a but, Sam knew . . . Tory was a woman, and as such she was vulnerable. His daughter possessed beauty, youth, and an enormous fortune; on his death, she would also have the land and the autonomous power of the Encantadora. She would be a target for any unscrupulous *Schweinehund* should she remain a lone female, without the benefit of a husband's name. What he was doing was right. He was guarding her against an uncertain future.

"Tomorrow I want you to show our guest about the ranch. Get used to his company." Sam smiled. "Who knows, you may find that you have something in common. Perhaps even a liking for one another."

Recalling the heated exchange of glances in the earl's bedroom, Tory couldn't imagine that happening soon.

"Oh, Papa," Tory said with a sigh, "you are such a dreamer."

Sam dropped an arm across Tory's stiff shoulders. "Perhaps, *mein Engel*. If I wasn't, the Encantadora wouldn't be what it is today."

Tory rested her cheek against his hand. *My angel*. He hadn't called her that in a long time.

Sam guided Tory to a chair and took one

opposite her. His blue eyes took on a determined look. "Or what it will be in the future. And that future is you, Tory. You and your children will determine what the Encantadora is to be. That's my dream. A legacy that will survive long after we've gone."

He glanced towards the portrait that hung over the fireplace mantel of his father, the Baron Paul Frederick Von Reitenauer. Carved in the wooden frame were the words: *Freiheit ist nur in dem Reich der Träume.* Freedom exists only in the world of dreams. "Your grandfather dreamed also. His vision lead him to leave our homeland and join the other German immigrants in this new land. Here, in Texas, he found the dream.

"All I ask is that you honor my dream, to see you married."

Rebellion flared for an instant in her heart. Tory wanted to deny his request. Yet she knew that she wouldn't. Her gaze fell to the signet ring her father wore. Again she was reminded of what she had been brought up to accept and to cherish. Tradition. Responsibility.

Sam returned to his desk and sat down, finishing his meal. "Tomorrow I want you dressed properly for supper. No work clothes, understand? And, you are to offer yourself as a guide to your fiance," he reiterated.

Tory pursed her lips. "I do have other responsibilities."

"Forgo them."

"As you wish." Tory stood.

"Schlafe gut, Liebchen," Sam said as he kissed his daughter's cheek.

Sleep well indeed, Tory thought as she tossed and turned restlessly. Pushing her down-filled pillows up against the carved headboard, she scooted up, her knees tucked under her. Night was fast losing its grip on the sky; dawn would soon spread warmth and color across the darkness.

She eyed the door that separated *his* room from hers. Never before had it been locked. It would remain so from now on. The key was safely tucked away. Her knife was close at hand, just in case. Tory wondered what this fine *gentleman* would think if he knew she'd used it before?

Even though the incident had taken place several years ago, Tory could still see it clearly in her mind. The drunken cowboy thought no one had seen him drag the terrified servant toward the empty bunkhouse. But Tory had seen, and followed. She'd pushed open the door and witnessed him slapping the girl as he roughly shoved aside her skirt and prepared to mount her.

Her only weapon was the knife. She didn't hesitate.

The man screamed in agony when the blade struck his flesh, sinking deep. He lay there, blood oozing from the wound as the servant pushed herself out from under the weight of his body. Getting to her feet, the girl threw her arms around Tory, sobs shaking her body.

The wound she'd delivered hadn't been life threatening. However, her father's judgment, pronounced several days later, was. She could still see the man's incredulous face as Sam told him that he was through on the *Encantadora*, that he would never work again in the state of Texas. Hate burned in those eyes.

It served Tory as a lesson in punishment and power, in justice and mercy.

But where, she wondered as her thoughts returned to the present, was her justice? Her mercy? Certainly not in being forced into this absurd partnership with a stranger.

She needed desperately to talk to someone other than her father about the situation. On the bedside table was the note she'd received yesterday.

No doubt his *lordship* would sleep most of the day away, so she would be free to ride to Rancho Montenegro. Pilar was once again at the home of her father, having returned, she explained to Tory in her short letter, for the impending nuptials.

Sam Reitenauer had wasted no time in informing their friends and family of the forthcoming event. Acceptances and gifts came daily. Each was like a snap of a bullwhip to skin already flayed raw.

Tory felt angry, foolish, and a little afraid. Angry that so many good people were being duped into believing this was a happy event; foolish at the notion that she was being treated like a child; afraid of what changes this detested union would bring about.

Tory drew on her inner resolves of strength and pride. She was a Reitenauer. She'd always faced challenges head on. This marriage would be no different.

Chapter Three

It was just past eight o'clock in the morning and the day promised to be quite warm. Stopping at the stream that divided the Encantadora property from Rancho Montenegro, Tory dismounted and let her mare have a drink. She pulled a dark blue bandana from her hip pocket, dipped it into the cool water, and dabbed it around her face and neck.

Tory knew that her father would be upset when she wasn't on hand to greet his *lordship* when he woke. A perverse smile curved her lips. Too bad, she thought; she doubted that her fiancé would be awake as of yet. He didn't look to be an early riser.

Shouted greetings from several men interrupted her thoughts. They were workers from the Montenegro hacienda, most as familiar to her as the cowboys on her own ranch. She waved back.

Abendstern, the beautiful gray mare with a white star on her chest that Tory had named after the evening star, pawed the ground, eager to be off. She wrung out the bandana, then remounted and turned the reins in the direction of the estancia. Today she needed a friend to confide in and Pilar Montenegro y Valmont Sanchez fit the bill. Tory, herself an indifferent letter writer, hadn't realized until Pilar's note came just how much she missed her childhood companion. At seventeen, Pilar had married the son of a wealthy rancher in New Mexico. Since the wedding, Tory had seen her only twice, once at her home in New Mexico, and again when Pilar visited Don Sebastian last year.

Soon Tory rode through the magnificent stone gates of the estancia. As she approached the stables, a lad of about ten ran to take her horse.

"I will see to *la señorita's* animal personally," the boy assured her in Spanish.

"*Gracias*, Juan," Tory said as she gently ruffled the boy's thick black hair, then moved towards the huge carved doors of the main house.

Before she could knock, the double doors swung open wide. She was enveloped by a hurtling bundle of energy that almost knocked her over.

"*Por favor*, Mano," spoke a beautiful, dark-haired young woman from the doorway. "Give your *tía* a chance to enter the house before you attack her in such a manner."

Tory said with a smile, "It's all right, Pilar." She knelt down and hugged the boy, then stood up, swinging him around to delighted squeals.

"*Dios mío*, that son of mine can be like a savage at times," Pilar moaned, although the look of intense maternal pride in her eyes belied her words.

Shooing the tiny terror in the direction of the kitchen with the promise of a treat, Pilar and Tory embraced warmly, each woman loath to break the bond. It was Pilar who drew back first, taking Tory's hand and ushering her into a small sala where a tray of coffee and warm tortillas filled with fruit awaited them.

Recognizing the concoction from their childhood attempts at cooking, Tory grinned. "So you *were* expecting me this morning?"

"*Sí,*" Pilar answered, pouring the steaming brew into delicate china cups and handing one to Tory. The fragrant aroma of cinnamon filled the air. "When I sent you the note I knew you would come as soon as you could."

Tory bit into the fragrant apple tortilla. "Ah," she sighed, "a Mexican strudel."

Pilar laughed softly, then her face took on a more serious look. "*Amiga,* who is this man who is to become your husband?"

"A stranger," Tory answered, draining her cup. "Papa arranged it."

Encantadora

"He is a friend, perhaps, of your father's?"

Tory was well aware of the fiction that Sam Reitenauer was spreading about. The lie was for her benefit; it rankled nonetheless. She would go along with the pride-saving dishonesty of it, but not to her friend. With Pilar she couldn't hide the truth. "No," she said, placing the cup and saucer on the table, "when I said he was a stranger, I meant he was a stranger to Papa as well."

At Pilar's perplexed look, Tory quickly explained the entire situation to her.

"So that is it, Pilar. He in an unknown, except that he is a man with a price. A high one, I'll grant."

Pilar reached out her slim hand and touched Tory's in comfort. "Maybe, *mi amiga*, it will not be so bad."

Tory leapt from her seat and started pacing the room. Her blue eyes flashed with a cold fire. "How can you say that?" she demanded.

Pilar folded her hands in her lap. She could see clearly the distress her friend was feeling. It was evident in the taut pull of flesh over Tory's cheekbones, in the agitated movements of her well-shaped, slender hands. Tory, she knew, was used to being in control—of her life, of her fate. Now she was faced with a situation over which she had no control.

Pilar answered the question put to her. "Because I married a stranger, and I wouldn't want to change my wedded life."

71

"At least the stranger wasn't totally an un-known to you," Tory said, walking to the open doors that lead to a garden. She breathed in the scent of dozens of plants, including several types of roses, some of which filled vases placed in the room.

"I knew only what Papa told me at the time—the man I was to wed was the son of his friend. The betrothal was made when we were children. Both of us understood that it was binding."

"But didn't you ever want to ignore it, Pilar?" Tory now pursued the questions she'd wanted to ask all those years ago. "Didn't you ever want to be free?"

"Free to do what, my friend?" Pilar joined Tory at the open doors, facing her. "I am the daughter of a powerful man, as are you. Alliances of marriage have always taken place in my family, as I suspect that they have in yours. It is the way of our world." Pilar's smile was indulgent. The happiness she felt with her life and the turns it had taken were written on her serene face. "I would change nothing. While it is true that Pedro and I were virtual strangers to one another, we shared a heritage. We have become the best of companions, and, I must confess"—and with this Tory noted the deep blush that stained Pilar's creamy cheeks—"that he is all I could have ever wanted in a husband."

At that moment the Montenegros' housekeeper, Marta, came bustling into the room, trailed by a maid. She whisked the tray into the waiting hands of the girl, replacing the empty silver pot of coffee with another. Her motherly smile changed to a frown as she caught sight of Tory's work clothes.

Wagging a stern finger in Tory's direction, Marta admonished her in Spanish, "This is not the way a man wishes to see his *novia* dressed, *pequeña*. It is not proper," she said as she left the room.

Tory chuckled. "As fond of me as she is, Marta has always considered me a bad influence on your mode of dress, Pilar."

"Well, I must say that the first time my Pedro saw me in the cast-off pants of my brother he almost choked."

Instead of a lovely day dress such as Pilar wore, Tory was dressed in her denim pants and a deep blue chambray shirt. Yes, she ruefully admitted, she wasn't the demurely dressed female that Marta could have wished for. But of what practical use to her were the hordes of dresses and outfits that hung in her closet, many from the noted House of Worth? She couldn't ride fast and hard in a silk ballgown; a tea dress wouldn't do for a roundup.

Pilar sipped her arm around Tory's shoulder and lowered her voice to a husky whisper. "You must be curious to know what passes between a husband and his wife," she said, the blush deepening on her face.

Tory stiffened. "Of course not," she protested, thinking that *that* was the last thing on her mind.

He wasn't going to get that close to her. She fingered the sheath that held the knife. Of that she was sure.

Pilar misinterpreted Tory's stiff, proud stance. "It isn't quite the frightening experience that one is led to believe it is; not, of course, if the man is a tender lover."

"Pilar, you don't have to. . . ."

"*Sí*, but I do," she insisted. "If I do not explain this to you, who will?"

"Mama told me about such things when my time began," Tory said quietly, recalling the conversation she'd had with her mother, who'd gently told her about the changes in her developing body as best she could. As to the role of wife, her mother had picked her words carefully, keeping to the basic facts. Tory shrugged her shoulders philosophically. "Remember, Pilar, I have been raised on a ranch. I do know how animals mate."

"*Sí*, so do I. Although," she added with a conspiratorial smile, her dark eyes flashing with mirth, "at times we must pretend that we don't." Pilar continued in a more serious tone. "I am not talking of things that happen between animals, but of things that take place between a man and his woman.

"We must hope that the man who is to be your husband is as tender, and as handsome, as my Pedro. He must be experienced in the ways of women; that is *muy importante*." Pilar grasped Tory's hand in her. "I was so scared the night of our wedding when we were left alone. My own mother's words came back to me, but at that moment they were cold comfort."

Tory interrupted her. "Please, Pilar, I don't need to hear this."

"*Sí*, you do."

"No," Tory stated vehemently. "It will not be the kind of marriage that you have."

"What kind will it be?" Pilar asked, puzzled.

"A marriage in name only."

"Victoria!" Pilar gasped. "Do you not intend to honor the vows that you make before God?"

"I don't want this marriage!" Tory protested.

"Oh, *mi amiga*," Pilar said softly, "you must honor your *novio* once he is your wedded husband. He will expect that you will be a true wife to him."

Angry, Tory said through gritted teeth, "I don't give a damn what *he* expects. I will marry him as I must and that is all."

"And if he forces the issue?"

"Then he may not remain a man for long."

"Tory, *calma, por favor*. You must not be like this. It can be beautiful between a husband and wife."

Her eyes focused once again on the flowers outside, Tory's mind replayed an incident she'd witnessed several weeks ago. It had been a very warm night. She'd been restless, in need, she thought, of a cool swim. Leaving the house, she'd thrown a blanket over Abendstern and rode, the moonlight a bright beacon, to the stream where it formed a pool shaded with live oak trees. Tethering her mare, she'd walked through the trees and heard a noise. Carefully, she'd edged her way until she could see two figures in the moonlight. It was Marshall Kincaid, the foreman of the Encantadora, and his wife.

Tory's smothered her gasp of surprise with her hand as she watched them emerge from the depths of the pool, both dripping water down their naked bodies. Marsh scooped up his wife in his powerful arms, his manhood erect. They dropped to the colorful Indian blanket on the bank, both laughing softly.

Unable to look away, with hot color tinging her cheeks a fine shade of pink, Tory saw Marsh's mouth meet Janet's in a deep kiss, observed Janet grasping the long, wet strands of Marsh's dark hair as she brought his head to her breasts, heard the triumphant cry that sprang from Janet's mouth as Marsh slid into the welcoming body of his wife and Janet wrapped her legs around her husband's slim waist.

Embarrassed, Tory had fled as quickly and as silently as she could back to her waiting horse, unable to explain the sudden deep ache in her belly, the tenderness of her breasts beneath her shirt.

Without conscious thought, her mind now saw a different image. The silvery slivers of moonlight played upon another body, also naked, emerging from the pool. It was Rhys Buchanan, smiling, beckoning to her. He hunkered down on the bank. Instead of the blanket that Marshall and Janet employed, his knees rested on the star quilt from her father's office, and he was stroking one lean-fingered hand over the material, inviting her to join him.

Shaking her head to rid herself of the image, Tory shivered.

"I won't deny that it can be beautiful, Pilar. I'm sure it is for you and Pedro. But not for me."

"Then you will miss much, my friend," Pilar stated. "The sharing of love is but one precious aspect of marriage."

Tory laughed, a bitter, brittle sound. "Sharing of love? There is no *love* in this union."

"There could be if you allowed yourself to be happy."

"I was happy until my father came up with this ridiculous scheme."

"Perhaps when you see your *novio* you will change your mind."

"I have seen him."

"You have? When?"

"He arrived yesterday."

Pilar digested this important piece of news. "And?"

"And what?" Tory asked, walking back into the room, taking a seat.

"Is he pleasing to look at?" Pilar queried, joining Tory inside. "What manner of man is he?"

"He's passing handsome," Tory answered.

"Indeed?" Pilar said, one dark brow rising in interest.

"Not to mention arrogant," Tory continued. "He is, after all, an *English*man."

77

Pilar couldn't repress a smile at Tory's re-marks. With the same words Tory could also be describing herself. Forcing herself back to the matter at hand, Pilar said, "Do not permit your stubbornness to ruin your life, *mi amiga*."

"I refuse to be subjugated to some man's will."

Pilar's lips curved sweetly. "At times there can be joy in the act of submission."

"Only because you love Pedro," Tory re-minded her.

"*Sí, es verdad*," Pilar admitted. "Yet, you may come to love this man."

"Never!" Tory insisted.

"Then," Pilar said with a trace of sadness in her tone, "I feel sorry for you, Victoria. You will never know the delight of a man's embrace. To see in his eyes all the beauties of this world, to feel in his arms as if the secrets of heaven were revealed." Pilar slid a sideways glance at Tory, who sat stiffly on the couch. She wanted to wrap her arms about her friend, to assure her that all would be well, as she did for her son when Mano was upset. Regrettably, she could not. Tory wasn't a child for whom a hug and a kind word would right the world.

From outside they heard the sound of a child's excited laugh. Both Tory and Pilar got up and went into the garden, where they saw Mano sitting perched upon Pedro's shoulders.

Pilar questioned them. "Where are you go-ing?"

"To the stables. *Abuelo* has promised me,"

Mano said, urging his father on.

"My son has finally gotten one of his wishes," Pilar said. "He persuaded his grandfather to let him witness the birth of Diablo's first offspring."

"Isn't that the stallion Tío Sebastian purchased last year?"

"*Sí*," Pilar answered, aware that Tory was carefully avoiding reopening the subject they had been discussing.

"I think I might like to breed my mare, Abendstern, to him."

"Papa says he's a wild one."

"A hellion?"

"*Sí*, a hellion. Untamed and proud. Used to having his own way."

"That's how it is with most stallions," Tory acknowledged.

"You must always remember that," Pilar said in an admonishing tone.

Tory shot her a quick look, her blonde eyebrows lifting.

"Come, let us go see the birth of the little one," Pilar said. "I must make sure that my son does not cause more of a disturbance than I am sure he has already created. We will finish our talk later."

"There is nothing to finish, Pilar."

Pilar laughed, a crystal sound, pleasant to the ear. "I must not neglect my responsibilities to you, and" . . . she paused, a particular gleam in her dark brown eyes . . . "I must reveal a secret to you."

* * *

No matter how many births Tory witnessed, each one was still a wonder to her. She and Pilar stood outside the birthing stall, watching. The mare was beautiful, and eager to bring forth her offspring.

Beside the panting, heaving mare was Dr. Hans Schmidt, the veterinarian who serviced this area of the hill country. A former Union Army officer during the War Between the States, Dr. Schmidt had been Tory's brother Travis's commanding officer. It had been his sad duty to inform the Reitenauers of their loss.

With the doctor, his snowy white lace shirt streaked with dust and dirt, was the *patrón* of Rancho Montenegro Don Sebastian Tomás Montenegro y Torres. Shirt sleeves rolled up, he was assisting Dr. Schmidt in the delivery.

Mano was silent, his dark eyes wide with amazement. He held his father's hand until he saw his mother and Tory.

"Tía Victoria, come," he urged, indicating that he wanted her with him.

At the sound of his grandson's voice, Don Sebastian's head rose. He threw a warm glance in Tory's direction. "Victoria," he greeted her, his voice deep and smoothly soft, "it's been too long since you've visited the rancho."

Impulsively, Tory joined Don Sebastian in the birthing stall, falling to her knees amidst the straw and bestowing a quick kiss on his lean brown cheek.

"I know it's been too long, Tío Sebastian. Will you forgive me?"

The warmth in his tawny eyes matched his words. "Always."

Pilar's gaze went from her son to her father with that exchange. She caught the deep-seated longing visible in her father's eyes. A sudden suspicion nagged at her. Could she be wrong? It was only a momentary glance. Yes, she must be mistaken. Had to be mistaken.

At the excited whinny of the mare, Tory stroked her neck and murmured soothing words of encouragement. Occasionally, Tory exchanged glances with Don Sebastian; her smile was always generous, her eyes sparkling.

"How much longer will this take, *Abuelo?*" Mano asked.

Don Sebastian gave his grandson a small lecture on man's place in the scheme of nature, that man must adjust to nature's timetable.

Mano persisted. "But when?"

"In good time," Don Sebastian answered.

"What is 'good time,' *Abuelo?*" Mano questioned.

"God's time," Don Sebastian replied. That finally seemed to satisfy the young boy.

Tory noted how very good Don Sebastian was with children. His daughter and son had provided him with the extended family he had always longed for. She knew he must be missing his son and daughter-in-law and their three children, who were in New Orleans visiting relatives.

"May I have the new horse, Grandfather?" Mano's eyes pleaded eloquently.

Don Sebastian shook his head. "Not this time, Manolito." He saw the slight trembling of his grandson's lips. "You may have one of Diablo's future offspring."

"Why not?" he asked.

"Because your grandfather has said no," Pedro answered. "It's not as if you don't have a horse, my son."

"But this is special," Mano said. "Please, *Abuelo*."

"I cannot, Mano. He, or she, is to be a gift."

"For whom, *Padre?*" Pilar asked, thinking that she knew the answer before her father spoke.

"It will be a wedding present, for Victoria."

Tory's head jerked upright at that remark. "Oh no, *Tío*, I couldn't allow . . ."

"It is not for you to allow or disallow. It is *my* gift," he said softly.

Tory felt the prick of tears in her eyes as she silently nodded her thanks.

Several moments later the 'gift' arrived; it was a striking, solid black colt.

Don Sebastian watched the subtle joy come over Tory's features as the new baby took his first tentative steps. Wavering, he plopped down on the straw before endeavoring to get up again. This time he was successful.

Tory wrapped her arms around his slender neck, bringing him to his mother, who nuzzled her baby with a welcoming whinny of affection.

"He's superb, *Tío*."

"What will you name him?" Pilar asked, knowing how very important the name of any of her animals was to Tory. Each was special and had to have a name that reflected that fact.

Tory thought for a moment before giving her answer. "Raven," she said simply, "in honor of Houston."

Those assembled understood her reasoning. Sam Houston, who'd been Tory's godfather, had also been known by his Cherokee nickname of "The Raven."

"An excellent choice, Victoria," pronounced Don Sebastian. "Now I think we should leave Raven to his nourishment." He stood up, wiping his hands on the towel that Pedro handed him. "Doctor, a brandy?"

"*Gracias*, Don Sebastian. I believe I will," Schmidt responded, snapping shut the leather satchel that held his instruments.

"Come, Tory, I want to show you the dress I had made for your wedding fiesta," Pilar said, taking hold of Tory's hand.

"You shouldn't have gone to any trouble, Pilar," Tory responded, giving the colt one last look.

Pilar pretended shock at her friend's remark. "Not take advantage of the occasion to order a new dress? Nonsense," she said. "Wait till you see it."

Opening the door to her suite of rooms in the estancia, Pilar went directly to a large pine armoire that dominated one wall. She carefully removed a dress and held it up to her neck.

It was stunning, Tory thought. Made of moire

satin, it was the deepest shade of wine, changing shades as the morning light played upon the fabric. "To say it's beautiful seems a waste of breath, Pilar, but it is."

"*Gracias,*" she responded and returned to re-hang the dress. She produced a lace mantilla next, also of deepest wine.

Tossing that onto the huge bed, Pilar held up one finger to indicate that she was not yet done. She bent down and removed a carved silver box from the bottom of the armoire. Taking a key from the gold keyring that lay on her dressing table, she opened the box. It contained her jewels. Not all of them, of course: a woman in Pilar's position would have enough jewelry to fill many large silver boxes. These were her favorite pieces.

She brought out a necklace, bracelet, and earrings. All were of gold and rubies.

Tory admired the set. She knew that the bracelet had been a gift from Pedro to Pilar on the occasion of their betrothal; the necklace was given on their wedding night; the earrings were in honor of the birth of their son. Tory picked up the feather-thin hair ornaments studded with ruby chips. Birthday gifts. Love tokens. Symbols of an on-going love, a marriage strong and secure. To herself Tory admitted a sense of envy—not for the costliness of the gifts, rather for the sentiments expressed by them.

"I thought you had something to tell me?" Tory questioned. "A secret."

"Not just yet," Pilar responded. "First, I must

give you a small token of my love for you."

Tory protested. "Pilar, you don't have to give me anything. The colt was enough."

"That was from my father. This is from me to you. Now sit down and close your eyes." She pointed to a small chaise in the corner of the room near the open windows.

Tory did as she was requested. A moment later something was placed into her hands.

"Open it," Pilar commanded.

Tory quickly untied the huge bow of blue ribbon that secured the bandbox. It was made of striped watered silk with tiny pink and white roses. Removing the lid, Tory gasped at the contents. Inside was a gossamer-thin nightdress of palest ivory, trimmed with ribbons of midnight blue.

Tory held it up, a blush staining her cheeks. "You can see through this!"

With a knowing smile, Pilar acknowledged that fact. "*Sí.*"

"It's beautiful, but . . ."

"It is meant for your wedding night."

"I couldn't wear this," Tory protested.

"Why ever not?"

"This is . . . it's meant for . . ." Tory couldn't complete her sentence.

"It is meant for a bride to wear for her husband," Pilar finished for her.

"Precisely," Tory stated crisply, her hand loving the soft feel of the material, noting absently how well the color blended with the pale golden tone of her own skin.

"It's not proper."

Pilar laughed. "Tory, *mi amiga,* since when have you cared for what's proper?"

Tory threw her a look that silently acknowledged that fact.

Curiosity getting the better of her, Tory suddenly asked, "Did you wear something like this when you wedded?"

Seating herself on the bed, Pilar nodded. "*Sí.* It was much like this, a gift from my aunt in New Orleans, except that there were more ribbons, in red. I wore this, and the rubies." Pilar's tone was wistful. "I was so nervous. Pedro had left me alone so that I might have time for myself. My maid helped me undress and then I dismissed her. As I slipped the gown over my head I caught sight of myself in the mirror. A part of me wanted to remove the nightdress before Pedro returned and saw me in it. *Dios mío,* I didn't want him to think me a wanton, lacking the proper respect for my vows and my position.

"Yet, ere I could change, Pedro came through the door that joined our rooms. He stood so still, so quiet, that I thought he must be very displeased. I couldn't look him in the eyes until he called my name softly." Pilar's mouth curved gently. "When I saw what was there, in his eyes, I knew I had nothing to fear."

"Our situations are very different, Pilar," Tory said, standing. She knew that to give back the gift would be an insult. And it was so exquisite. But of what use would it be to her? It was yet another reminder that this marriage was a mockery.

"I know this union is not what you want," Pilar said, crossing to where Tory sat. "Yet there are compensations. Do you not want children?"

A baby. Babies. Tory liked children, but when she thought of having her own, it was always in the nebulous future, when she was wed to a man she loved, a mate of her own choosing. Someone to help her pass on the legacy of the Encantadora.

"The ranch needs heirs; I know that."

"I'm not talking about what the rancho needs, Victoria. What about what you need?" Pilar touched Tory's cheek as she sat beside her. "Do you not long to feel the force of life within your body? To give what only you can? To create something unique?" Pilar's hand strayed to the fabric covering her stomach.

From the corner of her eye, Tory caught the movement. "You're going to have another child?"

There was a deep, contented glow in Pilar's onyx eyes. "*Sí.*"

Tory hugged Pilar tightly. "Pedro and Don Sebastian must be so pleased."

"*Sí*, both are overjoyed." She stood up and returned to her jewel casket, removing a velvet-wrapped package. Opening it, Pilar slipped on a magnificent ring of gold with a large deep red ruby stone. She turned so that Tory could see it. There was no need to explain to Tory who had given her the ring, or for what occasion. "Papa also made such a fuss." She closed the lid with a snap. "I wish sometimes that he had married again, to a woman young enough to bear him children. She added thoughtfully, "He loves them so."

"He loved Doña Anne dearly. I do not think he could find it in his heart to replace her."

"No, I agree that no one could take the place of my mother. Still, I think that he is lonely. And loneliness is harder when it is coupled with pride." Keeping her thoughts unspoken, Pilar realized that Victoria was just as lonely and as proud as her father. She hoped that this man who was to become Tory's husband would recognize her friend's sweet arrogance and cherish it, along with the woman. For if he trampled the pride, he would destroy the woman.

Don Sebastian Montenegro poured himself a large splash of tequila. Having left his son-in-law and grandson to their ride, and having provided Dr. Schmidt with an excellent brandy from his cellar, he had entered the house and heard the soft, feminine voices coming from Pilar's rooms as he walked up the stairs to his own apartments.

The sting of the tequila felt comforting as it slid down his throat. All he could think about was that he wished he hadn't had to share the moment of the colt's birth with anyone but Victoria. Her pleasure in the renewing of life gave her face an incandescent glow. She *was* life; she had all the vitality and spirit one woman could possess.

Another splash of tequila filled his glass. He tossed the drink back and decided that he was a fool. An *old* fool. A man enamored of an idea that could never become reality. The anger he felt was at himself for allowing his thoughts to be swayed from their proper channels for even a second. Don Sebastian was a man who didn't suffer fools gladly, most especially when he considered himself the chief fool.

However, that didn't stop the fantasies, or the frustration that he was suffering now.

Tío, Victoria called him. He was like an uncle to her. Victoria didn't know the extent of his feelings, and she musn't. He held her respect. That must never change.

Sebastian fingered the empty glass in his hand. He longed to throw it against the white wall, smashing it into little pieces, as broken as the dreams he had no right to dream. He refrained. The proud Sebastian Montenegro did not permit emotions to override his good sense. He must . . . what? Not think of himself as a man still? A man who ached to possess the one woman who brought youth to his heart?

He removed the gift he had selected for Victoria's wedding from the bottom drawer of his desk. The colt was a public gift; this was to be private.

Tory was leaving the estancia through the courtyard when she heard her name called from the open door that lead to Don Sebastian's study. She halted and retraced her steps, walking through the doorway.

"You wanted to see me, Tío Sebastian?"

"*Sí*, Victoria. I have something for you."

In her hands Tory held the bandbox containing the present from Pilar. Thinking of the colt he'd already given her, she wondered what more Don Sebastian could have for her.

"Your family has been too generous, *Tío*."

"It is your family, too. Do you not feel that way?"

Tory smiled. "*Sí, Tío*."

"Then there must be no talk of being too generous. Our families are for spoiling." He waved her into a chair. "I know that I must not keep you. This will take but a moment. Indulge me," he said in his deep, softly accented voice.

Tory sat, or rather, perched, because she was conscious of her attire, most especially contrasted with that of Don Sebastian, who wore an elaborate, albeit everyday, suit. Tory noted that he was a handsome man—truly, she thought, in his prime. His dark head was barely touched by silver, the hair still thick. His fine features bore the marks of his years well; age only added to the strong character of his face.

Tory gasped when she beheld the gift.

It was a bracelet, but not a simple piece of jewelry. It was wide, a band of silver with carved designs, and in the middle was a large stone that captured her fascination. It was turquoise. Tory remembered seeing this very bracelet in the portrait of Doña Pilar, Don Sebastian's mother and Pilar's namesake.

"I can't accept this," she said, her blue eyes focused on the stone. She thought it beautiful beyond compare, and she longed to have it on her wrist, though she knew she shouldn't. Her fingers caressed the workmanship, feeling an unexpected harmony with the piece.

"Please, Victoria. I insist," he said, taking hold of her slender arm. He felt the warm skin, the softness of her flesh. Stilling the trembling of his hand, Don Sebastian placed the bracelet on her wrist. "It was meant to be worn by a woman who would appreciate it."

"Shouldn't it be Pilar's?" Tory couldn't resist tracing once again the cool, smooth silver and the asymmetrical stone. It was perfect. Too perfect. "It's obviously a family heirloom."

"Pilar has her mother's jewels, not to mention those from Pedro's family. She does not need this. It was my mother's, made for her by a Navajo silversmith. My father wanted her to have something extraordinary on the occasion of their betrothal.

"It was given in love. Accept it in such."

Tory rushed out of her seat, wrapping her arms about Don Sebastian, whose face registered his surprise. The feel of her lushly curved body against his produced a traitorous response that he tried to hold at bay. His arms hung limply by his sides through sheer force of will.

"*Gracias, Tío. Muchisimas gracias,*" Tory said fervently. "I will treasure it always." Her eyes filled with tears, and before the Don could reply, she ran from the room, leaving her bandbox behind.

Even knowing that he shouldn't look, Don Sebastian could not resist the temptation. He opened the lid. Removing the material, he held it in his palms, allowing the light to filter through, absorbing the texture. His heartbeat quickened. A bridal nightgown.

His hands involuntarily crushed the garment, as if trying to obliterate from his mind the images it conjured. He dumped it quickly back into its container.

Turning, Don Sebastian directed his sudden surge of anger toward his desk, sweeping one arm across the surface and scattering the objects on it to the floor. Papers flew; an inkwell of Irish crystal crashed to the ground, splintering and spilling its dark contents onto a section of both the bare floor and part of a white rug.

He looked at the chaos and felt empty. "Victoria," he said in a whisper, his voice choking.

Chapter Four

Rhys awoke slowly, orienting himself to his surroundings. The room, instead of being filled with the acquisitions of several hundred years, contained the barest masculine essentials. The furnishings were well-crafted yet utilitarian.

He was in Texas, far away from the cosmopolitan streets of London, soon to be wed to the spitfire he'd met last evening. Christ, but she'd taken him by surprise.

Victoria. A regal name, worn by his queen. It was well suited to the proud woman who'd shattered his earlier expectations of a quiet, retiring girl whom he could easily bend to his will.

No matter, Rhys thought, he would still be the victor in this battle. And battle it would be, of that he had little doubt.

He glanced at the clock. Eleven. If he were in London, Twinnings would just now be bringing in the *Morning Post,* along with his favorite breakfast blend of tea.

Rhys looked around the room, noting that there didn't seem to be a bellpull to use to summon the servants. If he wanted food, he supposed he was going to have to go in search of it.

Throwing aside the sheet, he rose from the bed. Naked, he stretched his body, still feeling the ache of sore muscles in his thighs from the extended ride. Rhys ran a hand casually over the night's growth on his face as he headed for the bathroom.

As Rhys stroked the blade of the straight razor across his jaw, a soft knock sounded on the outer door.

"Come in," he called out.

He heard the door open. When no one spoke, Rhys stepped from the bathroom, wearing the borrowed robe, soap lather still heavy on one side of his face.

A slender girl of about fourteen was making his bed, humming softly to herself as she smoothed the sheets into place and plumped up the down pillows.

When she turned around, her mouth formed an "O" of surprise at the man standing before her.

"Good morning to you, sir," she said, her youthful eyes drinking in the sight of this new-comer.

"And who might you be?" Rhys asked amused by the girl's intent gaze.

"I'm Ruth, sir," she said, finishing her task. "My pa's the foreman here. My ma runs the house."

"Does she?" he asked. "Then how does one go about getting breakfast?"

"You're to come right on downstairs, sir. Morning meals ain't too formal here, as one never knows when they'll be getting it, 'cept for the hands. They get theirs regular like 'cause they'll be working regular. As for Miss Tory and the *patrón*, well, Kristen found it better to have something always on hand, seeing as they both eat whenever they want.

"Will you be needing anything else?" she asked.

"Where is my—Miss Reitenauer?" Rhys queried.

"Miss Tory rode out early this morning, sir. More n' likely she'll be at Don Sebastian's place."

"Don Sebastian?"

"Yes, sir. He's a great friend of her father. But don't worry, I'm sure she'll be back soon. You and she are going for a ride, I hear."

Which was more than he'd heard, Rhys silently acknowledged. "We are?" he asked, one black brow raising.

"Miss Tory's gonna show you around these parts."

By *these parts* Rhys assumed his financée was going to give him a tour of the property. He could feel his muscles protesting another long, strenuous ride.

"If you want anything else, let my ma know and she'll get it for you," Ruth said as she headed for the door, then added, "Welcome to the Encantadora, sir. I hope you enjoy your stay."

Enjoyment, Rhys thought as he finished the task of shaving, was going to have nothing to do with his tenure here. He wiped his face, realizing that without Twinnings and his bags, he had no clean clothes to put on. The thought of wearing the same trail-dusty clothes that he'd removed last night caused the fastidious Rhys to give a shudder. Damn! What was he to do now? He couldn't appear downstairs in a bathrobe.

Rhys opted for trying to get someone's attention downstairs, and just as he opened the door, he bumped into Ruth, carrying clothes.

"These are for you until your own gear gets here," she explained, laying them across the bed. "The shirt's pa's, one of his best. Pa's a mite taller than you, so he couldn't lend you any pants. Ma found these set aside in a trunk. They were Miss Tory's brother's."

"Thank you," Rhys replied. When she left, he removed his robe and picked up the shirt, a plain woven cotton, bleached white and smelling of sunshine. He slid his arms into the sleeves. This was another new experience for him. Rhys had never worn anything that hadn't been made expressly for him. His shirts, of only the finest materials, usually silk, were hand-sewn to his specific measurements, as were his trousers, jackets, and evening wear. His bootmaker, whom he shared with the Prince of Wales, was the best in London.

All that was behind him for now, he thought, as he fastened the buttons of the trousers and buckled the thick leather belt.

Tory strode into the house, heading for her father's office. She opened the door and found the room empty. Turning, she was just leaving when she saw Janet.

"Have you seen my father?"

Janet paused, her arms cradling a mixed bouquet of roses. "He's gone off with Marsh. Best as I can tell, a few head of longhorns are missing," she said as she arranged the red and white blooms in a vase, which rested on an oak table in the hall.

"And his lordship?"

"I believe he's eating his breakfast about now." An appreciative gleam formed in Janet's blue eyes. "He's a looker, that one," she said as she pushed one hand through the short, tumbled brown curls that surrounded her face. In her usual blunt fashion, Janet proclaimed, "Shouldn't be too difficult to wake up to that. Seems as though your pa picked a showy thoroughbred."

"I'd rather he'd chosen a man I could ride the river with," Tory said.

"How do you know that you won't be able to?"

97

Tory's blonde brows rose as her face reflected the chagrin she felt. "Janet, do you honestly think he looks the type to stay the distance?" Tory's voice was laced with scorn. "The Earl of Derran is a transplanted hothouse flower, fit only for the ballroom, the weekend hunt, and the trivial, idle pursuits of pleasure. He doesn't *belong* here. He never will." She turned on her heel, heading for the dining room.

Pushing open the door, Tory walked in and caught sight of Rhys as he stood by the sideboard. He was pouring coffee from the heavy silver pot. Smoky gray eyes clashed with crystal blue. Silence prevailed as Rhys returned to his seat and Tory took a china plate, heaping it with fluffy eggs, browned potatoes, and several thick slices of smoked ham.

An earthenware jug provided Tory with cold milk. Rhys recognized the workmanship of Waterford craftsmen as Tory poured the chilled beverage into a glass. He observed her as she tucked into her morning meal with great gusto. All the while neither spoke a word. They sat opposite each other at the table, Tory's eyes focused on her food, Rhys's on her. She was pretending that he didn't exist; her own version of the *cut direct*, he surmised.

She wiped her mouth with a linen napkin, replete and satisfied. A few of the pearl buttons of her shirt were undone, exposing the long, slim column of her throat and the whiteness of the cotton chemise she wore beneath her masculine attire. A deep breath drew Rhys's gaze to the swell of her full breasts as they rose and fell. He imagined peeling away the shirt, leaving only the chemise, cupping and stroking the flesh against the material, creating a teasing friction.

Her voice was a slap of cold water on his thoughts, dousing the smoldering sparks of desire he felt.

"Papa has asked me to show you some of the ranch. Are you ready?" Tory asked as she rose from her seat.

Rhys took due note of the icy tone of her voice: it was cold and impersonal. "Whenever you wish."

"Follow me," she said, leaving the room.

The day, which had begun so brightly, was now touched with clouds. Wind rustled through the stand of fruit trees by the house, snapping the branches and waving the leaves.

"Have Abendstern and Javert brought out," Tory called to a stablehand.

"Javert? What an odd name for a horse," Rhys remarked.

As the horses were each led from the stone barn, Tory answered him. "A personal quirk of mine. I had just finished reading *Les Misérables*," she said while swinging into the saddle on the gray mare, "and since I found that character so intriguing, I thought the name appropriate for a horse that was both black and white." She arched a brow as she waited for him to mount the prancing paint stallion. "Don't you agree?"

Rhys settled himself into the still unfamiliar saddle, recognizing the high-spirited stallion that he'd ridden previously. "I honestly wouldn't know, since I haven't read the book."

She was surprised that this man would admit that fact. Expecting a simple acquiescent "yes," whether he'd read the book or not, Tory was curious.

Rhys found he had to ride hard to keep up with his fiancée and her swift gray mare. They'd been riding for at least an hour, the terrain changing from softly rolling, flower-strewn hills to the dense greenness bordering a wide stream where they stopped briefly to water their animals.

"Just how big is your ranch?" Rhys asked as they rode towards a group of cowboys who were branding several young cattle.

"Close to two hundred thousand acres," Tory answered as she headed for the chuckwagon.

Rhys was astounded. He had known it was large, but he'd never imagined just how large. Indeed, it was a grand fiefdom, a kingdom in itself. His gray eyes carefully assessed the weapons each of the cowboys wore. Colts aplenty were in evidence, along with Winchester rifles. Tory, he saw, carried only a rifle; it rested in a scabbard of fine leather, made to match the workmanship of her saddle.

"Patches," Tory called, waving to the giant of a man who was pouring coffee from an enormous battered pot into an earthenware mug.

"Howdy, Miss Tory," he answered, holding out the mug to her.

"Just what I needed," she said, swinging from

the saddle and reaching for the hot brew.

Several of the men stopped their work to come over and join Tory in a cup. Patches's coffee, strong and black, laced with chickory, was renowned.

"That there your man, Miss Tory?" Patches asked softly, pouring her another cup.

Tory sliced a glance at the man sitting stiffly on the paint horse. She saw the flare of his nostrils as he caught the scents of men and cattle, of sweat and dung. Even in borrowed clothes he managed to look imperious, as if somehow removed from this particular group of humanity. That rankled her. Casting a glance at what was simmering in the pan Patches had over the fire, a smile tugged at the corners of her mouth.

"My lord Derran, if you would be so good as to join us?" she said, her voice silky and inviting.

The men surrounding Tory all focused their eyes on the stranger as he dismounted and walked to where they stood.

"Would you like a cup of coffee?" she asked.

"I would be pleased to have one," he answered, surprising her by taking the mug from her gloved hand. There remained about half a cup. He put it to his lips and drank from the same spot as Tory had, finishing it all. The taste was different, unique. "Another, if you don't mind," he said, holding out the mug.

Patches happily poured a refill, glad that this fine gent was enjoying his coffee.

"Patches," Tory spoke, "how about a plate of

prairie oysters for his lordship? I'm sure he'd enjoy sampling a local delicacy," she said, striving hard to keep laughter at bay.

"Are you sure 'bout that, Miss Tory?" Patches asked, his dark brown eyes acknowledging his comprehension of what she was planning.

"Of course I am."

Patches fetched a clean plate and plain fork from the wooden box at the back of the wagon. Bending over the fire, he spooned a heaping portion of the food onto the plate. He handed it to the stranger, who was the focus of all eyes.

Rhys lifted the fork, not at all sure of what he was going to taste. Gingerly, he opened his mouth and chewed, conscious that somehow he was again being tested. His Fitzgerald Buchanan pride rose to the fore. "Quite an unusual flavor," he pronounced, eating another forkful.

Several of the cowboys grabbed their lean stomachs, gripped by guffaws. Tory's hand flew to her mouth, trying valiantly to stop the chuckles.

Rhys focused his cool gray eyes on her face. "What is the joke?"

"Do you know what prairie oysters are?" she asked when she could compose herself enough to get out the words.

His gaze sliced around the assembled company. "I would hazard a guess that they are not really oysters?" His voice was slightly chilled, and very formal.

Laughter broke out again, very loud.

Patches watched the man carefully. The gentleman's precise enunciation, his rigid stance, reminded Patches of bygone days in his native Louisiana, when Creole gentlemen held sway. Here was a man who wouldn't take too kindly to being made to play the fool. What would be considered harmless fun, a way to initiate a greenhorn, might be construed as an insult to him.

"No, they're not real oysters," Tory said.

"Then what, pray tell, are they?" Rhys held the plate, his knuckles white with the force he was exerting.

"Bull testicles," Patches said, supplying the answer quickly.

"Indeed?" Rhys questioned. He lifted his right hand and speared the fork into another piece of the meat. He brought it to his mouth and began to eat, earning claps of approval from all there—all, that is, except Tory, who watched in silence.

She knew that he knew she'd done it deliberately. She'd believed that once he discovered exactly what he was eating, he would either throw it down in disgust or lose his temper and shout.

Rhys Buchanan did neither.

She watched, instead, as he continued eating; never once did he surrender his dignity. It took grit, she admitted, to follow through. This simple action gave Tory pause. She recalled her own first taste of the dish. She, also, had forced herself to finish the plate, pretending nothing was amiss. After all, didn't the hands eat this?

No one had ever, or would ever see her bow to pressure. Admiration for his ability to preserve his own dignity clashed head-on with her own reluctantly admitted sense of childishness. She, who found it hard to apologize, tasted the unspoken thought.

Rhys demured when another serving was offered, knowing that if he had to eat any more he would surely lose the contents of his stomach. He handed the plate to Patches and hunkered down to retrieve the mug.

Surprising him, Tory bent down to grab the hot pot of coffee, filling the mug half-way. Their eyes connected, each direct and intent. He swallowed the coffee quickly, allowing the hot liquid to rid his mouth of the taste of his dubious treat. Then Rhys held out his arm, the mug empty. Tory poured another splash into it and hung the pot back over the flame. This time Rhys indicated the coffee was for her. She followed his example, downing the coffee swiftly, the heat scalding the petty taste of hollow foolishness from her.

"I think we'd better be heading back," Tory said, giving Patches the mug.

"Yes, I rather think that would be a good idea," Rhys echoed, "as I expect Twinnings should have arrived by now with my things."

One of the cowboys approached Tory. "Tell your daddy, Miss Tory, we found another carcass on the eastern edge of the property."

"Same as last time?"

"Yep. Shot the mother and took the calf."

"Damn," she muttered under her breath.

As they rode from the camp, Rhys asked, "What did that pertain to?"

Tory pulled back on Abendstern's reins, forcing her horse to slow her pace to a mere trot so that she could talk freely. "Several of our cattle have been slaughtered recently. Whoever it is kills the cows and takes the unbranded calves."

"Is that the reason your men were so heavily armed?"

Tory stopped short at that question. Of course, to an outsider, especially to one such as he, it would appear that her men were overly cautious. "This is not England, my lord," she said. "Here a weapon is necessary just to survive. Most men would feel undressed without a gun of some sort."

"And what about you?"

"What about me?" she demanded.

"I noticed you carry a rifle."

"Yes."

"Have you ever used it?"

"Do you mean have I ever had to defend myself or my property with it? Yes," she said, her eyes focused on the hills beyond, "I have." Tory watched his gray eyes widen in comprehension. Her tone became harder as she explained, "This is not the polite world that you're obviously used to, my lord. Here, there are different rules. One must be ready and willing to protect and defend what one owns. If you don't, you lose it. It's as simple as that."

Rhys thought of his home farm in Dorset,

considerably smaller in recent years, but still his. The idea of riding the boundaries of that property armed was ludicrous. Poachers were apprehended by the local sheriff. "You have no officials whose duty it is to see to poaching?"

Tory shot him an incredulous look. "Poaching? My God." A short burst of harsh laughter erupted from her. "It's called stealing. *Stealing!* And as for the law—well, there isn't any. The ranches here have to provide their own security.

"If you plan to live here, my lord, you'd best get used to the idea." With that she kicked her heels lightly into the mare's ribs and the animal took off at a gallop.

Rhys did the same, his stallion responding quickly in an effort to maintain the pace of the other horse.

A sharp rain drenched them a mile from the house. Soaked to the skin, they rode their mounts hard, eager to get to shelter. They entered the stone barn together, ducking to get through the doors.

Tory quickly dismounted and removed the saddle from her mare, tossing it to the floor as she fetched a blanket to rub the flanks of the quivering mare. Looking up, she was surprised to find that Rhys had done the same for the piebald. Grooming a horse was natural to her, as it was to all hands on the ranch. A cowboy who neglected or mistreated his animal wasn't a man worth having. Surreptitiously, she glanced at him, noting the way his long fingers stroked the horse's sides, soothing as he rubbed the animal down.

Tory led her mare into one of the stalls, listening to the nickers of the other horses in the barn. Satisfied that Abendstern was secure, she closed the door and threw the lock.

Rhys, having secured Javert, watched her. She'd removed the soft suede jacket she'd worn; it hung casually on a hook, drying. His borrowed jacket was wet also, but it would at least provide her with some warmth and comfort as they made their way back to the house. But before he could offer it, Tory was at the doors of the barn, peeping through one of them, checking the weather.

"If we run fast, it shouldn't be so bad," she said over her shoulder as she sprinted out the door into the raging storm.

Rhys followed her, judging her too optimistic by half. The steady blast of wind and rain pelted his face without mercy as he raced toward the comfort of the open doorway.

Once inside he slammed the door and leaned against it. Tory was talking with Janet. The shirt she wore clung revealingly to the curves of her body. When she turned around at his entrance, he noted the fullness of her breasts, outlined seductively, the nipples hard and visible. The heat in his loins was at odds with the damp cold of his flesh.

Tory shivered as she watched his gray eyes lower. She felt that intense gaze as if he'd actually touched her. The well-worn material of her shirt and pants was suddenly confining. She shivered again.

"Best you get upstairs and out of them clothes, Miss Tory," Janet said. "I'll fix you a hot toddy to ward off a chill." She sliced a long glance at Rhys as Tory quickly bolted up the staircase. A small puddle had formed at his booted feet. "Your man is upstairs, waiting. You'd best be getting out of your duds also."

Rhys complied, hating the clammy feel of the wet garments.

Janet couldn't wait to share her observations about the couple with Marsh. If they'd stood there any longer exchanging heated looks they'd have dried out all by themselves.

"My lord," Twinnings gasped, his happiness at seeing his master shattered by the appearance of the disheveled man who entered the room.

"Twinnings, thank God you're finally here," Rhys said through gritted teeth. "Fetch me my own robe, and a whisky." Rhys, tired and caught off-guard by his strong reaction to Victoria, wasn't in a gracious mood. *"Now*, Twinnings."

Twinnings came out of his surprised stupor and fetched the silk robe, holding it out so that Rhys could easily slip his arms into it. A bottle of scotch whiskey was produced from one of the capacious traveling trunks. Twinnings poured a large measure into a squat crystal glass and handed it to his lordship.

The whiskey warmed his throat as it went

down. So smooth. Would her skin be as smooth to the touch?

"Shall I draw you a bath, my lord?" Twinnings asked as he proceeded to pick up the wet clothes, holding them away from his body as if they were contaminated.

"No. I've had my fair share of water this day." Rhys indicated that he wanted another whiskey. He sipped the beverage this time, slowly, enjoying the taste. "A towel wouldn't be amiss, though," he said as he walked to the window. He watched the splash of rain against the panes, heard the violent rumblings in the sky. Twinnings gave him the towel and took the empty tumbler in its place. Rhys ran the dry cloth over his head till his hair was merely damp. All the while his thoughts were on the woman in the next room. He couldn't forget the look on her face as she watched him eat the so-called oysters. And then there was the startled admiration he saw in her eyes as he finished them.

What was she doing now?

The gleaming copper tub was filled with warm water, scented with the essence of roses. One slim foot rested on the rim as Tory sipped the potent hot toddy. She wiggled her toes, casting a glance at the pile of clothes that lay in a heap on the tiled floor. *Her* clothes, and she'd felt a stranger in them.

A rumble of thunder shook the windows in the bedroom. The flicker of the candles added to the strange mood that gripped her. Tory normally wasn't the sort to linger in her bath; she never wanted to waste time. Tonight, it seemed somehow important.

The soft strains of a piano drifted through the closed door that lead to the hallway. Chopin, Tory mused, relaxing to the vibrant richness of the melody.

Then, without warning, the mood changed. Instead of a polonaise, a darker piece was being played. Beethoven. She recognized her favorite of his sonatas, the *Moonlight*. She let the music drift around her, filling her with a sense of wonder and joy.

It spoke.

She listened.

But who was playing? The only person who'd used the piano was dead. The niggling question forced her from her bath.

She dried herself with one of the thick towels that Janet kept in abundant supply in her bathroom. Removing the silver pins that kept her hair in place, she shook it free, eager to find the source of the hauntingly beautiful music.

His fingers flew along the keyboard, echoing his mood with the sounds he brought forth. It had been Christina Reitenauer's music room, Janet explained to him when he saw her enter carrying fresh-cut flowers. And tonight, for some unknown reason, Rhys craved the solace, the comfort that music afforded him. It was serenity, rebellion, freedom—most of all, expression.

Rhys was suddenly aware that he wasn't alone. His head bent and he glanced to the side, seeing the outline of a form standing in the doorway. He continued playing, knowing somehow that if he stopped, she would disappear.

Oddly, he wanted to share this with her—he, who had never shared his music with anyone before. It had always been his, a welcome sanctuary from the world.

Tory brushed aside the unexpected tears, backing away from the doorway when he finished. She turned, seeking the solitude of her room.

Once inside, she shivered, this time not from cold, but in reaction to the music.

Tory sank into a chair in front of her dressing table. There, in the oak mirror, she saw reflected her flushed face and bright eyes. She raised her hand to brush back a thick strand of strawberry-gold hair as she wondered what other surprises her husband-to-be held in store for her.

Chapter Five

"How many more head did we acquire?" asked the man standing by the mantel, a large drink in his hand.

"About thirty head, I reckon, boss," reported the skinny cowhand.

"Excellent." Talbot Squire took a long swallow, and his prominent Adam's apple bobbed as the drink went down. He was happy. Anytime he could steal as much as even one cow from the herd of the Encantadora, he was thrilled. He would do anything and everything he could do to put that bitch in her place.

The damp weather was playing havoc with his shoulder. It ached unbearably; always would. She'd sunk her blade in good and deep, almost rendering that arm useless. One day he'd have her right where he wanted her, screaming for mercy, begging him for her goddamned life. He smiled, his teeth revealed as his lips slid back in a feral grin. Destroying Victoria Reitenauer and her sanctimonious father was a pleasure he'd promised himself ever since they'd damn near destroyed him; Tory with her blade, Sam Reitenauer with his words. No amount of time would ever erase those days from his mind: the stabbing, the public humiliation as he was tossed off the ranch with no money, no food, and most importantly, with a threat to his very life should he seek work again in Texas. And all that pain over a stupid greaser whore who didn't realize that he would be doing her a favor by taking her.

Well, he'd showed them, Talbot thought. Seven years had passed since then. He went up Oklahoma way, changed his name, drifted from job to job. During that time he discovered he was skilled at parting people from their money, whether by fair means or foul. Every dollar stolen was an added incentive, a reinforcement to his notion that money was power; with it he could achieve whatever he wanted.

With money Talbot purchased an aura of respectability. It was his fine clothes and ready cash that persuaded old man Rayburne that Talbot was a proper suitor for Rayburne's daughter Martha. Not that the old man had much choice. Suitors for a tarnished woman with a breed brat weren't exactly thick about the Hill country. Talbot had done some checking into the Rayburne family. Their property was for the most part isolated, and they kept to themselves. The ranch was perfect for his plans. From here he could watch, waiting for the right moment to strike back at his enemies.

The only drawback was that he had had to marry skinny, pasty-faced Martha to get ownership. She had been easy to dupe. The fact that he had to take a breed's leavings gave him one more reason to hate the Reitenauers.

And hate was another thing that Talbot Squire was good at.

He forced his thoughts back to the present.

"Miss Reitenauer's fiancée arrived yesterday," his cowhand was saying.

So the bitch was getting married at last, Talbot thought. Another one to be rid of. One day he'd own the Encantadora. He'd beat Samuel Reitenauer and he'd take his daughter, in every way possible. That notion alone brought ripples of pleasure coursing through his thin body. He would make her suffer, as he had suffered. Thought she was Miss God Almighty Reitenauer. Uppity slut! He would show her that she was just like any other woman, good for only one thing. Pain, Talbot knew, was an important lesson to learn. He'd make sure that before he was done with her she understood it well.

"Another thing, boss . . ." The cowboy shifted his weight from one foot to the other.

"Yes?" Talbot inquired.

"We caught the boy tryin' to get away again."

"Where is the bastard?" Talbot rarely spoke of his stepson without rancor.

"Got him in the barn, chained up like usual."

"Good." Talbot smiled again. He supposed the brat needed another lesson. A thick whip hung on the wall. He lifted it down, hefting it in his hand. A few more snaps of this against the kid's flesh should suffice. Maybe he should make his wife watch. Then she could grovel to him to spare her brat. A sinister smile thinned his mouth.

"Keep the kid there for now. I'll take care of him later."

The cowboy took note of the cold certainty in his employer's eyes. As he backed out the door, he heard Squire bellow for his wife, "Martha! Come in here."

Martha Squire was a thin, pale woman, her weariness evident in her tired, lackluster blue eyes. Any spirit she'd once had had been effectively beaten out of her, until she was now a shell of her former self. The one person she loved, who made life bearable, was her only child. For him she clung to her miserable existence.

"What do you want, Talbot?" Her voice was barely above a whisper.

"Your son has tried to leave again, madam."

"Where is he?"

"Waiting for me to mete out his punishment," he said smoothly.

Sheer terror transformed Martha's face. "Please, Talbot. He's only thirteen."

"I don't give a damn how old he is. The bastard tried to run away. I warned you, and him, what would happen if he tried that again."

Martha knew Talbot didn't want her son carrying tales about what really went on in this house. She'd tried her best to shield her son from just how disasterous a mistake her marriage had been. When she thought of how stupid she'd been to be trapped by Squire's lies, by his smooth words, she wanted to scream. Concern for her son stopped her. She licked her dry lips. "What do you want?" she asked.

"I'm open to persuasion, madam, should you want to try."

Bile rose in Martha's throat. She knew what was expected of her. Her stomach threatened to eject its contents. She fought the urge. When it was over, she could escape to her refuge. One day she was sure she'd go there, find her peace, and never return.

Talbot's hands went to the fastening of his trousers, unbuttoning them quickly. "On your knees, Martha," he said, "now."

The rawhide ropes dug into the boy's wrists. They'd been dipped in water so that when they dried, they would tighten. Rafe kept silent, preferring not to give his enemy the satisfaction of seeing him struggle. And the smug look on Talbot's face compounded the fury he felt.

Talbot strolled over to the lad, who was held immobile by the bonds. He grabbed a handful of the boy's black hair. He could see the hatred in the dark blue eyes of his stepson. Talbot returned that hatred. This brat was a reminder that his wife could bear a child, something she'd never done for him. This arrogant little bastard actually thought he counted for something. Talbot sneered. The kid's blood was tainted as far as he was concerned. He was nothing but a Comanche half-breed. He tightened his grip on Rafe's hair, tugging, wanting to make him break.

"You've been warned about trying to escape, boy," he said, slamming the boy's head against the wall.

Pain knifed through Rafe's head. He held on to consciousness by a slender thread.

"When are you going to learn that what *I* say counts around here?" Talbot asked. "Look here, breed, you ain't fit to associate with decent folks. How many times I gotta tell you that?" Talbot signaled to a man standing with a rifle at the entranceway to the barn. "Take him down and tie him between those two posts."

Talbot grabbed the rifle, giving Rafe a taste of the butt of it against his side. A small moan escaped Rafe's lips. "Human after all, eh boy?" Talbot mocked.

When the hand finished his assigned task, Talbot returned the gun to him. Then he uncoiled the whip he'd brought with him, snapping it a few times to test it.

Rafe knew what was coming. His back already bore scars from earlier beatings. He snapped his mouth shut, determined not to show any weakness to this man. The sting of the whip sliced through his cotton shirt, tearing his skin. Tears seeped from eyes squeezed shut.

A lone figure slipped through the barn door, standing, listening. When she saw what was happening, Martha ran to Talbot, grabbing his hand.

"No!" she screamed. "You promised."

A glint of pure malice worked his face. "I did, didn't I?" he asked, his smile cruel.

Martha hated him. The memory of what he'd demanded of her earlier distressed her, but not half as much as the sight of the one good thing in her life, suspended by leather ropes, bleeding in silence. She made a move towards Rafe.

Talbot was quicker. He grabbed her arm and flung her backwards into the dirt of the barn floor. "Get out," he thundered, snapping the whip.

Martha crawled to her husband, her face streaked with tears and smudges of dirt, hay clinging to her hair. She ignored the pain of the bruises beneath her dress. She'd done what he'd asked—hadn't she always? Why then did he have to treat Rafe so? He was just an innocent boy.

"Please," she begged, her arms wrapping around the thin legs of Talbot Squire. "Please," she reiterated, clinging tightly.

Talbot looked down at her. His small mouth curled. He raised his hand and brought the whip snapping through the air, placing it squarely on the back of the boy.

Martha screamed again, earning a back-handed slap from her husband. She collapsed, retreating from the horror she couldn't prevent.

Rafe couldn't see his mother; he only heard her terrified pleas for mercy, then silence. Before he lapsed into unconciousness, he promised himself that he would find a way to make his stepfather pay for all he'd done to them.

Talbot dropped the whip, fighting to control his heavy breathing. He turned to his wife, who sat huddled in the dirt, staring vacantly into space. The bitch had gone loco, he thought.

Shit, he cursed silently, just when he could have used a woman. He needed relief. Ignoring the man who still stood watching, Talbot yanked his wife to her feet, dragging her into an empty stall.

Chapter Six

Unable to sleep, Tory crept silently down the stairs so as not to wake anyone else. She proceeded to the library, one of her favorite rooms in the house, thinking that she could lose herself in a favorite book. She entered her sanctuary, content to stand for a moment, loving the atmosphere therein. What would his lordship think? she wondered. Would he find this relaxed room a contrast to what she knew would have been the oh-so-very-formal library in his London house? This was a place used and cared for, smelling of beeswax and lemon oil. She doubted that in his townhouse the library floor would be covered in rugs as varied as hers: one large one made of cowhide, which matched the brown-and-white shading of the couch, another of thick brown buffalo fur, a gift from her godfather

Houston. Several quilts, made by her mother, herself, and Janet, lay scattered over the various pieces of furniture.

The room was comforting and comfortable.

The wild storm that had erupted earlier was just now calming. Tory unlatched the windows and threw them open, breathing deeply of the cool, moist air. It was the music, she decided. It was all the fault of the beautiful music that she couldn't fall asleep. The music and the man.

No, she chided herself, I won't think about it.

Selecting a leatherbound volume, she curled up in a chair to read. *Jane Eyre.* Tory lost track of the time as she became absorbed in the tale of the lonely governess and the proud, brooding Mr. Rochester.

Sam Reitenauer found her asleep when he investigated the light coming from the room when he finally returned home. He watched her for a few minutes, his heart swelling with pride.

Tory awoke with a start when she felt the hand on her shoulder.

"Come, *Liebchen,*" her father admonished, "you should be in bed."

"What time is it?"

"After eleven."

Tory replaced the leather bookmark into the book. Setting it on the chair, she went to shut the windows. "Are you just now getting back?"

"Yes," Sam said with a sigh.

"What did you and Marsh find?"

"More than thirty head missing."

Tory saw the weary, drawn look on her father's face. There was a sadness in his eyes. "What else?" she asked softly, padding on bare feet across the carpet to join him. She linked her arm through his, fixing him with direct blue eyes.

"We lost a man."

Her breath hissed inward. "Oh God, Papa, who?"

Sam's leonine head bowed. "Adam."

Tory's hand gripped her father's arm tighter. Adam was a younger brother to another of their hands, a young man just a year older than Tory, with a wife and baby on the way. "Did you tell Delia?"

Sam nodded. "One of the hardest things I've done. Bad enough when it's a legitimate accident, but this was murder. Deliberate, cold-blooded murder. If I catch the son of a bitch . . ." His voice trailed off, leaving no doubt in Tory's mind what Sam would do.

"I'd better go to her."

Sam decided not to attempt talking her out of it. "Marsh sent Janet to see her, but I think she'd like to see you, *Liebchen*."

Tory flew up the wide staircase, thoughts of sleep pushed from her mind. Just as she reached the door to her room and slipped in, lighting a lamp, the door that connected Rhys's room to hers opened.

"What's wrong?" he asked, standing there.

Startled, Tory turned to face him. "I thought that door was locked," she stated.

"Apparently you forgot," he answered, his

eyes taking quick inventory of her slim body. Just how many sides were there to this woman? he wondered. Now, standing there in the semi-darkness, he thought she resembled a young postulant. Her hair, which heretofore she'd worn in braids, was undone, flowing freely down her back and shoulders to well past her waist. Her nightdress was prim, starched white cotton, with tiny buttons covering the area from neck to waist. Innocence and worldliness; strength and fragility. His hands clenched as he tried to ignore the involuntary hardening of his body. *Bloody hell,* he thought. He wanted her.

How could she have forgotten to lock that damn door? Or had someone else engineered it? If it was Janet or Ruth, she would have to have a word with them. A flutter of something stirred in her breast as she scrutinized the intensely male animal in the doorway: his hands, the long, slender fingers which had brought forth magic only hours before; his legs barely concealed by the floor-length silk robe of pure black; and his eyes, those pale eyes of coolest gray which now seemed to burn hotly.

Nonsense. It was all a trick of the light. His eyes were no different than before. She was being fanciful. And Tory had no use for that.

In terse terms she explained the situation. "Now I would appreciate it if you would vacate my room," she said stiffly.

Rhys obliged. "As you wish," he said, closing the connecting door behind him. He waited to see if she would lock it.

When no sound came, he smiled broadly. To lock the door now would be to admit weakness, and that she would never do.

As he slipped beneath the sheets he recalled her bedroom. The room was feminine, yet not oppressively so. Two could fit quite comfortably in that large sleigh bed. Rhys had always abhored endless geegaws cluttering up every available space in a woman's room. He'd felt trapped, smothered by incidentals whenever he'd been in one such. His casual observation of Victoria Reitenauer's room revealed something different . . . a sense of freedom and warmth.

Odd, he reflected, that he would choose such terms to illustrate his impressions.

"It's been a rough couple of days," Tory admitted, answering the question posed to her by Pilar. She pulled off the buckskin gloves and tucked them into the pocket of her pants. From her saddlebag she extracted a canteen filled with fresh lemonade. She uncapped it and took a long swallow, offering Pilar a drink.

Pilar smiled and took the canteen. "You still have no idea who is doing this to you?"

"None whatsoever. Papa and Marsh have been investigating, but with no luck."

"Perhaps it was just a passing band of renegades."

Tory shook her head. "I don't think so. There have been too many incidents for it to be just someone stealing from us as they were passing through." She sank down on a flat rock, trailing her hand through the clear, cool water, watching it flow in rushing action over the smooth rocks that formed the bed of the stream. "Papa's warned Don Sebastian in case they try and raid his herds." Tory stood up abruptly. "We buried one of our men yesterday." She could still hear the cries of his wife, Delia, as the news of her husband's murder forced her into delivering her child a month prematurely. Delia had collapsed after the difficult birth and was unable to attend the funeral. Just as well, Tory thought. Delia would be forced to deal with the demands of a new life, which would keep her mind, for large portions of time, from dwelling on her pain.

Pilar watched the play of emotions on Tory's face. More than a mere funeral was plaguing her. "What about him?"

There was no need to identify *him*. "That's hard to explain, Pilar. He's all I said before and more."

"How so?" Pilar took another drink of the lemonade and passed it back to Tory.

Tory couldn't bring herself to tell Pilar about the night she went to the music room and listened as Rhys played. Or later, when he appeared in her room. Her own perceptions were confused, cast askew. Tory didn't like that. It wasn't safe. She wasn't in control.

"Make your own judgment tonight," Tory responded.

"Ah, *sí*" Pilar said, "you are all coming to dinner."

Tory rolled her eyes. "Yes. This should be very interesting."

"I cannot wait to meet your *novio*." And, Pilar thought silently, to find out more of what caused the restless uncertainty that she observed in Tory's eyes. Since last she saw her friend, Tory had undergone a subtle change. It had to be due to this Englishman. Of course, Pilar decided, Tory was still somewhat spoiled and headstrong, a law unto herself. That would always be Tory; there was, however, a fine shade of difference in that honest face.

Pilar stood, brushing off the back of her split skirt. Grasping the reins of her horse, she prepared to mount. "Until tonight then, *mi amiga*."

Tory, her thoughts elsewhere, responded, "Ah, yes, tonight. Very well, Pilar."

As she rode back to the Encantadora, Tory decided that tonight would be the perfect opportunity to wear Don Sebastian's elegant gift.

"A formal dinner, my lord?" Twinnings questioned.

"Yes," Rhys answered, gulping down the cold glass of lemonade that Janet had fetched for him after his own ride. When she'd suggested that he try Kristen's lemonade, he had looked askance, claiming never to have formed a habit of drinking what he considered a weak beverage consumed only by elderly women and insipid schoolgirls in lieu of wine.

The strong flavor of the beverage, its bite and taste, changed his mind. His full mouth curved into a gratifying smile. The drink was like the mistress of the ranch. Tart and strong, with an underlying hint of sweetness. Unexpected.

"We are to spend the night, I've been told," Rhys said, finishing the glass.

Twinnings raised his bushy eyebrows. "Another trip?" he grumbled.

"It would appear so, Twinnings," the earl affirmed, returning to the letter that he was writing to his younger sister. He missed Gillie terribly, more so than he thought possible. What would she make of this place? Another smile traced his mouth. His sunshine-souled sister would adapt quickly. As long as there were animals for her to "doctor," she would be happy.

With a flourish, he signed his name. He folded the thick cream paper, embossed with his personal seal, and slipped it into an envelope. Another seal was added to the back of the envelope, this one of wax with the impression of his signet ring.

Twinnings was already hard at work picking his wardrobe for this evening. At least tonight would relieve the boredom Rhys felt. If he were in London, he would have so many choices of how to spend his day: he could look at the selections of cards and invitations sent to him; spend a few hours at his club, a ball, or an evening at the theatre; perhaps enjoy a tryst with his mistress; or even spend some time at the House of Lords.

A fond memory crossed his thoughts. When

last he attended Parliament, Lady Anne had sent a footman with a note that she had a surprise planned, and to please follow him. As it was an especially boring session, he was eager to find an excuse to leave. A barge was tied up at Westminster awaiting him. On board was a cold supper and a warm Lady Anne, who'd arranged the rendevous.

Tonight he was sure to have a hot supper and a cool companion.

Her small traveling trunk packed, Tory checked to make sure she hadn't left anything behind. Satisfied, she grabbed the trunk and opened her door, just in time to see Rhys emerging from his room, his manservant behind him carrying his bags.

"Is there no one to fetch your case?"

Tory threw him a sidelong glance. "I can do it myself."

"My," Rhys noted, amused, "we are in a belligerent mood, are we not?" With this he cocked one black brow.

Tory pursed her lips. "No, *we* are not in a mood, belligerent or otherwise," she snapped.

"Leave your case then, and I'll have someone see to it," he commanded softly.

"I think not," Tory responded, grabbing the fabric-covered trunk and making her way down the wide staircase.

"As you wish, Victoria."

A shiver rushed down her spine with his

pronunciation of her name. Ignoring it, Tory continued.

Outside, a carriage was being loaded with baggage. Sam stood next to it, talking softly to Marsh, who nodded in agreement.

Sam took Tory's trunk and placed it with the others. He saw his daughter's puzzled frown at the number of men who were mounted and ready to ride.

"You think we need an armed escort, Papa?"

"I take no chances, *Liebchen*," Sam said. "Who knows what could happen between the Encantadora and Rancho Montenegro. It's better to take no risks."

"I suppose that's wise," she said, agreeing. "Are you going with the carriage or will you ride?"

Sam drew his child into his embrace. "I won't be going."

"Why, Papa?"

"I think it best not to at this time." He withdrew a letter from his jacket pocket and gave it to Tory. "This is for Don Sebastian. It will explain all to him."

"I wish you were going," she said wistfully.

"So do I, *Liebchen*. Especially since I was looking forward to a grand game of poker with the Don."

"Did I hear you mention cards?" Rhys asked.

Sam nodded, giving Rhys a quizzing look.

Rhys interpreted the nuances of that glance correctly. "I fancy the game as an amusement, even a challenge if you will. Lest you think I follow my father and brother's inclinations, I assure you that I do not."

Tory looked from one man to the other, realizing that her father had information regarding her future husband that he hadn't bothered to share with her. Gambling debts, she reckoned. A *lot* of gaming debts, she supposed, forcing the Earl of Derran to wed wealth. Perhaps, she decided, this could be a point of prospective leverage.

"I shall give your regrets to Don Sebastian and his family," Tory said, kissing Sam's cheek and grabbing Abendstern's reins. She watched as Rhys indicated that he would ride also, his man choosing the slow comfort of the carriage.

Sam watched the caravan ride out, his daughter in the vanguard, as always. Word had come earlier that his wedding surprise was almost finished. The limestone mansion he was building in San Antonio needed only the finishing touches before it was ready. Sam would give Victoria the deed the day of the ceremony. It would be the perfect spot for a wedding trip. He was quite pleased with himself, he thought as he returned to the house. Quite pleased indeed. Each day convinced him more and more that his daughter and the Englishman would fare well. There was nothing tepid between them, which he judged good. Time would tell, he knew, time and the natural affinity of two proud aristocrats.

* * *

The horses thundered into the courtyard of the hacienda. Tory knew that she and Rhys were at least a half hour ahead of the carriage. Two hands from the Encantadora kept pace with them. Normally she would have headed for the stables, but since she knew her men would see to the two animals, Tory rode to the house entrance.

Leaping down, she patted Abendstern's neck, hugging the animal briefly before handing the reins to one of the men. The other man waited for his lordship to do the same.

As the animals were being led away, Tory spoke softly, "This way."

Rhys's curiosity got the better of him as he surveyed the stuccoed walls of the ranch. Terracotta pots filled with bright red flowers hung alongside the doorway. The heavy, dark wood doors swung open, revealing an older man and a stunning woman whom Rhys assumed was close to Victoria's age. There was a vague resemblance between the two, so he dismissed the idea of a man and his wife. Rhys watched as Tory was embraced warmly by both the man and the woman, saw the love and the laughter that lurked in their eyes.

Tory stood between Don Sebastian and Pilar, taller than Pilar by a few inches, and equal to the Don.

"Don Sebastian and Doña Pilar, may I present my . . . fiancé, Rhys Fitzgerald Buchanan, the Earl of Derran." The hesitation between the words was duly noted by all present.

131

"My Lord Derran," Tory drawled, "may I present Don Sebastian Tomás Montenegro y Torres and his daughter, Doña Pilar Montenegro y Valmont Sanchez."

Rhys extended his hand and met the steely strength of the older man's. They exchanged glances, each silently assessing the other, with neither giving quarter. All was polite, but beneath the surface each recognized a tension that ran through their introduction. With Pilar, Rhys was his charming self, lifting her soft white hand to his lips. "My great pleasure, madame," he said in a caressing tone. In her large dark eyes, the color of a fine sable pelt, he saw a gentle quality of friendship. That surprised, and pleased, him.

"*Mi casa es su casa,*" Don Sebastian said, standing aside to permit his guest to enter.

With a nod of his head, Rhys walked into the house. Big square tiles in rusty red extended throughout the hacienda. A low, gleaming wooden bench, upon which lay a bright, multicolored blanket, held two guitars—one obviously a child's, the other an adult's. Above hung a portrait that caught Rhys's interest. It was of two girls whom he had no problem identifying as Tory and Pilar. Merriment warred with dignity in each pair of young eyes.

The chatter of voices speaking Spanish reinforced his sense of strangeness.

"You must forgive us, my lord," Pilar explained, "if we forget our manners and converse

132

in Spanish. We do not mean to exclude you."

The twist of Tory's mouth made Rhys think otherwise. Tory knew exactly what she was doing by switching to Spanish. He would deal with her games at a later date. For now, he bestowed on Pilar his most beguiling smile.

"This must seem so very strange to you, does it not?" she asked.

"Well," Rhys admitted, "it certainly isn't what I'm used to."

"Have you traveled extensively?" Pilar questioned as she escorted him, leaving her father to partner Tory, through the house to the courtyard. There on a small table were food and drinks. A woven rug in blended tones of red, cream, and blue covered a large part of the pale brick floor.

Rhys answered, "Only to France and Italy for my Grand Tour when I was much younger." He cast a swift glance in Tory's direction before returning his gaze to Pilar. "Whilst I was traveling by train to Texas I had a chance to see some of your country."

"Isn't that train superb?" Pilar asked. "The baron demanded the best and he obviously got it."

"Baron?"

Pilar's gaze clashed with Tory's, wondering what she was supposed to say.

"My father no longer uses his title," Tory said simply. "For *us* such formalities have no place."

"I thought," Pilar said, indicating that everyone should be seated, "you would both enjoy something to eat as dinner won't be served until much later."

Pilar and her father, she explained, observed the custom of late meals, with dinner often starting after nine p.m. Rhys assured her that he found no problem with this, as he was used to eating later in the evening. He was, however, hungry right now and glad of Pilar's hospitality.

Don Sebastian, keeping his own counsel, poured the wine. Envy crept insidiously along his veins, serrating his innate sense of what was seemly. His eyes focused on the younger man, haunted by what his mind could conjure—rich, colorful imaginings of male and female, lost in the pleasures of love. There was no denying the obvious fact that this Englishman was handsome. Physically he was a match for Victoria. But would he care for her as she deserved to be cared for? Would he cherish the part of her that needed to be cherished—though she would be the first to deny it? Sebastian wanted to take this stranger aside and caution him to treat Victoria gently. For all her apparent wildness, there existed within her a virgin's heart and soul.

Rhys watched Tory pop a tiny red object into her mouth. "What is that?"

Tory sliced a sidelong glance at him, watching those elegant long fingers as he sampled one of the three cheeses. "A pepper, my lord."

"I should like to try one."

Pilar spoke quickly, "I don't think that you should."

134

"I've watched you and Victoria eat them without harm."

"That's because we're used to them," Tory stated. She was tempted to advise him to eat several, knowing the certain reaction they would produce. Pausing, she thought better of it, remembering the episode with the prairie oysters. "They're hotter than he—hades," she ammended.

Rhys's mouth quirked in a grin. She didn't know that he had a fondness for curried dishes, so this wouldn't, he assumed, present a problem. The jalapeño pepper was hot, no doubt about that. Rhys enjoyed the taste, reaching for another.

Tory watched him carefully, her blue eyes never wavering from their intense perusal. For some reason, one she didn't wish to examine too deeply, she was intensely proud of Rhys just then. From her friends she didn't want sympathy or reproach. She needed their understanding and support, for she knew that this man was her destiny. Her father had seen to that.

One of Don Sebastian's *vaqueros* interrupted the gathering. He removed his hat, waiting for a signal from the Don that he had permission to speak. *"Patrón*, the carriage from the Encantadora has arrived."

"Gracias, Pedro." Don Sebastian stood up, as did the others. "I will have Marta show you to your rooms so you may rest before our evening meal." With that he left the room, followed by

Tory, who went in the direction of the carriage.

"If you would prefer not to rest," Pilar said, "then, my lord, you may indulge your fancy in our library, or perhaps you would like a tour of the rancho."

"If you don't mind, once my man is settled, I do think that I would enjoy taking a walk."

"Please, feel free. Treat this as your home."

"You are most gracious, Doña Pilar."

"Nonsense. You are to wed with my dearest friend. I could do nothing else."

Rhys stepped close to her, dropping his voice. "You and I both know that that is a polite fiction. Should you wish, you could make my visit here quite unbearable."

His percipience surprised Pilar. She lowered her lids for a second, hiding her eyes, then lifted the thick fringe and met his gaze full on. "I love Victoria," she said, her tone conveying just how deeply that love was felt, "and I do not wish to see her hurt in anyway. You must allow her time to get used to the idea of being"—she paused, her hand gracefully gesturing—"a *wife*."

"She is lucky to have such a staunch friend in you."

"As I am lucky, my Lord Derran, to have her." Pilar's dark eyes glowed warmly. "You would do well to take heed of the fact that she has many friends in Texas—powerful, influential people among them."

"Your point is well taken, madam," Rhys said, once again bringing her hand to his lips. He envied Victoria this wellspring of concern, and the fact that she could command such deep loyalty.

Marta bustled in, ready to show him to his rooms. Rhys left Pilar and, as he was making his way up the stairs, he wondered if the hand of friendship would also be extended by his host. Rhys sensed an undercurrent of unexplained, veiled hostility between himself and the Don. There was nothing overt; yet it was there, in the eyes. A distinct coldness, at odds with his formal manners.

For what reason?

Chapter Seven

"So, Papa, what do you think of Victoria's *novio?*" Pilar asked when her father handed her a glass of wine. She sipped it slowly, delighting in the rich bouquet, in the subtle taste.

Don Sebastian tilted his head to one side, considering the question, as he had been since earlier that evening. What *did* he think of the Earl of Derran? There was no denying that the Englishman possessed a handsome exterior, facile charm, and . . . youth. Logically, Don Sebastian knew that Rhys Fitzgerald Buchanan presented an attractive package, and for any woman content with the trappings of surface beauty, he would more than suffice. However, no matter how gaily decorated the accoutrements surrounding the man were, the certainty was that Victoria would look beyond.

A thought occurred to him. Suppose there was no beyond?

"Papa?" Pilar spoke again.

Don Sebastian apologized for his lack of concentration. "*¿Quién sabe?*" he shrugged. "As to his character, I must reserve judgment."

"Well said, Don Sebastian."

At that utterance, Rhys strolled casually into the room, sartorially the epitome of the classic English aristocrat. Impeccably attired in black evening clothes, beneath which the snow-white shirt was cut to fit his broad shoulders perfectly. The silver-gray silk of his tie matched the color of his eyes at that very moment. Gold cuff links, engraved with his initials, adorned the cuffs of his shirt. A thin band of gold stretched from one pocket of his black silk waistcoat to the other. Rhys gently removed the watch and checked the time.

"Wine?" Don Sebastian asked.

"Thank you, yes," Rhys responded, taking the elegant crystal glass from his host.

Pilar, dressed in a gown of deepest wine, which set off the magnificent set of rubies she wore, was on the arm of a man whom she brought to Rhys. Hands interlocked, Pilar said, "Pedro, I would like you to meet the man who is to wed Victoria." She made the introduction, smiling as the men shook hands.

"I wonder what can be keeping Victoria?" Don Sebastian queried. Tonight he was also dressed in one of his finest suits. Unlike the English cut of his guest's clothes, Don

139

Sebastian's suit was cut in the fashion of the Southwest. The short black jacket, edged in braid of silver and turquoise, was worn over matching black trousers. A frilly shirt of milk white, the cuffs dripping lacelike from the confines of the jacket, contrasted with the style that Rhys wore. Pedro's suit was similar, although more subdued.

Several minutes passed as polite observations and standard responses made up the conversation. No one sought to break the charmed spell while they waited for Tory Reitenauer to make her appearance.

Tory stood at the bottom of the stairs, her velvet-slippered feet making no sound on the tiles as she crept towards the open door of the drawing room. She could feel the race of her pulse as she neared the entrance. Doubt suddenly seized her. A yearning to turn around and flee back up to her rooms and remove this dress assailed her. It was daring, far more so than anything she'd ever worn before. She'd ordered it on an impulse, brought it with her today on the same, unnamed whim. A flash of bravado.

And now it was time to face the consequences.

Tory found herself the focus of all eyes as she made her way into the room.

Pedro blinked.

Pilar clapped in delight.

Don Sebastian nodded in approval.

Rhys was simply stunned.

By God—the thought hit him forcefully—she *is* beautiful. Gone was the brazen amazon replaced, however temporarily, by a young woman who would have graced and captivated any court, or courtier. He recognized the expensive Worth name, the signature use of color and design. The blending of black and midnight blue brought out the color of her skin, cool cream with a touch of golden peach.

Tory remained momentarily frozen to the spot, her gaze locking with Rhys's.

He held her eyes for a brief space of time before his dropped to the expanse of soft shoulders that were exposed by the low neckline of the gown. Black lace lay across her skin, drawing the viewer's eye to a comparison between the fabric and the flesh. His gaze dipped lower still, to the ripe fullness of her breasts. And soon it would all belong to him, to sample at his leisure, though his aching flesh tightened in response even now.

Black ribbons were loosely threaded through her upswept strawberry-blonde hair, several curls of which cascaded down her back.

Rhys's ears picked up the softly spoken response he recognized as coming from Don Sebastian—"Encantadora."

Pilar also heard the low whispered comment of her father. Her eyes flashed to his strong face, seeing the unmistakable signs of naked hunger there. What she'd thought she'd seen that day in the barn had been true. This revelation stunned her, dismayed her, frightened her. She shifted her eyes and caught the gleam of the bracelet on Tory's wrist. Her grandmother's bracelet.

Don Sebastian walked towards Tory, his ebony eyes unable to shadow completely the love he felt. He bowed over her hand, touching his warm lips to her fingers.

"Samuel would be so pleased."

"Do you think so?" she asked, his sincerity bolstering her courage.

His smile was reassuring. "There is no doubt, Victoria."

Pilar and Pedro joined them, leaving Rhys standing a short distance away, observing the closeness of the group. He'd be damned if he would sit back on the sidelines and wait to be included. Undaunted, he strode over and when a young maid came in to announce dinner, he slipped his arm around Tory's waist, much to her surprise as he felt the slight stiffness, and escorted her to the dining room.

At a table big enough to hold more than twenty guests, Don Sebastian presided at the head. Victoria and Pedro sat at his left, Rhys and Pilar at his right.

"I must compliment you on your choice of wines, Don Sebastian," Rhys said, his voice soft, pitched low.

Don Sebastian smiled and replied, "I am happy that you find our wines to your liking." He slid a glance to his left, catching Tory's eye. "They are from Texas."

Rhys's eyes widened in surprise. "Remarkable. I would have judged them to be French."

"German, actually," Tory spoke up, wiping

her lips on a linen napkin edged in lace.

Rhys watched the movements of her hand as she slowly brought the material to her mouth, which was bare of any color, save for the natural shading of a rose in blush. He concentrated on the shape of her lips, taking note of the fullness. What would they taste like? he wondered. Would they tease? Hold delights of desire? Her small tongue wet her lips with a careful quick flick. His hand gripped the stem of his wine goblet so hard that he thought it might snap.

Christ, what was wrong with him? He'd had women before. She was no different, he told himself. A cynical thought arose. He supposed he should be grateful that he did find her attractive. It would make the wedding and bedding of her that much easier. If he could dispatch his duty with a modicum of pleasure, than so much the better.

"The vineyard is a joint venture," she stated. "It was started when a German native, who came over with my father to Texas, suggested that the soil in this area would be right for certain wines. He explained what he wanted to do to Papa and Don Sebastian."

"And we deemed it a worthy investment," the Don responded. "A few of our friends thought the same, so the winery was started."

"I have a friend who would enjoy this. I should like to arrange to purchase several bottles and have them shipped back to England."

"Nonsense," the Don said, "you may select

143

what you will from my cellar."

"We also have wines at the Encantadora," Tory volunteered.

"Excellent," Rhys pronounced. "It will make a unique gift."

Don Sebastian signaled for the maid to remove the last course. "Your friend is a collector?"

Rhys's mouth curved gently into a smile. "You could say that. Anne's wine cellar is amongst the best in London, if not the best."

"Anne?" Tory's brows rose as she spoke the name.

"Lady Anne Beckworth-Bridge," Rhys pointed out.

"She is a close friend of yours?" Tory asked, staring straight across the table, fixing Rhys with her frank blue gaze.

"A good friend, yes," he confessed. Rhys ended the conversation, concentrating instead on the next course served, a thick cut of steak.

Tory could tell that she would get no more from him, but that mattered little as she had got what she wanted. It was in his eyes as he spoke the woman's name. Close friend indeed, she scoffed. His mistress, more than likely. Did he think she was a naive child? Far from it, Tory thought. She knew that the male of any species craved physical release. She was aware that men from her ranch visited brothels for that purpose. Rich men kept women.

Tory wondered what this "Anne" looked like. What kind of woman would appeal to this man?

She lowered her lashes, focusing on cutting a slice of meat. Dark or fair? Short or tall? Plump? Thin? Demure or demanding?

Covertly, she raised her eyes and gave him a quick glance. She watched his hands as he manipulated knife and fork. They were slender. Strong. Sure. Suddenly, the shield of thick black lashes rose and she was speared by the direct gaze of his gray orbs. Tory gripped her own utensils tighter as the silent byplay continued. She could feel a chill feather along her arms; conversely, she felt a warmth flood her body. Her breathing deepened; her breasts seemed too constrained by the fabric covering them; her nipples rubbed achingly across the silk of her camisole.

She was the first to look away.

Rhys sighed. Her blush of color intrigued him. One minute she was brazen, the next shy. The physical ache in his loins remained constant, making him more aware, more in control. He relished this challenge, enjoyed the stimulation because it was not perfunctory. It was deep . . . dark . . . dangerous.

Pilar's gaze darted from one to the other. A sense of satisfaction crept over her. Her friend wasn't as immune to the demands of her body as she would wish. And neither, she surmised, was he. This fine English lord was no phlegmatic illusion of a man. *Sí*, he was cool, she thought with a mentally dismissing shrug, but he wasn't cold, especially if the heated look he cast in Tory's direction was any indication.

She slowly reached out a slippered foot in Pedro's direction, under the table. "If you'll excuse me, I think I will retire now." She stood up, as did the men at the table, her husband adding that he would join his wife. She kissed her father's cheek, and then did likewise to Tory's, murmuring, "We will talk again in the morning." She turned to face Rhys. "It was a genuine pleasure to meet you, my Lord Derran. Enjoy the rest of your visit." With that she and Pedro left the company, hand in hand.

"Your daughter is very beautiful, Don Sebastian, and seems quite fond of her husband," Rhys said thoughtfully.

"Indeed, you are correct on both counts. This is a special time for her."

Tory explained for Rhys. "Pilar is expecting another baby."

The broad smile on the Don's face told Tory how he felt about another grandchild.

"You must be so happy."

"Yes." He sighed. "Children are a blessing, a reason for joy. They crown life. For what else do we strive to build a legacy?"

"Personal ambition?" Rhys volunteered.

"Sí, I grant that there are some for whom family is not their primary motive. For them I have pity. For myself, I am content."

What a pretty lie, the Don thought. He was forced to be content, lest he shock all who knew him. He could never let the truth be exposed. When Pilar told him her news, he had been very happy for his child—and, he admitted to himself, envious. She was about to present her husband with the most precious proof of their commitment. For one painful moment he allowed himself the fantasy of thinking of Victoria, as his wife, carrying their child.

"But don't you think that some men," Tory proposed, "see a child as a proof, a badge of their virility?"

Rhys's eyes widened with her frank question. By God, he thought, Victoria would certainly set London on its ear. He could very well imagine his mother's reaction had she said that at one of her dinner parties. The countess would be calling for her smelling salts. He noted that his host seemed immune to Victoria's candor.

She directed her next question to Rhys. "Is that not the case in England, my lord? Do titled men there not boast about their by-blows? Is it not seen as a rite of passage?" Her tone left little doubt about her feelings for anyone who subscribed to that philosphy.

"For others I cannot say. In truth, I have known some men who are considerably careless and who deem it a particular challenge to see how many progeny they can produce." From the breast pocket of his evening jacket he produced the silver cigar case, offering a smoke to the Don, who accepted. "With your permission?" he asked Victoria. At her nod, Rhys lit his cigar with one of the candles on the table. He drew in the smoke and exhaled deeply. "I, however, think it takes much more strength, if you will, to see to it that no children are created." Rhys recalled an

147

incident from the past when he was only a boy. His brother, Tony, had slept with two of their housemaids, and both girls had gotten pregnant. The young women were both dismissed from the household: one commited suicide; the other, he later found out, became a prostitute to support herself and her child, since Tony offered no money to either.

Tory was again taken by surprise. She'd aimed her question, expecting to score a hit, hoping to find another weapon to use against him. His unforeseen answer shattered that notion. In her mind, she thought he would admit to seeing no harm in fathering children, in having physical proof of his virility. It would show how shallow he was, how vain and selfish. Instead, his answer revealed a man of moral purpose, whether he was aware of it or not.

Could it be that she'd misjudged him? Or, perhaps, not given him an honest chance?

"I was going to suggest a game of cards," Don Sebastian offered. "Or would you also like to retire, Victoria?"

"No," she answered, "I would love a chance to play." Her eyes went to Rhys's face. "What about you?"

"I fancy it, yes."

"Good," Don Sebastian declared. "Let us go into the sala where a table has been set up, just in case." He rose, offering his arm to Tory.

Perforce, she accepted. Then Rhys came round the table, offering his. She flashed a look at each man, then slipped her right arm through Rhys's left.

Brandy and port were set out on a small table nearest to Tory. She poured each man a snifter of brandy, pouring herself a glass of port. She took charge of the deck of cards, shuffling expertly and dealing the first hand. "Five card stud," she said in a quiet, commanding voice, "and nothing's wild."

"It'll cost you to find out," Tory said, trying to stifle a yawn. The game had lasted several hours and she was tired. Exhilarated too, she admitted. Neither man gave her any quarter because of her sex, which was how she liked it. She was an honest player, as were they. It was between her and Rhys, the Don having dropped out about a half hour earlier, having lost badly to one of her hands.

"I think you are bluffing," Rhys repeated.

"There's only one way to be sure," she countered.

"I know," he said. The pile of chips in front of each was about equal. He narrowed his lids, dropping his gaze to the exposed cards. She was showing two kings, one ten, and a queen. He had two queens, a three, and a four.

She had him beat now, she thought. Tory steepled her fingers and rested her mouth against them. She was sure he could still see her smile of triumph.

"Well?" she queried.

There was already a sizable amount between them on the table. His face a mask of calm, he pushed forward all the chips that had lain in front of him. "I call your bet, and raise a thousand."

Tory couldn't contain her gasp of surprise. He was bluffing, she thought. He *must* be. He was waiting for her to fold out of fear. Well, she'd be damned before she did that. She counted out her chips and found that she was one shy of a thousand.

"Do you see my bet?" Rhys asked.

"I'm twenty dollars short," she said, her teeth gritted in frustration.

Now it was his turn to steeple his hands and look at her, frankly assessing.

"Will you allow me to write a note?"

"No."

Tory's eyes widened in amazement.

"I will give you the money," Don Sebastian said.

"No," Rhys admonished. "Please be so good as not to interfere. This is between Victoria and me."

"What will you take then?" she demanded, unwilling to allow this hand to slip from her fingers.

"Only your word."

"My word?" she repeated.

"Yes." He took a long drag on his cigar, forcing the smoke upwards.

"If you should win, you have my word that I will repay you."

"Do you agree, then, that I shall have the right to choose when I demand payment?"

"You may have it, should you win, when we return to the Encantadora."

"That's not what I said."

Tory flicked another quick glance at the cards exposed on the table. He was playing some sort of game with her, trying to get her to fold. This was his stratagem, make her doubt. It wouldn't work. She had him.

"I agree," she answered, pushing forward her chips until they met what was already there, forming an enormous pile. She turned over the face-down card. It was another ten. "Two pair," she stated proudly, reaching for the chips.

Rhys reached out one hand to stop her. The touch of his flesh on hers was kinetic. "Not so fast."

Her face wore a look of puzzlement.

Rhys turned over the remaining card in his hand. The queen of hearts. "Three royal women," he said.

Shock registered on Tory's face. He hadn't been bluffing.

"Congratulations," she said, her voice low but strong.

"Luck was indeed with me tonight," he quipped.

"You were certainly in her debt," Tory pointed out. A quick guess had her owing him almost three thousand dollars, give or take the extra twenty.

Rhys stood up, stubbing out his cigar, leaving

the chips on the walnut table. "I bid you both a good night," he said and strolled lazily from the room.

Tory watched him go, throwing a glance in Don Sebastian's direction.

"An interesting man, your *novio*."

"Without a doubt," she concluded. "I think I shall also turn in. Thank you for a lovely evening, *Tío*." Tory placed a kiss on his cheek.

The Don's heartbeat quickened. "You're welcome."

He stood there after she had gone, smelling the lingering traces of her perfume, his skin still able to feel where her lips had touched. He picked up the half-empty decanter of brandy. It would be a long night.

Rhys had been given the rooms across the hall from those that Tory occupied. When he left the drawing room, he was satisfied on one level and empty on another. The longing to sample a kiss from Tory's mouth was still gnawing at him. He was cognizant that this wasn't the time nor the place. But damn it, she owed him, and he wanted to collect. Now.

It wasn't long after he came up that she followed, moving quietly so as not to wake anyone. He heard her address someone in Spanish, most likely the same maid who helped her dress for the dinner party.

Disavowing propriety, he waited in the dark, his door slightly ajar. Tearing off his tie, he removed the silk waistcoat, tossing it heedlessly to the bed. Twinnings, asleep in the small adjacent anteroom, would grumble. Let him. Rhys slipped several buttons loose from his shirt. Finally, he saw the maid slip from her door and walk toward the stairs.

Casting the caution his brain urged on him aside, he slipped out the door. Slowly, he turned the knob.

Tory was glad to be out of the dress. Taking a deep breath, she put her hands to the back of her waist and sighed, stretching slightly from side to side. Untying the ribbons that held her petticoat, she stepped out of it, leaving it on the floor in a crumpled dark heap. Tory placed one foot on the bed, rolling down the silk stocking. She did the same for the other, not aware that someone was watching her, observing her rituals. A sigh escaped her lips. She was beginning to feel freer. More herself.

Her hands went to her hair, unpinning the artfully done curls. Her back still to the door, she bent forward and shook her head, then stood, working her fingers through the loose mass of thick waves. It needed to be brushed, she thought, but she was too tired to bother.

"Don't scream," the voice warned her as a hand cupped her mouth, and another slid around her waist.

Tory stood stock still. She knew who it was; there was no mistaking that compelling voice, or that accent. What the hell was he doing here?

As if he read her mind, he whispered against

153

her ear, his breath a tickling caress, "I've come to collect my wager."

"Are you mad?" she demanded when he relaxed his hand. If she had her knife she would have driven it into his other hand, which rested possessively around her, pulling her closer against his body.

"No, just determined."

"Can't this wait till tomorrow?"

He pulled her even closer, so close that Tory could feel the warmth of him through the thin silk drawers that she wore. His hand splayed across her waist, fingers extending. Then, abruptly, he released her. "Turn around," he said, his tone resembling a growl.

Tory did so, slowly.

"What the hell do you want?"

Even her use of a profanity didn't deter him. Rhys knew what he wanted and he would have it. "What's due me."

"You keep saying that," she said stiffly.

"And I've come to make my claim."

"Just what is it that you want if it's not money?"

How naive she sounded, Rhys thought. He detected no fear, just confusion on her part. "A kiss."

"What?" Her voice rose a fraction.

"Just what I said. A kiss."

"You *are* mad," she repeated. As she made to walk away, his hand stayed her.

"Let go of me," Tory demanded.

"Not till I get what I came for." Now his

cultured voice was rougher; there was an edge to it. He dropped his gaze, took in the high breasts straining against the silk, saw the way the material cupped every curve, exposing the hard points of her nipples. He longed to untie the dark blue ribbon that held the camisole together, unbutton the tiny row of satin-covered buttons and put his mouth to her. The nectar of roses; he could smell the essence on her, rich and warm from her skin.

Perhaps she should humor him, she decided. What risk was there in one kiss? He'd take it and go. "Very well," Tory said, resigned, "you may have your precious kiss." She leaned up and quickly touched her closed mouth to his.

Rhys stood there for a moment before he laughed, softly.

"What do you find so funny?"

"You."

"What for?" she inquired.

"Has no one in Texas ever had the courage to claim a kiss from you?" He saw the uncomprehending look in her wide blue eyes. Was it possible that she was a virgin? Rhys tunnelled his hand through her blonde hair, anchoring her head. Slowly, he put his face towards hers, so close that Tory blinked. His lips, warm and solid, feathered across hers at first, lightly brushing. Next, his mouth opened, stealing a taste of her as he sucked at her bottom lip. Tory was acquiescent, passively standing there. Rhys was hot, and getting hotter. "Open your mouth, damn it," he said.

Her response was to ask what he wanted her to do that for, but before she could form her question, he'd captured her mouth and proceeded to show her what an adult kiss could be like.

His mouth was strong. She was pulled along by the sheer force of it, her breath somehow mingled with his, so that she couldn't tell if they each breathed apart or if he was doing it for both of them.

A touch of his tongue against hers startled her as Rhys deepened the kiss even further. She felt as if she were being carried away by a twister, tossed and turned inside out. Her breasts began to ache again, and she found herself pushing forward against his chest, feeling the solid wall of warmth there. His shirt and her camisole rubbed against her straining flesh.

Rhys released her mouth, taking a step backwards. He was shaken to the core, and all from a kiss. Damn, he derided himself. He felt like a schoolboy, anxious for his first woman. A few more minutes of that intensity and he'd have shoved her to the floor, dispensed with her garments, and taken her there. Like any forbidden fruit, he had to have a taste, no matter what. Well, he'd had his taste. And now it only whetted his appetite for more.

His breathing was ragged, stretched. He looked at her, lashes fluttering open, her eyes bright and questioning. He dropped his hand from its grip on her hair, forcing himself not to touch her.

The sound of her hand connecting with his cheek echoed in the room, shattering the moment.

Silently, reluctantly, Rhys turned and left the room.

Tory stood there, not knowing what to do. She touched her lips, stroked the swollen flesh. He'd only touched her mouth, and yet she felt odd, as if she'd been claimed. Anxiety and awareness jostled for favor in her brain.

She was frightened. Tears welled in her eyes.

He'd stormed her senses, leaving her temporarily stunned by the force of his possession.

Shaking, Tory walked to the bed and collapsed, curling around a large pillow, hugging it close. For the first time since she was a child, she left a lamp on.

Rhys could still feel the tremors in his body as he closed the door. Tonight he'd been touched as no one before had ever touched him. With her kiss Victoria had somehow reached inside him and pulled at his guts, twisting and tangling, becoming in that instant an integral part of him.

That wasn't part of the bargain.

Chapter Eight

Tory's attempts at sleep had been broken by strange, erotic dreams, each one different, each one leaving her with a feeling of unease. Where had the strange images come from?

She slowly pushed herself up, fluffing the pillows, brushing the tangled mass of hair from her sleepy eyes. Her breathing was now under control. In one dream she remembered running through a series of doors, each of which slammed shut after she went through, while hands tried to grasp at her, to restrain her. She eluded each pair, only to face them again as she tried to make her way to the source of the music that called to her. It had been a struggle, but she'd finally attained the final door, bursting through, following the music, searching for she knew not what, and finding only the soft embrace of a gentle, swirling fog, hearing a voice that whispered her name softly. As she went to turn to the sound, instinctively, the dream vanished and she awoke the first time.

The second dream had taken an event she'd witnessed clinically many times and juxtaposed it into something wanton and abandoned. Tory shivered in recollection of the dream. She'd heard noises coming from one of the paddocks. As she went to investigate, she discovered the ranch was deserted, save for her and the two animals who were creating such a fuss. A storm cloud threatened overhead; nevertheless, she soon found herself outside, at the railing, in her cotton nightdress, the wind wiping it around her tall form. Her mare, Abendstern, was trying to evade the black and white paint, Javert. Each horse pranced and snorted, screamed and pawed the air. Finally, the paint cornered the smaller horse. He reared again, the sound coming from his throat a triumphant cry. Tory watched as the male made to mount the female, nipping at her, forcing her to accept his weight and possession.

Tory was determined to stop the horses from mating. However, she couldn't move. Two hands were holding her, the long fingers lightly resting on her shoulders, forcing her to stay. Kisses feathered across her back, along the column of her throat, exposed and vulnerable. She made to move again. And once more her movements were forestalled by the hands which maintained their vigilent power. A low voice whispered in her ear, mixing with the wind, "Observe. Understand."

Tory watched with new eyes. This was not a controlled, sterile incident, staged for breeding purposes alone. It was pure, wild and free, as nature intended. And exciting. She could feel the primitive energy surge around and through her. The wind drew chillbumps along her arms, yet she was warm. Her breath heaved on a deep, released sigh as she saw the act to its completion. She herself felt drained, exhausted.

That was when she awoke the second time. It was morning now.

A soft rap on the door heralded the maid, who brought a silver tray laden with tempting treats for the morning meal, which she placed on a small table near one of the windows. *"Buenos días, Señorita Victoria."*

Tory replied to the cheerful greeting in Spanish, asking if Pilar was up yet.

As the young girl opened the drapes to let in the morning sun, she responded that indeed, Pilar was awake, and she and her family had attended a private mass in the family chapel.

Tory threw back the sheet that had covered her, drawing on a wrapper of cotton. It was cream-colored, patterned with tiny flowers of pink, rose, and blue.

"Would the *señorita* like for me to brush her hair?"

Tory nodded yes, pouring herself a cup of hot chocolate. In Don Sebastian's household, this was the morning beverage of choice. She sampled some of the fine locally grown fruits, enjoying the taste.

"*La señorita*'s hair is beautiful," praised the maid. "It is like the peach, touched by fire."

Tory smiled and said her thanks. "A legacy from my *abuela*," she replied, relaxing to the soothing rhythm of the brush as she finished her meal.

"Shall I braid it for you?"

Tory's hands stilled as she poured her third cup of chocolate. One side of her argued in favor of leaving her hair free, unencumbered. She was, she admitted, proud of it. But the more practical side of her nature won over. "*Sí*," She responded. Funny, she thought, in the dreams her hair had been unbound.

"Are you sure that you are all right?" The Don queried, worried by the tired, drawn look on Tory's face.

"*Sí, Tío*, I am fine," she reassured him.

"Your *novio* is still abed?"

Tory blushed, and said, "I guess so."

Don Sebastian noted the becoming color on her cheeks. He stayed his hand from tracing the curving line of her cheekbone. Something was bothering Victoria. Yet it was not his place to demand an answer, much as he wanted to.

"I was so pleased that you wore my gift last evening."

"You know how much I cherish it," she replied. "It is one of the loveliest gifts anyone has ever given me."

You deserve all that and much more, Don Sebastian longed to say. The words, however, remained unspoken.

"Is Pilar still in the chapel?"

"I believe so," the Don responded.

"Good, I need to see her." They were standing at one of the paddocks, watching the antics of her colt, Raven and his mother. The mare watched as her son scampered across the grass and crossed to the fence, where Tory was holding out a carrot for him. He approached her warily, at first shying away, then returning, nuzzling her hand in search of the treat. His mother ambled over, keeping an eye on her baby. Tory reached out and stroked the mare's forehead. Her voice soft and wistful, she said, "I can't wait to take him home."

"He will be a fine addition to your breeding stock," the Don said.

At the mention of the word breeding, Tory blushed again, recalling the dream. She quickly turned and made her way to the white stone chapel, leaving the Don to wonder at her hasty departure.

Tory entered the building. It was cool inside. Thick, whitewashed walls and stone floors kept it that way. There was an essence of calm in this place, a peace and harmony she could respond to. She did not consider herself overly religious, but Tory nonetheless respected her friend's faith. She saw Pilar in the front pew, her head bowed in prayer.

As silently as she could, Tory walked up the aisle.

Pilar turned her head at Tory's approach. She thought it ironic that Tory should choose to come here, now. She'd been praying, seeking God's blessing on the convoluted skein of lives surrounding her. First, for her father, convinced that he was trapped and suffering from a love that could never be; second, for her best friend, forced to surrender her will to another's, all for love. And third, strangely, for the man who was to wed her friend.

Tory noted that in Pilar's hands she carried the milky-white rosary beads that she'd given Pilar on her wedding day. Around her neck hung a cross of gold, set with precious stones. A white lace *mantilla* covered her head. Tory envied the tranquil look on her friend's face. All Pilar needed was a baby in her arms and she would be the perfect representation of a madonna.

Tory entered the wooden pew, sitting next to Pilar.

"You are troubled?"

Tory knew that she could just as easily lie, pretend that all was well. Somehow, in here, it seemed wrong. "Yes," was all she said.

Pilar touched her hand to one of Tory's, both of which lay curled into tight balls of flesh on her thighs. "Do you wish to speak of it?"

Tory wanted to babble on about her strange dreams, to discuss them openly and ask Pilar what she thought. No, she decided, better to keep them hidden. "I don't know where to begin."

"Perhaps with the obvious," Pilar said, "your *novio*."

Honestly, Tory answered, "He confuses me."

"And that frightens you, doesn't it?"

Tory sliced a glance in Pilar's direction. "Yes."

"Is that so very bad?"

Tory retorted, "Of course it is." She was silent for a moment before continuing. "Why can't he be what he is supposed to be? Simple. Stupid. Someone to despise."

"Would you really rather he was?"

"It might be easier then."

"What? To hate him?" Pilar turned Tory to face her. "You can't hate him, can you?"

Blue eyes locked with brown. "No, I honestly don't hate him, Pilar."

"Then give this marriage—and him—a chance."

"I just don't know." She turned her head away, staring at the small stained-glass windows above the altar. In a whisper Tory added, "He kissed me."

Pilar's interest was piqued. "When?"

"Last night."

"Where?"

Tory quickly explained the circumstances, beginning with the card game and finishing with his intrusion into her room.

For Pilar, this was a serious breach of etiquette. A man did not seek out his intended bride in her bedroom, with no chaperone

164

around, especially when he was a guest under someone else's roof. "Was that all that he did?"

"Wasn't that enough?" Tory countered.

"I agree that it was impetuous . . ."

"Impetuous?" Tory questioned.

"*Sí*, impetuous," Pilar opined. "And ill-timed. Suppose someone had seen him?"

"Well," Tory said dryly, "he certainly couldn't have been forced to marry me."

"That is beside the point," Pilar explained. Her voice lowered. "He didn't hurt you, did he?"

Tory knew what Pilar meant. Had Rhys been brutal? "No," she answered honestly. He'd been persuasive, coercive, and unrelenting in what he wanted, stripping away the last vestiges of her girlhood with the command of his mouth.

"Pilar," she began, wondering if a holy sanctuary was the proper place to be asking this question, "what do you feel when Pedro kisses you?"

"That's easy," she said, laughing lightly. "Safe. Warm. Protected."

None of which Tory felt when Rhys kissed her. "What about you, *amiga*?"

"Unsure."

"How so?"

"Because I felt things I've never felt before."

"Such as?"

"It's difficult to explain." Tory stood, her back to Pilar, her arms wrapped around her waist. "It was as if I were caught up in a raging storm. Powerless. And yet, powerful." She laughed. "Does that make any sense?" She turned and

165

faced Pilar, resuming her seat. "Of course it doesn't," she said, answering her own question.

Pilar heard the conflicting emotions in Tory's voice, along with the fear. Shifting the conversation from the kiss and Tory's obviously storm-tossed emotions, Pilar asked, "You haven't mentioned your wedding dress."

Tory blinked. "I hadn't really given it that much thought."

"Your wedding is only a week away," she reminded Tory.

"I know," was the terse reply.

"Do you not want to wear something special? This ought to be an occasion to remember."

"I'll go through my closets and see what I have."

Pilar shook her head. "That won't be good enough," she scolded her friend gently. "Your Janet is an able seamstress, is she not?"

Tory nodded. "The best."

"*Bueno!*" Pilar pronounced. "I will accompany you back to the Encantadora this afternoon. We shall go through your wardrobe together and see if there is something suitable for a bride to wear." She stood up, as did Tory. Pilar linked her arm around her friend's. "Now let us return to the house and a much needed cup of coffee, eh?"

"No tea, I'm afraid, my lord," Twinnings intoned as he handed Rhys a cup of coffee instead.

"It doesn't matter," Rhys replied. "What time

is it?" He drained the cup in one long swallow, giving it back to his manservant for a refill.

"Gone ten, I'd say, my lord."

Rhys ran his fingers through his thick hair. Christ, but he could still remember with the utmost clarity the feel of her mouth under his: the texture; its wild, sweet taste; the innocence and the outrage.

He traced one lean finger down his right cheek. That had been no weak-willed blow. She'd meant it. Smacking him because he had kissed her. He'd succeeded in tweaking the baroness's pride. He'd beaten her at cards, shown her in no uncertain terms that he wasn't bluffing.

"Your bath is ready, my lord," Twinnings announced.

Rhys got up from the bed, unselfconscious about his nudity. He walked the short distance to the other room, sinking into the brass tub with a fluid, graceful movement. He looked forward to the time when he would show Victoria the delights to be found in bathing together. He imagined that he could see her now, shy, hesitant, that long curtain of hair cascading around her exquisite body. Last night those bloody silk underthings had outlined in perfect detail what they purportedly covered. This time, there would be no barriers between them as she stepped into the water. A bar of fragrant soap could contain magic. The texture of a piece of cloth stroked over the skin could heighten pleasure.

He'd wed her, woo her, bed her, making her acknowledge that she too recognized the raw intensity they shared. He felt a lust for her unlike any he'd ever experienced.

And that's what Rhys believed it to be: lust, more potent than any he'd heretofore known. It went beyond merely wanting a woman to just share his bed, to relieve a physical need.

This Texas-born colonial was different.

"Hold still!" Janet said as she carefully stuck another pin into the dress, pulling it tighter in the waist.

Tory stood on a small footstool, her face reflecting the boredom she felt. "Can't we hurry this up?" she demanded.

"No," Janet said, "not unless you plan to be married in your petticoats."

"How about my pants?" Tory asked flippantly.

Pilar, her arms akimbo, a bolt of lace draped over her shoulder, said, "The sooner we get this done, the sooner you can step down. Janet, what do you think about this as a trim?"

Tory stood as still as she could, all the while wishing she were anywhere but here, being fitted for her wedding gown. What a lot of fuss, she thought, all for show. She would wear the family pearls, smile as best she was able, and pretend that this was a marriage she intended to honor, that this was the man of her choice.

So what if it was getting more and more difficult to pretend an indifference to this Englishman. She could be honest and admit she was marrying for love. There was no lie in that. She was. Love of the land and a tradition she wanted to maintain.

"I think that's it," Janet proclaimed, relaxing back on her heels.

"Finally," Tory said, stepping down from the pedestal.

Janet warned her, "Be careful you don't ruin what I just finished."

Tory gave her a solemn look. "I promise to be careful. Just get me out of this thing so that I can breathe."

"You will be the loveliest bride, *amiga*," Pilar said as she helped unlace the back of the gown. "Your *esposo* will have a *condesa* that all will envy."

"*Condesa?*" Both Tory and Janet spoke at the same time.

"*Sí*," Pilar pointed out, "what you in English call a countess, no?"

Tory slipped on a shirt of pale blue chambray cloth. She pulled on her denim pants, fastening the buttons. Her moccasins followed. She laced them tightly. Lastly, she secured the silver belt around her waist, touching the knife in its sheath. "*Ich bin wie Ich bin*," Tory stated, first in German, then she repeated it in English. "I am what I am. Victoria Reitenauer."

It was, Pilar thought, as if her friend had just admitted that she was the Queen of England. Such was the pride with which she uttered her name. Pilar shrugged her shoulders. "Be that as it may, when you wed you will add *his* name and *his* title."

Tory responded with, "The title that means the most to me is that of *patrona* of the Encantadora. And that," she pointed out, "I already possess."

Sam watched the men herd the small band of mustangs into a corral. There were about ten mares, one stallion, and a few offspring. This was the third such corral on his property, helping to insure that his men would have fresh mounts and that he would have additional horses to sell to the Army. Cattle and horses were important cash crops to Sam. His ranch depended on what the market demanded.

A wry smile etched his mouth. He was glad that it wasn't the only thing he depended on. Astute investments, and an occasional risk-taking venture, assured Sam a wealthy life. His business empire was far-flung, an enviable holding of property and commerce. All of it would be Victoria's. Hers and her heirs'.

Had he chosen correctly? Would this Englishman provide, in the long run, what his daughter and this ranch needed? In a matter of days his child and this stranger would be wed. Forever tied. They were the future. Its hope and bright promise. Trust in his own judgment had taken him far. After all, hadn't it lead him to abandon his secure heritage in Germany? Granted, he acknowledged, had he failed, he could have returned to his homeland and simply become once again a part of the fabric of his past. But Sam hadn't failed. And he wouldn't have gone back.

His blue eyes surveyed the land, its majesty and grandeur. Texas soil held his blood; it contained his pledge.

Once again he would do what had to be done.

Scattered over the desk in the library were newspapers and books galore. Several volumes were in a lopsided pile on the floor next to the oak chair that contained Rhys Fitzgerald Buchanan. Poring over the collection of material, Rhys was astounded by the wealth of information he garnered about this area, and about the family he was aligning himself to. He expected to find local papers; included also were newspapers from various cities in the States: San Francisco, New Orleans, Philadelphia, and New York, as well as several from London, Paris, and Germany. One paper from San Antonio contained the engagement announcement. Several interesting items about the Reitenauers were part of the rather lengthy story, discussing their background, past tragedies and triumphs, and, Rhys noted, some of their other holdings. He'd thought that Samuel's huge fortune was a result of the ranch; that proved shortsighted. These were not the insular provincials he'd first imagined. Instead, their wealth owed much to diversification. The story hinted at interests, both in properties and businesses, in not only other states, but other countries.

A cynical smile twisted his mouth. His mention was brief. Just his name, title, and the fact that he was the scion of a noble family, the last male of his line.

Gathering the papers to one side, Rhys focused his thoughts on Victoria, his bride-to-be. Since leaving Don Sebastian's ranch earlier that day, she'd been distant and aloof. It was if she'd pulled on an invisible carapace, once again donning the shell for protection, to keep herself inaccessible. No words were exchanged between them on the brisk ride back. Silence was broken only when one of their armed escort asked a question. Rhys was ignored, something he was unused to.

Darkness began to intrude upon the room. He reached out a hand, bringing the light forth from an oil lamp. How odd to be the peripheral person once again in a household.

Well, he'd be damned before he'd allow his bride to shunt him off to the side, as if he were so much extra baggage she could claim at a later date.

Victoria would have a few lessons to learn. And he was just the man to teach her.

Tory entered the house through the kitchen, her feet making no sound on the stone floor. As soon as Pilar left and Janet returned to her own house, Tory took off with Marshall in search of her father. Even though she was tired, she didn't want to stay in the house for fear of running into her *guest*.

Taking a seat at the round kitchen table, she grabbed an apple, sinking her white teeth into the solid, juicy flesh. Her nose caught the scent of chicken frying in a large iron skillet.

What would his *lordship* think of so plain a meal?

Kristen came bustling into the kitchen from her own connecting room. "Ach, baroness, do not spoil your supper," she admonished.

"As if I would, Kristen, since you're making one of my favorite meals." Tory disposed of the core, then bent over the stove, lifting the heavy lid from one of the frying pans. "Mmm, delicious," she pronounced.

"Do you think that it will be to the liking of your *verlobte*?"

Tory recognized the older woman's use of the German word for fiancé. "I suppose it will have to be," she said. "Either that or he'll starve."

"Ach, *nein*, baroness." Kristen threw Tory a curious glance. As tempted as she was to ask if Victoria was happy, she declined to do so. Such a question would overstep the bounds Kristen believed in. "In the larder there is beef and venison. He may have whatever he wishes. It will be no trouble, I assure you," she hastened to add.

"Be that as it may," Tory said, "serve him the same as anyone else. My lord is no longer in England."

"As you wish, baroness," Kristen nodded her head. Her mistress was obviously not intent on pleasing her husband-to-be. Kristen was led to believe that this was a match eagerly anticipated by both sides in the union. Her stolen glance at Tory revealed otherwise.

"It will be ready in about an hour," Kristen commented as she bent over to see about the pies she was baking in the oven.

"Peach?" Tory asked.

"*Ja*, baroness. Also one of apple, and another of blueberry."

Tory hugged the older woman who, being much shorter, came only to mid-chest on Tory. "You do spoil us, Kristen."

"Ach, it is my pleasure, *Herrin*."

"An hour gives me time to go over some accounts."

Since her father was now ensconced in his office, Tory carried the work she wanted to finish to the library. It would be quiet there, she thought. A place to retreat and regroup.

A surprise awaited her as she entered. Rhys was sitting at the desk in the corner.

He looked up as she walked in. "Hello," he said.

"I didn't know you would be here," she replied.

Rhys stood. "Else you wouldn't have come in?" he asked, walking around the desk to face her.

Tory stood her ground, ignoring a desire to

flee this situation. She cast her glance at the desk and the materials collected there.

Rhys watched the look of disbelief on her face.

Tory wondered what he was doing with the assorted newspapers and books. Reading? Why?

Rhys correctly interpreted her questioning look. In a voice slightly rough, he said, "You needn't look shocked, Victoria. I was merely taking the time to catch up with events and to familiarize myself with this area."

"Whatever for?"

He leaned back on the desk, crossing his arms across his chest, narrowing his lids, his gray eyes intense. "Contrary to what you may think, I am neither stupid nor a dilettante." Rhys straightened, making a move towards her. Her instinctive reaction of backing away angered him. "I need something to occupy my time. Can you understand that?" He resumed his position leaning on the edge of the desk. "Just doing nothing is boring. And," he drawled, "I abhor being bored."

"I'm sorry that you do not find us stimulating enough."

"Liar," Rhys said softly. "You couldn't care less if I do or not. However, I do find your company most *stimulating*."

The last word was uttered honey-smooth and full of promise.

Tory lashed out at him. "I imagine your life in London left you little time for boredom, what with a full social calendar."

A lazy smile kicked up the corners of his wide

mouth. "It had its moments," he confided.

"Oh, I'll just bet it did," she said, her tone scathing.

"Jealous?"

"Jealous?" she repeated. "Are you perhaps making a grand joke?" Her hands gripped the leather portfolio a little tighter. "How did you spend your precious time? What kept boredom at bay? Hunts? Balls? Visits to one of your mistresses? Time spent in idle pleasure?" she demanded.

"Pleasure is never idle time spent, I've found," he countered. In a silky tone he observed, "What a little puritan you are, Victoria."

"I am not."

"Oh, but you are."

"You know nothing about me."

"Just as you know nothing about me," he stated.

"I know what I need to know."

Rhys's smile deepened. "I think not."

Tartly, Tory said, "If you will excuse me."

Rhys nodded. "Certainly."

Tory stood outside, a tremor skittering along her limbs. Damn him! she cursed silently. Why does he affect me this way?

Damn her! he raged in mute protest. Why did he feel the need to justify himself to her?

"It's called fried chicken, my lord," Tory stated.

Rhys looked at the platter that was piled high

with various pieces, each crisply golden.

"What would you like?" Tory asked, a large fork in her hand, poised over the platter.

Sam sat without making a comment, content to watch the byplay. He'd noted the tension that once again crackled in the room when his daughter and Rhys were seated.

Rhys's eyes met Tory's. He paused to take a sip of chilled white wine, his gaze still focused. "I fancy the breast," he said softly.

She stabbed the fork into a large piece, plopping it onto his plate. "I rather thought that you would," she agreed, breaking eye contact to give her father several legs. She placed a plump piece of breast on her own plate, before spooning a drizzle of honey onto it.

Rhys watched in fascination as, instead of using a knife and fork, Tory picked up her piece of chicken and bit into it.

"Feel free to eat it anyway you please," Sam said, attacking a leg with gusto.

"I shall," Rhys promised. He opened the pot of honey, spooning some onto his plate. It was thick and fragrant. Unbidden, he entertained a fantasy—pouring the golden substance slowly over Victoria's breasts, letting it run, then following each trail with his mouth.

Tory scrutinized his eating of the chicken, observing how carefully he cut each slice, dipping it into the pool of honey on his plate. A little honey dripped off the end of his fork. She looked on as one lean index finger caught the thick droplet. An urge to lean over and clean his finger with her mouth seized her. What would honey-dipped flesh taste like?

Tory shook her head. What was wrong with her? These conjectures weren't proper. Hot color crept into her cheeks.

Rhys saw her blush and wondered at the cause. But Sam's grin was cheerful and spontaneous. *Wunderbar!* he thought, as he bit into another leg. He recognized the blush for what it was. Attraction was a powerful factor in any equation, especially a marriage.

Chapter Nine

The house and immediate grounds of the ranch were filled with the sounds of laughter and music. It was the eve of the wedding of Victoria Reitenauer and Rhys Fiztgerald Buchanan. Guests from all corners of Texas had come. In deference to Tory's wishes, Sam had kept the invitations to a select group. He'd had to turn down two governors and three senators who wanted to come and share in the happiness of the couple, as well as several of Tory's relatives on her mother's side from Philadelphia. Telegrams expressed the regret of some at not being on hand to wish the couple well.

It was the curious mixture of people who made the party such a success, Sam thought as he watched guests move from the little-used ballroom at the back of the house to the tent set up outside.

The only sour note of this evening's festivities was the news he'd received earlier that day. One of the herds of mustangs that he'd set aside for sale had been destroyed. It appeared that somehow the water supply had been poisoned, killing all the animals. Clearly, someone was out to get him. But who? Who could hate him enough to destroy human and animal life with no compunction?

Soft, lilting laughter wafted over him. He recognized his daughter's voice. Tory was dancing in the arms of the vet, Dr. Schmidt. Her fiancé was nowhere in sight.

"I think that I could use a glass of champagne," Tory said as the dance was completed. Her companion agreed with her and they went in search of a servant. After finding one who was carrying a silver tray laden with glasses, Tory and Hans Schmidt approached her father.

The sky was clear, the moon full. Stars dotted the blue-black darkness, twinkling like the diamonds that studded Tory's elaborate coiffure. She wore the same dress that she had worn to Don Sebastian's dinner party.

Tory saw the worried frown furrow her father's brow. An hour ago Marsh and Janet had joined the party. Marsh had immediately rushed to join her father and had whispered something in Sam Reitenauer's ear. Someone had distracted Tory before she could find out what was the matter. Her father was wearing his concern well; only someone as close as she could have read the signs. She was determined to find out what was wrong as soon as she could.

"Enjoying yourself, Hans?" Sam asked, foregoing a glass of champagne for a stein of beer.

Dr. Schmidt cracked a smile, which melted several years away from his sometimes stern face. "Great party, Sam. Everyone here seems to be having a good time."

Sam wasn't so sure that the statement included his daughter. "That's what I hope," he concluded.

"Is something wrong, Papa?"

Sam looked at Tory. *Mein Gott*, he thought; she is lovely. And he was so proud of her. He reached out his rough hand and stroked her soft cheek. "Nothing, *Liebchen*."

"I think you're lying."

"Ach, my friend, what do you do with a child like this?" Sam inquired.

Hans chuckled. "I think it's probably too late for a convent."

"Indeed," Sam replied, pulling Tory into his bearlike embrace.

"As if I would have gone," Tory protested, returning her father's hug with one of her own. She was determined to ferret out whatever her father was keeping from her. "You're evading my question."

"What a termagant you are," Sam said softly, removing the sting from the word.

"Nevertheless, there is something troubling you."

"Yes," Sam admitted.

"What?" Tory questioned.

He took another long swallow of beer. "One of the herds was slaughtered."

The glass dropped from her hand, shattering onto the stone below, splashing the hem of her dress. "You can't be serious?"

"I wish that I wasn't," he said. Sam watched as a servant hurried over to clean up the mess, noting the glances they received from several of the guests.

"How? When?"

"Yesterday, from what we can tell. One of the men went to check and found the herd. Seems as though they were poisoned."

"Poisoned." Tory was stunned. "It wasn't a freak accident, was it?"

"No," Sam said wearily, "it wasn't, I'm afraid."

"Who would deliberately destroy livestock? For what reason?" Tory couldn't fathom someone carefully planning to destroy magnificent animals.

"I wish I knew just who was responsible," Sam muttered.

"Still no idea?" asked Hans.

"No," Sam replied, his features tightening. "Whoever it is, he's damned clever. No clues. No traces."

"Who could want to do this to us?" Tory questioned, her hand on her father's arm. She could feel the tension beneath his sleeve.

"They'll pay dearly when I catch them," Sam

vowed. He lowered his voice as several guests approached. "Very dearly."

Rhys danced with a few of the women at the party. Excusing himself from his latest partner, who was properly impressed by having a member of one of England's premier families step out with her on the floor, he went in search of fresh air—and of his intended. She'd danced with almost every male present—except him.

He lit the thin cigar carefully, inhaling its rich fragrance, his eyes alert for signs of Tory. He spotted her, her face close to her father's, obviously deep in conversation with him and Hans Schmidt. He watched as a few more people joined them and then saw their mood change.

Tory sliced a sideways glance and saw Rhys's approach. She'd been avoiding him all evening, but she couldn't maintain this separation forever. They were expected to dance at least one dance with each other. Tory supposed that Rhys was coming to claim her.

Claim her. Those two words sent a chill cascading along her spine.

Conversation ceased abruptly when Rhys arrived. Grinding what remained of his cigar beneath the heel of his elegant leather shoes, he spoke in a tone both insistent and full of promise. "Our dance, I believe?" Rhys nodded his head toward Sam as he crooked his arm for Tory.

Her gloved hand slid caressingly across the fabric of his jacket as they linked arms. She caught the eager looks, the barely concealed stares as they walked onto the floor. The musicians hired for the weekend's entertainment had just completed a spirited Virginia reel.

Rhys stopped in front of the players. "A waltz," he commanded softly.

They complied.

Rhys took Tory in his arms, surprised at the way her slender body molded itself to his. It was as if they'd danced before, so smoothly did they execute the steps together. Rhys was used to dancing automatically, his body trained and honed from years of social experience so that he could divorce himself from the process if the companion proved too boring or insipid. With Tory in his arms he felt as if he were rediscovering the pleasures of the music and the rhythm.

They were alone on the dance floor; all eyes were on them. Sam and Hans stood framed in the doorway, watching the couple glide smoothly, sensually, across the polished oak boards. At the far end of the room Pilar stood between her husband and father, rooted to the spot, her gaze riveted on the man and woman who possessed such grace and finesse.

Don Sebastian watched the couple; a bittersweet smile sketched his lips. The handsome prince and his lady fair, the unawakened princess, on the threshold of experience. A sleeping beauty that a husband's tender loving would bring to full flower.

Sam cast a hasty glance around the room, examining quickly the faces of the assemblage before he returned to the couple. He wished his beloved wife were still alive to witness this moment. She would have shared his immense pride in their child.

Tory, her face flushed with a soft glow, accepted the applause at the end of the waltz. In a suddenly playful mood, her hand in Rhys's, she curtsied to the crowd, a genuine smile of enjoyment on her lips. Heretofore, her experiences with the waltz were as perfunctory duty dances, just as this had started out to be, before changing, evolving into something deeper. It went beyond rote steps memorized and executed flawlessly. This was feeling, absorbing the music, and silently communicating with one's partner. A strange, invisible, irrefutable bond.

"Splendid!" Sam declared.

Tory accepted the compliment. "The dancing lessons weren't a waste after all, I suppose."

"Far from it," Rhys intoned. "You would have taken Marlborough House by storm," he said, referring to the Prince of Wales's London residence. And she would, he thought. Not to mention capturing, Rhys had little doubt, the prince's highly selective, and roving, eye.

They were soon joined by Pilar, Pedro, and Don Sebastian, who took possession of one of Tory's gloved hands and raised it to his mouth, saluting her with a kiss. "Victoria, tonight, as I watched you, I discovered just how special a waltz can be. You were magnificent." As an afterthought, Don Sebastian tagged on, "As were you, my Lord Derran."

Pilar wondered if her father were aware of just how much he was revealing of himself and his feelings. Or was she being overly sensitive? Sam and Pedro seemed to notice nothing untoward. Her eyes flashed to Rhys, who wore a cynical smile. *He* was aware, and none too pleased.

"You are *too* kind, Don Sebastian," Rhys responded. He slipped his arm around Tory's waist, pulling her closer to his own body. Her perfume was subtle, evocative.

Sam was beaming. His party was a success. "*Liebchen*, I insist on the next dance," he declared as he removed her from Rhys's embrace. A shadow of sadness formed around his heart. After tomorrow Victoria would be a married woman, no longer his "little girl." Rationally, Sam was aware that Tory hadn't been a little girl in some time. He'd seen to it that she had an education, was exposed to culture and travel, and understood all there was to know about the land and power she would inherit. He'd completed all his responsibilities with love. The man he'd handpicked to be her mate would complete the last phase, instructing her in the ways of a wife.

Partners were chosen for the dance, with Rhys escorting Pilar onto the floor. As they twirled to the music, Pilar spoke. "May I offer a word of advice?"

"I have the distinct feeling," Rhys commented, "that you will no matter what I answer." He was beginning to like this woman. It was refreshing to hear a female speak her mind, and most especially to defend a friend.

Pilar greeted his response with a gentle laugh. "*Sí, es verdad.*" She looked up into his eyes, searching for compassion. "Treat her kindly."

Rhys digested the simple request. It stayed with him the rest of the evening, in the forefront of his mind, no matter what he was doing. He thought it odd that Pilar had phrased her entreaty in such terms. It wasn't fear he'd heard in her voice; rather, it was caution.

A glass of champagne in his hand, Rhys observed some of the differences between the world that he had left and this: here, again, the men who did the work on the ranch were included in the evening's festivities. He recognized a few from the episode of the prairie oysters. He watched as each man stood in line to dance with "Miss Tory," as he heard her referred to. A jolt of surprise hit him when she danced with two of the black ranch hands. That they were permitted to attend this function was surprising in and of itself; that they should dance with the daughter of the owner was astonishing.

"'Scuse me," said the deep voice of the man to his right, who edged his way past Rhys to a keg of beer. Rhys watched the tall man fill his glass and take a long swallow, finishing half the contents.

"You're Marshall Kincaid, correct?" Rhys asked.

Marsh, finally able to get a good, close-up look-see at the man who was to wed his boss's daughter, answered in a deep, rumbling bass, "Yep, I surely am." He stared point-blank at the man his wife had deemed a "mighty handsome fellow." When he'd first heard the news, he'd been skeptical, thinking that Sam Reitenuer had gone and done something loco. A few of the boys had told him about the prairie oysters. Sure, that spoke well, but Marsh preferred to reserve judgment. This English greenhorn still had a lot to prove before he would be accepted.

"You are the bailiff, are you not?"

"The what?" Marsh asked, his mouth, beneath the thick moustache, slightly curled.

"I do believe," said Dr. Schmidt, "he means the foreman, Marsh."

Rhys inclined his head. "I stand corrected," he replied.

"That I am," Marsh answered.

"Are there no sheep on this property?"

Marsh choked on the beer he was drinking, managing to gulp the contents instead of spewing them. "Sheep? Why would we have them ornery critters on a cattle ranch?"

"To provide a change in diet?" Rhys suggested.

Just then, Tory joined them. "Never mention sheep to a cattle rancher, my lord," she said. "It just isn't done."

"I would think that a little variation would be welcomed."

Hans Schmidt chuckled. "Not in this part of the country."

"So, there is no source of mutton in the area?"

Hans stroked his chin. "Well, there is someone who sells his sheep to one of the hotels in San Antone. The spread is northeast of here." Schmidt paused. "Can't say as there is much call for the meat in these parts."

"You fancy it, my lord?"

"I enjoy it, yes. But then, perhaps my tastes are rather more sophisticated than yours." His smile mocked her. "I would be glad to broaden your . . . appetites."

That infinitesimal pause. The scorching look in those eyes of gray. "I am content, my lord," she shot back.

"Merely content?"

"Happily content."

"Really?"

"Yes!"

At that moment, Sam interrupted. "Marsh, your wife is looking for you."

"Best not keep Janet waiting," he said, leaving the group. "Damn fine party, Miss Tory."

It had been a damned fine party, Tory thought as she headed for her father's office, a glass of champagne in her hand. She knew he hadn't retired for the evening, and she wanted to have a private moment with him before the ceremony on the morrow. A glance at the large carved clock in the hallway made her correct herself. It was already tomorrow. Her wedding day.

The guests had all retired, most to the large quarters in the back which Sam had added to his ranch about ten years ago. Since guests were apt to travel long distances for a visit, he thought it best to keep rooms ready.

She heard the sound of hushed voices. Pausing in the doorway, she listened. It was her father and Hans Schmidt.

"The conditions there were truly appalling, Sam. I was called in to check on one of their horses, and I found all in poor condition. Some had obviously been beaten, broken, and generally abused."

Tory pushed open the door, saw on Sam's face disgust at such treatment of animals. A man was judged by how he treated his animals, especially his horses.

"What did you do?" Sam asked, his eyes now focused on the chessboard in front of him.

"I had to put it down. Nothing else that I could do," Schmidt said sadly. "The gashes made by the barbed wire were too deeply infected. A real pity, as that had been a fine horse. An appaloosa stallion, with an unusual star design on his forehead."

Sam's brows knitted in concentration. He recalled such an animal. It had disappeared from his north range over a month ago. The unusual markings and fiery spirit promised a valuable stud. "What was the name of this man?"

"Talbot Squire."

A look of revulsion crossed Sam's features.

"Talbot Squire," he repeated, his voice spitting out the name as if it were a curse.

Tory questioned, "Why does that name sound familiar?"

"Don't you remember, *Liebchen*, he married Martha Rayburne?"

Tory sank to the oak settle. Yes, she recalled the gossip about the union, and about Martha, the snide snickers whispered about Martha and her son. Tory remembered seeing the woman once when she and her family were in San Antonio. In her mind Tory still could see the way other women crossed the street, or swept their skirts out of the way when Martha Rayburne passed. She remembered the pain etched on the woman's face. Martha possessed none of Tory's "damn the world" defiance.

Once, during that visit, Tory had chanced to meet Martha Rayburne in a small bookshop. Tory had selected several volumes and, her arms full, the women literally bumped into each other, spilling their books to the floor. Bending, Tory commented on the woman's choices. Martha, her thin face flushed, was shy, Tory noted. A slim volume of Shakespeare's sonnets in leather and gold caught Tory's eye. She smiled and handed it back to the woman, who said that it was a gift for her son.

That, she recollected, was the extent of their conversation, but Tory remembered the air of sadness in the woman's eyes, the timidity of her voice. Returning to her room in the Menger, she'd questioned her mother, who explained to her about the gossip surrounding Martha Rayburne. The woman had been keeping company with a neighboring rancher, a widower. They had even announced a wedding date, when, to everyone's surprise, the marriage was called off. Martha Rayburne, it appeared, was to have a child, and her intended was not the father. Kristina explained to Tory, who even now could remember her beloved mother's dulcet tones, that Martha Rayburne had been violated by a stranger, a half-breed gunslinger. The man had been caught and killed by Martha's father and her erstwhile fiancé.

Tory demanded to know why the man who was to marry Martha didn't keep faith with his promise.

Her mother explained to her that according to some people, Martha was now less than acceptable in polite society. He simply went along with the majority opinion.

Tory was outraged, protesting that it wasn't Martha's fault if she was attacked.

Sam's voice brought Tory back to the problem at hand. "With her father dead, and her son still too young to run the place," Sam continued, "she needed a husband."

Tory knew Sam was correct in that assessment. The woman she'd met all those years ago couldn't have handled running a ranch, even a small one. So, she'd had to barter herself in marriage, which gave her a modicum of respectability. But if, as Hans Schmidt contended, her husband was cruel to his livestock, what kind of a man was he? How did he treat Martha and the boy?

Seeing that her father and the veterinarian were so wrapped up in their game, Tory decided to forget about talking to Sam. Instead, she got up from her seat and bent, her arms around Sam's thick neck. "I love you, Papa," she said, kissing his beard-stubbled cheek.

A glitter of tears in his eyes, Sam patted the hands that wrapped around him. In a voice hoarse with rising emotion, Sam said, "And I love you, *mein Engel*."

Tory found sleep elusive. She'd tried reading, but found nothing which could hold her interest.

Recurring thoughts about the Rayburne woman made her reflect on her own situation. In several hours she would become a wife, bride to a man she still didn't completely know, or trust.

Her father's words were still with her. "Needed a husband." And there were so very many ways to interpret *need*. Obviously, Martha Rayburne needed a husband for practical, economic, and social reasons. But what about the things Pilar stressed: what about emotional and physical needs?

Needing left one vulnerable.

Hadn't she been susceptible to *him*, there on the dance floor? Tory twisted her thick braid of hair around her fingers. In the darkness of the night she could remember what his hands felt like sliding around her waist, drawing her close to the heat of his body.

Her fingers tightened around the thick rope of the braid.

He was here, now, in her mind.

A presence.

A need.

The light from the lamp in the next room was visible beneath the door. He stared at it as the smoke from his thin cigar curled into the air, and the moving light made patterns on the bare floor.

Rhys reached over, pouring another glass of wine. Tory had been correct when she boasted about the contents of her father's wine cellar. The wine was excellent. Twinnings had fetched several bottles for him to choose from before he retired, promising to be back early to get his lordship "outfitted properly for the big day."

His wedding day.

It was only hours away. Rhys drained another glass of the deep ruby liquid. He wasn't drunk; merely, he observed, mellow. And unable to sleep.

He quit the chair, moving instead to the wide bed, looking at the empty space, at the crowd of down pillows. Big enough for two. As was her bed.

His stray thoughts went again and again to the waltz, to the way her body fitted against his, to the excited beat of her pulse, the glow of her body in the candlelight. His flesh had responded with alacrity to her nearness. That boded well for their union, this merger of mutual benefit.

He relaxed on the bed, this endless night almost banished by the coming dawn. His nocturnal musings turned to fantasies, sweet, aching fantasies involving his bride.

Today the accounts would be tallied and paid.

Part Two: *To Pay the Price*

Chapter Ten

Today was her wedding day.

Tory sat still, dazed. Janet was fussing with her hair, her daughter Ruth was darting about and Pilar was chattering gaily as Tory stared blankly into the mirror. An open pot of lip rouge lay on the dressing table; nearby a crystal bottle of fragrance stood, waiting. Various hair pins, both plain and fancy, were scattered about, waiting their turn to adorn the bride.

Tory wiggled her toes in the elegant silk stockings. Instead of her comfortable moccasins, or her weathered cowhide boots, she would be wearing soft, supple shoes of finest leather, crafted for her alone.

A curling iron, properly heated, was applied, transforming her hair into a mass of tighter curls. Janet swept up the sides, anchoring the hair in place with several of the fancy pins.

Tory's knife lay close at hand, carefully sheathed. Tory slipped it from its casing, running her fingers lightly across the blade. It was such a part of her that she knew she would feel naked without it today. But a knife was not a necessary part of a bride's wardrobe. What use was it to her today? No use, Tory decided, save as a link to who she was. The cold feel of the metal was an odd comfort.

Pilar watched her friend toy with the deadly weapon. Softly, she chided, "You have no need of that thing today, *amiga.*"

Tory's head snapped up, her blue eyes focusing on Pilar's reflection in the mirror.

Janet, her work completed, said with a sly wink, "Of course she doesn't need it. Tonight she'll be handling another sort of blade."

Janet's bawdy remark brought a flush of color to Tory's cheeks and a hearty laugh from Janet and her daughter Ruth. Pilar, however, was thoughtful, her dark gaze meeting Tory's in the mirror.

Tory shivered. How aptly Janet put it. As Rhys's wife she would be expected to sheath her husband's blade whenever he chose. That was part of her duty; part of the obligation she accepted when she married him.

But not tonight.

Damn his expectations! Damn everyone's expectations, she thought defiantly. She couldn't just wed him and bed him as if it were a normal occurrence. She wouldn't be forced to seal this contract in such a way. She could not bear the thought of the cold, clinical joining of their bodies for no other reason save that it was *expected*. She was too private a person for a casual physical union with a virtual stranger. She needed first to trust.

A soft rap sounded on the connecting door between her suite of rooms and Rhys's. Pilar opened it a fraction.

It was Twinnings, holding something in his hands. "For the baroness," he explained, seeking entrance.

Making sure her wrapper was secure, Tory gestured to Pilar to let him in.

Twinnings approached her, his sharp eyes taking in the feminine preparations for the wedding. With a nod of his head to Tory he spoke. "Madam, his lordship charged me with the deliverance of this to you." He handed Tory a box, which was very old and carved from fine, rich wood.

She placed the object on her dressing table, marveling at the workmanship. It was a jewel casket. Her mother had had one, which she now possessed, made also of fine inlaid wood. A key was in the lock. Tory turned the key, opening the lid to reveal the contents. Instead of the ostentatious family jewels that she had presumed would be in the box, she saw only a single brooch. It was beautiful, Celtic in design, made of gold, resting in a bed of plush midnight blue velvet.

Tory reached in and drew out the brooch,

taking delight in the gasps of the women assembled. Her fingertips traced the flowing lines of the piece, loving the feel of it. Turning it over, she saw inscribed there words foreign to her.

"It's been in his lordship's family for over two hundred years," Twinnings declared. "Given by *the* Buchanan to his Fitzgerald bride."

"What does it say?" Tory asked, holding out her hand with the back of the brooch visible.

"That you'll be having to ask his lordship, madam, as the words are in Scots," Twinnings pointed out.

"I shall," she whispered, admiring the craftsmanship. It was simple yet unique.

The three other women in the room all expressed interest and delight in the piece, but Tory felt their surprise. No doubt they were thinking that her husband had chosen a rather insignificant gift. A union such as theirs demanded a grand gesture such as a large collection of wildly expensive gems.

Had she received such a gift from him, Tory knew that she would have refused it.

She turned her head and looked Rhys's man straight in the face. "Twinnings, isn't it?"

"Yes, madam," he responded with the deference due her.

"Twinnings, please tell his lordship that I am pleased with the brooch. I . . ." Why was she finding it so hard to say what she was feeling? "I thank him." With that she turned back to her dressing table, her eyes on the small enameled clock.

"Very good, madam," Twinnings intoned, giving her a nod of head as he left the room.

Tory placed the brooch back in the security of the box, reaching for the larger chest that held some of her jewels. Pulling open a tiny drawer, she selected a pair of earrings and quickly fastened them into her ears.

Janet watched Tory make her selection, her head cocked to one side. "How about a fancier pair? And what about a necklace?" she offered.

"No, I don't think so," Tory said quietly. She gently removed the silver and turquoise bracelet from her wrist.

Pilar observed how carefully Tory handled the bracelet, treating it with special care.

Reaching for the crystal bottle of scent, Tory removed the stopper and dabbed some onto her wrists and behind her ears.

"You're not gonna stop there?" Janet asked, hands on hips.

Tory shrugged her shoulders. "Yes, I am."

"But this is your wedding day."

"So?" Tory threw her an arch look.

Janet made a clicking sound with her tongue. "Trust me, there are other spots that can be more effective."

Tory wanted to dismiss Janet's attempt at help. Instead, knowing that Janet wanted only to make this day even more special, she merely inquired, "Where?"

"Loosen your wrapper and stand up," Janet insisted.

Tory went along with the request.

"Place the scent between your breasts."

"Are you serious?" Tory questioned.

Janet nodded. "Quite serious. Do it."

"I don't think . . ."

"This is not something that you have to think about, Miss Tory."

"Fine," Tory said defiantly, "I'll do it." She took the stopper and drew it down her throat and between her breasts.

"Now," Janet urged, "place some behind your knees."

Tory once more dipped the stopper in the fragrance, and bent to do Janet's bidding.

"There," Janet pronounced, "that should bring a smile to your groom, if he's half the man I suspect he is." Janet paused as she helped Tory step into her gown.

Tory took a deep breath as the gown was fastened. No going back now. "Will I do?" she asked, the merest trace of cynicism lacing her tone.

"Of course," Janet declared.

"You're so lovely, Miss Tory," Ruth said, her young face aglow with excitement.

"There was never any doubt, *amiga*," Pilar answered, placing her hands on Tory's shoulders and hugging her friend close.

"No," Tory replied, sliding her feet into the satin slippers, "there never was, was there?"

"I almost forgot," she said, stopping to go back to her dressing table as the others filed out the door. Tory picked up the brooch and fastened it onto the bodice of her gown. Why had he given it to her? she wondered. And why now? Was it really for tradition's sake as his manservant explained? Or did Rhys have another motive? And if so, what?

"She took it straight away, my lord," Twinnings reported, helping Rhys don his velvet waistcoat.

"Did she say anything?" Rhys asked as he fastened the buttons covered with black silk, adjusting the gold pocket watch and chain.

"Just that she was pleased with the gift, my lord," Twinnings said as he held up the earl's evening jacket so that Rhys could slide his arms in.

"Nothing more?"

Twinnings stood back to admire the way the cut of the entire outfit suited his lordship. He found it a pleasure to dress a man who was born to wear fine clothes. Aye, Twinnings thought, the ladies in London would have been swooning tonight over the earl. Rhys Fitzgerald Buchanan was a handsome fellow who looked more the part of a prince than he who occupied the position, Twinnings believed. "Aye, my lord," Twinnings confessed, "the baroness did say that I was to tell you thank you and that she was wanting to know what the inscription on the brooch meant."

"And what did you say?" Rhys quirked a black brow in amusement.

"That I didn't understand the Scots, my lord. I suggested that she ask you."

One corner of Rhys's mouth rose in his lop-sided smile. "Good."

"I did tell her that it's been an heirloom of your family since *the* Buchanan gave it to his bride."

Rhys paused. What would his soon-to-be-bride make of that story, and the translation of the inscription? As he slipped the Buchanan clan colors around his shoulder, he felt oddly close to that long-ago ancestor, who had also found himself bartered for money. Had he too wondered if he was doing the right thing? Did his mind haunt him with questions? Or had that long-ago laird done what was expected of him with no second thoughts? Rhys's slim fingers touched the soft, multicolored wool plaid, emblem of his family. Once, wearing of the colors had been outlawed. It was only because the Queen herself favored the plaids that clan colors were now allowed, even considered fashionable. Were he Scots-born, he would have worn a kilt for the ceremony today. He could well imagine the startled looks he would have received from those assembled below if he had done so. The tradition of his family decreed that he honor his family colors, at least in some way, so he'd had this long length of wool made in the Buchanan plaid with its rich hues of green, red and yellow. He fastened it with a smaller version of the brooch that was his gift to Victoria.

What did she truly think of the brooch? Had she anticipated a larger, more ornate collection of gems to wear? More fool she if she had, Rhys thought. Doubtless the Buchanan jewels, which had been sold or traded as payment for debts owed, were adorning some rich tradesman's daughter, wife, or mistress. He'd tried to get some of them back after Samuel's bank draft reestablished his financial well-being, but to no avail. Repeated inquiries had been fruitless. Another piece of his heritage cut away, leaving only the scar tissue of memory behind.

And now he was the last family jewel, so to speak, to be pawned.

The subtle irony of his situation wasn't lost on Rhys. It was his choice. He'd known others who lived quite comfortably off the charity of friends and were happy to do so, having no compunction about using their position and connections as bargaining chips. Their name, their very heritage, meant nothing more than a means to an amiable existence.

His pride demanded better. His respect for those who had shaped the past would not allow him to wantonly trample on their efforts.

The account was due. And full value would be paid.

"With this ring I thee wed."

Rhys's deep, clear voice carried through the room, his tone soft and sure as he slipped the thick band of gold onto Tory's finger. He expected her hand to be stiff; it was warm and flexible, fitting into his comfortably.

With the permission to kiss the bride, Rhys lifted the veil of lace that kept Tory's face concealed. The material was soft and delicate; the face beneath was strong, and yet, he saw in the crystal-blue eyes a suspicion of vulnerability. He had expected coldness, perhaps hate or disgust. Instead her eyes betrayed determination and candor.

Rhys cupped her chin in his hand, tilting her head up to meet his lips. He'd considered making the kiss long and hot, forcing her to respond. He knew now that he couldn't, wouldn't do that to her. Slowly, his head dipped so that his mouth touched hers in a warm salute. The contact was vibrant even though of short duration. Rhys could feel the reaction of his bride with the leap of the pulse in her throat. His own response was swift and sure, tightening his flesh even as he released her.

Rhys watched silently as Tory accepted the kisses of her father and other well-wishers. God, but she was breathtaking, he thought with a groan. She wore his brooch on the low-cut bodice of her gown, and the ornament seemed to highlight the magnificent swell of her breasts. Tory's wedding gown was of cream silk moire, with pale roses adoring the material. The puffed and tiered sleeves gave the dress a Georgian look, as did the bows of muted rose pink. In her hand Tory carried a bouquet of roses, deepest red mixed with a soft blush color.

She was his own briar rose to bloom for him alone.

That thought was like a thorn in his mind; he inhabitated a world that didn't expect faithfulness. After the nursery was filled with an heir and a spare, a woman's life was her own. Now, somehow, the idea of someone else touching Tory filled him with anger. His wild rose was his and his alone.

Absently, his fingers stroked the pin that held his plaid in place. Rhys smiled.

Tory accepted the congratulations, thanked everyone till she thought her mouth would freeze in a perpetual smile. She turned her head and saw her husband. It was then that she noticed for the first time the small piece of gold that fastened the multicolored strip of material crossing his wide chest. It was a mate to her own brooch.

Excusing himself from Pedro, who offered his felicitations, Rhys approached her. "I see that you wear my gift."

Tory's eyes were direct as she looked at him. "What does the inscription mean? Your man told me it was Scottish."

"It is. Scots Gaelic to be precise."

Again, she prompted, "The meaning?"

" 'My own is mine,' " he quoted.

Tory threw him a sharp look, her brows raised. "You don't say?"

"It's true." His gray eyes were keen, so intense that Tory was unable to break contact.

"How quaint," she retorted, her voice a soft drawl.

Rhys reached out his slim-fingered hand and lightly touched the brooch. "Quaint or no, it is something we both believe, is it not?" His fingers strayed and skimmed her flesh.

"Enough," she protested.

"For now," he promised, using his hand instead to summon a servant with a tray of champagne. He handed one of the crystal goblets to Tory, then took one for himself. "A toast, sweet wife."

"To what?" she asked.

"To whom," he corrected. "To us." His voice was a low, seductive whisper, meant for her ears alone.

Clinking her glass to his, Tory echoed Rhys's words, "To us," and drained the goblet, her eyes still focused on his.

Don Sebastian stood aside as the bride and groom were fêted by well-wishers. His goddaughter smiled, though he detected a strain in her polite expression. His hands remained at his sides, fists unconsciously clenched. Suddenly, he felt another hand, a feminine hand, take his and give a squeeze of comfort. He turned his head and saw Pilar.

Her voice was soft and low. "I know, Papa, how much of a strain this is is for you."

"I don't know what you mean."

"*Sí*, I think that you do. You are in love with Victoria."

"Nonsense," he protested.

Pilar tightened her grip on her father's hand. She could feel his tension. "Papa, please," she begged, "do not lie to me, or to yourself. You love her."

He took a deep breath, admitting honestly to his daughter, "*Sí, es verdad*, I love her."

Pilar gave a heartfelt sigh. "Witnessing this must cost you a great deal."

Don Sebastian's voice remained calm, his manner controled. "I could not have stayed away. I am Victoria's godfather and Samuel's best friend." His gaze remained on the bridal couple. "They are a handsome pair, are they not?" he said without rancor. He was simply stating a fact as he saw it.

"*Sí*, papa, they are indeed well-favored." Pilar noted the sadness on her father's face, though he tried hard to maintain his dignity. It was important to him that others not see what his own child did, most especially Victoria. He didn't want pity, nor did he wish to inspire the laughter of others who couldn't comprehend the deep emotions that he struggled to keep buried.

"We must offer our congratulations to them. Come," Don Sebastian said, taking her hand in his, striding towards them. His heart was heavy, tinged with an envy he loathed. Bitter thoughts crowded his brain, brooding thoughts about Victoria and this man who was her now legally

211

wedded husband. No bride ever looked more beautiful, he acknowledged. Or more ready for loving.

Loving.

Don Sebastian felt that word like a knife thrust to his heart. To fill and be filled with a woman like Victoria. To show her all the patience and kindness his love urged him to give. To share a bed and a future.

But truth spoke clearly, dispassionately to him. Such was not to be.

"Tío," Tory's warm voice rang with love.

Don Sebastian leaned over and placed a tender kiss on each of her cheeks; then his lips touched hers for a brief salute. "Much happiness, Victoria. Now and always."

Tory returned his kisses. Here was familiarity and security, much as her own father provided. A man like Don Sebastian would have made her a correct choice for a husband. *"Gracias, Tío,"* she said, her eyes touched with tears.

"My best to you, my lord," Don Sebastian intoned, giving Rhys a slight nod of his head, along with a firm handshake.

"Thank you for your kind words," Rhys drawled.

"Bien hablar no cuesta nada," the don replied.

Tory quickly translated for Rhys. "Kind words cost nothing."

"Oh, but in some cases they do—very much," Rhys affirmed, his cool gray eyes meeting the darker gaze of Don Sebastian. That the man was in love with his wife was obvious to him. Rhys could well imagine what it must have cost such a proud man as Don Sebastian to have uttered those words. He glanced at his wife, who was speaking with Pilar and the housekeeper, Kristen. He'd seen the look that Pilar had passed to her father on their approach. She too was aware of her father's feelings. His wife, he judged, was blissfully ignorant of the depth of Don Sebastian's passion. And there was passion there, Rhys admitted. He could read plainly the stamp of desire in the eyes that gazed so adoringly at Victoria.

Well, he reasoned, Don Sebastian could look all he wanted; it would progress no further. Victoria was his wife.

The wedding supper was festive, with animated conversations holding sway between the courses. The long, polished table, agleam with the glow of silver and china, held large platters heaped high with selections of prime beef, baked chicken, and roast pork. Bowls of fresh hot vegetables and cold fruit provided further treats, along with warm breads. Champagne and wines were abundant.

Tory, who normally took only one glass of wine with dinner, found herself imbibing several glasses of champagne. Once or twice her gaze shifted to the other end of the table, observing her husband's charming manners as he chatted with the guests flanking his seat. Outwardly, he looked to be having an enjoyable time. Yet, what thoughts occupied his brain? Did he dwell on what the night was supposed to bring? Perhaps he believed without question that tonight he would claim his bride.

Well, husband mine, she mused, that won't happen.

Rhys watched as his lovely countess chatted gaily with her father and Don Sebastian, who sat opposite her. She was warm, laughing with gentle abandon, animated. He couldn't hear what she was saying. Was she caustic or careful? What thoughts lurked beneath the careful mask of her face? Did she dwell, if only for a passing moment, on the significance of this night? Was she ready to become his bride, his wife in fact? Had it been only months ago that he'd thought to perform this function as quickly and effortlessly as possible? To do the deed and ignore the consequences? Now, duty's face was fresh and exciting.

Sam's face was aglow with his triumph, and with the pride that he felt for his daughter. His scheme to see her married had come off without a hitch. There was no room for doubts or recriminations tonight. He firmly believed that he'd acted for the best. Security for his daughter was important, as was continuity for the dominion under his control. The vitality of this union must be tested to see if it would hold secure. And if it did not, Sam was ruthless enough to see it dissolved with the same haste as it was joined. He had the time. He had the patience. What he hoped was that he now had the right combination.

Sam rose to his feet to propose a toast. His voice was steady and sure as he said, "To my beloved daughter Victoria, and my newfound son, Rhys: may every happiness be yours!"

A chorus of voices echoed the words, leaving the bridal couple exchanging sharp glances, both wondering about that illusive chimera styled happiness.

Chapter Eleven

An old Spanish proverb stole into his thoughts as he stood talking with his goddaughter: *Bien ama quien nunca olvida*. He loves well who never forgets.

And how could he? Tonight Victoria was incomparable. *Hermosa. Muy hermosa*. And she was legally wed to another.

As the soft strains of chamber music played around them, and he listened to Victoria's animated voice as she replied to something his son-in-law said concerning his grandson, Don Sebastian was taken back through the years to her christening celebration. How time sped by, as if being pulled along by the fleetest team of horses, without pause. Back then, this ranch was simply referred to as the *Hochburg*. The stronghold. The young woman who danced in his arms last evening, and who would soon lie in the embrace of another, had once been held in his hands as the water annointed her. It was then, holding the infant Victoria, her blue eyes wide, her mouth bowed in a tiny smile, that he spoke aloud the word, *encantadora*. Her mother heard the word and asked her husband to use it for the ranch. "In honor of our own little enchantress," Don Sebastian remembered her saying. And Samuel Reitenauer, who adored his wife and baby girl, eagerly complied.

Another tray of champagne was passed among them, and each took a glass.

"One more toast, if I may be permitted?" Don Sebastian asked, his mind once again on the present.

"Of course," Tory declared.

"To my godchild, Victoria."

"To Victoria," was the reply.

"Gracias," was her answer.

"There is no need for thanks," Don Sebastian said.

"Oh, but I disagree," Tory insisted. "Had I not had the support of my family, I don't know how I would have gotten through this," she confessed.

Pedro grinned, his thin moustache a slash of black against the white of his teeth. "You would have managed. More than that"—he paused to take her right hand in his, saluting it with his mouth—"I know that you would have survived —and triumphed. It is your way. Like the mountains that surround my home." Pedro's face became more serious. "We are as God made us."

"Still," Tory responded, "I am glad that you were all able to be with me." Draining her glass, Tory asked, "Anyone for another?"

"No," Pilar answered, "we must be leaving."

"So soon?" Tory demanded, the careful mask of gaiety slipping from her face as she reached for Pilar's hand.

"*Sí*," Pilar said.

"Stay," Tory spoke the word softly.

Pilar sighed. "We have to return to our own *hacienda* the day after tomorrow."

"Perhaps you and your husband will come to stay with us soon?" Pedro asked.

Tory shook her head. "I don't think that would be a good idea."

Pedro looked puzzled. "You know that you are welcome at any time."

"I do know, *gracias*."

Pedro excused himself from the gathering to see to their carriage.

Pilar and Tory embraced each other warmly, clinging, tears wetting their eyes. "I shall miss you," Tory said, reluctant to break contact.

Pilar whispered, "And I you, *amiga*." They hugged again, with Pilar pulling back ever so slightly. "*Por favor*, give yourself time, Victoria."

"I cannot promise . . ."

"Do not promise me, *amiga*. Promise yourself. Do not throw away what could be happiness."

"*Could* be."

"*Sí*, could be."

Don Sebastian stood waiting, wishing that he could hear what the two women spoke of, aware that it probably had to do with Tory's marriage.

Pedro returned at that moment, joined by Rhys and Sam.

"I've ordered an escort for your journey," Sam said, shaking hands with both Pedro and Don Sebastian. He bussed Pilar warmly and helped her into her light cloak.

Don Sebastian's brows rose a fraction. "You think it necessary, *amigo?*"

"A precautionary action only, old friend." Sam's blue eyes narrowed slightly.

"As you wish," Don Sebastian agreed. He took Tory's left hand, stared at the unfamiliar ring, and brought it to his mouth for a soft salute. "Victoria, be happy." With that he stepped back and walked away, his back straight and stiff.

The Montenegro carriage awaited them, along with ten armed men on horseback.

Rhys, a silent observer, decided to allow actions to speak for him. As his bride stood watching her neighbors prepare to depart, he moved to stand behind her. Gently, he slipped his arm around her bare shoulders, his hand splayed across the sleeve of her gown, his fingers light but possessive. He felt his wife's body tense. However, Tory didn't move. To the people in the coach, with the muted light from the open doorway behind them, Rhys knew how very intimate it looked, and what message it conveyed. His smile was lazy and sensual, ripe with promise.

The three stood there until the carriage vanished into the night, and Sam, a look of contentment on his features, left the couple, closing the door behind him.

"Please remove your hand," she stated.

Rhys complied with Tory's request, slowly, so that his fingers lazily skimmed her bodice. In a somewhat husky voice, he asked, "Are you going to return to the party?"

It must have been the warm breeze that caused her to shiver, she decided. That, and nothing more. "No. But don't let me keep you from celebrating." Tory moved down the steps, away from him, away from the urge to relax against his strong body. "I'm tired and I'd like to go to bed."

As would I, dear wife, Rhys thought. He murmured politely, "As you wish, Victoria."

She walked toward the garden, listening to the sounds around her—the music; the snippets of conversation that poured from open windows; the familiar night noises—unaware that she was the focus of attention of two very different observers.

One was watching with curiosity from behind a silk curtain; the other stalked her with malevolent intensity.

Tory stopped, a sudden chill moving over her flesh. She spun around, looking in all directions, hearing only the whicker of a horse, the bark of a dog. Nothing out of the ordinary. She rubbed the chillbumps on her arms and continued her walk.

There was nothing keeping her company except her apprehensions. A stone bench provided a place to sit and she willingly took it. Her gaze shifted first to the sky, counting the stars, then to the heavy weight of the unfamiliar ring on her finger. The representation of the joining in matrimony of two strangers. What would the rest of this night bring? she wondered. Confrontation? Certainly not consummation, she vowed.

The murmur of low-pitched voices caused her to shift her position on the seat to see who was approaching. It was only Janet and Marshall, who stopped to kiss before hurrying to their own place. One would think they were the newlyweds, Tory observed.

Hoping to avoid putting on a happy face for any other guests, Tory made for the kitchen entrance.

There, sitting at the table, were Kristen and Rhys's valet, Twinnings, having a cold supper.

Twinnings jumped to his feet, his napkin spilling to the floor. "My lady," he began, giving her a formal nod.

Tory waved her hand. "Please, finish your meal," she insisted.

"Do you have need of anything?" he asked, not quite knowing if he was overstepping his bounds with her, but thinking it wouldn't hurt to offer, especially seeing that she was now the Countess of Derran, and not just any ordinary American female.

"No, thank you," Tory answered, eyeing the food enviously.

Kristen caught the look and interpreted it correctly as Tory reached for a piece of ham. She said with a grin, "*Liebchen,* I have fixed a private supper for you, for later." A blush stained her cheeks.

"And the wine that the earl ordered earlier is properly chilled, my lady," Twinnings informed her.

Tory demanded to know, "What wine?"

Twinnings bent to retrieve his napkin. "Why, the champagne, of course."

Tory's blue eyes narrowed consideringly. "How very thoughtful of him," she said with a forced gaiety.

Twinnings, alert to the change in her tone, asked, "Would the countess perhaps prefer something else?"

It was on her tongue to reply scathingly, *not to be married*, but she resisted. "No," she said, knowing that Rhys's man was only following his instructions, "that will be fine." Tory headed for the back stairs and paused, one slippered foot on the first step. She addressed herself to Kristen. "Fetch Ruth for me and send her to my room, else I won't be able to get out of this dress."

"As you wish, baroness," Kristen answered,

her voice floating up the stairs as Tory made her way to her room.

Opening her door, she was quick to note the changes made since last she was in there. More plump pillows had been heaped upon the bed, along with scented candles in the wall sconces and in various candelabra scattered throughout the room. Vases of fresh flowers had been added.

Pilar's gift lay strewn across the bed, which was already turned down, waiting, the invitation explicit.

Snatching the artfully draped garment, Tory flung it into the open wardrobe. It was then that she noted the table set for an intimate supper for two, with a silver bucket in which rested the bottle of champagne.

She recognized Kristen's handiwork, aided and abetted, she had no doubt, by Janet. Crusty loaves of bread, the smell fresh and tantalizing, were heaped in two baskets lined with cloths. Thick slabs of cheeses, a selection of cold meats, apples and peaches and candied orange peels, a treat Tory loved—everything that two lovers could want, she thought morosely, awaited them.

Except that she and Rhys weren't lovers; nor were they likely to be, she decided. His lordship would be in for a big surprise when he came to take his marital prize. His *prize* was in no mood to be taken.

A knock on the door spun her around, her pulses racing. "Enter," she said, her stance rigid, her heartbeat increasing.

It was only Ruth, come to help her undress.

The girl was excited, chattering inconsequentially as she unlaced the gown, which only served to irritate Tory further.

"Please, Ruth," Tory snapped, "be quiet."

The younger girl fell silent for a moment as she hung the wedding dress in the wardrobe, picking up the discarded nightdress and folding it before she slipped it carefully into a drawer. "I'm awfully sorry, Miss Tory," she said quietly as she bent to retrieve the voluminous petticoats from the floor where Tory had left them.

Catching the hurt look on Ruth's face, Tory experienced a twinge of guilt for her outburst. She reached out her hand and placed it on the girl's, saying, "Pay no heed to my words, Ruth. I meant no harm."

The words changed the girl's face; now it beamed knowingly. She answered Tory as she stored the petticoats in a chest, "That's okay, Miss Tory. Ma said you'd be nervous, this being your first time and all."

Ruth's plain speaking caused Tory's eyebrows to raise.

"He'll be getting a fine lady, Miss Tory," Ruth said as she held out Tory's robe so that she could slip into the garment. "Ma thinks he really fancies you."

"Fancies me?" Tory questioned, removing her earrings and placing them, along with the brooch, in her jewel box, putting the silver and turquoise bracelet back on her wrist.

"Yes," Ruth continued, "I heard her telling Pa this evening that she caught the Englishman watching you whenever you wasn't with him. Just as if he was eatin' you up with those frosty eyes of his."

Which is about all he'll be able to do, Tory thought as she dismissed Ruth, tying the sash to her robe and popping a few of the candied orange peels into her mouth, savoring their sweet taste.

The final guest had retired for the evening as Sam proceeded down the hall. Tonight he'd made sure that guards were posted around the perimeter of the ranch and the house. There had been too many accidents of late for him to feel as if he could not take measures to protect his own.

Sam saw a faint light coming from the library. Deciding to investigate, he made his way carefully down the hall, feeling a trifle foolish. If it was anyone intent on harm, they surely wouldn't leave a light on.

As he opened the door, he saw his son-in-law, his evening jacket and sash tossed negligently across the back of the wing chair, a snifter of brandy in his hand.

"Strange way to be spending your wedding night, boy," Sam said, closing the door.

Rhys acknowledged Sam's presence with a salute of his glass before taking a large swallow, finishing the contents of the snifter. He reached down and picked up the bottle of brandy from where it had been placed on the floor, refilling the cut glass. Handing the almost empty bottle to Sam, Rhys stared at the prisms of light reflected in the well-crafted piece. His voice was deep and even when he spoke. "I think we both know that this is anything but a typical wedding, sir."

Sam emptied the brandy bottle into his glass, coming to stand next to the empty fireplace. "But this *is* a wedding, all legal and proper."

"I know."

"So?"

Rhys focused his cool gaze on Sam, a measure for measure. "I have a plan."

"Which is?" Sam asked, his curiosity aroused.

"To woo my wife," Rhys announced.

Sam laughed heartily at Rhys's words. *"Mein Gott,* but you are a rare one, my boy. Woo her indeed." He tossed back a drink of the warm liquid. His regard for Rhys was increasing. Another man might have made the mistake of trying to storm the bastion of his daughter's virginity without care for her feelings. In truth, he'd worried how this stranger would approach his girl. The unexpected sensitivity that his son-in-law exhibited pleased Sam greatly.

"Victoria's stubborn," Sam said, "even I'll admit to that. But she's got heart, my girl has. Deal with her fairly and she'll return the same to you." He finished the brandy in one gulp, walking across the room after leaving the snifter on the mantel. "I want you to wait here for a few more minutes, my boy," Sam said. "I have something for you that I think will please you."

Rhys nodded his consent and Sam left the room, pausing outside, his hand still on the doorknob. He'd planned on giving this surprise to Rhys at a later date; however, tonight it seemed somehow appropriate. A fitting signal of his sudden trust in the other man.

Stubborn, her father had confessed. Rhys smiled lazily at that word. At the very least. It was a war of wills that he and his countess were engaged in. He had no doubt that Victoria would eventually be his wife in every sense of the word. His promise to himself as he left the Menger came vividly back. It would take more finesse to bring his proud bride to submission. She needed some time to wait, to brood over what would happen. Time was his ally. Besides, claiming her tonight as his wife wasn't part of his plan. To get her used to his touch, that would suffice. To allow her to feel the pull of the senses; to make her tremble with the need that could slowly burn in the skin while it scorched the blood. For all her bravado, Victoria was a virgin. A novice.

A smile of wicked delight curved Rhys's mouth. One thing that he wasn't, was a novice to the pleasures that could be shared between a man and a woman. Instead of a practiced partner, one who was well aware of the act, he would have to be tutor to a recalcitrant student whose ignorance was a barrier to be broken.

To do so without proceeding to the final culmination would prove an exercise in concentration and strength, as Rhys was well aware of the demands that such a sacrifice would cost him. He was a man used to a woman's body. Used to the release that it offered. And he did crave that. Strangely, the woman he wanted to share that with was his wife.

Sam finally returned, bring with him a wooden trunk. Placing it on the desk, he beckoned Rhys over.

Rhys joined Sam, who drew a key for the lock on the trunk.

"Open it," Sam demanded.

"What is it?" Rhys asked.

Sam repeated himself. "Open it and find out."

Rhys took the key and fit it into the lock. He lifted the trunk lid; surprise widened his eyes.

Inside the silk lining of the oak chest were numerous velvet pouches. Rhys reached in and pulled them out, inspecting the contents. They contained the jewels that had once belonged to his family, which he'd been forced to sell. "Why?" was all that he could ask, dumbstruck.

Sam was pleased by Rhys's reaction. "I understand the value of heritage, my boy. When Jason explained to me about your losses, and what they meant to you personally, I decided to try and get back what I could. I instructed him to act again as my agent and purchase what he could." Sam picked up one collar of pearls, the clasp of which was a diamond. "These objects are family history, and as such are to be respected and cared for. They are tradition."

"I am in your debt, sir," Rhys replied. In

truth, he felt somewhat awkward, at once beholden and angry.

Damn, he thought, what was he complaining about? The property was back where it belonged. What matter who secured its release and how?

Inside one of the velvet bags was a man's ring and a lady's necklace. Rhys picked up the ring, a large sapphire set in gold. He had no reason to turn it over and read the inscription inside; he knew it by heart. *In gratitude: Carolinus Rex.* It had been a wedding gift to Cameron Buchanan from Charles Stuart, as the matching sapphire necklace had been for Marisa. How fitting that they were restored to him now. He slipped the heavy ring onto his slim finger, feeling firmly connected once again to his ancestor.

"Tory will do full justice to that necklace," Sam declared.

Rhys's thoughts returned to what Sam was saying. He lifted the necklace in his hand, the gems catching and reflecting the light. He doubted that he and Samuel Reitenauer were envisioning her wearing the jewels in quite the same way. Rhys's concept of doing the necklace full justice would be to have Victoria, his splendid amazon, totally naked save for this piece. He dropped it carefully back into its secure niche, then left that bag on the desk as he re-packed the others into the trunk.

"Thank you," Rhys said quietly.

"My grandchildren deserve to have all that is theirs," Sam stated.

Children. The getting of children. Another particular of the marriage compact. Heirs. Continuity. Planting his seed into Victoria's body.

"I shall secure these once again," Sam said, picking up the trunk.

Absently, Rhys murmured, "Yes, please do," as he hefted the deep blue velvet pouch with the drawstrings of gold thread, catching it in one hand. It was even embossed with Cameron's motto.

Tonight Rhys felt the kinship across the years. His own was his.

Tory was sleeping, confident that Rhys wouldn't be coming. She'd waited, wondered, and finally dismissed the chance of his actually trying to establish some sort of marital harmony. Satisfied, and exhausted, she made sure the locks were secure before she slid between the scented sheets.

Rhys's smile was a satisfied half grin as he strode into the near-dark room. He suspected that she would have the foresight to lock her doors, as if that would have stopped him. The key that he'd found pushed to the back of the drawer of the desk in his room had proved a godsend, else he would have had to bribe or steal another to make a copy.

His bare feet made no sound as he walked to the bed. His new bride was fast asleep, her thick braids spread upon the pillows. He bent and lit the brace of candles by her bedside with the single one he carried. It was then that he noticed the pile of small plump pillows in white velvet and silk that littered the floor.

Bridal offerings. Made for the marriage bed.

She looked like a comfortable, secure child, tucked up in her safe cocoon, except that she moved in her sleep, exposing for one moment a glimpse of her naked flesh beneath the quilt. There was nothing remotely childlike about that.

Rhys turned and saw the table laid for a wedding supper. He strolled over, relighting the candles. He reached for one of the candied orange peels. They brought back memories from his childhood, when Cook would make them for holiday treats. He sampled one. Delicious.

He picked up the bottle of champagne and opened it, making use of the simple silver corkscrew. He poured a small measure into the fluted glass and sampled it. Satisfied, he filled both glasses, leaving his on the table. Taking the other, Rhys once again approached the bed.

Awakening with a start, Tory blinked several times. No, it wasn't a dream, she admitted. It was her husband, sitting bold as brass on her bed, offering her a glass of champagne. Her eyes widened. He was clad only in his black silk robe, open just enough to expose the hair that furred his sleekly muscled chest.

Arrogant bastard! she thought. How did he get in?

Remembering that she'd gone to bed without a nightdress, Tory pulled the quilt a tad higher about her shoulders.

Her glance skittered to the knife that lay on the nightstand.

Rhys watched her eyes, saw where she glanced. "You won't need that," he said smoothly.

"How did you get in?" she asked, voicing aloud her thoughts.

"With a key," he answered.

"I assumed that," she shot back. "Where did you procure a key?"

"From your brother's desk drawer." Rhys leaned over and handed Tory the glass. He stood up in one fluid movement, his eyes narrowing. "Did you really think a bloody lock would have stopped me?" He moved silently to the table, picking up his own glass. "It wouldn't have, you know."

Tory heard the truth in his words. He *would* have broken through had he not found a key. Beneath that fine exterior, she glimpsed a very determined man, one who wasn't used to being thwarted. Oddly enough, she could admire his tenacity.

Rhys couldn't believe his own words. Would he have carried through on his threat? Would he really have broken the lock if he hadn't found a key? *Yes*. He mentally dismissed the notion of playing the obedient husband who respected the imposed barrier. With another woman, perhaps. With her, never. She inspired no half measures, no polite gestures.

"Will you join me?" he asked, seating himself.

Tory was well and truly awake now. No use to try and go back to sleep until she could get rid of him, she thought. Besides, she was hungry. She downed the contents of her glass and leaned over to place it temporarily on the nightstand. Scooting up on the bed, she made to reach for her robe from where it lay at the foot of her bed.

Before she could reach it, Rhys was there.

God, but he was quick.

He held the garment in one big hand as she watched, fascinated. Slowly, he lifted his other hand, and drew it across the fabric.

Tory shivered beneath the quilt. It was as if he had just stroked her flesh, so intimate was the caress of her robe. She found that she couldn't tear her eyes away from the subtle motions of his long fingers.

Rhys tossed her the garment. It was then that she saw that he wore another ring, on his left hand, a rich, deep blue stone set in gold.

He turned his back to her, returning to the table to fix himself a plate of food.

Tory pulled the robe on beneath the protection of the quilt. Somehow it felt different against her skin. Or was she just more aware?

Padding to the table, the glass in her hand, she sat down opposite him.

"More champagne?" he offered.

"Yes," she answered, pushing her glass towards him.

Rhys refilled it, handing it back to her, observing how careful she was not to make contact. He took the large silver serving fork and speared slices of ham and beef onto her plate as she sat quietly, sipping the bubbly liquid. A few slices of cheese, along with a dollop of the mustard, completed the fare.

Tory reached for a handful of nuts to add to what Rhys had already put on her plate.

His hand covered hers.

She froze.

"Don't be afraid," he murmured softly.

"I'm not," she assured him.

"But you are, I can feel it," he said. His voice was smooth soothing, coaxing.

"What do you want?"

"To get to know you," he responded, freeing her hand.

"Why?"

"We are man and wife."

"So?"

Rhys smiled at her. "Humor me."

Tory shrugged her shoulders, using her fork to stab at a piece of ham, dipping it in the mustard. "As you wish," she said, chewing her food calmly, wondering what he was about.

They finished their meal in companionable silence. Replete, Rhys asked her. "Now, that wasn't so dreadful, was it?"

Tory managed a tremulous smile. "No," she admitted carefully, "it wasn't."

"If we'd been in London tonight, I'll wager the Prince of Wales would have sponsored a dinner for us."

"You move in rare circles."

Now it was Rhys's turn to shrug. "Not quite so rare." He stood up, circling to her seat. "Spare me the humble peasant girl pose."

Tory twisted in her seat. "I don't know what you mean."

"Of course you do." Rhys laid one hand on her shoulder, the warmth permeating her wrapper. "I observed the guests at our wedding; I even know who was informed, who sent gifts. Senators, governors, merchant princes, families of quality; I hardly think they count as typical, my dear."

"I suppose you're right," she admitted.

"You know I am," he countered, removing his hand from her shoulder. He reached into the pocket of his robe, drawing out the necklace. "I have something for you."

Wearily, she asked, "What is it?"

"Close your eyes."

He noted her reluctance. "Just do it," he insisted.

"All right," she conceded, feeling the weight of something around her throat and the warmth of his fingers as they lingered momentarily on her skin.

"Go and look," Rhys said, stepping back, catching sight of her long legs as the robe flapped softly about her as she made her way to the full-length mirror.

She stood and stared at her reflection, her hand going to the stone. It matched in color and clarity the one in the ring that Rhys wore. A pair.

Designed for male and female. Each piece alone was marvellous. Together, they formed a unique bond.

Rhys joined her, surprised to see a single tear threaten her cheek. Her vulnerability touched a chord deep in his soul. One part of him thought it best if he quit the room now, leaving her alone. The other felt the need to be inside her, to possess her, if only by a kiss. He yielded to that, sweeping her into his arms before she could protest. His hungry mouth was on hers, exploring the mystery, tasting the fantasy.

Her defenses were down. He grasped the opportunity. He'd never tasted a mouth so sweet, so wantonly innocent.

He pulled her hard into his embrace. Her lush body fit into his easily. One hand held her still, in the small of her back, pushing, pressing her against his eager flesh.

And still it wasn't enough. His other hand moved between their straining bodies, sliding across the fabric, pushing aside the thick rope of her braid, searching for her breast.

His mouth muffled her gasp when his hand met her barely covered flesh. He cupped the mound, fingers teasing a path along and around, tracing, learning, memorizing, as if he were a blind man.

His lips broke contact, moving for a brief moment to her throat, staking territory.

In a hoarse voice, he whispered darkly, "Touch me," as he took her lips again, his tongue driving deep.

Tory gasped. What was happening to her? Once more he was controlling her senses, forcing her to give in, to recognize this other side, as if he had pulled her through one mirror and forced her to look into another, one which exposed a deeper, intense need that had simmered quietly, waiting to errupt. His voice, rough and deep, called to her before he captured her mouth again.

Why wasn't she fighting this overwhelming possession by his ravenous lips?

Because, Tory realized as she wound her arms about his neck, she wanted this too.

Curiosity, coupled with his demand, led her to place her left hand on his chest. The crisp feel of hair, the warmth of his skin, fascinated her. She found the hard nub of his nipple and heard his groan. Had she hurt him?

Rhys thought he was going to explode. Her untrained hand had almost cost him his control. His chest rose and fell with the rapid breaths he took. Their gazes locked. He saw the blink of confusion in her honest eyes.

Rhys reached out his hand and touched her cheek. He could press home his advantage, force her to accept him in her bed.

And if he did, what then?

He would lose.

"I think it best if we say our good nights now," Rhys said.

Regaining her composure, Tory agreed. "Yes, that would be for the best."

Tory heard the soft click of the connecting

door shutting, leaving her alone. But she wasn't alone: memories flooded back, sweeping her along in their powerful current.

She touched the stone around her throat.

A reminder.

A warning.

A promise.

Chapter Twelve

Dearest Pilar:
   A month has passed since my marriage.
And in that time, amiga, *I have become*
more and more confused as to the
marriage and to my husband.

Tory paused in writing the letter, putting
down her pen. She wondered just how candid
she dared be? Could she admit to her friend that
what really bewildered her was Rhys's attitude
towards consummating their relationship? In
these past weeks since they'd exchanged their
vows, he had yet to demand that she yield in
anything to him. In some ways he seemed content to play the role of friend or brother. Then,
Tory would catch a scorching look directed her

way, or his hand would linger whenever he had an excuse to touch her.

I ask myself if he is playing some kind of game with me. Why? Because he has yet to insist on his rights as my husband.
I don't know what to think.
Is he sincere?
Can I trust him?

Trust.
Such a small word.

But what do I really know of him? Yes, I will admit that he is not the ineffectual wastrel that I first thought him to be. On the contrary, Pilar, at times his perspicacity surprises me.

Tory recalled an incident that had happened only a week ago, over breakfast. It was rarely that she and Rhys, as well as Sam, were eating together. She had been having a heated discussion with her father, and Rhys, until that moment a spectator, had offered his perspective. His remarks cut to the core of the matter and made sense. Since then, Tory found herself sharing more of her thoughts with her husband, eager to sample his ideas.

The deep, stirring chords of a Mozart sonata wafted down the hall to her ears. Tory stopped, went to her door, and opened it just slightly, listening to the achingly sweet music.

Quickly, she hurried back to her desk, putting pen to paper once more.

> *I must share with you something that I discovered about Rhys: he plays the piano. He isn't just a dabbler, content to merely plunk the keys. What he produces from Mama's instrument is beautiful; at times both sweet and sad, tender and strong.*
>
> *Can a man produce such music and not be affected by it?*
>
> *How very different he is.*
>
> *In consequence I feel different somehow. More aware; more responsive. And that frightens me. Does that shock you? It does me. Something strange passes between us whenever we're together. I can't say what it is exactly, but it's there.*

Honesty forced Tory into revealing part of the turmoil that she was experiencing.

Abruptly, Tory decided that she'd said enough about that subject and switched to something safer.

> *I hope that you are getting enough rest. I remember how tired you were during your last confinement. Pray, amiga, take time for your own care.*
>
> *Answer me as soon as you are able. Your letters are always a welcome diversion, for when I receive them you are not nearly so far from me. Again, I promise to try to*

241

become a better correspondent.
You remain in my heart, close and loved.
Give Pedro and Mano a hug from me.

Tory signed her name with a quick flourish, eager to put the letter into an envelope before she could give in to the urge to crumple the pages and throw them away.

* * *

Dear Gillie:
I thought it about time to let you know just how your older brother is getting along. First, scamp, he misses you terribly. Not a day goes by that I do not think of you and wish with all my heart that you were closer to me. I regret that I shall be forced to miss your birthday. Alas, that cannot be helped. My stay here is perforce to be an extended one. I do hope, however, to be home in time for Christmas.
I know that that seems very far away, but the time will pass quickly, I promise you.

Christmas. Rhys stopped and wiped a few beads of sweat from his brow. The air was especially hot today, with a muggy quality. He'd already removed his jacket and unbuttoned his shirt, to Twinnings' silent consternation. A gentleman should never give in to the elements. Rhys knew without being told that that was Twinnings' motto. Rhys mentally shrugged. He'd be damned before he would allow this foul

Texas weather to get the best of him. No, he'd ride it out as best he could, thinking instead of the sweet summers he'd spent in Devon, or of the scattered trips made to relatives; of the windswept ruggedness of the western coast of Ireland; of the sweeping grandeur of the Scottish border country or the quiet beauty of the north of Wales.

What have you been up to? Are you still playing at doctor with the estate animals? Or has our mother at last persuaded you to give that up for being a proper young lady?

Rhys smiled as he recalled his mother's attempts to turn Gillian into a model of decorum. The dowager countess couldn't understand how a daughter of hers could be happiest with animals.

What would his mother think of his bride, Victoria? And Gillie, how would she see his wife? He imagined that they might fare well together, both being independent-minded.

Are you satisfied with your new governess?

Rhys was well aware that his mother thought that Gillian should have been sent to an exclusive school for girls, her own alma mater. His sister's tearful pleadings told him otherwise and, as her sole guardian, he had the final say.

But in the haste of his leaving for America, Rhys relied on his mother in the choice of the governess for his sister.

Without a doubt you would find this place incalculably different from our home, scamp. This Texas is huge, unlike anything that you or I are familiar with. It is, in a strange way, magnificent.

Rhys thought about what he'd just written. His choice of words took him by surprise. Since arriving only scant months ago, this place had lost its strangeness. He could now accept the ways Texas was different from England. Riding the ranch with Tory and her father had given him this appreciation. Seeing through their eyes, and most especially those of his wife, altered his perspective.

Please take some time and write to me, so that I may hear how you are faring.
Don't ever forget, my dear Gillie, that I love you. Would that I were there to wrap you in my arms and show you.
your devoted brother,
Rhys

* * *

Don Sebastian poured himself another cup of morning chocolate. A rider had arrived late yesterday with letters from his daughter and grandson. He re-read Pilar's as he sipped the fragrant brew.

Encantadora

Dearest Pilar:

I am touched by your concern for my welfare. Pray, daughter, do not waste your time worrying about me. I am fine; more, I am a survivor, as well you know. Fate has alloted me a role in Victoria's life. I have long since accepted it.

You asked me if I had been to the Encantadora since the wedding celebrated there. I was invited to dine with Sam, Victoria, and her husband just last week.

Don Sebastian summoned the memory of that evening. It came clear and sharp. Over the years he'd grown used to the way Victoria dressed for dinner at her own rancho. That evening it was different. She had abandoned her customary denim trousers and cotton shirt, not to mention her ubiquitous knife. Instead, Victoria was dressed, he recalled, in a gown of deepest rose. Her hair was pulled way from her face by tortoiseshell combs, leaving the rest falling like a cloud around her back and waist. Around her throat she wore a new piece of jewelry, a superb sapphire pendant. It was a mate to the ring the earl wore.

His loins ached heavily with the memories. A sharp stab of jealousy caught hold of him as he rose when she entered the room on the arm of her husband.

I observed that night a change in Victoria's attitude towards her esposo.

*Before, there was a palpable tension
between the couple; not so that evening. It
was as if they had formed some kind of
bond. Her voice was softer, warmer, when
she addressed him, which she did often.*

And what of those blue-crystal eyes of hers?
Don Sebastian couldn't help but be aware of
how often her eyes sought those of her husband,
or how Rhys's sharp gray eyes silvered whenever
he focused on Victoria, making his desire obvious to anyone who looked.

*If this marriage brings Victoria
happiness, then I sha.l be content. That is
all I have asked of life for both of you, the
best that it has to offer. But, I wonder, is he
the best for her? ¿Quien sabe? My old
friend Sam seems much taken with him
lately. It was evident that night, and in
several conversations I have had with him.
Sam is not easily fooled. He is tough,
shrewd, and I must admit, however
grudgingly, so is this Rhys Fitzgerald
Buchanan.*

And, a man of infinite patience it would seem,
Don Sebastian granted. He decided not to in-
clude in his letter to his daughter the fact that he
was positive that Victoria and her husband had
not so far shared a bed. The glow of innocence
radiated still in her eyes. Nor did she wear the

face of a woman well and truly loved. Why? he wondered. Sealing the bargain was within Fitzgerald Buchanan's rights. Why hesitate?

Because he *was* shrewd, Don Sebastian decided. Anticipation only heightens the fulfillment. And with a proud woman such as Victoria, the extra time would work in her husband's favor.

Clever. Very clever.

He lifted his cup in a salute.

How is my grandson? And Pedro?

I had a letter from your brother only last week. It seems that he and his wife have decided to stay on in New Orleans for at least another month. Your mother's cousins have been most kind to them. Invitations have been extended for all of us to visit. I may accept their offer. As you know, I have not visited New Orleans since your mother and I were last there.

Perhaps a trip would do me good? I think that I could use a change. No, I would not be running away. Your papa is a realist, querida.

And the reality was that he was a lonely man; he had been since the death of his wife. His love for Victoria had shown him that he was a man who needed the comfort that a woman could give him. Realistically, he knew that he would have to settle for less than he wanted; such was life. Perhaps a warm widow to see to his house and his bed. A woman who could help fill the hours and ease the solitude.

Sí, it would be the best for all concerned. The rancho would be well looked after, the Reitenauers would see to that.

I shall bid you good-bye for now.

May the Holy Virgin keep you and your family safe and secure. You are forever in my prayers and thoughts.

Your loving papa.

* * *

Durston Harewood, Attorney at Law:

Enclosed are the papers pertaining to the codicil of my will, all properly signed and witnessed.

Sam sat back in his office chair, sure that he had taken the correct action for the future of both his daughter and his vast business empire. Not that he really need worry about the items he had altered. He was in good health and should live quite a while longer. The responsibility of what he'd accumulated wouldn't fall on Victoria's shoulders just yet. But he knew it was wise policy to make sure that all matters were taken care of, and that Victoria was protected.

The extra copy of the codicil will be sent to my man in London, Jason Beaudré. This detail I will see to personally.

*As to the other matter we discussed
when you attended Tory's wedding, I have
sent for the U. S. Marshal. The various
incidents which have occurred cannot be
considered mere coincidences. Small
numbers of cattle have been rustled; several
hands have been shot at; damage has been
done to several of my line camps.*

*I do have a suspicion as to the culprit,
but it is just that, a niggling suspision.*

Sam paused, the anxious hunch poking at his
mind. Suppose he was wrong? Suppose he
wasn't? Could he take that chance? No, not with
the lives of his people. Better to err on safety's
side.

*I want an investigation begun on a man
named Talbot Squire. Hire the best; spare
no expense.*

*I thank you for your time and efforts. My
best to your wife.*

Sincerely,
Samuel Reitenauer

Sam signed his note and slipped it into the
thick envelope. One of his men would be dispatched posthaste with these documents to San
Antonio. One copy of the document remained
with him, to be kept secure here on the
Encantadora. He stood up and went to his safe.

It was one of several that he had hidden in his house; this one contained the legal papers for his empire. The others contained ready currency, bars of gold, and jewels. He, Victoria, and now Rhys knew the combinations of those safes. But only he and his daughter had access to this one.

He returned to his desk, taking another thick cream vellum sheet with the Reitenauer R stamped on top. Sam began a second letter, this time to Jason Beaudré.

Dear Jason:

Enclosed with my letter is a copy of a certain document that I want kept in a secure place. Please read it first and familiarize yourself with its contents.

Our choice of a husband for Victoria has proved to be the correct one. Granted, she and Rhys did get off to a rather rough start, but I believe that, given time, they will each accept that this marriage is for the best. It is my fervent wish that this marriage bring fulfillment to each of them.

Yet, should anything untoward happen, Victoria is to be protected at all costs.

I have just finished reading your quarterly report on the European investments. Excellent work. A triple return on the capital expended was better than predicted.

As to that other matter: I support your dismissal of Grant. He knew my requirements when I purchased the wool mill. I don't care what he was used to from the previous owners; my workers will not be treated like offal.

In addition, please call on the gunsmith's, Purdey's, and see if the shotgun I ordered has been completed. I had thought to keep the weapon for myself, but I think it will suit Rhys. Have the initials changed on the stock from mine to his. It'll make a fine Christmas gift, don't you agree?

Sam finished the letter, holding the candle so that the wax dripped on the folded paper. Satisfied that he had enough melted wax to secure the flap properly, he pressed his signet ring into it. He repeated the procedure when he placed the letter and documents into a thicker envelope, and then secured them into a locked leather pouch, to which only he and Jason held a key.

The sound of his daughter's rich laughter, followed by the deeper tones of his son-in-law, produced a satisfied grin on Sam's blunt features.

The hot afternoon sun had taken its toll on Rhys. He relaxed with a cool bath while Twinnings fixed him a small plate of sandwiches and a pot of tea. Instead of milk, he added a lemon slice, and wolfed down several of the elegant little sandwiches. He noted that there were two thick slices of cake added to the repast, courtesy, no doubt, of Kristen. He'd managed, somehow, to find favor with her, and she never missed the opportunity of giving him a special sweet when he took afternoon tea.

Naked, except for a thick white linen towel wrapped around his slim hips, Rhys subsided into the chair at his desk. He slipped open the capacious side drawer and removed the stationery. His slim index finger traced the raised R. It was then that Rhys noted how much darker his skin had become under the Texas sun. He pushed a stray lock of black hair from his forehead. He hadn't had a trim in months.

He picked up the silver pen, planning to write to his estate manager, Randolph Biggs. Even though he was now in Texas, he was well aware that he couldn't ignore the business of his own holdings.

I will need a report sent to me at this address regarding my tenant farms. Have the improvements that I ordered been carried out?

After the outstanding debts on the estate were paid, Rhys had devised a plan to ensure a secure financial future for his heirs. Making his property yield a profit would be the first step. Seeing to a better educated work force was another of his plans.

Rhys stopped for a moment to consider what

he was planning on telling Biggs next. It was a decision that he'd mulled over and made alone, without consulting his bride or her father. But he believed his ideas had merit.

> *You are to select a small herd of sheep for shipment to Texas. Two rams and perhaps fifteen ewes.*

Rhys thought that the hardy breed of Exmoor sheep that were native to Devonshire and raised on his property would make a fine addition to the meat source on the ranch. The horned sheep were prized for their mutton. And they would need, as well, an animal that was trained to deal with the sheep. His beloved border collie, Champion, would be perfect.

> *In addition we shall require several dogs to handle the sheep. I want a few of Champion's trained offspring to be included with the shipment of the sheep.*
> *Please contact the tea merchant that our family deals with. I require several pounds of our special blend to be sent to me as soon as possible.*
> *That should suffice for the present. I await your answer.*
> *Derran.*

* * *

My dear Victoria:
Your letter was greeted with much

*enjoyment. My health is good, as is that of
the little one. I can feel him move inside
me, letting me know that he is getting
stronger.*

At that moment Pilar felt a strong kick. Her
hand rubbed rhythmically against the silk wrapper she wore; her face was a glowing tribute to
the love she felt for the child and the man who
had given her his precious seed.

*This, Victoria, I wish for you: to know this
joy, this sense of peace and purpose. How
special life is for me because I carry this
baby beneath my heart.*
It seems to me, amiga, *that your
confusion over your feelings for your
esposo are natural given the circumstances
of your marriage. It would appear that he
is indeed concerned with your sensibilities.*
*Have you given thought to the idea that
you are perhaps falling in love with him?
Do not reject the notion,* amiga.

Pilar thought about it, confident that somehow this state of confusion on the part of her
friend was indicative of growth. The Victoria of
only a few months ago could not have admitted
to being baffled about anything. She had been
supremely confident in what she would or
wouldn't allow to happen. Pilar let out a soft
chuckle. This Rhys was indeed a smart man;
he'd taken her warning words to heart.

*Just suppose that you are falling in love
with your husband? Would that be so bad?
I think not. Isn't it better to try and build
something warm and stable? Something to
last? A future filled with harmony and
purpose? Have you not wondered if this
was perhaps a match divinely inspired?*

Pilar touched the golden cross she wore,
confident that God's plan was at work for her
friend.

*Open the doors to the fortress of your
heart, amiga, and let this man who is your
esposo in. Give love a chance to flourish. If
you do not, you may very well regret it for
the rest of your life.*
Your loving sister,
Pilar.

* * *

Dearest Anne:
*I hope that this letter finds you well and
happy. It was ever my wish that we
continue with our friendship, for that is
what brought us together, and that is what
remains important to me.*
*How different this Texas is from what I
first thought. When I came here I rather
expected that I would be anxious to leave
and return home; that I would be terribly
bored. Not true.*
*Things are rather more complicated here.
It would seem that my father-in-law is*

*involved not only in ranching; his interests
(and holdings) are varied, making for a
large portfolio of business concerns.*

Rhys left it at that. Having studied some of
papers that Sam had given him, he suspected
that he was being shown only a little at a time,
parcels of information to consume and digest.
Sam was obviously astute, as was Tory. A few of
the papers that he allowed Rhys to see contained
the handwritten comments of both Sam and
Victoria. Their business acumen impressed
him, especially Victoria's. She was shrewd,
thoughtful, and scrupulously fair. A woman
blessed with both brains and beauty, who
flaunted neither.

*Indeed, Texas holds many surprises. I
have sent on to you a case of wines that
are produced here. I have already sampled
some of the vintage and find it to be most
pleasing. You must let me know what you
think.*

Rhys poured himself another glass of a rich
red wine and sipped. Splendid, he thought,
wishing that he was sharing this bottle privately
with his wife.

*I know that you must be curious about
my wife. Suffice to say, Anne, I think that
you and she would get along. Victoria
possesses intelligence, humor and pride.*

> *She is not at all a proper lady as we are*
> *used to defining the word*

(he imagined that Anne would get a chuckle out of that, as Anne had always maintained that neither was she),

> *all stiff and proper, terribly formal, content*
> *to follow. She cares very much for the*
> *people who work and live on the*
> *Encantadora.*

And, Rhys thought, she wasn't afraid of getting dirty. He took another sip of wine, recalling an incident that had happened only yesterday.

He'd been ensconced in the library, content to seek shelter from the heat of the day. Several papers had arrived from London, and he was reading when he heard the sound of raised voices. His valet, Twinnings, appeared with his lips compressed tightly to stifle the laughter that threatened to erupt.

"What's wrong?"

Twinnings replied, valiantly keeping a sober face, "It's the countess, my lord."

Rhys leapt from his reclining position. "Has something happened to my wife?"

"Nothing to fear, my lord. She hasn't been injured."

"Then," Rhys demanded, his tone bordering on exasperation, "what is it?"

"It would seem that her ladyship has met with a sort of accident, more damaging to her pride than to her person." He added pleasantly, "She's got a proper vocabulary when she's angry, too."

Rhys decided that he'd better investigate for himself. Twinnings volunteered the information that the countess might be found in the kitchen.

Rhys found Victoria there, covered from head to foot in mud. She was in the act of pulling off her knee-high moccasins, swearing colorfully under her breath as Kristen watched.

"What happened to you?" Rhys was trying hard to keep a straight face. She looked like a child caught in a mud fight.

Tory threw him what he assumed was a defiant look. "I fell into a mud hole trying to free a calf that had fallen in. He was frightened, and heavy, so it was a struggle to wrestle him out of the mud. He got out and I went tumbling in."

Rhys couldn't contain his laughter any longer.

Tory stood up. Her tone was defensive. "Just who do you think you're laughing at?"

"Not at," Rhys protested, "with. You do look bloody ridiculous."

Tory smiled as she ran a glance down her body. "I guess I do look pretty awful at that," she replied and burst out laughing herself.

"*Ja*, baroness, you do," Kristen said, "and so please take off your clothes so that they can be washed now. You don't want to track all that mud upstairs."

Tory hesitated.

Kristen insisted, holding a towel, and telling

Rhys to please turn his back for a moment.

"I have a better idea."

"Which is?" Tory asked.

"Suppose I carry you upstairs. That way you won't have to undress here in the kitchen."

Tory declared, "I don't think that's a good idea."

Kristen interrupted. *"Ja,* I do." She pointed to the stairs. "You can go up the back way, there. Your bath should be ready, baroness."

"You'll get dirty," Tory protested.

"I can wash up, too," he responded.

"You won't be able to lift me."

"Come now, Victoria, you can't weigh more than nine stone. I promise you that I shan't drop you. Trust me." With that he scooped her up in his arms, making for the stairs.

Rhys walked into her bathroom, releasing her gently.

"You're covered in mud now, too," Tory pointed out.

"No matter," Rhys replied, looking at the tub and imagining her naked flesh warm and slippery against his. The steam rising from the hot water, with its softly sensual essence of roses, relected the rise in the temperature of his blood.

Rhys clenched his hands at his sides lest he willfully reach out and help her undress, quickly, by ripping the mud-splattered clothes from her body.

Back in the relative safety of his own room,

Rhys paced back and forth. Twinnings had laid out a fresh shirt, along with a carefully pressed pair of trousers and a jacket. Once he would have donned them without a second's hesitation. Instead, he went now to the wardrobe and selected something different, more in tune with his mood.

The shirt was white, made soft by frequent washings. It smelled of the sun and fresh air. He slipped it on, reaching for the pants. The denim material slid over his long legs, hugging his slim hips as he fastened the buttons.

He strode over to the mirror, looking at his reflection there. What differences were wrought by mere change of habit.

Rhys put away thoughts of yesterday and returned to his letter.

It has not always been easy here. I can see the resentment evident in some people's eyes. To them I am a very different species indeed. I must relay an incident to you that will illustrate, dear Anne, just what I mean. A week or so ago I went for a ride with my wife. As we returned I heard her greeted by some of the hands at the ranch with the Spanish word patrona, *a sign of their respect. The foreman of the ranch, Marshall Kincaid, happened to be standing at the corral when Victoria and I dismounted; she went to see Janet, Marsh's wife, and I was leading my mount, Javert (I shall tell you about his name another time), to the barn when Marsh stopped me.*

He said, "just because you're married to the patrona *doesn't make you the* patrón *in their eyes. It is a title that has to be earned."*

To these people my titles and lineage mean nothing. I am to be judged on my character alone. Refreshing, eh?

Time has come for me to draw this letter to a close. I trust that you will reply and tell me the latest on-dits; you always did manage to hear the best and most interesting scandals.

I remain your friend, as always,
Derran

* * *

My Dearest Papa:

I am sorry that it has taken me so long to reply to your letter. We have had guests at our rancho, three of Pedro's cousins from Los Angeles; and there has been no time.

Since your letter arrived, I have also heard from Victoria. She has, I think, finally decided to give her marriage a real chance. This pleases me, as I know, deep in your heart, it does you. It must, for there is simply no other alternative. Don't think that I don't understand your pain, papa; I do. You are an honorable man, and had Samuel not seen fit to arrange this union for his daughter, I would have supported your wish to have Victoria as your bride because I love you both. But, Papa, that is not to be.

Don Sebastian read that last paragraph over again before continuing.

I do think it best if you travel to New Orleans. The trip will give you a chance to visit with old friends and see family. It will do you good, of that I am certain. And, Papa, it will spare you some of the pain of seeing Victoria and her esposo. It cannot be easy for you, I realize.

You are daily in my thoughts and prayers. I am proud to be your daughter.

Don Sebastian sat quietly in his study as he finished Pilar's letter. He dropped it to the desk, steepling his hands over the bridge of his nose, his eyes closed for a moment's reflection. When he opened them he stared straight at the golden frame in front of him. Inside was a miniature of the portrait that held pride of place in the hall. The faces of his girls as captured by the artist—youthful, glowing, radiant with life. What his late wife called *joie de vivre.*

A solitary tear blurred the ink on the paper.

* * *

My dearest brother Rhys:
I'm never sure if I am allowed to use your name in my letters or if I should be addressing you as Derran. Both Mama and the new governess insist that I am too informal with your name.

I miss you terribly!

Mama is much happier now that people have begun visiting the house again. I would be just as happy if they didn't, as I have to be on my best behavior and can't ride my pony. And I do love my pony, Rhys! Thank you!

I had a cake and quite a few nice gifts for my birthday, although I wished that you could have been there to share it with me. Mlle deClare and Mama organized it, so that I had to be the hostess. I had more fun when I took the extra cake to the stables and fed my animals. The marmalade cat has six new kittens and the pups are getting bigger and stronger. Biggs told me that you asked for two to be sent to you in this place called Texas. I have picked out the best of the litter for you.

Rhys looked over the sheets of paper in his hand, watching his wife, who was curled on the chair opposite him, reading a book. Sam had long since retired, leaving Rhys in sole possession of the library, until Tory, not being able to sleep, decided to join him. It was a measure of her changing attitude toward him that she felt comfortable enough to come in her nightwear. He saw the rise and fall of her chest with every breath she took. Her long hair was braided in two thick plaits, falling over each breast. Beneath her robe she wore that same high-necked nightdress; except this night the buttons were undone, exposing some of her flesh to his eyes.

He thought it safer to go back to his sister's letter.

As I told you, Mama hired a new governess for me and I don't like her very much. She is far too strict (which Mama seems to think I need) and she has no sense of fun. Mlle deClare makes lessons a bore. Besides, Rhys, she detests animals. She told me that I wasn't a proper young lady because I sometimes get dirty whilst playing with the animals and some of the farm children. Mlle deClare thinks it isn't respectable to be so informal with those that she deems beneath me.

Can you not find someone else for me, Rhys. Please? Even Biggs doesn't like her. He called her a "martinet." I had to look that word up and when I found out the definition, I agreed.

Please do have my new sister write to me so that I can get to know her. If she is your wife I am sure that I will like her, else why would you have wed her? You must have loved her ever so much to have left our home and gone away to America.

I miss you. Won't you send for me or tell me that you plan to come home soon for a visit?

My candle is almost gutted, so I must go

*before Mlle deClare comes to check and
finds me still awake.*

I love you.
Gillie

"What's wrong, Rhys?"

Tory's voice broke into his disgruntled
thoughts, as did the touch of her hand on his
shoulder. He hadn't noticed that she'd moved
from her chair. His head snapped up. "This
letter that I received today from my sister has
me vexed."

Tory reached down for the sheets of paper in
his hand, her subtle rose perfume working
its spell on him. "May I?" she asked, her voice
soft.

He gave up the letter, waiting as she read the
contents.

"Dismiss the woman," she stated.

"Just like that?" he inquired.

"Of course," Tory said. "Obviously your sister
is quite unhappy. Hire a governess who will
expand her horizons, not try to limit them. I'd
never tolerate a woman such as Mlle deClare
around a member of my family, even if she is
your mother's choice."

A wide smile was Rhys's answer.

"What's so amusing?"

"I had already decided that I must let the
governess go. I will write to my mother and tell
her that as my sister's legal guardian, it is *my*
responsibility to select a governess. In my place

I will ask a friend to see to the task immediately."

"Who?"

"Who what?" Rhys inquired.

"Who are you planning on asking?"

"Lady Beckworth-Bridge."

A tremor of resentment ran across Tory's flesh. His damned *mistress*. She should have known. He would not trust his own mother; instead he would ask the woman whose bed he'd shared.

"I trust her judgment," he explained.

"Of course," Tory replied.

Rhys quirked a black brow in amusement at her tone.

"Are you still keeping her?" Tory demanded bluntly.

Rhys stood up, his gray eyes focused on Tory's blue ones. Did he possibly detect a note of jealousy in his bride's voice? "I never *kept* Anne."

"She was your mistress, wasn't she?"

Rhys answered truthfully. "She *was* my lover; she was and is my friend."

Tory moved to the couch, sitting down. Her gaze maintained its hold on his. "Didn't she resent your marrying?"

Rhys sighed. "Anne knew that I had responsibilities."

"How convenient for you," Tory said.

Rhys laughed. "If you imagine that Anne is pining away for me, please, let me dissuade you."

266

"You think she's found another?"

"I certainly hope so."

"You do?"

"Of course," Rhys answered, sitting alongside her on the couch and taking one of her hands in his. "I am very fond of Anne and I want her to be happy. She deserves it. Besides, she's much too vital to be alone." His voice lowered to a seductive whisper, evoking vivid images as if he were a painter. "What we shared was very special. The idea of Anne alone, no longer enjoying the sweet pleasures that two lovers can experience, is unthinkable." He lifted her hand, palm up, to his mouth, placing the lightest of kisses there, and on the pulse that beat at her wrist, before releasing her.

As he started to rise, Tory reached out and swiftly wrapped her arms around his neck, bringing her warm lips to his.

Rhys didn't hesitate to take advantage as her mouth opened and he deepened the kiss, pulling her closer, savoring the taste and feel of Tory. Within seconds he had loosened her robe and placed his large hand on the cotton covering her breast. Her nipple rose against his palm.

A shimmering spear of excitement burned deep inside her when Rhys broke the kiss to place his open mouth on the material, wetting it with his tongue, before sucking both cloth and flesh into his hungry mouth.

She gasped aloud.

He fought to control his own ragged breathing.

"Go!" he said roughly, standing, his back to her so that she wouldn't see the tangible proof of her affect on him.

Tory made her exit with all the dignity she could muster.

To himself, he muttered in a husky growl, "Not yet. But soon, I promise."

* * *

September 10, 1877

Dear Rhys:

Your letter reached me and I have seen to the matter of a new governess for your sister. The dowager countess was less than pleased, but your mother could do nothing since I held your letter of intent. The young woman came highly recommended from the Bennett household. Her name is Maeve MacGuire, and she is, as I'm sure you've guessed, an Irish lass of gentle birth.

Anne took another sip of the Texas wine Rhys had sent her. He'd been right; it was quite good. Perhaps she's start a new vogue by introducing it at her dinner party next week for the Prince of Wales.

A noise from the bed behind her made Anne turn her head. It was only Patrick, moving in his sleep. Her stable master. How lucky she'd been to find both a governess for Rhys's sister and someone to take care of her stables at the same time. Patrick MacGuire's lyrical voice and gentle hands were what both she and her horses needed. Now her stables had been returned to their former glory, and she was sure to be breeding champions again. The boy had an eye for the best, no doubt about that.

Now for a bit of personal news. There is a new man in my life. He is also Irish, brother to Gillie's governess, and as our country estates are quite close, they are able to see each other. Patrick is his name. He's witty, irreverent, and makes me feel like a girl again. In some ways, Rhys, he reminds me of you. He's filled the lonely places with laughter. And, as I can be honest with you, dear friend, he is a superb lover.

Much as you were, Rhys, Anne thought. She'd read his letters to her over again, realizing just what Rhys was saying beneath the lines of prose. He was a changed man. Though he might not admit it to himself, he was in love with his wife. This Victoria Reitenauer must be a remarkable woman to have captured Rhys's heart. He thought so and Rhys was nobody's fool. And it wasn't only his wife who was having an unforeseen influence on her former lover—it was Texas, also.

Before I end this epistle, I thought I would relate one interesting story: It seems that at a recent tea, a guest was overheard to remark that Lady Pennington's third child, another daughter, looked

*remarkably like her cousin's husband, Lord
Topston. Rather bad form to have voiced
what was so obvious to all, don't you
think?*

*I wish you well, dearest. Please keep in
touch.*

As ever,
your Anne

"Annie, me love, are ya coming ta bed?" spoke
the lilting voice of her lover. "It's lonely without
ya, lass." Patrick patted the empty spot beside
him. "Come on now, I'm waiting for ya."

Anne, a glowing smile on her face, said softly,
"The wait is over."

Chapter Thirteen

"So what are you waiting for?"

"I don't know what you mean."

Janet arched her brows, throwing Tory a skeptical glance. "Yes, you do," she answered as she continued polishing the silver.

Tory's blue eyes dropped to her plate, where she stabbed her fork into a thick slice of smoked ham.

"Honey, you've been right lucky that he hasn't let his eye go a-wandering. Nobody's gonna blame him for looking elsewhere if his wife ain't providing what he needs—not even your papa." Janet put down her cloth, pulled out one of the chairs, and sat down facing Tory. "I'm speaking plain to you, Miss Tory; he ain't going to wait forever."

"Janet, this is none of your business," Tory stated.

"Maybe it's not, but I can't stand seeing you like this."

"Has Rh . . . my husband said something to you?"

Janet was actually surprised by the question. "My Lord, no," she said, reaching out her hand to Tory's. "Your man wouldn't say anything; that's not his way. He's like you in that respect."

"Perhaps he just expects, as I do, to have his privacy."

Janet laughed. "Honey, you know that's just about impossible on this here ranch. People got eyes and ears, and they talk."

Tory's body stiffened. "What are they saying?"

"Well, no one's outright gossiping about you. People have noticed, however, that you and your husband are still, in a sense, strangers to one another. The fact that you aren't increasing yet has cast some doubts on your husband's virility."

Tory's color heightened with that remark. "You heard that?"

"Marsh told me that he heard a couple of the men talking."

"How dare they?"

"It isn't a question of daring, Miss Tory. They care about you, and about the future. Naturally they take an interest in seeing that your papa's line continues. I reckon if any one of them thought that the earl wasn't doing right by you, he would meet with an unfortunate accident."

"No," Tory protested, realizing that what Janet said was true. She *did* possess the loyalty of the people who worked and lived on the ranch.

Janet was reluctant to repeat other conversations, speculations that Rhys wasn't quite man enough for Tory, or that Tory perhaps wasn't woman enough for him. Janet knew both suppositions were wrong: this was a well-matched pair if ever they could put aside their stubborn pride.

Tory recalled that conversation later that day when Rhys accepted her invitation to check some counts on the herd. As they galloped across the rolling hills Tory slanted a glance in his direction. No one looking at him now would ever guess that he hand't always ridden mounted on a western saddle. He wore gleaming black knee boots, polished till they shone. His buff-colored buckskins hugged his thighs like a well-made pair of gloves, smooth and snug. His hair, under the new hat he'd gotten in San Antonio, was longer now, falling past the collar of his white shirt. The sun had darkened his skin so that his eyes stood out even more in his sculpted face like silver ingots in a burnished golden frame.

He was still the same distinctly proud English aristocrat that she'd been forced to wed; yet, there was more, so much more to him.

"I'm glad you chose to accompany me," she said, her voice low and soft.

"The pleasure, dear wife, is all mine," he answered smoothly, his own voice soft as silk sliding over bare flesh. He pulled on the reins to halt Javert. In the lush grass of the valley below, hands were herding the cattle. One man sat on a horse with a long rope held in his hands, his fingers working deftly. "What is he doing?" Rhys asked, pointing to the cowboy.

Tory, who was watching someone else, turned back to Rhys. "Him? He's taking a count of the herd."

"Rather a time-consuming bit of work, I would imagine." He paused, narrowing his eyes to focus better. "Where is his tally book?"

Tory grinned. "He's holding it in his hands."

Rhys looked again. "The rope?"

"Correct," Tory replied. "It's called a tally string. He ties a knot in it for every hundred head counted. It's amazingly accurate. For our purposes we need a general idea of how many cattle we have, so that we can determine what portion we sell directly to the forts we supply, how many head are to be shipped north, and how many we'll have to feed come winter."

"It's also the only way to determine if someone is stealing from you."

"Right you are." Tory mentally reviewed the losses the ranch had suffered in the past few months. There was no real pattern to the thefts; they were not confined to one specific geographic location, nor were they always large losses. Just a few head disappeared here and there or they were slaughtered uselessly, as had happened on several occasions. Her father was still waiting for the report from the detective their lawyer had hired.

Tory scrutinized the men working below, watching and remembering other times when she had been with the hands, helping with the fall roundup, pitching her bedroll under the stars, sharing their camraderie. Now so much of her work was confined to the ranch office, reading papers, sorting through contracts, discussing new ventures. The direction her life was taking wouldn't allow her to be that free and easy again. She patted Abendstern's neck, soothing the restive mare with the motion of her hand. She was a wild child no longer; and for far too long, she had put off what must be faced, choosing to ignore another responsibility that she had knowingly assumed. It was past time to become a wife in deed as well as in name.

Rhys observed Tory closely. He could see that his wife was deep in thought, so involved with whatever occupied her mind that she was temporarily unaware of anything, or anyone, else. On the journey here, they'd stopped to water the horses at a secluded stream. A perfect spot for a tryst, especially if it was with one's own wife. He wanted to make love to her in the open, with only nature surrounding them and hearing her cries, with sun and grass as their bed and blanket.

Amusement curved his mouth. He used to be so fastidious, preferring his experiments in love to be cushioned with the proper degree of comfort. Now, comfort be damned! He desired her with a craving so hot he cared little whether the time or spot was propitious. In his imagination he'd made sweet, aching love to her wherever and whenever he chose. And loveliest of all, she came to him with a need as great as his own, demanding, pursuing, an eager and talented pupil.

Suddenly, Tory seemed to break free of her thoughts. "I hear that you are learning to handle a pistol?" she asked. She found the notion of Rhys with a Colt strapped to his thigh slightly incongruous.

He nodded his head once, acknowledging the fact.

"Why?"

"I thought it about time," was his reply.

"You did?"

"You're shocked?"

"No," she answered slowly, "I think I would use the word stunned."

"It seems to be the weapon of choice here and I believe it will be useful for me to know how to use it efficiently."

"Marsh is a good teacher."

Rhys agreed. "He's very proficient."

Tory slanted him a glance. "He had to be. Marsh was once a sheriff. He gave it up after he got married to Janet. He was ready to settle down and the Encantadora needed a top hand to help run things.

"So, are you comfortable with it yet?"

"I'm beginning to be," Rhys confessed.

She gave him a piece of advice. "Don't worry about being fast, just accurate."

Rhys smiled, revealing his white teeth. "Marsh gave me the same instruction."

"That's because it's true. No use being fast if you don't hit your target. Fancy shooting's for exhibitions and dime novels."

A cacophony of strange sounds greeted them as they rode back into the ranch compound.

It didn't take Tory long to identify the bleat of sheep. "What in blazes are sheep doing here?" she asked as she reined in her mare and leapt from her saddle.

"Surprise," Rhys said, joining her on the ground and tossing the reins of his paint to a stablehand.

Tory rounded on him. "What do you mean, surprise?" she asked, her tone vexed.

"Exactly that. A surprise, which I hope you will like." He took her gloved hand in his, pulling her along behind him to the pasture behind the barn. There, in one of the paddocks, surrounded by curious cowhands, was a flock of very big sheep. Keeping an eye on the woolly creatures were two small black-and-white dogs, who circled and barked, maintaining order.

The hands gave Tory's husband sharp looks, having a cowman's disdain for anything besides cattle.

A wiry, bowlegged man, who Tory judged to be in his late fifties, called out orders to the two young dogs, who immediately left their charges and ran to the fence, sitting perfectly still.

The older man gave a tug on his cap when Rhys approached. "Good ta see ya again, me lord," he said.

"And you also, Avon." Rhys bent down and fondled the head of each dog. "They're Champion's get all right."

"And doing a fine job they are, me lord," Avon added.

"What are they called?" Tory asked, joining Rhys. The pups sniffed and licked her hand as soon as she pulled off the buckskin gloves.

"This is my wife, Avon," Rhys said by way of introduction.

Tory put out her hand and the older man just looked at it. She blinked and waited, as he realized that she wanted to shake hands with him.

Avon wiped his hand across the rough material of his workpants and skittered a glance in Rhys's direction, not sure if his lordship would permit this. The slight nod of Rhys's head was all he needed. He reached out and took Tory's hand. "Nice ta meet you, your ladyship," he said, nodding his head in her direction. He faced Rhys. "As for the names of the pups, me lord, your sister, the Lady Gillian, said that was best left ta your lordship as they were ta be yours."

Rhys, leaning over and picking up one of the dogs, scooped it into his hands. "What say you, Victoria? What will you name our border collies?"

Tory saw that all eyes were on her. "Rochester

and Darcy," she replied quickly.

Rhys laughed at her literary bent. "Rochester and Darcy it is then," he agreed, placing the squirming pup in her arms.

Sam stood a bit away from the paddock, watching, observing the closeness the pair seemed to be sharing. At first, he couldn't believe his ears when one of his hands told him a man was here to deliver sheep ordered by the earl. He put aside the letter that he'd just received from Don Sebastian to personally investigate.

Sheep. Here on the Encantadora.

Tory was thinking the exact same thing. She looked at the animals, wondering how they would fit in with the cattle. They wouldn't, she decided. It didn't enter her mind to return the sheep to England. They would have to make an adjustment, keeping them away from the cattle herds. It was a good thing that Rhys had someone to take charge of the sheep. She knew of no self-respecting cowhand who would.

Putting the pup back into the paddock, she stood up, noting the expectant looks on the faces of the hands. She also saw her father.

"Well, Papa, it looks as though we shall be varying our diet."

His face crinkled as he smiled. "It would appear so, *Liebchen*."

Marsh, casting a cool eye on the new occupants of the enclosure, said, "You plan on keeping them here?"

"Not quite here," Tory explained, darting a

Gail Link

quick glance at Rhys, who was listening, as were all the others, even Samuel. "I think on a ranch this size we can find a place for them. For the present, until they can be moved, they will remain here." She looked at Sam. "Papa?"

"As you say, daughter," pleased at her decision.

The hands then dispersed, mumbling under their breath.

Rhys was also pleased by her decision. He hadn't been sure just how Victoria would react. He had been prepared for a tirade. Her amiability was a surprise.

"Don Sebastian has returned," Sam said.

Rhys snapped to attention, focusing his gaze on his wife. He knew Tory had been hurt when she'd found that Don Sebastian had quit his ranch without saying a word.

"Did he say why he left so abruptly?" Tory inquired.

"No," Sam answered. "A rider from his rancho arrived with a note from him. I haven't had a chance to read it yet."

"It isn't like *Tío* to do something so rash."

"Maybe he just wanted to indulge in a bit of traveling," Rhys suggested. He could well imagine why the man had left. Faced with the same situation, Rhys was sure that he, too, would have taken the opportunity to put some distance between himself and the object of his unspoken affections.

"I want to see his letter," Tory demanded.

"Come with me," Sam said, walking back towards the house.

"I will," Tory answered, leaving her husband to watch her back as she kept pace with Sam, sharing a private joke with him, her arm linked companionably through her father's.

Tory sat on the oak settle in her father's office, reading the letter from Don Sebastian. She read it slowly and carefully. It said that he was inviting them to a special dinner party at his rancho to formally introduce his wife to them. Tory still couldn't grasp the fact that Don Sebastian was now married.

Tory exchanged glances with her father. "Very sudden, wasn't it?"

Sam agreed. "He is a man too long alone, Tory, and he was too long wed."

"But you never remarried, Papa."

"I never found anyone to replace your mother, *Liebchen.*"

Tory stood up, handing the letter back to her father. "I wonder what Pilar thinks of this?"

"The same thing that you would say, *mein Engel.* If the woman makes him happy, then I share that happiness. Am I right?"

Tory hugged Sam. "Of course," she insisted.

"And you, Victoria—has your marriage made you happy?" Sam asked, concern furrowing his brows.

She answered honestly. "At first, no, Papa. But now," she said, a softer glow in her blue eyes and a smile on her lips, "I think that it will."

Sam gave no apology for his choice; Tory expected none.

"A wedding gift," she announced. "What shall we get them?"

Sam shrugged his thick shoulders. "I have no idea. That I will leave to you."

"Perhaps I'd better wait till after we've had the pleasure of meeting her. Then I may be able to judge her taste."

"I think that a wise idea."

"Maybe Rhys will have a notion of what would be appropriate." Tory sat in Sam's big chair and reached for the pen, quickly writing a note in Spanish to Don Sebastian. "Is Don Sebastian's messenger still here?"

"He should be. I told him to wait should we need to send a reply."

"Good." She addressed the envelope and heated the sealing wax.

Moments later, Tory had located the *vaquero* and given him the letter for his master.

From his seat in the garden Rhys observed her talking to the cowboy. He was sipping a glass of wine, celebrating the success of his surprise and contemplating the end of his self-imposed fast.

Rhys caught Tory's eye and she joined him.

"Shall I procure another glass?"

"That won't be necessary," she said as she reached over and took the crystal from his fingers, draining the contents. "Mmm," she said in a tone which resembled a purr.

"What news from Don Sebastian?" Rhys

asked as he took back the glass, their hands lingering as if reluctant to break the contact.

"*Tío* Sebastian is married."

Rhys hid the fact that he really wasn't surprised from Tory. "Really? To whom?" he put the question casually.

"To a woman he met in New Orleans while visiting relatives."

He refilled his glass. Rhys believed he knew why Don Sebastian had married so hastily. It was, he surmised, to put more distance between himself and Victoria, to find forgetfulness in another woman's arms. Hot blood demanded a release, and this society would not tolerate the convenient mistress.

Rhys lifted his glass. "To Don Sebastian and his bride." He drank half the glass before relinquishing it to Tory, who tossed back the remainder.

Don Sebastian struck a match and lit the cigar, inhaling deeply. He was alone, in his bedroom, having left his wife in the room she had earlier selected for her own. His lean body was covered by a film of sweat and a plush robe. He stood on the balcony, watching the night sky.

He'd found physical release in Michelle's arms; but there'd been no release for his heart. Even as he made love to his wife, slipped into her willing body, he could think only of someone else. This was his private penance, for he would not bring shame on Victoria's name by confessing to his own sin.

Gail Link

But was he truly contrite?

Don Sebastian was completely honest with himself. No, he was not contrite, for if he admitted that, then he would be denying what he felt in his heart of hearts. He would see that Michelle never knew; he owed her that.

Michelle was everything Victoria was not; she was dark, short, quiet, and deferential. She accepted his presence in her bed as her duty. Try as he might to ignite her desire, there was no spark of passion beneath her calm surface. When he'd entered her room tonight, he'd found her on her knees in prayer. She was too modest to remove the nightgown she wore, preferring to keep it on as she went to the bed, blowing out the candles so that the room was plunged into darkness.

Michelle would undoubtedly make an excellent mistress for the Rancho Montenegro and would provide for his comfort as she had been brought up to do.

It wasn't her fault that she wasn't Victoria, could never be Victoria.

"Time to stop playing cat and mouse," Talbot Squire said aloud as he casually pushed the blowsy prostitute who was sharing his bed onto the floor.

The action woke her up. "What the hell did you do that for?" she demanded, rubbing her sore hip.

Talbot reached over and yanked her by her dirty hair. "Because I wanted to, bitch."

The whore realized her mistake and scrambled back to the bed. It didn't pay to make this customer angry. She'd been witness to his treatment of other girls. "Hey look, honey, I'm sorry. Let me make it up to you." She wiggled her ample bottom at him. "We'll do it the way you like best. How 'bout it?"

"I've got a better idea." He jumped out of the bed, grabbing the woman by the arm and jerking her along the corridor. "We're gonna have a private party."

The prostitute rolled her eyes, wondering if she would get extra for servicing his friends.

"Wait here," he said roughly, shoving her against the wall as he entered a bedroom. He returned a minute later, dragging a woman along with him. She was thin, pale, and mute, her eyes staring straight ahead. "Come on," Talbot ordered.

The whore followed him and the woman he dragged along to the attic. It was warm, and the smell of unwashed flesh hung heavy in the air, along with the stale smell of food. A candle was lit and the prostitute gasped. Chained to a bedpost was a thin, black-haired youth, who'd obviously been beaten and starved. She saw food scraps lying on the floor. The boy's face bore the marks of abuse.

An evil grin slashed Talbot's face. "This here's my wife's boy. A virgin. Would you believe that?" He laughed and it was a sour sound. "Time he was learnin' what goes on." He grabbed the woman and shoved her in the boy's direction.

"Do him," he said. "Do him right in front of his ma and me."

She shot the boy a quick look. There was hate in those dark eyes. Then she glanced at the man. There was something unhinged about him. She approached the youth, who automatically pulled away from her.

Talbot Squire's curt voice cut through the silence. "Get on that bed, you bastard, or your ma will pay. Understood?"

Rafe stared at his mother, then at the naked woman. He swallowed, even though his throat ached and his stomach threatened to empty what little it contained. He slowly lay down on the bed.

"Good boy," Talbot said.

Rafe shut his eyes as the creature manipulated and then mounted him, tearing another rent in his wounded soul.

Talbot grinned evilly. His plans were coming along. He was now ready, and eager, to move to the next step. Once more he'd proved who was boss in this house.

Now it was time to show the Reitenauers.

Chapter Fourteen

"It is a well-constructed piece of furniture," Tory declared, commenting on a wedding gift that had just arrived from England. She walked around the item, looking at it from all angles. Rhys had had it put in the library after it had been uncrated. "And," she admitted, "quite beautiful."

"It's a Regency chess and backgammon table," he explained, removing the top so that she could see the backgammon board underneath. It was made of ebony, satinwood, and fruitwood, with folding sides.

"Lady Beckworth-Bridge has elegant taste." Try as she might, Tory could find no logical fault with the gift. It was, indeed, beautiful.

"Do you play backgammon?" Rhys asked.

"No," she replied.

"Then I'll have to teach you," he said, his voice soft and low, as he moved to her side, standing behind her with his hands on either side of the table so that he trapped her within the circle of his body.

Tory could feel the heat that came from his tall, lean frame, could smell the masculine fragrance of his cologne. "I'd like that," she responded, her voice taking on a huskier tone.

"So would I."

"Excuse me, baroness," Kristen said, standing in the doorway.

Rhys turned, his arm around Tory's waist, bringing her with him.

Kristen's broad face was wreathed in a smile. "I wanted to let you know that the supper you requested is ready."

Smiling, Tory said, *"Danke,* Kristen." She tilted her face toward her husband. "I thought that since it was just you and me tonight, simple fare would suffice?"

"Whatever you want, Victoria. I'm more than willing to oblige," Rhys said.

Why did she think that offer extended to more than a mere meal? Could it be because she felt the strength in the way his hand rested at her waist; or was it because she saw the way his gray eyes warmed?

"Shall we?" Rhys asked. Relinquishing his hold on her waist and stepping in front of her, he held out his hand.

Tory responded with a "yes," as she placed her hand in his.

The table had been set with care. Though the meal was to be simple, Kristen had decided to add a few elegant touches. A large silver bowl of fresh flowers, including several varieties of roses, was placed so that the fragrance from the blossoms added to the quiet atmosphere. Tory recognized the dishes and the cutlery from a set given to her parents by her godfather, Sam Houston. Napkins of Irish linen, hand-sewn with the letter R, rested on the table in rings of gleaming silver.

Kristen entered, carrying a large oak tray that held small dishes of vegetables to complement their main meal, which was a thick-crusted game pie of beef, pork, venison, and wild turkey. As Rhys and Tory seated themselves, she bustled in with a warm peach pie, which she placed on the sideboard.

"Is there anything else that you require, baroness?"

Tory smiled, taking in all that Kristen had placed before them. "I can't see that you've forgotten anything," she said. Casting her glance at Rhys, who sat opposite her, she asked, "Would you like some wine with dinner?"

He thought for a moment before giving an answer. His control was dangerously close to the limit, and tonight he wanted to maintain a clear, sober direction. No excuses; no artificial stimulants. And, he decided, he wanted Victoria aware and responsive. This hunger that grew must be fed on clarity, else a dark shadow of denial could be cast later.

"No, I believe that I shall dispense with wine tonight. A jug of spring water will do nicely."

Kristen nodded her head in Rhys's direction. "As you wish, *Herr Graf*."

Tory cut several thick slices of the fresh-baked bread as she listened to Rhys and Kristen. She would need no wine tonight, either, to cloud her judgment. This evening everything was to be simple, direct, honest. Removing a slice of the warm bread, she passed the wooden board to her husband. His hand touched hers, ever so slightly, as he took the tray. Tory felt the heat of his fingertips as they came in contact with hers. This tingling response was all so new to her, so unfamiliar.

Kristen entered the room again, carrying a large silver tray, on which rested the silver coffee service of Tory's mother's family. It was an heirloom, passed down from mother to daughter. That tradition was brought home to Tory anew as she watched Kristen place it with great care on the sideboard. She'd never given any thought to having a daughter of her own with whom she could share this bit of history. Now, perhaps that was a possibility. But to deliver this child of her flesh, she would have to take into herself the body of her husband. The ultimate trust. The ultimate sharing.

Would she do it?

Could she do it?

"Gute Nacht!" Kristen said softly as she placed a jug of cold water on the table and left the room, leaving the couple alone, a grin on her

face and a twinkle in her eyes.

"Will business keep your father in San Antonio for long?" Rhys asked as he began to eat.

"I'm not sure," Tory responded, feeling the need for a glass of cool water. With a steady hand, she poured a large splash of the contents of the earthenware jug into one of the crystal goblets. "I wish, though, that we'd gone with him."

"Yes," Rhys agreed, "I didn't see much of the town when I was there, except for the hotel."

"Now that Papa has bought a house," she said, referring to the wedding gift that he'd given the couple, the deed to a house in San Antonio, "I would like the opportunity to visit with friends and perhaps return some of the gracious hospitality that is always afforded me when I go there."

"I should like to see what it has to offer."

"Nothing as grand as London, but we manage," Tory responded.

Rhys leveled a look at her. "It wasn't meant disparagingly, I assure you."

She shrugged her shoulders. "Perhaps I'm being overly sensitive."

"I think, in this instance," he pointed out, "that you are." Again, he mused, the thorns of her pride formed a barrier around his Texas rose. No matter, he decided, he would simply pluck them aside. Any wounds would be minor and insignificant compared to what he would reap: a harvest of budding beauty unfolding for him in the sweet surrender of the night. "Besides, your father has told me that you've made the Grand Tour of Europe and are quite familiar with several of the larger cities in this country as well."

"That's true," she admitted, "though I have a special fondness for San Antonio." She took a sip of the water, her throat suddenly very dry. "It is so much a part of Texas to me."

Rhys put down his fork, asking, "Could you live anywhere else?"

"Truthfully?" she asked, resting her chin on her hands. "I don't think so. My heart is here," Tory said softly, raising her eyes to his, "as I imagine yours is in England."

Rhys was silent for several minutes. He wondered if that were indeed true. Was his heart still in England? The fact that he even posed the question stunned him.

Tory took his reticence for agreement. "Everyone and everything I love, or have loved," she explained, "is here." She almost blurted out, *Why do you think that I married you, if not to keep what is mine?* "My family has bled and died for Texas. While the War Between the States raged, my father sent me into exile with relatives, in Philadelphia. They were kind and caring. But it wasn't Texas, it wasn't Encantadora."

Rhys heard and understood the fierce love in her voice. He'd wed to protect what was his. So, he was sure, had she. Another forged link between them.

"I have been wanting to ask you why, if you

are German, does your ranch carry a Spanish name?"

Tory's mouth curved in a small smile. "Actually, it was named by Don Sebastian at my christening, in honor of me, or so I was told. And since my uncle had then recently married a girl from a *Californio* family who'd come to live at the ranch, Papa thought it a good idea, a blend of both worlds."

"Do your uncle and his wife now live in California?"

Tory's eyes grew misty with memories. "No. They are both dead."

Rhys uttered the required polite phrase of "I'm sorry."

Tory recognized the words for the socially correct response that it was. "I think had you really known them both, you would have regretted that they were taken from us too soon."

"How so?"

"When war broke out, Uncle Karl sent Doña Maria back to the safety of her father's house, promising that he would return for her as soon as possible. I was just a child, but I can still remember him. He was father's younger half-brother, a handsome devil who could charm anyone. My brother Travis was rather more like him than Papa. A group of German neutralists, in 1862, wanted to flee to Mexico during the war. They needed escorts to guide them, and Karl volunteered. Unfortunately, they were pur-

sued by a group of Confederate soldiers who
found them camped on the Nueces. While they
were sleeping, the Confederates attacked. Those
who survived being trampled or shot, who willingly surrendered, were still put to death."

"Your uncle was one of them?"

"Yes. It was after that that Papa made his
decision to send me away."

"What happened to Doña Maria?"

"We had word from her father that after she
received the news, she lost the child she was
carrying. Grief became to heavy a burden for
her, I suspect, as her father said there had been
an accident at the convent to which he had sent
her to recuperate. It seems as though she went
walking in a storm and fell from a cliff."

Rhys heard the words she wouldn't speak. His
wife believed her aunt by marriage had taken
her own life, despite the tenets of her religion.
He studied the woman opposite him. She too
had experienced pain in her life, and she'd come
through, he judged, stronger, with a steely determination. No easy leap off a cliff for her. No,
Tory would fight on, live on, as best she knew
how. Another link snapped in place.

He wanted to ask about her brother, but
decided that now was not the time to pursue it.
Instead, they both allowed the conversation to
drift to safer topics as they finished their meal.

"A slice of pie?" Tory asked, holding the silver
cutter in her hand, standing at the sideboard.

"Yes, I do believe I shall," Rhys said, watching
as she deftly cut the thick crust and placed a

slice on the china plate. He tried to imagine his mother performing this gesture, or for that matter, any other woman he knew. A footman would have been discreetly tucked in the corner, obsequious and silent. He would have seen to their needs without fuss.

"Coffee?"

Rhys nodded, observing Tory as she turned her back to him to pour. Her trousers clung tightly to the curve of her slender hips and bottom. His hands clenched as his loins tightened in response. Tonight her strawberry-blonde hair was done in a single thick braid, swishing back and forth with her movements. She was wearing a shirt which matched the color of her denims. Even in masculine attire, there was nothing remotely male about her.

"May I ask a favor of you?" she inquired, savoring the sweet taste of the peaches, soaked in brandy and touched with a hint of spice.

"Yes," Rhys answered without hesitation.

"A dangerous response before you've heard what I want."

He smiled, one corner of his mouth kicking up. "I think not." His gray eyes fixed on hers. "I trust you."

Trust. How odd he should use that word, she thought.

"What is it that you want?" he asked softly.

"Would you play for me?"

"Of course," he answered, "providing that you do something for me." This time his smile was broad. Rhys felt flattered that Victoria

295

wanted to listen to his music, especially tonight, when they were alone. Kristen had been dismissed for the evening, as had Twinnings. Sam had left for San Antonio on business the day before.

Tory wondered about Rhys's request. "What?"

The request caught her by surprise. "Let me unbraid your hair."

"That's it?" she queried, somewhat perplexed.

"Yes," was his deep-voiced reply. He waited, eyes focused on hers, for her response.

She dropped her lids, shielding her eyes, and brought her coffee cup to her lips, finishing the contents. Slowly, Tory pushed back her chair and stood, moving around the table till she came to where Rhys sat. She turned her back to her husband, her hands loose at her sides.

Rhys twisted his chair around slightly so that he could untie the piece of leather that held the braid in place. That done, he tossed it to the table. His large hands then went to work. He unraveled the skein of reddish gold carefully, his slender fingers working strands free until they lay like a shiny cloak across her back and shoulders. He reached out and brought a section of it to his lips.

Tory relaxed under Rhys's smooth ministrations.

Rhys rose, walking around her, extinguishing all the candles in the room, leaving only the lamp, which he picked up in his right hand. He faced her, struck anew by her soft beauty. Her strong features went beyond what he termed the "vapidly pretty." Victoria radiated confidence and, he suspected, a deep, untapped sensual nature.

"Come with me," he urged, holding out his hand, as he slid back the doors to the dining room. He moved towards the staircase, taking the light with him, waiting.

In the shadows, Tory heard her name called softly, "Victoria." Galvanized by the sound, she followed her instincts, joining her husband.

Hand in hand, they climbed the stairs.

The music room was in darkness as they entered.

Rhys gave the lamp to Tory while he struck a match to the silver branch of candles atop the piano. He then lit several of the wall sconces, choosing to keep the room in soft, low light.

Tory placed the lamp on the small table next to the comfortable leather wing chair. She sank into its cushioned depth, relaxing.

Then the music began. Tory was captivated by the various pieces he played with such skill and, she admitted, with a splendid passion. Rhys's fingers brought forth such beauty and power from her mother's instrument that Tory felt moved to tears. Schumann, Liszt, Mozart, and Beethoven—all poignantly felt and delivered so that Tory found herself being taken somewhere she'd never been before.

He knew when she left the chair. He could sense her soft steps behind him as he worked the keys. She shared this with him as no one before had or, he sensed, ever would again.

When at last he paused, momentarily drained, she responded with a simple gesture.

Tory captured his left hand in both of hers, soothing it with butterfly strokes of her fingers, before bringing it to her lips. She turned it over, placing a kiss in his broad palm. "You've touched me in a way I never knew existed," she confessed with an honesty born of the moment. It was true, and with that realization she made another: *she loved him.*

Rhys saw in the glow of the candles the sheen of tears in her pale blue eyes. And in their depths a woman's heart was revealed. Rhys knew he wanted Victoria. Everything she had to give. Now.

Tory saw the rampant hunger in Rhys's gray eyes. Both her body and mind demanded that she surrender. The time was right; the time was now.

"Rhys," she whispered, her voice a plea.

"Yes," he said, his tone resembling a growl. He stood up, pushing aside the stool, and gathered Tory into his arms, his mouth seeking hers. The union of their lips was hot and deep, each savoring the unique taste and flavor of the other. This was passion, bright and clean, like the most intense flame, which seared below the levels of ordinary pursuit to the very nerves of sensation.

"I want you, as my *wife,*" he said, lifting his head, tunneling his hands through her hair.

Tory spoke from her heart. "I want that too."

Needing no further words, Rhys bent and lifted Tory into his arms, striding down the dark hallway towards his own suite of rooms.

Once inside the secure haven, he shut the door with his booted foot. He bent, slowly, and released his wife. He lit the lamp beside his bed, leaving the rest of the room in shadow. Tomorrow there would be time to love her in full light; now he respected what he knew would be virginal fears. Slow and easy, he cautioned himself.

"What should I do?" Tory asked.

"Relax," Rhys assured her.

She stood, her hands anxiously moving up and down on her denim-covered thighs. There was no turning back, she knew. Nor did she want to. She would see this thing through, hoping that he wouldn't find her lack of experience a hindrance. He was a man of sophisticated tastes; a man who'd bedded women before. *Damn it*, she thought. How can he be so calm when I'm on fire inside?

Victoria looked like an angel in the muted light, Rhys thought, her hair a halo about her. She must never know how much it was costing him to keep his desire under control.

"Come here."

Tory responded to the soft command of his voice.

"Sit down," he said, indicating the bed.

Tory did so, and Rhys knelt in front of her. He began to unlace one knee-high buckskin boot, pulling it away from her skin, soothing the

299

denim-clad calf with his hands as he drew the boot from her foot. He tossed it into the corner, peeling away the plain cotton sock and holding her foot in the palm of his hand, lightly feathering it with his fingertips as he released it. He did the same to her other leg, smiling as he heard her indrawn breath. He stood up, abruptly consigning his own handmade leather boots to the same fate, along with his silk hose.

His informal smoking jacket of charcoal gray velvet was dropped to the floor, as was the white silk shirt he wore underneath.

Tory's eyes took in the expanse of skin exposed. She saw the rise and fall of his chest with each breath he took. Her pulses quickened yet again as he reached out a hand to her, pulling her from the bed. She stood stock-still as he unhooked the silver belt that held her knife.

"You won't be needing this tonight," he said, his voice soothing away her trepidation. "Now, let's get rid of this shirt," he declared, as he skillfully undid the buttons, slowly, one by one, till the shirt hung open. He reached for her wrists, undoing the buttons of pearl found there. "Remove it."

Tory pulled the material away from her body eagerly, discarding it quickly.

Rhys stepped back, his gaze running the length of her body. "Now . . . the trousers."

Tory unbuttoned the denim pants and pushed them from her hips, letting them slide down her long legs before she stepped out of them completely. The only thing she wore now was a pair of pantalets and a camisole.

"Permit me," he insisted as he took a step forward and reached out his hand, pushing aside the thick fall of her hair so that it was behind her. A small bow held the top of the camisole secure. He unlaced it, then dispensed with the buttons, all the while his eyes on the flesh he was revealing. The camisole joined the collection of garments on the floor as Rhys once more gathered Tory into his embrace, fusing his mouth to hers. He felt the push of her nipples against his chest. While exchanging pleasure-filled kisses, he permitted his hand to roam from the silken curve of her back beneath its curtain of reddish gold to the soft lushness of her breast. He cupped its weight and felt a stab of desire rush quickly through him.

Between the power of his skillful mouth and the warmth of his strong hands, Tory felt twisted and knotted with a strange yearning. Her legs buckled when his hand left her breast and skimmed along her stomach, eventually finding and caressing that spot at the apex of her thighs. Heat exploded in her body, sending a rush of sensation pooling there. His fingers rubbed and skimmed, back and forth, back and forth, causing her to gasp aloud with a strange sense of joy and wonderment. "Give in," she heard him whisper darkly in her ear as she swayed in his arms. "Trust me," he said, his voice a low, rough whisper as she moaned his name when he failed to undo the ribbons that held her pantalets and was forced to rip the material from her body.

God, she thought wildly, she did trust him—with her body and with her heart. More than she could have believed possible.

Rhys swung her up into his arms and laid her gently on the wide bed. He stood back and looked into her eyes. He saw there no artifice or pretense, only exactly what she was feeling—this same inescapable bond of communion that gripped him. His hands went to his trousers, removing them in haste.

At last he was as naked as she. He watched her eyes grow wide as she looked on him.

Tory lay on the soft comfort of the mattress, her gaze focused on the body her husband had revealed. He was so very male. And, like one of her prize stallions, he was eager to mate. That much she could recognize.

A frisson of anxiety raised a doubt in her mind. Would he be kind?

Rhys joined her in the huge bed, pulling her into the safety of his arms, holding her close. He could feel the stiffness of her limbs subside as he turned her face to him. He kissed her deeply, giving as much as she, and demanding more.

Tory wondered if one could be drunk on kisses. Each melding of their lips was more intoxicating than the last. Her fears subsided as she went with the tide that was sweeping her away. *Rhys*. All she could feel, all she could smell or touch, was Rhys. His skin was warm and smooth under her fingers; his hair was thick and soft as down. Their limbs entwined as once again his hand slipped between their bodies, testing, probing, bringing forth another excited, eager gasp.

"Now," he said, his voice hoarse.

"Yes," she cried, reaching for his broad shoulders as his slim hips eased between her legs.

Rhys could feel the tightness of her body as he probed. He was surprised only because she was a girl raised in the saddle, and he would have expected this barrier to have been breached accidentally before now. Better to get it over quickly.

"Victoria," he began, fighting for control.

"I know," she said, interrupting him, her breathing coming faster and faster. "I'm prepared for the pain." Pain she could deal with; it was this suspension betwixt pleasure and uncertainty that she wanted ended. "Please," she said.

With her words echoing in his ear, Rhys pushed forward, past the proof of her virginity, and held still, allowing her body to adjust. Her cry was muffled by his mouth, swallowed by the depth of his kiss. He withdrew slightly before beginning the rhythm of his thrusts.

She was on a journey of discovery, flying high over the clouds. The small pain that held her earthbound had vanished, shed like an unnecessary garment. Soaring, with her husband in her arms, until a final powerful thrust of his body sent her reeling into a world of sensation so intense that she lost control.

Rhys had brought other women to climax; as a lover he was used to hearing their cries and feeling their joys. But never had he seen the fresh face of a woman finding fulfillment for the first time. This was a privilege sweet and special. Never had his own pleasure been so sharp. When he released his seed, he shook with the force of his own abandonment, as if he too had just discovered all the secrets of making love. It was as if he'd always held something back. Not this time. Not with her. She took all, and gloried in it.

Feelings this intense, this special, were alien to him. He'd given before; he'd taken before. But never like this. *This* was complete union.

And he realized, with Victoria soft and warm in his arms, holding her close as her body gradually relaxed, he had made a vital discovery.

For the first time in his life Rhys knew a depth of emotion so complete that it shocked him. He was in love; deeply, unequivocally in love, with his wife.

Chapter Fifteen

Tory snuggled under the quilt, a smile on her lips. She felt so lazy, so completely relaxed. Her eyes opened slowly, adjusting to the light which flooded the room. Pushing back the tangled mass of wavy hair from her face, she blinked several times before she focused on the bedside clock.

It had to be wrong!

She couldn't have read ten o'clock.

She looked again.

It did read a little after ten o'clock.

Tory fell back into the mound of pillows with a groan. She wasn't used to sleeping this late. Her lassitude had a reason, she thought, as she reached out her hand to the empty space beside her. *Her husband.* Heat suffused her face as she recalled Rhys's hands stroking her skin lightly as she woke; his mouth raining gentle kisses across her neck and shoulders until he dipped his head and found her breast. Just thinking about it brought a heat to her loins and caused her nipples to tingle and tighten, exactly what had happened when his tongue laved her flesh with ardent strokes before his lips captured her nipple and drew it deep into his mouth, suckling. It was then that she once again lost control, her body tightening and exploding. While she was still caught in the throes of passion, Rhys slipped into her body, bringing her once more to the brink and beyond. Their mating was powerful and primitive, quick and deep.

A hard knock sounded on the door before it was thrown open, admitting Twinnings carrying a tray laden with tea and muffins.

Tory could either pull the covers over her head and hide, or she could face Rhys's man.

"Set the tray down there," she ordered, indicating the foot of the bed.

Twinnings, his face impassive, as if seeing the earl's wife in the earl's bed was a commonplace occurrence, did as she asked. He then bent and retrieved the scattered clothes, laying them carefully across a nearby chair.

"Is there anything else that I can do for you, my lady?"

"Yes, there is." She marveled at Twinnings' *sangfroid*, and resisted the urge to smile at how very, very proper he seemed. "I would like a pot of hot chocolate, if you don't mind."

"Certainly, my lady. Is that all?" he inquired in a smooth tone.

"Yes, Twinnings, thank you." Tory watched as he silently left the room. Her hand was reaching for a blueberry muffin when she heard a voice behind her.

"I do believe that you've made another conquest, my dear."

Tory's head turned quickly. Rhys was standing there at the entrance to his own bathroom. His only covering was his black robe. Gone was the stubble of dark beard which had left its mark earlier on her tender skin.

Daylight had stripped away the protective covering of the night, exposing both.

God, he hadn't meant to say "another." Yet what he could say except that it was true? She had conquered him with weapons both sensual and honest; the impact of her surrender was freshly stamped on his brain. Tory had held nothing back, and, in consequence, neither had he. She made an innocent demand for all his skill, all his energy. Rhys gave back in equal measure, and in so doing, freed himself as never before to the sublime reaches of passion.

Had she revealed too much of herself to him while in the grip of something stronger than anything she had ever known? One night in Rhys's bed, in his arms, released a tumultuous force previously unknown to her—a Pandora's box of feelings and sensations kept locked in the deepest recesses of her character. These heretofore secret enclosures were breached and plumbed. She who had once so blithely dismissed the union of male and female was now privy to the power it conveyed.

Rhys strolled casually around the bed, reaching for the cup provided and pouring himself some of the hot tea. He added a splash of milk and seated himself.

Tory watched Rhys settle his long body against the headboard, pillows propped against his back. He crossed one leg over the other. She recalled the feel of the hair on his legs against hers, tickling, oddly stimulating.

"Would you hand me a muffin?"

Tory shot him a sideways glance. Were they to pretend that the things they shared last night hadn't happened? The enormity of what had transpired between them in this bed wasn't lost on her. Was it on him? Had it been too commonplace? In this arena, he was the sophisticated player; she the amateur.

"Butter?"

"Yes," he answered, his voice a lazy, contented drawl. A smile creased his mouth as he observed how carefully Victoria secured the quilt under her arms as she leaned forward, balancing on her knees. Her hair provided a thick curtain to shield her back, though he could occasionally catch a glimpse of her pale flesh. It was the same skin his hands had smoothed and skimmed. Soft. Supple.

Tory spread the soft golden butter abundantly across the muffin halves, handing him the china plate, before doing the same for herself.

Awkwardness hung in the air, keeping each silent and wondering.

Doubts resurfaced and swirled in Tory's head. Pride made her question. Did he think about the other women he'd had while with her? Had she compared favorably? Was he used to silent females? To women who remained passive and pliant?

The circumstances and culmination of their passion remained ingrained in his mind. Victoria's sweet abandon had both humbled and excited him beyond measure. The first taste demanded more, feeding on what it consumed so that he was eager to repeat the experience, showing and sharing all the possibilities.

Twinnings appeared once again, after knocking, with Tory's chocolate, setting the small tray on the desk and pouring her a cup of the hot beverage. He walked to the bed and handed it to the countess.

"Thank you, Twinnings," she said, her tone soft.

"My pleasure, to be sure, my lady," Twinnings intoned, his silent thoughts focused on the earl and his lady. How right they looked together. His lordship was relaxed, with a contented glow on his features; the countess was quiet, with a soft glow about her face as she sipped her chocolate and nibbled on her muffin.

"Is there anything that you require, my lord? Shall I draw a bath?"

Rhys cast a swift glance at his wife. She was what he required now, another sampling of their unique duet. "Nothing more now, Twinnings, except that you may remove the breakfast tray."

"Very good, my lord." When the manservant took his leave of the couple, he was whistling a happy tune under his breath.

Rhys waited until he saw that Tory was finished with her chocolate. "Do you wish another?" he inquired.

"No. Not right now."

"Good," he said, removing the cup from her fingers and placing it on the bedside table.

"I should be getting dressed," she began.

"Why?"

"It's late and there's work to be done," she said.

"It can wait."

Tory let out a sigh. What did he want?

As if by some coincidence he'd read her mind, Rhys replied, "I want you."

A thrill shivered over Tory's skin with his husky, whispered words. "Now?"

"Yes, now." He could see the dawning comprehension in her face, see the creep of blush stain her cheeks as she realized that he wanted her here, in the light, without the protection of the darkness.

"There's nothing to be ashamed of, sweetheart," he said, untying the sash of his robe and shrugging out of it. "Let me show you." He gently drew back the quilt she had hold of, exposing her body to the sunlight, and to his avid eyes. "Beautiful," he murmured, reaching out his hand to stroke the skin of her arm. Instead of a full caress, Rhys used only his middle finger, skating along the surface, joined then by his thumb.

She trembled.

He shuddered.

His embraces grew bolder, deeper, more acute. With each touch he shared the warmth, fanned the flames. Her gasp was deep when he reached the reddish-blonde curls. In this portal their essences had mixed: her blood, his seed. Her innocence, his experience. Their lips met hungrily as he continued his journey, exploring the riches her body had to offer. A mild explosion seized her when the probing increased.

Rhys could feel the intense pressure of his own flesh, hard and eager. He grabbed one of her hands and brought it to him.

Tory, her body damp with sweat, felt the object in her hand. She gave in to her own curiosity, running her fingers along its length. It was warm, hard, alive. She heard Rhys's breathing quicken, saw the gleam of silver in his eyes darken.

"Mount me."

His words were raw, needy.

"What?" she asked, not sure exactly what he wanted of her.

He repeated his words, his voice ravishing her senses. *"Mount me."*

Her look of bewilderment forced him into action.

Tory found herself lifted so that she was now

stradling his prone body. With a quick thrust of his hips, Rhys brought their bodies together. So deep was he in her that she instinctively reached out her hands for his, linking their fingers as the driving rhythm overcame them both.

They rode out the storm, each surrendering to the ultimate abandonment.

Tory collapsed onto Rhys's body. Her cheek rested in the hollow of his throat; her breasts nestled against the crisp black hair of his chest. Her tongue flicked out and tasted his skin. Salty. When her breathing was under control, she lifted her head, her eyes staring deeply into his. Tentatively, she bent and kissed his lips, offering a gesture of trust.

Rhys responded, anchoring his hand in her hair, pulling her deeper, closer into the kiss. His body, still joined to hers, stirred quickly to life once again, surprising even him. He rolled her under him, never taking his lips from hers, and began again the steady, thrusting rhythm.

Her short nails scored his back as she held on, spinning further and further out of control. Her only reality was the potent force of Rhys's mouth on hers. Each searing kiss they shared was a glimpse of heaven, a promise kept.

When she awoke again, Tory found herself in her own bed. A delicious languor crept over her. She stretched like a contented cat, enjoying the feel of the cool linen sheet against her naked body. The caress of the material brought back memories of Rhys's large hand gliding along her flesh.

A soft rap sounded on her door.

She moved upright, thinking that it was her husband, then dismissed the idea, since he would have entered from their connecting door.

"Come in," she called out.

Janet poked her head around the door, a sassy grin on her face.

"Do stop hovering, Janet," Tory said, running her hands carelessly through the mass of her hair, a slow, sweet smile on her own mouth.

Janet closed the door, unabashed in her curiosity. "So, you've finally become a wife?" she asked, opening the curtains and letting in the last of the sunlight.

"Is nothing a secret around here?" Tory queried.

"Not much so's you'd notice," Janet answered, making herself comfortable on the bed. "Are you all right?"

"What makes you think I wouldn't be?"

"Well, it being your first time and all, could be that you'd be a mite sore. Or," and she slanted a penetrating glance in Tory's direction, "a trifle disappointed."

Tory blushed, feeling the heat creep up into her cheeks. Disappointed? Oh no, she thought, she could never have felt that.

She reached out her hand and touched Janet's. "There was no disappointment, I can assure you."

"Deep down I had a notion that you wouldn't be."

"Did you really?"

Janet nodded her head. "It was easy to see that he wanted to be a husband to you. Men are men under the skin, be they highborn or not." She got up and went in search of Tory's robe. "I had a bath prepared for you. Best you soak some of the stiffness out of those muscles, seeing as how you'll be needing to be fresh for later." A knowing wink accompanied her words.

Later. The word conjured up fantasy images in Tory's mind of her and Rhys happily ensconced in a bed, any bed so long as they were together.

"You love him, don't you?" Janet asked as Tory rose from her bed.

As Tory slipped her arms into the robe Janet was holding out, she responded softly. "I never believed that I could care this deeply about him when first we met. He was the man foisted on me by my father. A handpicked stud for hire, albeit a wellborn one. A man overly arrogant and proud."

"Of course we don't know anyone like that, do we?" Janet questioned.

Tory gave her a quizzing glance before continuing. "Yet these past months I've come to see other sides to the Earl of Derran. He's an intelligent man, Janet, and he respects that in others. He cares about his heritage, just as I care about the Encantadora." She soothed the sheets of her bed, then her hands plumped the pillows. Janet had been the recipient of other confidences, so Tory felt no hesitation in sharing this also. Besides, she wanted to tell someone, to test the sound of the words to ears other than her own.

"I didn't expect to love him, but I do." In an attempt to occupy her hands, Tory set about braiding her hair. "It was more of a quiet surprise. While we were in the music room, I suddenly looked at him and I just knew." She turned and faced Janet. "Does that sound odd?"

Janet took both of Tory's hands in hers. "Not odd, honey. Just human." She traced Tory's cheek. "You're too fine a woman to be alone. Besides, this isn't the country for it, as you're well aware. Out here a woman needs to know she can depend on her man, just as he needs to know he can count on her."

"A matter of mutual trust," Tory said.

"Yes, that's a good enough word for it," Janet responded.

"And Marsh has never broken that bond, has he?"

Janet smiled, her eyes full of love. "Never. He's kept the faith of our love." She walked away from Tory, in the direction of the wardrobe. "I'm sure you'll be wanting to wear something extra special to dinner this evening."

A change from her usual shirt and denims, something softer, more feminine, for Rhys. He'd like that. Moreover, it was something she now wanted to do, both for him and for herself. Rhys's masculine appreciation of her body compelled Tory to acknowledge the pleasure that could be gotten from dressing not merely to cover decoratively, but for enhancement.

Tory sat at her dressing table, selecting a bottle of perfume. She removed the sapphire pendant and the gold brooch from their storage. It was important that she wear them tonight. More than her wedding ring, they were visible symbols of her marriage, and of her acceptance of the same. She touched them reverently. "Have you ever doubted Marsh?"

"No."

Tory was surprised by Janet's swift answer. There was no hesitation, no uncertainty. "Never?"

"I love Marsh, and loving him, I know him well." Janet opened the wardrobe door and brought out a long-sleeved white blouse and a skirt of deep rose, as well as a few petticoats. "I'm not a fool, Miss Tory, and Marsh ain't a saint. He's sure enough a man, and I reckon he's done his fair share of looking and thinking about other women. I can accept that."

"You can?"

"Sure enough," she answered, laying out the clothes. "Because I know that where it counts, in our bed, I have the truth. You can't be as close as Marsh and I are, and have been all these years, and not have trust. Yeah, I reckon some folks can say they believe and let it go at that. But they don't, not truly. It's easy to love someone if you've a mind; it's having the heart to love that can be tough."

* * *

Rhys took a deep drag of the cigar, inhaling the rich fragrance. He blew out a thick ring of smoke, and his lids narrowed as he observed his wife. She was pouring them both an after-dinner drink. Her hands on the crystal brandy decanter made him ache to feel them on his body. The breath caught in his throat as he recalled her untutored fingers skimming his flesh and, conversely, the pleasure he got from holding her in his arms and watching her explode with the force of her capitulation.

She was wearing his jewels tonight. The brooch gleamed brightly over her heart. The sapphire necklace rested against the crisp material of her blouse. He considered as he took the snifter that Tory handed him how the blue stone would look contrasted with the creamy flesh of her breasts.

He glanced quickly at the door to the library. There was a key in the lock.

Rising from his chair, Rhys stoked the fire. The evening had turned colder, with a continual rain which pelted against the long windows. He walked to the door and twisted the key, slipping it into the pocket of his smoking jacket before dispensing with the garment altogether, folding it carefully and placing it on the chair he had recently vacated. Next, Rhys picked up the quilt that lay on the couch. With a snap of his hand he laid it on the floor in front of the fireplace, levering himself down on top of it.

His eyes met hers, and he held out his hand in invitation.

Tory read the request and answered the summons, linking her hand to his. The sensation of flesh meeting flesh warmed her within and without. Without words their lips met and clung, both delving deep. It was an elixir so potent that each felt the melding of mouths as if one of the frequent lightning bolts that lit the night sky had zigzagged its way into their souls, cutting to the bone and beyond.

Deftly, Rhys undid the buttons of her blouse, pushing it down and off her arms. He sucked in his breath. The cunning little witch had provocatively left off her undergarments. His wish was fulfilled: her breasts had the luster of pearls in the fire's glow. The sapphire rested in the valley, enhancing the contrast of colors. He sought the crest of one breast, tugging and teasing the nipple. He heard her low moans. One hand captured her wrists, holding them above her head while he luxuriated in her body, captivated by the lingering aroma of roses, by the liquid response of her body, touched by the unabashed sensuality she possessed.

He needed to have her now, without waiting for the security of a bedroom. His weight shifted and he rested his body against hers. He locked his mouth once more onto hers as he slid his other hand up and down the skirt she wore of soft merino wool, outlining her thighs, easing the fabric up and back. When her legs were exposed, the sharp blade of desire drew blood once more in him. The curling nest of reddish curls beckoned.

Tory moved sinuously, her legs opening. The hot core of her desire was centered there, eager to contain once more the full weight and length of his masculinity. Her eyes fluttered closed.

Rhys released her wrists and leaned back on his haunches. "Look at me," he insisted.

Tory's eyes opened quickly. She saw her husband, his hands resting on his lean, muscled thighs. His shirt hung open, disarranged by her eager hands. Glancing upward, she stared at his broad chest, with its fine carpet of black hair. A thrill raced along her body.

Rhys, his gray eyes focused on her face, quickly undid the buttons of his trousers, freeing himself. He observed the slow drag of her tongue across her full mouth and longed to have Victoria measure him with the same artful strokes. Soon. Someday. But for now, he was eager to plumb the silken sheath she offered.

Tory couldn't take her gaze from Rhys as he lowered himself once again to her. She welcomed him eagerly, sliding her arms under the silk shirt, clinging to his back as he brought their bodies together in one expeditious move, sending her reeling with the force of his possession. This was no gentle loving; rather it was fast and unrestrained, savage in its untamed beauty. It was a mating of equals, each taking and demanding; each giving and receiving.

Rhys kissed the tears that wet her cheeks, oddly humbled by her response. He levered himself onto his arms, gazing down into her luminous blue eyes. Christ, he thought, every time with her was like the first as he discovered something new. As no other woman before, Tory had shown him the completeness of making love.

The incongruity of their situation brought a smile to Tory's face. Just days before, had anyone even suggested that she would be lying in front of the fireplace in her library, her skirt pushed up, exposing the long length of her legs, her torso bare, a clothed man between her thighs, she would have deemed them mad. Yet, it had happened. There, on the floor, wild and free. Beyond reason, beyond any barrier her mind could devise.

Now, gathered in the safety of his strong arms, Tory gave voice to the formidable feeling swelling inside her. She reached over and touched his mouth in a soft, calm kiss. It seemed so natural, so right, to say simply, "I love you, Rhys."

He'd heard the words in times past, murmured through a haze of sex, words said because they were part of the ritual, words lost in the shuffle of expectations, sometimes real. This time, however, the words were genuine, spoken honestly, from the heart of a woman without lies. Rhys realized the rarity of the gift, and in so doing, treasured it all the more.

Just as he was ready to acknowledge that his own heart had also been moved, there was a loud, incessant pounding on the door.

Tory bolted from Rhys's arms, scrambling for her blouse, pulling it on as she hurriedly did up the buttons. Rhys stood up, fastening his trousers. Grabbing his jacket, he flung it on, removing the key from the pocket. He went to the door, giving a swift look over his shoulder to be sure that Tory was all right. She looked the part of a woman well loved: her eyes slumberous, her lips swollen from their impassioned kisses, her nipples puckering the material of her shirt as she hastily tucked it back into her skirt.

When Rhys opened the door, Marsh stood there. The tall foreman's frame was covered in a long oilskin coat. Everything he wore was wet. His boots dripped puddles on the carpet. When he spoke, his low voice was barely above a cracked whisper. "I need to see Miss Tory."

"What's wrong?" Rhys demanded.

"Is she in there?" Marsh asked, attempting to push aside the Earl of Derran, all manners forgotten.

The sheen of tears were evident in the foreman's dark, red-rimmed eyes as Tory rushed to the door. Fear struck a cold cord in her heart. "Marshall, what's happened?" she implored, her arm reaching for the solid grasp of her husband's flesh.

Marsh could well imagine what he had interrupted. Clothes put to right in haste, faces that wore the aftermarks of passion well spent, the undeniable scent of love. His big hands clenched. "Miss Tory . . ." he began, swallowing the emotion that threatened to overwhelm him.

"Oh God, just tell me what's happened," she pleaded.

"Your father . . . he's . . ."

"Papa? Where is he? Has there been an accident?" Her words rushed out, a sick dread settling in her stomach.

"No accident, Miss Tory. He's dead."

Had Rhys's arm not held hers so tightly, Tory could well imagine that she would have sunk to the floor in a faint. The breath was knocked painfully from her chest.

"Victoria," Rhys said, his voice a cherished balm at that moment.

"Where is he?" she asked, fighting for control.

"The barn."

Tory threw off Rhys's hold and ran past the two men, out into the storm, running as quickly as she could. By the time she got to the barn, her clothes were mud-spattered, her velvet shoes were ruined, and she was soaked through, her shirt clinging to her body. She burst through the open doors.

All assembled there, black, brown, and white, silently formed a path through which she could proceed.

Sam Reitenauer had been placed in a buckboard, on a bed of blankets. Tory walked automatically forward until she reached where her father lay. Bruises covered his weathered face. She could see the large stain of red that covered his white shirt. The rain had faded the brightness of his blood. A hole was ripped in the fabric over his heart. A gunshot, her mind registered.

Tory reached out her hand, tracing the thick hair at his temple. "Papa," she cried, her voice breaking as her heart was shredded by grief.

Rhys and Marsh were only seconds behind her. They joined Tory, who stood, her proud head bent, Janet at her side.

"Where did you find him?" Tory turned and stared into Marsh's eyes, as if there she would find a reason, some sort of credible explanation.

"On the trail to San Antonio."

"What about the men with him?"

Marsh shook his head. "Diego is barely alive; the other man, Preston, is dead. They were bushwhacked near as I can tell."

"Who?"

Rhys listened to the cold, solitary words as it came low and bitter from Victoria's lips.

"I don't rightly know, Miss Tory," Marsh answered. "If Diego recovers enough to talk, I'll question him."

Rhys edged closer to Tory, his arm sliding around her slim waist. He realized that Sam's death brought more sadness to him than had the death of his own father. Sam was a man Rhys had grown to respect and care for. Without Sam he wouldn't have had the money to rebuild his heritage, nor would he have had something of even more value than mere money—his wife, who'd somehow rebuilt his heart.

Rhys watched her fight to maintain her composure, to put on a brave face as the men and women there sought her out, giving her what little comfort they could impart from words.

"Marsh," Tory said, turning away from the

lifeless body, "would you bring my father back to the house?"

Marsh nodded his head.

A chill so pervasive that even a roaring fire couldn't warm her invaded Tory's bones. Too late to tell her father just one more time how much she loved him. And how much she would miss him. Like a hole in her heart, the gap would never be filled.

Tory paced restlessly around the confines of her darkened room, her eyes red and swollen from all the tears she'd shed in solitude. All her close family was gone now. She was the last of her line.

Tory was grateful that Rhys had insisted that Twinnings give Janet a hand in preparing Sam's body. Arrangements had to be made for the funeral services; letters written to friends and relatives; always endless details. Janet had insisted that she must wash the grime of the night's storm from her body else she might have just kept herself in the mud-stained clothes. After her bath, she'd gone back to Sam's room to be with him. It was there Rhys found her, on the floor by Sam's bed, her cheek resting against Sam's cold hand. He pried her hand loose from her father's and made her leave, stressing that she needed rest.

Some joke, Tory thought as she once again paced back and forth. At least in the privacy of her room she'd been able to give vent to the torrent of tears. Right now she felt as if she'd been frozen, unable to accept the fact that she would never share anything with Sam again, that he would never know she and Rhys were now really husband and wife, in every sense of the word.

Grief wasn't the only emotion making her feel so cold. It was a consuming anger towards the person who had robbed her of her father. That person, whoever it was, would pay dearly for that, she vowed. She would use all the resources at her command to find the culprit and see that justice was done. Slowly, painfully—that's how this person would be dispatched. Without hesitation. This unseen enemy would welcome death before she was through with him.

The rain had ceased its relentless tattoo against the windows. The first streaks of dawn were pushing at the darkness. Tory stood before the flames, watching the flickering colors. She concentrated so keenly that she didn't hear the connecting door open and close.

Rhys moved soundlessly on the floor, his bare feet covering the distance between him and his wife effortlessly. He'd held back and let her have the time he thought she needed alone. Sleep was as impossible for him this night, as it was for Victoria. His beautiful amazon stood alone in the shadows of the room.

But, she wasn't alone any longer. He was here. "You should be in bed," he whispered in her ear, his hands pushing aside the thick fall of her hair.

Tory relaxed against the solid wall of her

325

husband's chest. Here was warmth; she could feel it seeping into her through the cotton of her nightdress. Rhys was alive. She could feel the steady beat of his pulse as her fingers made contact with his wrist as his arms wrapped around her stomach.

"All my family are gone, Rhys. All dead."

"Not all, Victoria," he responded, pulling her chilled body closer to the heat of his. "I'm your family now. You've a sister in England eager to meet you. And, my love," he said, his lips moving slowly up her shoulder to her throat, tasting her flesh with teeth and tongue, "one day you will carry our child in your womb." His lean fingers stretched and caressed. She could already be pregnant with his child, he thought, his seed taking root.

Rhys silently cursed himself as he felt the kick of his body, its heady response to being close to her. What had began as comfort was rapidly changing.

"Come you to bed now," Rhys said as he bent and scooped Tory into his arms, walking the short distance to her bed. He placed her carefully there and backed away.

"Don't leave me," Tory implored. She had to have his warmth once again. Without it, she wasn't sure that she could keep the demons of this night at bay. Her often-vaunted self-reliance seemed to be failing her now. Was it so wrong to want to share this burden?

"If that's what you really want?" he asked.

"Yes, Rhys." Tory held open the cover that

he'd placed over her, making room for him in the bed.

Rhys unloosed the belt to his robe, letting it fall in a black puddle on the floor. The state of his arousal was in evidence as he slipped between the sheets. Where his wife was concerned, his body reacted faster and more intensely than with any other woman. Yet now was not the time. Her need was for comfort, and that's what he would provide.

Tory sought Rhys's arms and nestled close to the heat of his body, burrowing in the strength of his embrace. Here, now, in this bed, with this man, there were no empty spaces.

Rhys kissed the top of her head as it rested on his chest. He could hear the even tenor of her breathing, signaling that at last Victoria had succumbed to sleep.

Satisfied, he too closed his eyes.

Chapter Sixteen

Two days later, Sam Reitenauer was laid to rest in the family cemetery. The sloping hill was covered by a throng of mourners, each quietly remembering the man just interred. A lone sound broke the stillness of the day as a solitary singer raised his voice in a bittersweet spiritual.

Tory's face was visibly pale beneath the black lace *mantilla*. Her head ached, and there was still the will to be read, not to mention dealing with all the people assembled here. She lifted her eyes heavenward; the sky was a bright, clear blue, with white, puffy clouds. The air was crisp despite the warmth of the sun. All she wanted to do now was to saddle Abendstern and ride as fast and as far as she could. That, however, was now out of the question, as the person who murdered her father could be lurking even now on her own ranch. Until they found the villain, she would perforce have to remain a virtual captive in her own home. Marshall gave her strict warning just that morning. She'd bristled at the challenge to her freedom even while recognizing the wisdom of the judgment. Her foreman was doing his best to look out for her well-being. He'd vocally reiterated exactly what she had thought: "You're the last of the Reitenauers, Miss Tory. You owe it to them who've come before to stay alive. Your pa would have wanted it that way and well you know it."

Even Rhys, who was included in the meeting at Tory's request, agreed with Marsh's pronouncement. "He's correct, Victoria. You must be kept from harm's way."

Her thoughts shifted back to the present as the crowd began to disperse, each returning to their own lives. Only a few people would be going to the main house.

Don Sebastian, his new wife at his side, watched Tory. When a messenger from Victoria had arrived with the news, he'd been stunned. His first instinct had been to get dressed and ride to the Encantadora to be with her, to give his adored Victoria whatever comfort he could. Knowing that he couldn't give free rein to his feelings made him heartsick. When he did arrive, his eyes beheld a subtle difference in her, despite the inundation of sorrow. It was there in the half-glances that she cast toward her husband, in the touching of their hands, the whisperings between them. Don Sebastian recognized the hungry look that the earl gave his countess. Rhys's gray eyes glowed with possession whenever they rested on his wife.

Despite his pain, Don Sebastian put a proper face over his hurt, masking the true depth. Now he must assume the mantle of surrogate father in Victoria's life.

"Words cannot begin to express my sorrow at this moment, *querida*," he said, taking hold of Tory's hand.

Tory went into the welcoming embrace of Don Sebastian, once more fighting back the tears. She took solace from the powerful arms that wrapped around her, sheltering, holding her close. "Oh, *Tío*, I miss him so much."

Automatically, Don Sebastian switched to Spanish. "I know."

Tory answered him in his native tongue. "I want to think that this all a nightmare, that I will wake and find it's all been a bad dream, and Papa is alive."

"Sadly, I wish I could say that too," Don Sebastian replied.

"Give me your word that you will stay the night. Please?"

"Of course, my dear, if that is what you want."

Tory nodded her head. "My invitation includes your wife, of course." Tory felt obliged to extend his new bride every courtesy, even though she and the lady were virtual strangers. Her parents would have been aghast had she neglected the fundamental courtesies of hospitality.

"I wish circumstances had provided me with a better means for an introduction between you and she."

"No matter, *Tío*," Tory declared. "I have no doubt that we shall be friends. How could we be otherwise if she is your wife?"

Don Sebastian, his arm around Tory's shoulder, led her away from the gravesite.

Rhys, standing silent and solitary, a part of the tableau, yet somehow distant, narrowed his eyes in speculation. He heard the words Don Sebastian spoke to his wife. Even though they were uttered in Spanish, Rhys could tell by the inflection in the man's deep bass voice that they were words of comfort. Every gesture marked him the concerned "uncle," save for the Don's eyes; those black eyes yielded a much stronger emotion.

And, Rhys realized, that was as far as the Don would take it. In the months since his arrival, Rhys had become cognizant of the situation and the people involved. This was no cosmopolitan setting where sophisticated partners went their own way, each turning a blind eye to the other's indiscretions. Here in Texas, one's honor, and the good regard of those one held dear, were durable enough barriers should one even consider overstepping bounds.

His thoughts drifted to the early morning hours of the day before, when she had begged him to stay. He'd checked the hot blood of his desire for her until much later, when Victoria awoke, her hands busy exploring his body, her lips bold and magical. It was loving slow and sweet, keen and prolonged.

More than her body, he'd come to realize, his wife had shared her soul. Once that idea would have seemed fanciful to him. All his life Rhys had taken for granted that his wife would share her body and her social life with him, and there would be an end to it. It would be all he'd need, or want. Until, that was, he met Victoria. In her he discovered a woman who gave, and in turn demanded, much more.

Rhys saw the Don's wife. She was standing alone, finishing a prayer. In her broad hands she held a rosary, the black beads well worn.

He stepped over to her, holding out his arm.

Doña Michelle accepted with a grateful nod of her head.

Kristen, her face creased by sorrow, made sure that the food was laid out correctly. She had to keep busy, or she would find herself crying again. To be found by the baroness, of all people, as she was preparing the morning meal, with her hands constantly in the pocket of her white apron as she reached for the linen handkerchief she kept there. The baroness had walked into the kitchen, intent on procuring another pot of chocolate, while Kristen was sniffling into her square of linen.

Victoria had put down her silver chocolate pot on the kitchen table and drawn the cook into her embrace, comforting her.

Kristen felt such a fool, to be unburdening her

grief onto her mistress's shoulders. "You must forgive an old woman, baroness."

"There is nothing to forgive," Tory assured her. "I know that you loved my father, Kristen. You miss him, just as I do. That is as it should be."

Tory's words had given Kristen the measure of comfort that she needed. Now, as she laid out thick slices of smoked ham, she cast her glance in Victoria's direction. She was proud of her mistress, of the courage that she exhuded in this most difficult time. To Kristen, Victoria was the epitome of the true aristocrat. She voiced as much to Janet, who stood next to her, pouring cups of coffee into the delicate porcelain cups.

"The baroness is strong," Kristen declared. "See how she conducts herself," Kristen said proudly.

Janet busied herself fixing the coffee as each person had requested. She glanced in Tory's direction and saw her talking with her guests as if this were a formal salon instead of a wake. Janet was slightly skeptical. "I'm not sure that she needs to be." Adding a splash of brandy to Tory's *café au lait*, Janet continued. "Better to bend so as not to break."

Kristen brushed imaginary crumbs from her starched white apron. "The baroness is a von Reitenauer," she stated.

Janet answered her with, "Victoria is also a young woman of deep flesh-and-blood passions, make no mistake about that."

"She is a survivor," Kristen argued.

"But at what cost?" Janet mused to Kristen's chagrin. Janet's blue eyes focused on the two men who stood flanking the seated Victoria. Each, she surmised, was in love with Tory. She slid her glance towards the Don's wife, who was talking to Dr. Schmidt. A quiet, safe mouse, she decided. She could not be more unlike Tory, who, even in the stark black of mourning, was alive and vital.

Tory ate from the plate that Kristen had fixed for her. Her stomach, so long without food, growled and rumbled with hunger.

"You must eat to keep well and healthy, baroness," Kristen admonished.

"I know what I must do," Tory said as she lifted another slice of the ham into her mouth. And that was true. Tory was well aware of her responsibilities. She and the family lawyer, Durston Harewood, had gone over certain business matters for a brief time this morning. People depended on her. Her own innate sense of loyalty and duty were sharp. Now, also, she'd found the man to match her and realized the depth of her love for him—having placed in Rhys's care her trust and faith—believed that he loved her even though the actual words had yet to pass his lips. Her head argued that he was her "husband for hire." Her heart said, "So what?" Rhys Fitzgerald Buchanan was a loving husband, who had shown her a world she never knew existed. When she'd accepted him that fateful night, she'd made her choice. She had followed her heart.

"Perhaps you would care for something a bit stronger than coffee, Don Sebastian?" Rhys inquired, indicating with a wave of his hand the well-stocked bar which had been set up.

"*Sí*, I would like that very much," the Don replied, walking with Rhys.

"Brandy?"

The Don shook his head. "I would rather have either a bourbon or a tequilla, *por favor.*"

"As you wish," Rhys answered, handing the Don a small glass of clear liquid. He opted for a tumbler of bourbon with splash of cold water. In the months he'd resided in Texas, Rhys discovered a fondness for the brew known as bourbon. In England, his liquor of choice was either Scotch whiskey or French brandy. He tossed back the contents of the glass with one long swallow.

"She'll be fine," Rhys assured the Don, his gray eyes seeking and finding his wife across the room.

"It is my most fervent wish," Don Sebastian replied. "I want only what is best for her."

"As do I." Rhys fixed both of them another drink. As he handed Don Sebastian his, their gazes clashed. In a soft voice, Rhys said, "I know that you love her."

Don Sebastian drank the tequilla before answering. "I would never do anything to dishonor Victoria."

Rhys shot a quick glance at Michelle Montenegro. "I believe that."

Don Sebastian weighed carefully in his mind

the words that he wanted to say before he uttered them. "Have you truly come to care for Victoria? To love her and cherish her, as a man must for the one precious thing entrusted to his care?"

Rhys's eyes narrowed. Had it been any other man questioning him, he would have been tempted to call him out. He noted the hard edge to the Don's voice even though the tone was silky. Yet, Rhys respected the man's honesty. In time, he could well imagine that they might even manage a friendship, of sorts.

"Yes," Rhys admitted, "I love Victoria."

"Without doubts or questions?"

"Without doubts or questions," Rhys answered. He fixed his gaze on the older man, deciding to be brutally frank. "All misgivings were shed on the night that she gave herself to me, finally, freely, without hesitation."

Pain stabbed through Don Sebastian's dark eyes even as he held his face held in control. He looked to see if the younger man had said it deliberately. The Englishman was only stating the hard facts. Nothing more. Nothing less.

Across the other side of the room, Tory sat, her mind thawing gradually from the numbing cold that had come over it. She responded politely to the questions or comments made to her, wishing only that she could turn back the stale hands of time. Such, she knew, was not to be. Illusion must not be allowed to outweigh reality. Reality was that Sam was dead and that she was sitting here entertaining his mourners, when all she wished was to be left alone. Well, perhaps not completely alone. She searched for her husband and found him. Tory watched as he made a point with those elegant hands of his, sweeping and punctuating the air. Hours before, they had made his references on her skin, taking her to dizzing heights.

"I'm sorry, what did you say?" she asked.

"That at this time you must be especially glad that you are a married woman," Michelle repeated.

"Yes," Tory responded, missing the point that the older woman was making. Tory could see only that comfort that Rhys's strong embrace provided. He'd given her safe harbor during this time of storm.

"With a husband to secure your holdings, this loss should seem easier to bear."

Tory looked at the older woman in stunned surprise. She took a deep sip of the brandy-laced coffee. *"Madame,"* she addressed Don Sebastian's wife in flawless French, "I have no need of a husband to secure my property. I shall see to that myself."

Doña Michelle's dark eyes went wide with incredulity. "You wish to handle your own business affairs?"

"Of course," Tory scoffed. "My father trained me for this day."

"But you are a wife."

"An indisputable fact."

"It would be much easier to have your husband settle your estate."

"Easier for whom?" Tory countered.

Doña Michelle's face began to flush. "Why, easier for your man. Will you not consider his pride?"

"What about my own?"

"It does a woman no good to be overly proud, my dear," she confided.

"Nor," Tory responded, "does it do a woman any good to behave like a bonded servant in her own home. I bend the knee for no one, madame." She stood up, plate and saucer in hand. "If you will excuse me, Doña Michelle." The last remark was placed in the form of a statement of intent rather than a question.

Rhys observed Tory as she made her way to the table laden with food. She stopped to say a few words with Marsh and the veterinarian, who were engrossed in conversation. She glanced his way briefly and he was cut to the quick with desire for her—aching, gut-tearing longing that almost cleaved him where he stood. He could actually feel his hands trembling. *Christ*, Rhys thought, he was once again like a schoolboy with his first woman, eager, his flesh hard and urgent. He mentally stripped the black gown, beautiful as it was—a Worth original without question—from her body, exposing the lush curves she hid beneath the velvet fabric. Those milk-white breasts pushed higher by the cut of the gown would one day swell even more with nourishment for their child. Even now she could be carrying the seed of their union within her womb. An heir.

But, his mind questioned, for which estate? His title was old and demanded a son to keep it alive with the Fiztgerald Buchanan blood.

However, this wild, raw land also made substantial claims of its own.

Another packet of letters had arrived from England just yesterday; among them were missives from his sister, who reiterated her sadness at his continuing absence, and words from his estate manager, with pointed inquiries into matters concerning the farm. He would have to return to his native land sometime soon. For far too long, he'd put off thinking about the details. Perhaps this trip would be just what Victoria needed. A chance for her to break away from the bitter remembrances of these past few days. A chance to make new memories to replace those sorrow-tinged ones.

Tonight, when they were alone within the shelter of their bed, he would proffer his suggestion regarding the trip. Besides, he concluded, it was time to show off his American wife to London society.

And tonight would be the proper time to make his overdue confession of love to Victoria. She had waited far too long to hear the true expression of his feelings for her.

Tonight that would all change.

Everyone mentioned personally in Sam Reitenauer's will was gathered in the library, sitting or standing, anxiously awaiting the words the lawyer would speak.

"I think it best if you begin now," Tory told him, eager to get this last bit of business over with. Her head was aching; her temples throbbed.

Dunston Harewood cleared his throat while he opened the leather satchel. He knew that certain parts of what he had to read would bring great changes in the lives of the people here in this room. He and Sam had discussed it with great care.

"First, may I take this opportunity to say that we shall never see a man the like of Samuel Reitenauer in our lifetime again. I counted him not only a client, but a personal friend. He was tough, hard, but always fair. A man brave enough to take risks.

"I shall begin by reading the bequests he made to those that do not concern the bulk of his estate.

"To my great and dear friend, Don Sebastian Montenegro, I leave my collection of dueling pistols, which he has so long admired. I also bequeath to him my share of the vineyard we jointly owned, with the proviso that he is to select bottles from each harvest for the cellars of the Encantadora.

"To my foreman, Marshall Kincaid, and his wife Janet, I give free title to one hundred acres of the Encantadora, the site to be determined by consultation with my daughter, along with $20,000. For their daughter, Ruth, I leave her money, $3,000, sufficient to establish herself in whatever she chooses."

Janet and Ruth both gasped at their late employer's generosity, while Marsh stood stiffly, not quite believing what he heard. His hazel eyes became misty with tears.

"To my faithful servant, Kristen, whose loyalty and love have provided me with comfort these long years, I leave the sum of $10,000. How you chose to dispose of this money is up to you. I say that because I know that you will never willingly leave the service of the house of Reitenauer."

Kristen, her eyes filled with tears, dabbed at them ineffectually with her crumpled linen square.

"There are other bequests, mostly concerning the ranch hands, which I shall skip for now. That is, if you don't mind, Mrs. Buchanan?"

Tory sat quietly in her chair, lost in thought, and unused to her new name.

"Victoria?" Rhys prodded.

She responded. "Sorry. What were you saying?"

"That if it meets with your approval, I will leave the other dispersals of gifts, which concern those who work on the Encantadora, plus assorted business associates and relatives, until later?"

"That is fine," she said.

"Then," he continued, "the last and most important bequests are for you and his lordship. I would suggest that these be made in private."

Tory shrugged. It mattered little to her. She knew basically what would be included in the document; she was her father's sole heir. Her

Gail Link

gaze caught Rhys's and automatically she
smiled. It was most kind, she thought, of her
father to have included his son-in-law in his will.

"I would like my godfather to remain," she
stated.

The lawyer cleared his throat again. "If that is
what you want."

He waited till all other occupants had left the
room before he began. "I feel I must preface
this reading by saying that Sam made a few
alterations in his will in the last months before
his untimely death."

Tory interrupted. "What changes?"

"Certain financial and property arrangements
heretofore made have been . . . altered."

"Altered?" Tory's voice took on a decidedly
frosty tone. She rose from her chair with deliberate calm. "What are you talking about?"

"Perchance we should allow him to proceed
with the reading so that we may find out?" Rhys
suggested.

Tory glanced quickly at her husband. Rhys
was right. "Please," she said with a wave of her
hand, "continue."

"Your father did nothing without reason."

"I know that," Tory stated.

"Then you must allow that he knew what he
was doing when he made these alterations."

"We are agreed then, I think, that my father
was in his right mind when he made these
changes of which you speak," Tory conceded.

"Sam loved you very much."

"I'm well aware of my father's love for me."

342

"Good," the lawyer said. "Keep that in mind."

"I shall," she said, "Now, if you don't mind, read on."

"The codicil to Sam's will is dated August 1877, superseding all previous documents as to the dispersion of the bulk of his estate." He picked up the thick vellum sheets and proceeded to read Sam's words.

"To my most beloved daughter, Victoria Reitenauer Fitzgerald Buchanan, I leave the control of my various and sundry businesses. In her hands I place the reins of power. All judgments on such are her responsibility alone. My faith and trust in her ability is without question.

"I would wish that she see to the establishment of a scholarship in the family name to the newly established seat of higher learning, the Agriculture and Mining School."

Tory relaxed somewhat. No real surprises in her father's will so far. They had discussed recently a program providing funds for students too poor to pay for their own tuition.

"To my son-in-law, Rhys Fitzgerald Buchanan, the Earl of Derran, I bequeath the sum of £1,000,000 sterling. As he will find, the sum has already been transferred to his private account in the Bank of England. This is given freely, without conditions. In the months since he married my only daughter, I have judged his mettle most carefully and find that picking him as a husband for Victoria was one of the wisest business decisions I have ever made."

The lawyer paused to drink from the large

glass of water in front of him.

Rhys was struck dumb by this event. With the stroke of a pen his fortune was restored and bettered. Sam had given him both a measure of freedom and a heavy responsibility. Months ago he would have viewed it as a bribe, as another vulgar payment for services rendered. Not now. Not having come to know his father-in-law as he had. This was indeed a surprising gift of the heart.

Tory, too, was caught off-guard by the generosity of her father's gift to Rhys.

Don Sebastian took a deep breath. He marveled at his friend's foresight. A man of Rhys's breeding would need some measure of independence from his wife's purse strings. Victoria was wealthy beyond belief. Now, thanks to Sam, her husband was also a man of substance.

"Is that all?" Tory inquired.

"No. There is something else."

All three in the room exchanged hurried glances. In each mind was the question: what else?

"Continue," Tory and Rhys both spoke.

"As you know, the companies owned by your father, and now you, have some real estate holdings among their assets. The only property that was privately owned was this ranch, the Encantadora. It belonged wholly to Samuel Reitenauer."

"And now it belongs to me," Tory declared, wondering why the lawyer was repeating information already known.

"No, Victoria," he said, using her Christian name.

Tory's blue eyes sharpened and gleamed like polished chips of cold stones. "What do you mean?" she demanded.

"The ranch is not yours alone."

"Who else has claim to it? My brother is dead."

"That is true, sad to say."

"Then who?"

He cleared his throat again. He had argued with Sam that Sam should have let his daughter know of this change. Now it fell to him to break the news.

"As per your father's written statement, you and your husband are to have joint control over the Encantadora."

"What?" Instead of the shout the lawyer had expected, her word was soft, barely audible.

Don Sebastian observed the looks on the couple's faces. Rhys's was shocked astonishment, held in reserve. Tory's was open in its puzzlement.

"Has there been some mistake?" she asked.

The lawyer chose to read from her father's words once again. "I know that what I am about to propose will come as a shock. I do it for reasons for my own, without coercion, for what I deem the best interests of all concerned.

"The ranch called Encantadora in the state of Texas, is hereby to be divided equally between my daughter, Victoria, and her husband, Rhys. All decisions regarding the ranch must be shared. The only condition to this is that should there be no heir born of their union within five years of the date of their marriage, the property be sold and the money divided between the two."

"There must be some mistake," Tory said, feeling as if the breath had been struck from her body.

"I assure you, Victoria, there is no mistake. See for yourself," the lawyer advised, handing her the handwritten documents.

She swiftly scanned the contents, recognizing her father's handwriting. It was no joke. No mistake. Samuel Reitenauer had meant every word he wrote. But why?

Chapter Seventeen

Tory couldn't believe it. She just couldn't fathom the words she'd heard. What could have possessed her father to have changed his will? And to have given Rhys a share in what was rightfully hers alone? It mattered little to her at that moment that she controlled the vast Reitenauer business interests; her home had been purloined. The very same ranch that she had married to secure.

Had this been Sam's idea of a cruel joke?

If so, why?

Rhys must have known about it. That particular thought hammered at her brain. Doubt went deeper, like a nail driven home with great force. Had Sam discussed it with him?

Tory reached behind her back and undid the buttons on her dress in a hurry, not really caring if she tore the material. She wanted to remove the garment as quickly as possible.

Her husband was now a very wealthy man, by anyone's standards. The money alone that Sam gave him was enough to ensure that. But as half owner of one of the largest ranches in Texas, he had power and influence.

She kicked the gown aside as if it were offensive, little caring about the damage she might do. Her gaze fell onto the bed, covers still tossed. Her stomach lurched sickeningly. They'd shared this bed, her bed, these last two nights. Lain in each others arms, and sought comfort.

Cold comfort, Tory thought now.

Had she meant anything to him besides a way to recoup his finances? Had all his apparent honesty about his motives for wedding her been a careful ploy, part of a larger, more grandiose scheme to win a bigger slice of the Reitenauer fortune? Had his lovemaking been only a means to an end? A way to gain a hold over her?

All a lie, she thought. All his tender gestures and kind words. And the worst lie of all was that she *believed*, that she *trusted*.

She'd been a damned fool; she had made it all so easy for him.

Images came back with clarity to haunt her, to mock her. His hands, those purveyors of magic, skimming over her naked flesh, conjuring up a response from deep within her; those lips, murmuring words of delight, spoken in that liquid gold tone, lush with hidden meaning; that lean, hard body driving into hers, at times with slow care, at others, with powerful abandon.

Was it all a ruse?

He could see her mourning clothes scattered across the floor as he stood in the doorway that connected their rooms. Here the dress, there a silk stocking or a petticoat, carelessly abandoned.

Rhys was as shocked as she when he heard the will. He hadn't expected either the money or the interest in the ranch. That Sam was so generous to him came as just as big a surprise as it did to his wife. He'd seen the look of astonishment on her features before she schooled her expression to one of calm. Now that he knew Victoria, he knew that that outward appearance of calm was just a mask. The calm was dangerous.

What must she be thinking?

Her appearance led him to think once more of the proud amazon of their first meeting. One foot was on a chair as she leaned over to fasten the ties of her knee-high moccasins.

He'd come to tell Victoria that he didn't care a tinker's farthing about his so-called inheritance. The money didn't matter to him. He was willing to relinquish it all to her. At their first meeting, he had told Sam that he wouldn't take any further funds from him. Rhys meant what he said. All he wanted was his wife and a life together.

"Victoria."

Tory turned to face him, hating the effect the sound of his silky voice had on her. She could recall her name said in the heat of passion, and her reaction, shivering with all the need he'd brought to the fore.

In her eyes Rhys could see the cold fury of her temper. He had to make her see reason. But could he?

"Get out of my room," she said, her voice dripping frost.

"No." He wasn't going anywhere until she listened to him.

"According to my father's will, you are entitled to half the Encantadora. Well," she said, looking every inch the imperious lady of the manor despite her mode of dress, "this is *my* half and you are not welcome."

He watched in silence as she tugged the wedding ring from her slim finger and dropped it on her dressing table.

"We have to talk."

"About what?" she snapped. "I would have thought you'd be celebrating your astonishing good luck. You're a very rich man, Rhys. Money *and* property."

"I didn't know about your father's plan."

"Oh, no?"

"You can't believe I would have kept this from you had I known?"

She shrugged her shoulders. "Why not?"

"Can you honestly dismiss what we felt for each other?" he asked, knowing that he was fighting for their future happiness.

"Oh, that," Tory said coldly, lashing out at

what she perceived was a betrayal of her trust. "A tumble was all it was to you. A way to relieve your boredom and secure your position."

"You don't really believe that?" Rhys reached out his hand to Victoria and saw her flinch from his touch and step back. That gesture hurt.

"You despicable bastard," she hissed. "I gave you my trust. It makes me sick to think that I also gave you my body." And, she thought, not able to say the words aloud, her love. All she had to give.

"Victoria, I love you," Rhys stated.

"A very nice touch, my lord. So very sincere." Her voice was laced with a sneering overtone.

"What have I done to deserve this?"

"Robbed me of my home."

"You can have the bloody place for all I care," he shouted. "Will that satisfy you?"

"No."

Rhys approached Tory again, trying to make her see that he was sincere, that his love for her was real and completely honest. What happened next came so fast that he didn't have time to react. He could only feel the hot sting of metal across his arm, slicing through the fabric of his coat and the shirt beneath.

He stared at the knife in her hand, at the blood, his blood, that wet the tip. His gaze went to the wound she had inflicted.

"Keep your distance," she said through gritted teeth.

"All right," Rhys conceded. He took a step

back from her, thinking that she was like a wounded vixen, striking out.

Tory replaced her knife in its sheath. She hadn't thought, merely reacted. When he went to draw her into his embrace, she knew that she couldn't allow him to touch her, and she instinctively drew her knife in defense. Her blade hadn't gone bone deep, just enough to make him keep his distance.

Why didn't he leave? Or shout? He didn't even seem angry.

Rhys made no move to staunch the flow of blood that seeped from the wound, so Tory was forced to act. She went to her wardrobe and flung open the door, removing the first item she found. She tossed it to him.

Rhys caught the bridal *mantilla* and wrapped it about his arm. Both watched as the blood stained the white material.

"What do you want, Victoria?"

"To be left alone, my lord." There was a trace of sadness to her tone.

Rhys sighed. "Don't let what you're feeling now destroy what we had." He began to walk towards his own room. He stopped and turned to face her. "I love you," he repeated softly. "Trust me once again, Victoria. That's all I ask of you."

"Trust?" She had trusted him and where had it gotten her? "I *did* trust you. My mistake."

"It was no mistake. Listen to your heart. I did," he admitted. "Then you will know the truth."

"The truth is that you married me for gain. I

forgot that, as you wanted me to, when you seduced me."

"I didn't force you."

Tory blushed. His words brought to mind her fervent response to his skilled lovemaking.

"Suppose you are with child?"

Tory's hand went instantly to her flat stomach. Her face drained of color.

"Oh my God," she exclaimed.

"You could be carrying our baby, even now."

"Do you want it?"

"What?" he asked blankly.

"Do you want it if I am?"

Rhys came closer. "What kind of question is that?" he demanded.

"An honest one," she said. "Would you want a child enough to sign over your share of the ranch?"

Now it was Rhys's turn to blanch. *Christ*, he mentally swore, she couldn't mean it. "You're joking."

"I'm serious," she insisted.

"You would barter your own child?"

Said like that, the ugliness of it hit Tory square in the chest, making her stomach twist and bile rise in her throat. She could never do that, she thought. But he didn't have to know that.

Her silence seemed to speak volumes to him. "You coldhearted bitch!" Rhys said, all stiff formality, his left hand gripping tightly the piece of cloth on his right arm. "If you will excuse me, *my lady*." He left the room.

As long as Tory lived, she would never forget the look of abject horror in Rhys's gray eyes. She wanted to call back the silence and deny she would ever willingly give up her child. Their child. But it was too late.

It was too late.

Worse than the slice of the blade was the slash of her words. Did she hate him that much? So much so that should they have a child, she would want to divest herself of the responsibility?

"My lord," Twinnings gasped, "what has happened?" He rushed in the door, careful not to spill the decanter of brandy that Rhys had ordered brought to his room.

"Get me a wet cloth," Rhys ordered.

Twinnings set down his burden and hurried to the adjoining bathroom. He returned moments later, a thick towel and a bowl of water in hand.

Rhys had removed his jacket and was in the process of stripping off his shirt. He looked at the track that the blade of the knife made in his skin. His wife's handiwork would undoubtably leave a scar.

Twinnings dipped the cloth in the cold water and washed away the blood, trying not to exacerbate the wound further. His lordship remained silent throughout the procedure. Only one person could have inflicted this damage on the earl. But why?

Rhys knew that Twinnings was bursting to ask about the circumstances. Only strict training held his manservant in check.

"Find something to bind the wound," Rhys insisted.

"What about this, my lord?" Twinnings asked, picking up the *mantilla*. "I could cut off a clean section."

"No!" Rhys protested. "Take one of my shirts instead." He held out his hand, demanding the piece of material.

Twinnings gave it back to Rhys while he went to the capacious *armoire* to fetch a shirt.

"It will have to be cauterized also, my lord," Twinnings stated.

"Yes," Rhys agreed. "I thought as much."

"Perhaps you'd best have a large snifter of the brandy, my lord."

"A very good idea, Twinnings. I think I would like that." Brandy to numb the senses, though naught would numb the pain that was etched in his soul.

Damn you, Samuel Reitenauer, Rhys thought. *Your kindness has cost me dearly. It is all so ironic: those you sought to push together have been torn apart.* While Twinnings attended to heating the poker in the flames of the fireplace, Rhys clutched the lace in his hand, not letting it go even as he drank the brandy with what he would once have considered indecent haste.

"Are you ready, my lord?" Twinnings asked, the tip of the poker red-hot.

"Do it," Rhys said, placing the glass on the floor next to his chair, holding out his arm, his fist clenched tightly. His left hand grasped the arm of the chair, the *mantilla* spilling over the

355

furniture and over his thigh. Rhys clamped his mouth shut, his teeth gritted. He endured the pain of the hot metal as it sealed the wound. How he wished, at that moment, that he could still the flood of bitter memories from his heart, to cauterize them with as much skill as Twinnings employed on his flesh.

Rhys sat as Twinnings finished his task methodically, deciding that he should put some distance between himself and his wife. A return to his estates in England seemed a good idea. Time would serve them well, giving each a chance to sort through the unexpected crisis that had befallen their marriage.

"Twinnings, fetch me some of my private paper. I have a document that I want you to witness after I've finished drafting it. And," Rhys demanded, "pack a bag; enough clothes to see me back to England."

Twinnings couldn't hide his satisfaction. "We're finally returning home. Very good, my lord," he said, setting about his task with a smile.

Home.

He watched as Twinnings went about packing a small traveling bag. On the side, stamped into the leather, were his initials and his motto.

He moved to the small writing desk and dipped the pen into the crystal inkwell. The stamp of his heritage was also deeply imprinted on the paper he chose. It was a deliberate choice, as the desk was filled with stationery, all embossed with the Reitenauer **R**. No mistake must be made. The message he was to leave must be clear.

Rhys read over what he'd written. Satisfied, he summoned Twinnings.

"I need your signature."

Twinnings took the pen from his master's hand and hesitated when he saw what the document contained.

Rhys saw his man's hesitation and the look of concern that shadowed his face. "Do it," he said.

"My lord . . ." Twinnings began to speak.

"Do not put a voice to your fears. This is as it should be," Rhys responded.

Twinnings saw the fierce look of determined pride in the gray eyes of the earl and obeyed with haste.

Rhys pushed back his chair and rose. "Fetch me Kincaid. I would speak with him."

Waking from a fitful sleep, Tory crept quietly down the wide stairs, anxious to find a place of refuge, of solace. Her bedroom no longer afforded her that. It was instead a place full of insidious memories. If she closed her eyes she was assailed by either graphic remembrances of her and Rhys, locked in passionate embraces, their bodies blended; or she would see again the clear picture of herself holding her Bowie knife, the blade red with her husband's blood.

The door to the library was open.

Don Sebastian needed time to himself. Leaving his wife sleeping in the bedroom they had been assigned, her soft snores piercing the otherwise silent night, he hastily dressed and slipped out.

He sat alone in the darkness, thinking about the events of the last three days. So much had happened, so much upheaval in their lives, especially those of his godchild and her husband.

He recalled not so much the look on Victoria's face when the will was being read as the change in the color of her eyes: from grief's paleness to anger's intensity, from soft water to hard stone. And then he cast his glance at her husband, whose eyes also reflected the turbulence that his well-schooled face could not.

Had he been less an honest man and more of a selfish one, he would have rejoiced to see the chasm that had opened up in the foundation of their marriage. However much it gave him inner pain, Don Sebastian could not ignore the force of the formidable desire between Victoria and the earl. Nor the salient fact that they were in love. Lust alone was not the motivating factor, for lust, as Don Sebastian understood it, was clean and simple; love, on the other hand, could be dark and complex, depending on the individuals. It was that way, he observed, for Victoria and Rhys.

Even though the room was cloaked in the blackness of the night, he saw the movement of a shadowy figure in the room as the door opened. Alert, he waited.

Encantadora

The room was bathed in a soft light as the figure lit a nearby lamp.

Her gasp was audible. *"Tío,"* Tory said, her hand to her throat.

"Sí," he said, rising slightly in his seat.

Tory waved her hand, indicating that she did not wish him to rise on her account from what appeared to be a comfortable position.

"It would seem that we both are in need of shelter," he stated.

"Shelter?" she asked in a quiet tone, walking over to where he was, kneeling on the floor at his feet. "Perhaps," Tory said as she shifted position and drew her knees up, resting her chin on them as she leaned back against his trousered leg and the chair.

Don Sebastian reached out his brown hand, marking the contrast between his skin and the color of her unbound hair, like golden fire. He lightly touched the crown of Tory's head before folding his hand tightly into a fist and drawing it back.

"Tío," Tory began, "I don't know what to do." Her voice was low, more of a whisper.

"About what, *niña?*" he asked.

"I miss him so much," she said, "and yet I don't understand why he did what he did."

"Your papa was a wise man, *cara,* and a fair one. He did what he thought was best."

"What about what *I* think is best?"

At that, Don Sebastian's thin mouth curved into an amused smile. Neither of his children would have thought to ask that of him. And that was not because they were weak-willed or lacked courage; they trusted his judgment, respected their traditions. Victoria's iconoclastic upbringing, coupled with her own stubborn determination, led her to question. It was, he recognized, an essential part of her nature.

"So," he inquired, "what do you think about it?"

Tory answered truthfully. She knew no other way. "I was hurt, *Tío*. Papa should have told me."

"Was the *rancho* his to dispose of?"

"Yes," she admitted honestly.

"Then we agree that he was free to leave it as he instructed. My friend Sam was a man who believed in his own ability to judge people. For him to split the *rancho*, he must have had great faith in your *esposo*. Sam, as well you know, was no one's fool."

"In that he is much like you, *Tío*." Tory turned so that she was facing Don Sebastian. "I have always looked to you as if you were my second father."

"You do me much honor, Victoria," Don Sebastian said. His silent heart knew the wound her gentle, loving words were inflicting. They were splinters of kindness, sinking deep. "As to what I would have done . . . perhaps the same as he."

Tory was shocked. "Really?"

"Why not?" he insisted. "This *Inglés* is your wedded husband. Sam knew what this land means to you. Perhaps it was his way of solidifying your marriage. To give you and the earl something to share besides a name."

Tory stood up, her arms wrapped around her middle. "You think so?"

"Even I can see that the *Inglés* has deep feelings for you. It is there in the way that he watches you, in how he speaks of you, in his every gesture."

Tory was surprised by Don Sebastian's comments. "How can you be so very sure?"

Don Sebastian rose from his chair and took the few steps that would lead him to her. He placed a hand on her arm, feeling the weight of the turquoise and silver bracelet beneath the white linen shirt she wore. "It is easy to recognize a man in love."

"Why wouldn't I have seen love in him?"

"My dear child," Don Sebastian began and then paused, as if gathering strength, "because at times, Victoria, you are indeed a child. A sweet, wild child who sees life as she chooses it—on her own terms." He took a deep breath, fully aware that he would have to give her an example, aware too of what this would cost him, and her. "I, too, love you."

Tory smiled, her hand squeezing his. "I know, *Tío*. I love you, also."

"*Amada*," he said, "you still do not see, do you?"

Tory stared at him, blinking slightly. "What are you talking about?"

"See with your woman's heart, not with a

child's eye." He stepped closer to her and bent his head, touching his lips to hers. Sliding his arms around her waist, he drew her close.

Tory was momentarily shocked. She couldn't believe what was happening. Her beloved family friend, the man she thought of as "uncle," was kissing her deeply, with a lover's passion. Frozen to the spot, Tory could only stand there.

Don Sebastian lifted his face from hers and ran his hand in a soft caress across her cheek, catching the tear there. "Do you *see* now?"

Tory met his gaze, eye to eye. Stripped of any illusions, in those dark orbs she recognized the love he had for her: not that of a relative, but rather a man's for a woman.

Tory leaned forward, one hand on his broad shoulder, and sweetly touched her lips to his. Softly, she said, "I'm so sorry."

Don Sebastian was right. Tory had seen only what she wanted to see and was impervious to all else. In her heart, she saw how much it must have cost Don Sebastian to toss aside his considerable pride and control to remove the blinders from her eyes. That, taken with his actions, humbled her.

"Do not be sad, *querida*," he said. "I know that you will keep my secret. And"—he smiled—"we shall never speak of it again."

"As you wish, *Tío*. Now, if you will excuse me, I think it best if I try and get some sleep."

"*Buenas noches*, Victoria."

"And to you also, uncle," she answered in English.

Upstairs in her room, Tory quickly stripped off her clothes. Climbing into her bed, she cast a long glance towards the door to Rhys's room. Such a relatively short distance separated them. All she had to do was walk through the battlefield of distrust, pride, and anger to reach her objective.

But not now. Not tonight.

She would marshal her forces for the reckoning to come.

Chapter Eighteen

Tory placed a single red rose on Samuel Reitenauer's fresh grave. The mid-afternoon sun was warm, penetrating the cotton shirt she wore. She shifted her position so that she was under the large live oak, sheltered beneath its branches. An air of serenity washed over her, bathing her in a feeling of calm.

She heard the sounds of the ranch going on around her. Her head lifted and her gaze scanned the rolling hills, catching sight of the mares and foals in one corral. Raven, her wedding gift from Don Sebastian, was frisking playfully with several other colts, prancing and preening.

The excited yap of the dogs as they herded the sheep in another corral drew her attention. Tory watched as the pups moved efficiently around the larger animals. A smile graced her face.

Tory's attention was drawn to several of her men working at various occupations. MacTavish was making a new shoe for Ace's horse, his burly body bent to his task, sweat staining his shirt. Freshly laundered clothes were being hung on the line, the slight breeze making them snap. A cowboy rolled a smoke while another worked on mending his lariat. A woman was digging in the communal garden, harvesting vegetables for her evening meal, with a happy toddler in tow, who wanted to join in with what her mother was doing.

All around her was life.

It went on, as she must.

Her hand slipped to her stomach. Perhaps, she thought, life existed there as well. Hers. Rhys's. A continuation of the legacy of the Encantadora.

Her gaze shifted once more to Sam's grave. Her father had been a man to take chances, make choices. So could she. Love was a choice: a courageous, challenging choice. And Tory loved a challenge. Rhys was that to her. An invitation to live deeply, to love passionately, to experience all that was possible. On so many levels he was the man for her.

Ah, Papa, she thought, you were right. He *is* the man for me. I *am* the woman for him. For I do love Rhys, for all that he is and more. No more doubts. No more hesitations.

She walked briskly down the well-trodden path, heading for the house. She and Rhys had to talk. So many things were clearer to her now.

"Miss Tory. Miss Tory," called Ruth, rushing after her.

Tory stopped, turning to see what was wrong. She could tell from the sound of Ruth's voice that it was urgent.

"You've got to come with me, now," the girl implored.

"What's the matter?"

"It's Diego."

Tory recognized the name of the young cowboy who'd been shot and left for dead, along with her father. "Has he come round?"

"Yes," Ruth said, taking a deep breath. Her heart was hammering, both from her run and from the fact that she was so happy. Diego was quite special to her; she'd volunteered to help with his care so that she could keep watch over him personally.

Tory was aware of the younger girl's feelings for the handsome *vaquero*.

"Papa said to fetch you so that Diego could tell you himself who it was that shot your pa."

That was all that Tory needed to hear. She turned towards the direction from which Ruth had come and began to run.

Tory burst through the door, startling the people gathered there. "Excuse me, *señora*," Tory said as she saw the look of stunned happiness on Diego's mother's face.

"It is a miracle, *patrona*," the woman declared.

Tory nodded and replied, *"Sí, es un milagro."*

Encantadora

She approached the youth's bedside in the next room.

Diego, his normally olive skin pale from his ordeal, managed to sit up. A bandage covered most of his left side.

Ruth hurried in, taking up a place at his side, her hand in his after giving him a drink of water. Marsh and Diego's mother followed.

"Patrona," Diego began, "I am so sorry about *el patrón."*

Tory accepted the young man's comments, feeling a twinge of guilt that she hadn't given any of her time to him. So much had happened these past few days that she neglected her duty to the welfare of one of her own. She went to his bed. Instantly a chair was pushed so that she could sit. "It is I who should beg forgiveness for not having come sooner," she said, reaching out her hand to take one of his.

Diego flushed with gratitude and pride. It was a lucky *hombre*, he thought, who could have two beautiful women at his bed.

"I understand you know who did this to you, and who murdered my father."

"Sí, patrona," he said, "I heard your father call him by name."

Tory gasped. "Had you ever seen this man before?"

Diego shook his head. "No, *patrona*," he answered, "but your father knew him."

"He did?"

"Sí." Diego took another sip of the water that Ruth handed him. *"El patrón* recognized him."

"Tell me what happened. From the beginning."

"Your father wanted to go to San Antonio, to take care of some business, as I understood. I asked to accompany him, to be one of his escorts so that I could call on my uncle and his family.

"We rode out early, with only a small force, never believing that anyone would dare to harm the *patrón* of *Rancho Encantadora*. Your father, he was most anxious to get to San Antonio. We rode quickly until the first shot."

"Who fired?"

"That I do not know, only that the man to my right was killed instantly. As I made to pull out my rifle, it was shot from my hand. Within seconds we were surrounded by a large force of armed men. It was then that I saw your father's face. He was shocked. I could tell by the look on his face that he knew one of the men. Such an evil face that one had. With the cold eyes of a dead man. The *patrón* demanded to know what this other man wanted, and why was his man harmed?

"It was then that this man laughed. Such a sick thing I have never heard before. This *malvado* looked at your father and spat at the ground. He said that he wanted revenge."

"For what?"

"For a past wrong, he said. It was then that your father spoke a name."

"Which was?"

"Tom Sanders. The man laughed and said that

he was once known by that, but no longer. Now he was Talbot Squire."

Tory repeated the name. "Talbot Squire." She too recognized the man's other name. She had thought him gone years past, a bad seed removed from their midst.

"*Sí*, patrona. That is the name. *El patrón* demanded again what he wantcd." Diego paused, recalling with horror what came next. "This man told your father he wanted *el patrón* dead. He continued by saying that he desired that more than anything in the world, except . . . " Here Diego paused once again in his narrative, his free hand working the cotton of his bcdsheet.

"Except what?" Tory queried, her blood chilling by degrees as she listened to the *vaquero*'s words.

"Except to have you, *patrona*, as his personal *puta*."

A shocked gasp was heard from almost all in the room.

"Go on," Tory insisted.

The youth's dark eyes began to fill with tears. "It was then the *el patrón* lunged for him. Another man hit your father with the butt of his rifle and knocked him to the ground. I went for my *pistola*. What happened next came very quickly. I felt two bullets hit me, knocking me to the ground. While I lay there, I saw the man called Talbot Squire pull out his gun as your father stood up. He fired at *el patrón*, who died instantly. It was then I lost consciousness. When I came to, I was alone with our dead."

Tory spoke, her voice cold and sure. "He will pay, that I can promise you. By his actions he has signed his death warrant.

"Now you must rest," Tory said, standing up. "I thank you for all your help, and wish you health."

Diego, exhausted from both his wound and from talking, managed to get out a warning. "Be careful of this man, *patrona*."

"Don't worry, Diego. It is this Talbot Squire who should beware," she insisted, her fingers straying to the sheath that held her knife, "for he is a dead man."

Tory walked back to her house through the garden, ignoring the delicious smell of the roses, her mind instead on what she had to do.

It would be too late to try and contact the Federal marshal. Besides, it was her problem and she would handle it. Talbot Squire would pay for what he did. She needed no one to give her permission to exact retribution. Her father's murderer would be caught and punished. After leaving Diego's bedside, she informed Marsh that she wanted men ready to ride within the hour.

She had to find Rhys and talk to him. So much had changed that she didn't know where to begin. Or maybe she did—simply saying that she loved him.

Tory entered through the kitchen, her soft

boots making no sound on the stone floor. There she found Kristen, her arms coated in flour, rolling out a pie. Tory noted these last few days that the smell of baked goods and the abundance of such was Kristen's way of working through her grief. She kept busy.

Tory called the cook's name softly so as not to startle her.

Kristen's head snapped up. "Ah, baroness. I did not hear you come in."

"No matter," Tory stated. "What I want to know is, have you served breakfast to my husband yet?"

Kristen looked at Tory with eyes that reflected her puzzlement. "*Ja*, baroness, some hours ago his man came to get him something before they left. I even fixed something for their trip."

"Left?" Tory stood, her arms akimbo. "For where?"

"I was not told the destination, only that they would be leaving after the *Graf* had eaten."

"What time was this?"

"Very early."

Where had Rhys gone? And why now?

"What about you, baroness, would you like something to eat?"

Tory, lost in thought, did not reply.

Kristen repeated herself. "Baroness?"

"Nothing, *danke*, Kristen." Maybe there was some kind of clue in his room. She dashed up the back stairs to the wing that housed their rooms, eager to see if there was something, anything, that would give her some explanation.

371

She flung open the door to his room. No longer would she think of it as belonging to her brother Travis. Rhys had so firmly placed his stamp on it that it would always be *his*.

She walked in, moving past the bed to the wardrobe. There were still clothes hanging there. She entered the bathroom. Gone were his personal grooming articles. No brush of silver rested on the lace covering of the low chest that held bath linens. No comb of ivory, nor pearl-handled razor lay there. His shaving mug and brush were missing also.

He *was* gone.

A spasm of emptiness gripped her. Her head bowed and her fists clenched, she walked back into the bedroom. It was then that she noticed her bridal *mantilla* on the bed—and something else.

Tory sank down on the mattress, reaching for the cream-colored envelope that bore her name. She turned it over, breaking the wax seal. Rhys's seal. She withdrew the single sheet of expensive paper that carried his crest. The words inside were simple, and so very direct.

Victoria:
I, Rhys Alexander Fitzgerald Buchanan, do hereby relinquish any claims to the property known as Encantadora in the state of Texas.
My honor is not for sale. It never has been, nor will it ever be.
Neither is my love.

Tory closed her eyes for a moment before focusing once again on the words so carefully written. The letter was signed with a bold masculine hand. *Derran.*

She saw also the other, smaller signature which witnessed the document: Albert Twinnings.

A legal farewell. That's what it translated to her.

Tears stung her eyes. She was damned if she'd just let him go, she thought. She raised her left hand, the hand that clutched the thick sheet of vellum. Her wedding ring was once more on her finger. Slowly, a smile on her face, Tory ripped the paper in half, then half again. A document was only legal if it existed.

She dumped the shreds onto the quilt, picking up the *mantilla*, noting the stains of blood. Her fingers caressed the material slowly. Tory brought it to her lips, kissing the crimson stains. "I swear by the blood of my honor and yours, we *shall* be together, Rhys. It is not too late. It will never be too late for us."

Chapter Nineteen

Goddamn his arrogance!

This thought was uppermost in Rhys's mind as he prowled the confines of the small room. He pulled at the thick metal manacles that bound his wrists, the chains rattling as he moved. His skin was rubbed raw from trying to break free from his bonds, and his arm ached from the still tender knife wound.

What utter, colossal foolishness had lead him here, trapped, a prisoner of a man who enjoyed destroying life?

Because of him four men had died. He was sure to be the fifth.

At least Twinnings' death would not be on his conscience. His manservant had been spared the slaughter so that he could deliver a message to Victoria.

Rhys's smile was edged with cynicism. This Talbot Squire was unaware of the true situation between him and his wife, else he would not have bothered to send a much distressed Twinnings back to the Encantadora to deliver the ultimatum. Rhys had to watch, helpless to prevent the men from being killed or Twinnings from being severely beaten. What sickened him was the knowledge that had he not demanded an escort, forcing Marshall to accede to his wishes, this might all have been prevented.

He thought he'd been leaving for all the right reasons, giving Victoria time to think, time to remember what had transpired between them. Returning to London would serve as a time of truce, a chance to settle family and estate matters.

He heard in the realm of his mind Squire's cold words to Twinnings. The message that the valet was expected to deliver was simple. An outrageous sum of money was named for his ransom, and it was to be personally delivered by Victoria Reitenauer herself. No force of men was to accompany her, else Rhys would be killed.

That Squire planned to kill him no matter what his wife did was evident to Rhys. He'd seen too much, and dead men bore no witness.

Rhys could appreciate the irony of the moment. Squire had no inkling of the reason for his leaving the Encantadora. Why should Victoria care if he was being held against his will? After all, had she not tried to wound him herself?

Didn't the words of contempt that she'd thrown at him still echo in his ears?

How long did he have left?

To have it all end here, a prisoner, ignominiously bound and treated with disdain . . . what irony. To discover love and lose it, along with his life.

Rhys dropped to the iron bed with its bare horsehair mattress. He hoped Tory was safe, that she would not be caught in this madman's web of lies and murder. He closed his eyes and filled his mind with pictures of her—how she looked when first they met, how her eyes sparkled with challenge when they argued politics, the intense sensuality she presented when she wore the Worth gown at Don Sebastian's, all the ways she was, pensive, happy, sad, triumphant.

Tory.

He bitterly regretted that he'd dismissed Marshall's warnings about traveling. He'd ignored the foreman's words, insisting that he would take an escort made from Don Sebastian's men instead of men from the Encantadora. This, he thought, would draw less attention. Four men paid the ultimate price for his demands.

Tory would have found the note he left her by now. Perhaps it would convince her that he meant what he'd said. He loved her more than his life.

The door to the hovel posing as a room opened and Talbot Squire walked in, confident that his grandiose schemes were coming to fruition. A sneer twisted his thin lips.

"Evening," he said, as if they were best of friends and this was no out-of-the-ordinary experience.

Rhys watched him carefully, never taking his eyes from the man. That Squire had come to gloat was obvious.

"Not so very fine now, are ya?" Squire mocked.

Rhys continued to stare at him in silence, contempt evident in his eyes.

"Doesn't really matter if your wife pays the money or not, I aim to kill you, just like I did her pa," he boasted.

Once the thought of killing another human being had been abhorent to Rhys; now, with this man, he was certain that he could do it cheerfully. He could dispose of this piece of human offal without regret, especially knowing how much of a threat he posed to Tory.

As he asked the question, "Why?", out loud, Rhys imagined putting his hands around the man's throat and squeezing.

Talbot felt inclined to answer the question, for he didn't fear his pampered prisoner. What harm could this dandy do him? Besides, it would give him pleasure to make this foreigner aware of his power.

"You want to know why?" Squire walked closer to Rhys. "To make them both pay for what they did to me."

He leaned over, his fetid breath making Rhys's stomach lurch, even as Squire's fetid mind made him recoil.

"The bitch knifed me," Squire stated, his eyes gleaming with implacable hatred.

Rhys could now understand such hatred; he felt it for this man. "Tory must have had a good reason," Rhys suggested.

"Good reason?" Squires said in a soft voice. He stepped back. "Good reason?" he said louder. "No, she didn't, the bitch."

"Then why would she have done such a thing?" Rhys posed logically. His ancestors would have known what to do to a man like this, Rhys thought. Drawn and quartered, with his head stricken from his body and perched on a pike. At times like these, he acknowledged, there was a lot to be said for the old ways.

"She did it over a woman. Some greaser slut who meant nothing."

"Obviously not to my wife."

"Your wife." Squire's mouth curled. "Well, fancy man, I will *have* your wife, and soon. She owes me and I intend that the bitch should pay. Think on that. The proud Tory Reitenauer being taken like any common slut."

Rhys's face was a portrait of cold fury. Hate darkened his eyes to slate. As he made to lunge for Squire, the butt of Squire's rifle hit him square in the side.

Pain exploded in Rhys. He fell back against the mattress, clutching his side, his breath labored.

"Maybe I'll even let you watch. How'd you like that, fancy man?" Squire said, his voice rising with an almost hysterical note.

"You filthy bastard," Rhys managed through pain-gritted teeth.

"Yeah," he added as he was walking out the door, "I think it'll be fun to let you watch. Hell, maybe I'll treat some of my hands and let them have a go at her. She won't be so high and mighty then, will she?" Squire slammed the door, his malicious laughter finally dissipating.

Earlier, Rhys had hungered for Tory's love; now he prayed that he commanded her hate, for that was the only way he could keep her safe. And that was tenuous at best, Rhys knew, for as long as Talbot Squire was alive he would pose a deadly threat.

The answer was simple: Talbot Squire must die.

Tory studied the map set out before her in what had been Sam's office and was now hers. She knew that what she was planning was risky, since it involved leaving only a small contingent of hands on duty at the Encantadora.

"I have already sent word to my *segundo*," Don Sebastian said over her shoulder. "He should be arriving shortly with the men that I requested."

Tory lifted her head, tilting it sideways to peer into Don Sebastian's face. "*Gracias, Tío*," she replied. "I will need them if my plan is to succeed. That this Squire has had spies at the ranch is without doubt. I don't want the dispersal of men to be noticed. If it appears that they are merely going about their usual duties, before meeting Marsh at the agreed rendezvous, then fine." Tory dropped her gaze back to the map, massaging the bridge of her nose with her thumb and index finger. She had a headache—and a heartache. Because of this information about who the killer of her father really was, she would have to postpone her reckoning with her husband. More than likely he'd gone to San Antonio, probably to secure whatever way he could to return to England.

No use trying to find him now, she thought. Her option was to make for England herself as soon as this ugly business was wrapped up. She had a small interest in a shipping line in New Orleans. She could book passage from there.

Her mind switched focus. She looked again at Don Sebastian. "You know that Rhys left me, don't you?"

Don Sebastian's brown eyes were somber. "*Sí*," I know," he admitted. "He came to me this morning and asked if I would permit him to have the use of some of my *vaqueros* to guide him safely to San Antonio." He shrugged. "I told him yes."

"Did he tell you why he was leaving?" Tory's face betrayed her concern. She wondered just how much of the story Rhys had related to Don Sebastian.

"He would tell me only that he had pressing

business back in England that could not be put off any longer."

"That's all?"

"No," he said, his tone soft, adding, "he spoke of his love for you, and asked that I keep watch over you, which I agreed to do." He looked at her. "Is there something else that he should have spoken of?"

Tory's long lashes hid her eyes from his view. "Just that we quarreled."

"And now you are sorry, is that it?"

"Yes," she responded, "so very sorry because I misjudged him."

"Then you must hasten to set the matter to rights," he advised.

"I intend to, *Tío*," she said, basking in the old feeling of comfort and amiability around him. "Just as soon as this other matter is resolved."

"You are determined to take this upon your own shoulders?"

"I have to. I cannot let my father's murderer, and the murderer of others on this ranch, get away. He must be caught and punished. It is justice."

At that moment a loud knock sounded on the office door. Before Tory could respond, it was opened and in walked Marsh. "Begging your pardon, Miss Tory, but you'd best be getting on outside and see who just arrived."

Tory stood, her eyes glowing. Rhys had returned.

She pushed past both men and ran down the

hallway and out the wide door. She scanned the area, looking for Rhys. What she saw was Rhys's manservant, Twinnings, being helped from a nondescript horse. He had obviously been beaten, for his face was puffy and discolored.

She gestured to two of her men. "Bring him into the house, quickly."

Summoning Janet, Tory instructed her to fetch water and bandages.

Twinnings was helped to a chair in the library. Marshall, Don Sebastian, and Tory hovered over him. "Brandy," Tory called.

Twinnings spoke in a small voice, "If you don't mind, my lady, I'd rather a strong cup of tea."

Janet was just entering with a bowl of warm water, a cloth, and a towel. Tory asked her to get Twinnings his tea.

Tory knelt on the floor by his chair, wiping the water-soaked cloth gently across his face, trying not to hurt him any further.

Twinnings was embarrassed by the fuss made over him, especially by his lord's lady. It wasn't seemly that she should be attending to him. He tried to summon the words. "My lady, please, you do not have to . . ."

Right then Tory wasn't interested in Twinnings' sense of class do's and don'ts. She wanted to know where Rhys was. "Tell me where my husband is," she demanded, ignoring the manservant's protestations.

Twinnings could see that she was upset—and

that she did truly care for the earl. It was in the tone of her voice. "I was sent," he said, gathering his strength to make his report, "to deliver a message to you. My Lord Derran is being held for ransom."

"Shit," was the succinct word that popped out of Marsh's mouth.

Tory rocked back on her heels. Rhys was a prisoner. A pain like the thrust of a knife sliced through her stomach. "No," she said in denial.

"He is, my lady."

"What about my men?" Don Sebastian asked. Twinnings' face was ashen. "They are all dead, sir."

"*Maldito sea!*" Don Sebastian cursed.

"What about Rhys?" Tory demanded. "Was he hurt?"

"Not so that I could tell, my lady," Twinnings said. She looked obviously distressed, more so than he would have expected after seeing what she had done to his lordship. In her eyes he could see the concern that shone through. It was not faked for the rest of the room. It was genuine and heartfelt.

"How much?"

Janet entered the room again, this time bearing a cup of steaming tea. She handed it to Twinnings as Tory stood up.

He sipped the strong brew. "Fifty thousand of your dollars was the sum the man mentioned."

The collected gasp echoed in the confines of the room.

"Fifty thousand," Tory repeated. "I don't keep that amount of money around. How long did he give me?"

"Till tomorrow, my lady. Begging your pardon, countess, I don't think he really wants the money, truth be told."

"What do you mean?"

"It was just the way he spoke, the look on his face. It was as if it were all part of a game that he was playing."

A chill invaded Tory's body. Up until now she had believed that the abduction of her husband was unrelated to her other problem; now, she was positive they were linked.

"Did he give his name?"

Twinnings shook his head.

"Describe him," Tory demanded.

Twinnings did so, to the best of his recollection.

"Squire," she said.

"Sure sounds like him, Miss Tory," Marsh agreed.

She strode quickly from the room. Marsh threw the Don a quizzical look. Don Sebastian returned the glance.

A few minutes later Tory returned. In her hands she held a velvet pouch. Opening up the gold ribbon that served as a drawstring, she emptied the contents onto the desk. The dazzling glimmer of diamonds sparkled brightly.

"This should suffice for his demands," she said.

"You can't be serious?" Don Sebastian demanded.

"Of course I am serious, *Tío*," she stated. "That *cochino* has my husband. Do you think I care this"—and she snapped her fingers—"for these stones?"

"*Sí*, he is a filthy pig, I agree with that, but what makes you think that he will honor the ransom that he has demanded?"

"I don't expect him to," she admitted.

"Then why the jewels?"

"Bait."

All eyes focused on Tory.

She directed her next question to Twinnings. "How was he to collect payment?"

"Two of his men escorted me to the borders of the ranch, my lady, before they released me. They are waiting for your answer at a grove of live oak that is due northwest of here."

"I know the spot," Tory replied.

"So do I," Marsh said. "It'll be easy to get them."

"No," Tory said.

"You aren't thinking about going with them yourself, are you?" Marsh asked.

"Of course."

"You cannot," Don Sebastian protested.

"I must." She leaned back on the desk, her face a mask of determination. "Don't you see that I must?"

"No, I don't," The Don replied.

"It's all perfect. Squire doesn't know that I

385

know he killed my father. He won't be expecting what I have planned for him."

"It's too dangerous, Miss Tory," Janet said.

"I have to," Tory stated simply. "He has my husband."

"Have you given thought to the idea that he may have already murdered the earl?" Don Sebastian asked.

Tory's face was pale; her hands gripped the edge of the desk tightly. She took a deep breath. "I have faced that possibility."

"And still you would put yourself in jeopardy?" Don Sebastian questioned.

"Yes."

The Don was sure that he knew the answer, but he felt he must ask. "Why?"

"Because I love him." Tory gathered the gems back into their container. "Besides, if Squire has harmed my husband, it will give me greater pleasure to kill him," she said softly.

All eyes in the room focused on her.

"I already have more than enough reasons to see him destroyed." She caressed the knife sheath. "If he's taken the most precious thing that I have left . . ." She let her sentence trail off, the meaning clear. "Now, it would seem," she said calmly, "that we have a few more things to discuss before we can put our plan into action."

Talbot Squire poured himself another large measure of whiskey, content that he was about to have it all. Everything had fallen into place.

Perhaps not quite as he planned it, but he was in control. The bitch didn't know he was behind the scheme to destroy the Reitenauers.

He gave a cursory thought to the man held in bondage. Didn't that prove that luck was with him? That he couldn't be stopped? To have the great fortune to have his bait fall into his lap?

Perfect.

Nothing could stop him now. Soon he would own the Encantadora. He'd already drawn up the document that would give him the property. He would force her to sign it, making, of course, false promises about sparing her if she did. Naturally, she would sign it. He had no doubts.

Nothing could stop him now.

She would ride into the lion's den, willingly.

Tory sat at her dressing table, staring into the image reflected back at her from the mirror which hung over it.

It was getting late.

She adjusted the light of the lamp, casting a soft glow about the room. Within the hour, dawn would break and she would be leaving.

Her strategy was, she hoped, foolproof. She'd adapted it from one of her brother's campaigns, recalling in vivid detail his letter explaining the maneuver to her. Travis had been a master chess player; military strategy was just another way to play a game.

A sudden shift in the wind blew the curtains. A feeling of intense peace seemed to settle over her, calming her fears. It was as if she could actually feel the spirit of her father and brother with her in the room, giving her their collective blessing.

She stood up.

It was time.

Chapter Twenty

Tory had been riding for nearly two hours when she and her men sighted the Squire property. She narrowed her eyes and inspected the general state of neglect. It was as bad as Hans Schmidt said it was, with not a care taken to the upkeep of the farm and its animals. The best thing to do would be to raze this entire place.

That was a promise that Tory made to herself and intended to keep when this business was finished.

Now to play out the hand. Well, perhaps not quite the hand that Squire believed he'd dealt her. She was gambling heavily, too heavily according to her friends. She had wagered that Squire thought her to be a fool, a lovesick female without sense. She was counting on him to swallow the lie that she was dumb enough to trust him to honor his word. A man like him didn't know anything about honor. Or love. She knew about both; they were what had led her to this place.

Tory didn't underestimate the danger inherent in her plan, yet she felt some risk must be taken to secure Rhys's freedom. She knew she'd admitted earlier the possibility that Rhys was already dead. She had, and then dismissed it. Somehow, some way, Tory was convinced she would have known it were it true.

A quiver of apprehension shook her.

There was no room for error in her plan of action.

No time for tears, fears, or backward glances. She took a deep, comforting breath, and prodded Abendstern forward.

Squire poured a large whiskey, congratulating himself on his good fortune. He stood by the window, watching as the Reitenauer bitch entered his trap. He downed the hard liquor in one deep swallow, wiping his hand across his thin lips.

Look at her, he thought, *riding in here like she was some kind of goddamn queen*. He refilled his glass. Well, Victoria Reitenauer wasn't gonna be so high and mighty when he was done with her. The idea of humbling her excited him. He could feel the tension seep into his groin, tightening his flesh. He slipped his hand down against the material of his trousers, thrilled with what he considered the absolute proof of his power. And he would use it against her. Slowly he stroked, visions of her helplessness giving him a shuddering thrill.

Rhys woke up.

He saw his reflection in the cracked mirror that hung to one side of the room. With a sardonic twist of his mouth, he considered his state. His silk shirt was torn, streaked with dirt, as was his face. He lifted his chained wrists and rubbed one hand across the black stubble on his face. He gave a little laugh and the pain ripped into his side, forcing him back to the thing that masqueraded as a bed.

Rhys tried to focus his mind away from the abyss of this nightmare onto other things.

As always, his thoughts turned to Tory. How natural that sounded now. Tory. Lady of his heart; woman of his soul.

He heard noise coming from outside and eased his aching body upward. He identified shouts and the sound of incoming horses. He hoped that it was Tory's reply to Squire's preposterous demands. Rhys could well imagine her messenger telling Squire he was welcome to go straight to hell for all she cared. He managed to maneuver himself around to the one small window, ringed by iron grills.

As if conjured up by his imagination, Rhys saw the figure approach. There was no mistaking the gleam of that hair or the straight set of that spine as she brought her mare to a halt.

A bitter pain, more intense than that which

afflicted his side, struck him in the belly. *No!* he wanted to shout. Not her. Not now. Not here.

He blinked. It was no dream. Tory was here. Yet, in the moment when despair scissored through him, hope was there to bind the wound.

She loved him!

That knowledge was both a blessing and a curse. For now *she* would be in danger. Sadly, Rhys decided that he could have been happier without her love if it would have guaranteed her safety.

Tory sat atop her mare, patting Abendstern's neck to soothe her. Her quick, darting gaze took in all of the surroundings. There didn't appear to be a surplus of men at this place. It had once been, she knew, a prosperous concern. No longer. What breeding stock she had seen was pathetic.

The door to the house opened and she saw him. He was older, but she recognized the man she had once stabbed in the back. Her gloved hands tightened on the leather reins. How she wanted to wipe that smirk off his face. This grinning animal had caused the deaths of too many good people, most especially her father, and justice for them weighed heavily on her mind.

But not yet, she mentally declared. The trap was not quite ready to spring.

Tory managed a cool, composed face. "You have something of mine that you wish to trade for?" she asked.

"You certainly get to the point," Squire said.

"No reason not to," Tory answered, still pretending that she didn't recognize him. She could see from the look on Talbot Squire's face that he expected her reaction to him to be different. Good. That gave her another advantage. Right now she needed every advantage she could muster.

"How 'bout you coming down off that horse of yours and into my house?"

"I would rather conduct my business in the open," she stated.

He laughed. "Still don't get it, do you, Miss Reitenauer? What you want here doesn't matter a damn." He snapped his fingers and several hands appeared with rifles drawn.

"What is the meaning of this?" she demanded.

"I'd have thought that was clear. You ain't going nowhere."

Tory managed to convey surprise. "What do you mean? I came here in good faith to pay the ransom you demanded for my husband who, I might add, I have yet to see."

"He's inside, waiting for you," Squire said, stepping back and indicating the opened door.

"I have what you want," Tory said, still maintaining her position astride her horse.

Squire's eyes gleamed with lust. "I know that you do," he responded, licking his lips.

Tory fought back the urge to purge her stomach of its contents.

"Get down," he snapped, losing what little patience he possessed.

Tory reached into her saddlebag and extracted a velvet pouch, tossing it to Squire. "That should be enough to secure my husband's release."

Squire caught the bag and hefted the weight. He then grabbed Abendstern's bridle. The horse responded by stepping back, pulling away.

Tory tried to calm the animal.

"You still don't understand, do you?" Squire asked. "What you want don't matter. Now, if you don't want this fine animal shot from beneath you, I reckon you'll be getting down and coming with me."

"What about my men?"

"They'd best be dropping their gunbelts before some of my men get a mite riled up."

"They'll want them back when we leave," Tory insisted. Could he seriously believe she was as naive as she sounded?

Talbot Squire gave her a false smile. "Sure thing," he said. *The stupid bitch!* Talbot was pleased that he had judged so well. She was far too proud and arrogant to suspect that he never meant to release her. So full of her her own importance, she thought all she had to do was ride in and demand and she would get. Not this time, he thought. It was his turn to call the shots.

Tory dismounted. She watched as her men surrendered their guns, happy that each carried a knife hidden in their boots. She gave a slight nod of her head as they were led away on foot towards the barn. Each man had been warned of the dangers should something go amiss with her plan. Her heart swelled with pride when all her hands volunteered to help her. Tory counted on the loyalty of her men. She doubted Talbot Squire could make the same claim.

Entering the house, Tory was struck by the darkness inside. It was damp and smelled musty. A fine coating of dust covered what little furniture she could see. A grimy oil lamp gave off a weak light.

"In here," Squire said, pushing open a door.

Tory followed. This once must have been a sitting room. A faded carpet showed signs of wear. The drapes, pulled against the midday sun, made it seem even gloomier. There were a couch and several chairs.

"Sit down," he ordered.

"I would prefer to conclude our business." Her tone was cool, brisk. "Where is my husband?"

Squire gave a tug on the curtains, flooding the room with sunlight. "There. Better, don't you think?"

He was stalling, Tory thought. Excellent! He was playing his hand as she believed he would, taking his time. He felt that she was the mouse and he the cat. His underestimation of her character would cost him.

"Didn't you think it may have been risky to come yourself?"

Tory faced him, her voice cold, her manner haughty. "I suggest we do away with conjecture and get down to the business at hand. You have my husband. I want him back, and I'm willing to pay what you ask.''

"So you say.''

Tory fixed her eyes on him. "See for yourself,'' she said, indicating the velvet pouch he still held in his hand.

Squire opened the drawstring and stared at the jewels that spilled into his palm.

"That is more than you demanded.''

"I guess so,'' he said, tossing the gems onto a small table that held a bottle of whiskey.

"Do we have a deal?'' she demanded.

"Not quite,'' he countered.

"What more do you want?''

"Your pride.''

"Are you insane?''

His laughter was mocking. "You stupid bitch,'' he sneered. "I could kill you now with no one the wiser.'' He opened the bottle and splashed some whiskey into a glass, handing it to her. When she didn't accept it, he drank it himself. "Too good to drink with me, eh?''

Tory could see the anger rising in his face. His eyes glittered with a nasty sheen. She willed herself to stay still, though her nerves were screaming inside her skin. She wanted to shout that she wasn't alone, that others knew where she was and with whom.

She called on that pride that he so carelessly damned for her strength. Caution. That's what she needed. And all the courage she could muster.

He walked over to her, his gaze running up

and down her body, lingering on the fit of her denim pants.

His look was like a dirty hand covered with mud, smearing her, soiling her.

When he reached out one of his hands to touch her, Tory batted it back. "Don't you touch me," she warned him.

"Or you'll what?" he retorted. "Use that fancy knife of yours?" Squire made a grab for it, ripping it from its sheath at Tory's waist. The thick blade gleamed. He held it up and waved it before her eyes, moving it closer to the skin of her cheek. "What would it take for you to beg, I wonder?" he asked, taunting her.

"You'll never know," she snapped.

"Wanna bet?"

Squire stepped back, calling out a name Tory didn't recognize. A man came to the doorway and stared at her.

"Fetch her husband," Squire commanded. "And," he added, "let's make this special. Drag Martha down here, and her bastard brat." The man departed and Squire smiled. He wanted Tory's humiliation to be witnessed by as many people as possible.

Squire poured another drink, dropping the knife next to the bottle. He hated Victoria Reitenauer for standing there as if she were better than he. He saw that in her eyes. He wanted to replace that look with fear, for then, he thought, he could control her.

"You don't know who I am, do you?"

She shrugged her shoulders. "Should I?"

With that casual remark, Squire struck Tory with the back of his hand. "Bitch!"

The blow knocked Tory backwards. She staggered against a chair, bracing herself.

"So, you don't even remember me, eh?" he persisted. "Well, I never forgot you." He walked over to her, bending down so that his face was close to hers. "I once worked for you." He stood up. "Maybe I shoulda showed you my back."

"Of what interest could that be to me?"

"Maybe if you saw the scar from your knife you would remember."

Tory feigned surprise. "My knife?"

"That's right, bitch. Your knife."

Tory stalled for more time, pretending to consider the matter before delivering her answer. "You're the pig that was trying to rape one of my servants. I remember now."

"Pig? You really are one stupid woman, do you know that?" Squire's twisted smile was filled with malice. "And like all women, you'll get what you deserve."

"Which is?" she asked.

A reply was denied to her as the door opened and two men with guns drawn escorted three more people into the room.

Tory's head turned and she saw a slender boy of about thirteen being shoved forcibly into the room. He lost his footing and sprawled onto the floor. Her gaze skimmed the boy's face. He had the look of a wounded animal; his eyes were dark blue, but there was a bleakness in them haunting in one so young. His face and body were thin, as if he hadn't been fed properly. A smell of unwashed flesh rose to her nostrils. She watched as the boy struggled to his feet. It was then that from the corner of her eye she caught sight of her husband being led in.

"Rhys!" The cry was torn from Tory's heart, so great was her joy at seeing her husband alive. That he was dirty, his hands bound behind him, his once fine clothes in tatters mattered little to her.

Tory leapt from her chair and ran to him, her arms sliding around his waist. She heard his deep, indrawn breath when she hugged him close. Her hand slipped upwards and felt the swelling at his side.

Rhys cared little about the pain. He thought he would never see her beloved face again, nor feel her warmth. But he would have gladly denied himself this most delicious of pleasures had it ensured that she was safe from this madman. "Oh, my love," Rhys spoke, his voice low and tender. "Why did you risk your life to come here?"

Tory tipped her head back, her blue eyes shimmering softly in the muted light. "I love you, Rhys," she whispered. "More, so much more, than anything." Tory knew that what she said to him was true. She loved Rhys Buchanan, and would have walked into hell itself if she had to to bargain with the devil for his life. He was, she had decided, worth any price, any risk.

"How very touching," Squire mocked. He signaled for his men to break Tory and Rhys apart. A blow from a rifle butt to his injured side brought Rhys to his knees. Squire grabbed hold of Tory's arm and twisted it, forcing her back.

She struggled to break his grip and succeeded. "Leave him alone!" she demanded.

"So," Squire considered aloud, "the bitch cares about him."

"Of course I do," Tory confessed, making her way back to Rhys.

"How much?"

Tory looked at Squire, not bothering to mask the hate that filled her eyes. "What do you mean?"

"How much is his life worth to you?"

"What more do you want?"

"I told you before. Your high and mighty pride. And you," he added, reaching out his hand to touch one thick braid, "as my whore."

"No!" Rhys shouted, getting to his feet, which earned him another blow from the man guarding him.

"Beg me," Squire demanded. "Beg me for his life."

Through the haze of pain that gripped him, Rhys managed to force the words from his mouth. "I shan't allow it, Tory. Not for me." The very idea of his wife on her knees to this scum was repugnant to him.

While Tory helped her husband to a chair, she saw someone else in the room. The woman sat on the faded couch, her eyes blank, hands folded primly in her lap. It was Martha Rayburne. The abused boy who stood numbly at her side must be her son, the child society had shunned her for bearing.

"Well," Squire insisted, "are you ready to bargain?"

Tory glanced at Rhys. Their gazes locked. His determination that she not humble herself to this man was evident in the direct appeal of his gray eyes. Tory looked away, her eyes drawn to Martha. For the flicker of an instant, she thought she saw the woman shake her head almost imperceptibly, indicating that she, too, believed it to be a wasted gesture.

"Do you need a lesson?" Squire asked. "Is that why you hesitate?" He walked over to where Rafe and Martha sat. He yanked the woman from her seat, his hand digging into her arm, bending it back as if to break it. He looked down at his stepson. "Go on, boy, beg me to let her go. Grovel like the dog you are," Squire taunted.

Rafe clenched his hands into fists so tight his bones stood out. If he refused, his mother would once more be subjected to his stepfather's cruelty. Rafe's own humiliation mattered little at this point. He would do what he must.

Tory and Rhys watched as the boy bent one leg, then the other, the struggle within him mirrored in the hard set of his young face. Tory could well imagine what it was costing this boy to submit to a man he hated.

"Let her go," Rafe asked.

"Please," Squire instructed.

His black head bent, the lad murmured softly, "Please."

Giving Martha's arm a vigorous twist, Squire let her go with an ugly laugh.

"Now, your turn," Squire insisted.

Tory stood up. "No," she said.

Squire's face screwed up in rage.

It was then that shouts from outside penetrated the room.

"Go see what's happening," he instructed the two men.

"You want one of us to stay here, boss?"

Squire gave them a dismissing look and placed his hand on the revolver at his side. "No need," he said. "I can take care of this lot."

The men trooped out, leaving Squire alone with Rhys, Tory, Rafe, and Martha.

Tory hoped that what had drawn the men outside was her men fulfilling their part of her plan. Diversions were needed for all of it to succeed. But she had others now to consider. It wasn't just her life and Rhys's now. Martha and her son were involved too.

"Maybe you don't believe me when I say that I'll kill your husband if you don't do what I say. You should," Squire said in a chilling tone, "since I've killed before."

"You have?" Tory asked, feigning horrified surprise.

He grinned, dirty teeth revealed. "Yes," he admitted proudly.

"Will you let us go if I do as you demand?" Tory took a step closer to her objective.

"I'll let your fancy man go." Squire took a step closer to her.

"What about your wife and her son?"

"I don't need them anymore," he said, not giving them even a glance, which was just as well, as Tory caught the slight movement of the other woman. "Both of them can go. I'm tired of them," he explained. "You, on the other hand could prove exciting, given the right opportunity."

Rhys, his gaze on Squire and his wife, also saw Martha's slow movements. The woman looked as if she were in a trance, obeying some unseen, unheard command. He moved his gaze back to Tory, wondering what she was up to. Squire was dangerous, and it appeared that Tory was deliberately provoking him.

"And you seriously think that I would allow you any opportunity?"

"Because if you don't, I'll gut-shoot your fancy husband right now. The choice is yours."

Tory knew he meant what he said. It was there in the bleakness of his eyes.

And what, she wondered, was Squire's wife up to?

"Will you oblige me now?" he snapped.

Tory turned her back on Squire, silently mouthing to Rhys, "Trust me," as she slipped the buckskin jacket she wore from her arms. She tossed it to the floor and turned around again.

Squire's greedy gaze fixed on Tory's high, full breasts, outlined by the shirt she wore. He licked his lips.

Bile rose in her throat again.

"You could persuade me to spare his life."

Rhys struggled as best he could against the leather bonds that held his wrists together behind his back; he forced his mind to ignore the pain from his side and arm in an effort to free himself. Hate, as cold as ice, made him want to kill this man. That he could not offer his protection to his wife, that he was forced to sit and watch, chilled him.

"Let Rhys go, now," Tory said in a soft voice.

"After," Squire promised.

"It's me you want, not him."

"That's true," Squire said, working closer to his goal. "But he has to witness your humiliation. Don't you understand?" he asked, his voice filled with a sick pleading. "He has to see you for the slut that you are. He has to know that the Reitenauers are no different from anyone else. Your pa wasn't any different. He bled when I shot him, just like any man. All his power didn't save him then." His eyes glittered with pure malevolence.

Suddenly, the sound of gunfire exploded around them.

Squire's attention was distracted. He turned toward the sound and came face to face with Martha, standing there, her hand raised. In it she held Tory's knife, which she brought straight down, slicing into Squire's throat. Blood spurted out in a rush as she hit her target and dragged the knife across his flesh.

The gun fell to the floor as Talbot Squire

tumbled over, astonishment quickly wiping the look of smugness off his face.

Tory retrieved the small knife that she'd secured in her knee-high moccasin and sliced through Rhys's bonds with quick strokes.

When his hands were finally freed, Rhys slipped them around Tory's waist and pulled her close. His mouth covered hers in a kiss so intense both felt it deep in their bones. It held love, forgiveness, hope, and passion. It was a promise and a rebirth.

They broke apart, gray gaze locked with blue. Anything was possible, each seemed to say, as long as they had love.

Martha, her white dress splashed with her husband's blood, stood there, staring down at him. Her hands hung limply at her sides.

Tory gave the knife to Rhys, who went to release Rafe. Tory went to Martha, whose face was pale, but somehow younger.

"I couldn't let him hurt my boy any longer," Martha said, her eyes pleading for understanding, her voice rusty from lack of use. "He would have finally killed Rafe. I couldn't let him do that. I couldn't," Martha cried.

Tory put her arms around the other woman, feeling the tension, sensing the frailty. "Of course you couldn't Martha. You saved all our lives," Tory said.

"Mama," Rafe spoke quietly, his mouth grim. His eyes, however, were gentle as they looked upon his mother, finally, ironically, returned to the land of the living through an act of death.

Martha grabbed Rafe and threw her arms around the boy. "Forgive me," she said through her tears.

The shooting was closer now, as was the smell of smoke.

"What's happening?" Rhys asked as he headed for the window. When he looked out, he saw that the barn was ablaze and men were scrambling for cover as a large contingent of men on horseback rode in, guns blasting. He recognized many of the riders from the Encantadora, as well as several from Rancho Montenegro. It was all over within minutes.

Tory joined him, a confident smile on her face. "Do you remember the story of the Trojan horse?" she whispered.

Rhys cocked his head to one side and flashed Tory a charming smile. "By Christ, my love, you are a wonder."

"Yes, I am rather, aren't I?" she agreed, slipping into her best imitation of his posh accent.

Oh God, she thought, it was good to be alive and to be loved. Briefly, she touched the rough bandage on Rhys's arm. "I'm sorry," she managed to say, her voice suddenly sad.

Rhys reached out one hand and cupped her chin. "Don't think about it, my love. I understand why you did what you did. Just push it to the past, where it belongs."

Tory's hand sought Rhys's, their fingers intertwining in strength. "Let's get out of here, she said.

They stepped around the now lifeless body of Talbot Squire.

Before Tory could bend to retrieve her knife, Rafe was there, pulling it free. He casually wiped it clean on Squire's coat, then handed it to Tory. As he stood up, the boy spat on the dead man's face. "I wish that it had been me that killed him," he said, his voice low and dark.

Tory paused, glancing once more at Martha. "You and your mother are coming with us," she announced. "Your home will be the Encantadora for as long as you wish."

When they all walked outside, they were greeted by the sight of numerous men on horseback.

"It's all done, Miss Tory," Marsh declared, still seated on his horse.

"What about our losses?" Tory asked.

"One man dead, four wounded," he replied, pleased that the raid had gone so well. When she'd first proposed her plan, Marsh hadn't been sure. Under his thick moustache, he allowed himself a rare smile. "Where's Squire?"

"Dead," Tory stated.

"So we're ready to ride back?"

"Just one more thing," Tory said.

Marsh nodded his head in understanding. "I'll see to it."

"Good." She turned to Rafe and Martha. "Are you both well enough to sit a horse?"

Rafe nodded. "We'll make it, Miss Reitenauer," he said, stubborn pride rising to the fore.

"Of course you will," Tory assured him. But please, call me Tory." She glanced at her husband. "And you?" she asked of Rhys.

Rhys touched Tory's cheek with one finger, lingering on the soft flesh. "Come love, let's go home."

Epilogue

London: Christmas 1878

The house was finally quiet. All the guests had long since left.

"Will there be anything else you require, my lord?" Kinsenning asked.

Rhys, who was busy pouring a brandy into a cut-crystal snifter, responded, "No, that will be all, I think." He handed the drink to his wife, who was adding finishing touches to several of the gaily wrapped boxes beneath the tree.

"Then I wish you and the countess"—he paused as the clock chimed one o'clock—"a very happy Christmas."

Victoria Reitenauer Fitzgerald Buchanan, Countess of Derran, raised her head from her task and said, "Happy Christmas to you, Kinsenning."

The butler departed and left the couple alone.

"The party went well, don't you think?" she asked as Rhys slipped his arm about her waist, leading her to the couch.

"Very well, indeed, my love," he pronounced.

She watched as he made certain that the door was securely bolted before returning to her side.

He shrugged off his elegant velvet jacket, tossing it casually to the couch. Next, he unbuttoned the patterned silk waistcoat, adding it to the jacket.

A smile of hungry anticipation curved Tory's mouth as she reached behind her and pulled out the jewelled pins that held her hair in place. She shook her head, letting the mass tumble free. Standing up, she stepped out of her shoes. "I think even your mother is resigned to our marriage."

"She could be nothing *but* resigned. You've given her a very handsome grandson and made her son most happy indeed."

Tory turned her back to her husband, pushing aside her hair so that he could play the lady's maid and unhook her gown.

His mouth sent shivers along her spine as he kissed her shoulders and back. He pushed the gown down her arms, his hands caressing all the while, helping her step from the silken heap it made.

Tory loved the feel of his hands on her flesh. They created magic wherever they touched.

She turned around and waited while Rhys

fetched something from behind the tree.

"Open it," he commanded softly, handing her a huge box.

She did so, uncovering a large quilt of deepest blue. Tory removed it, shaking it out to its full length, noting the cream-colored single star in the middle. She laid it on the floor in front of the fireplace. Slowly, she divested herself of her remaining clothing, then knelt on the quilt.

Rhys quickly stripped off his trousers and shirt, joining her.

Tory slid her hands through the thick mane of his long black hair and offered her mouth to his.

The fire flooded between them, seducing and enchanting until it was impossible to tell where one began and the other left off. Each willingly surrendered to the overpowering storm.

Later, wrapped in each other's arms, they shared the almost forgotten snifter of brandy.

"I've enjoyed our visit to your country, Rhys. Travis will be spoiled by the time we return to the Encantadora."

Rhys smiled at the thought of his son, asleep upstairs in his old nursery. How the servants had fussed when he introduced them to his child. Travis was never without someone doting on him. His mother and sister had adored his son on sight, as had Anne when she came to visit.

He explained to Tory that Anne had left her card while they were visiting his estate in Dorset, indicating that she wished to call on

413

them at their return to London. Tory agreed and invited Anne to join them for a small family supper. Rhys was pleased that the two women got along so well, finding other things besides him in common. It had helped, he thought, that Anne was much in love with her younger man, whose Irish charm was not lost on Tory.

"Have you spoken to your mother about Gillie's coming with us when we go back?"

Rhys sighed, his hand reaching out to cup the weight of Tory's breast, one finger teasing the nipple. It was heavy with milk, as she was still nursing their son. "I've told her that I want Gillian to spend some time with us at the ranch."

"Has she accepted it?"

"She has to, as I am Gillie's legal guardian." He'd missed his little sister and was thrilled when Tory suggested that Gillian spend time with them.

"She'll be good company for Rafe," Tory stated, running her hand along Rhys's chest, glad that she had persuaded the boy to accompany them on their trip to London. Though Rafe was slow to smile, this trip had given him pleasure, Tory was sure of that.

"Yes," Rhys said, "already Gillie has responded to him as if he were another of her injured animals."

Tory trailed her hand along the lean line of Rhys's chest, following with her mouth. She heard his hastily drawn breath and smiled. Then a thought struck her.

"Rhys, do you mind terribly leaving your homeland once again?"

Rhys shifted so that they were both sitting up, facing each other. He slipped his hands through the tangled mass of her hair, bringing her closer. "I love you, Tory," he said, his voice husky with passion and truth. "I made my choice happily. Yes," he admitted, "I loved being able to return to London, especially now that I could show you and our son off to my family and friends. But I do miss the ranch, and our friends there.

"Believe me when I say that there will be no regrets on my part when we leave after the New Year."

Tory showered kisses across his face, suddenly eager to have Rhys once again buried deeply in her flesh.

How far they'd both come since first agreeing to the bargain. Now, the bargain be damned, she thought, for love had given them something better: its own special enchantment that sealed their fates forever, together.

SPECIAL SNEAK PREVIEW!

PROUD PILLARS RISING

By Ana Leigh

"Ana Leigh's historical romances always captivate readers!"

—*Romantic Times*

Enjoy a selection from Ana Leigh's fabulous new historical romance, Proud Pillars Rising.

Fascinated by tales of the Wild West, Margaret Collingswood was thrilled to learn that she had inherited a ranch in the Dakota Territory from the father she'd never known. Traveling to Deadwood with her mother, stepfather, and sister, she longed to break away from the restraints imposed by her all too proper family . . . to discover real-life adventure . . . to finally meet the rugged Western hero she'd always dreamed of. . . .

**ON SALE IN DECEMBER—
AT BOOKSTORES AND NEWSTANDS
EVERYWHERE**

"Margaret, I insist you wear a dress," Katherine Collingswood demanded the following morning.

Maggie paused, jeans in hand. "But why do—"

"And I will not tolerate an argument," Katherine asserted. "My dear child, you were born a girl. It's high time you begin dressing and acting like one."

Diane's mouth curved into a vain smile. "What would be the purpose, Mother? She would still have a boy's haircut." She pulled a hair brush through her own long, golden strands. "Will you help me pin my hair, Mother?"

When Katherine turned away and began to

fuss with her younger daughter's curls, Maggie quickly slipped into her jeans and boots. "I'll be with Father." She sped from the room before her mother could voice any further objection.

Taylor Collingswood was not alone when Maggie paused in the door of the dining room. He rose to his feet and waved to her. "Here's Margaret now."

The man to whom Taylor spoke stood up and stared with curiosity at Maggie as she approached the table. Although he was as tall as Taylor, his body was heavier and more muscular. He had a thick thatch of gray hair, and bushy eyebrows dominated his face. Maggie guessed the man to be in his late fifties.

"Margaret, this gentleman is William Godfrey."

"How do you do, sir," Maggie said politely, feeling uncomfortable under the man's continued scrutiny.

"The pleasure is mine, Miss Harris . . . ah, Miss Collingswood."

"Mr. Godfrey is a local banker, dear," Taylor added as he drew a chair for her to be seated.

Maggie smiled nervously at the man, and after an awkward silence, Godfrey commented, "Your father and I were close friends, Miss Collingswood. Forgive me for staring, but you bear a remarkable resemblance to him."

Maggie had never seen a picture of her father. Intrigued, her interest in this man perked up considerably.

"I hope your trip to Deadwood was a pleasant one," Godfrey commented.

"Didn't Father tell you our stage got held up yesterday?"

"Good grief!" Godfrey exclaimed. "I hope no one was injured."

Taylor smiled cordially. "No, none of us are worse for the experience, and we even recovered all our valuables."

The conversation ended abruptly with the appearance of Katherine and Diane. As soon as Taylor dispensed introductions, William Godfrey donned his Stetson and shook hands with Taylor. "I will return shortly with a carriage to transport you and your trunks to Sam's ranch."

"A ranch! My father had a ranch?" Maggie's eyes gleamed with the excitement of this unexpected discovery, the fulfillment of her longtime dream—a ranch.

Godfrey nodded. "A horse ranch. Sam Harris ran the best horseflesh in the state." He paused momentarily and smiled down at Margaret. "I think you'll like the Lazy H, Maggie."

"My daughter's name is Margaret, Mr. Godfrey," Katherine sharply reminded him. "Sam Harris called her Maggie, that hideous name, to aggravate me."

"My apologies, Mrs. Collingswood."

Godfrey nodded politely. "Ladies, enjoy your breakfast."

Katherine cast a critical glance at the back of the departing banker. "He certainly doesn't look like any banker I've ever met, Taylor. And I think he was much too familiar with Margaret."

In an effort to appease her, Taylor patted Katherine's hand. "It was improper, Katherine, but Mr. Godfrey was a close friend of Sam Harris. Perhaps your late husband often spoke of Margaret with him."

"Well, he still had no business addressing Margaret so familiarly. And in public, too." She swung her disapproving glance toward her eldest daughter. "Of course, Margaret, your manner of dress invites such brash informality."

Maggie was only half listening to her mother's complaints. She had heard them often enough to recite the lamentations from memory. Maggie had to admit her mother might be right about William Godfrey. The way he stared at her was strange. And why would he call her Maggie? Or could Taylor be right? Possibly, Sam Harris *had* spoken of her so often to his friend that the nickname just slipped naturally through William Godfrey's lips. Maggie smiled with pleasure. Perhaps her father had cared for her, after all.

Anxiously awaiting the banker's return, Maggie barely touched her food. Her eyes remained riveted on the window. She jumped to her feet as soon as she saw William Godfrey approach in a shay. By the time they joined him outside the hostelry, Godfrey had a buckboard pulled up behind the carriage. "I'll drive the buckboard if you can handle the shay, Mr. Collingswood."

Taylor eyed the pair of spirited-looking black horses harnessed to the rig. "I don't see why not," he replied.

When the trunks had been loaded, Katherine and Diane seated themselves under the carriage's canopy, but Maggie climbed up onto the spring seat of the buckboard. With a flick of the reins, the wagon pulled away. Taylor followed behind with the shay.

Casting a grin at Maggie, Godfrey commented, "I can see what Sam meant. He told me you have a lot of mettle."

Her father's neglect of her still struck a sensitive nerve in Margaret Collingswood. "How would he know? He never knew me."

Her belligerent tone caused Godfrey to glance over at the girl. The man could see a lot of Sam Harris in the resentful expression on her face. She was a scrapper. This wasn't going to be as easy as he had hoped.

"I guess Sam figured a daughter of his couldn't be any other way," Godfrey responded lightly in reply to her feisty comment.

"Only he didn't think I was worth the effort to find out for himself, did he?"

Maggie fell into a brooding silence the rest

of the way to the ranch, asking only an occasional question about the sights. After an hour's ride, they reached the ranch.

Her expectations had not prepared her for the size of the ranch house. Maggie's eyes widened in amazement when she spied the long, double-winged log house stretched out before them. "It's . . . so big," she stammered.

"Sam added another wing just before . . . he left," Godfrey said slowly.

A small building, which appeared to be a smokehouse, stood near a large barn and the bunkhouse. Several horses romped in a mammoth corral several hundred yards from the main house.

Katherine Collingswood, just as astounded, gushed forth. "This all belonged to Sam?" she gasped as her husband assisted her out of the carriage.

William Godfrey appeared to be well-known to the household staff. An Oriental servant opened the door, nodded politely to the banker, and after a few whispered instructions, scurried off.

Maggie loved the interior of the house on first sight. Roomy and masculine, a stone fireplace occupied one complete wall, and a long dining table framed by a dozen chairs stood at the other end of the large room. Several leather sofas and chairs were dispersed throughout.

Braided, oval-shaped rugs, scattered over a

hardwood floor, which showed signs of a recent polishing with beeswax, added additional warmth.

William Godfrey motioned for them to sit down, then seated himself behind a large oak desk.

However, Maggie, attracted to a painting of an Indian hanging above the fireplace, walked over to have a closer look. The Indian's hair hung to his shoulders, and two eagle feathers dangled from a plait at the side of his strong, square jaw. The artist had captured wisdom in the dark eyes which seemed to focus on her, penetrating her very soul. Mesmerized, Maggie stared at the face in the painting.

"He's magnificent," she murmured. "Who is he?"

William Godfrey glanced up at the portrait. "Screaming Eagle. An Oglala chieftain."

"An Oglala?" Maggie asked.

"The Oglalas are a tribe of Dakota Sioux," Godfrey added as she returned her attention to the portrait.

The reappearance of the servant with a coffee tray interrupted the discussion. Godfrey quickly offered a cup to Katherine, then added a generous measure of whiskey to Taylor's cup, as well as to his own.

Unable to withdraw her gaze, Maggie remained entranced by the dignified face in the portrait.

William Godfrey settled down behind the desk and took a deep draught of the liquid.

"The ranch house is spacious, and I'm confident all of you will find it much more comfortable than the hotel," he declared. "I regret, however, you'll have to—" Suddenly, the words died in his throat, and the banker rose to his feet, his face creased in surprise.

All eyes shifted to the object of his attention. Maggie spun around, then gasped with pleasure at the sight of Dakota MacDonald framed in the doorway.

"Dakota!" Godfrey exclaimed.

"What in heaven's name is *he* doing here?" Katherine disparaged.

Ignoring her boorishness, Godfrey crossed to the door and shook hands with Dakota. Then forsaking formality, he pulled the younger man into his arms and hugged him. "When did you get back, son?"

"Last night," Dakota said succinctly.

Smiling sadly, Godfrey stepped back. "I can't tell you how badly I feel about Sam's . . ." His eyes shifted downward, unable to meet Dakota's pain-wracked stare. "He was my best friend."

"How did it happen, Will?" A deep huskiness edged the younger man's voice. "Yen Ching said you were with Sam when the accident happened."

Godfrey nodded. "Sam spied a herd of wild horses on the northern slope of Twin Buttes and took off after one of 'em. His horse stepped into a chuckhole and stumbled. They both went over the edge of the bluff."

"Was he riding Diablo?"

Godfrey nodded.

Dakota shook his head. "Can't understand it. That black of his was as sure-footed as a mule."

Katherine Collingswood's frigid voice shattered the exchange of grief. "Mr. Godfrey, may I ask why this . . . person . . . is being offered an explanation when my daughter and I are the two people directly affected by Mr. Harris's death?"

Anger flashed temporarily in Godfrey's eyes as he turned to the woman. "I beg your pardon, Mrs. Collingswood, forgive my oversight. This is Dakota MacDonald. Sam Harris's other heir."

"Other heir!" Katherine appeared to be on the verge of swooning. She drew out a handkerchief and began to fan and dab at her brow with the dainty piece of lacy linen. "Are you saying Sam fathered this . . . half-breed?"

Maggie was perplexed. She had heard the Army colonel refer to Dakota's father as a trapper, but Taylor had told her Sam Harris had been a soldier in the Army.

Her gaze lingered on Dakota. If, in truth, this man was her brother, she could understand why she had felt such empathy for him from the first moment she saw him.

"I don't believe this . . . Indian . . . is Margaret's brother." Katherine fired another insult.

Maggie's heart ached for Dakota MacDonald. To learn of his father's death was a tragic homecoming for the soldier, and her mother's insensitivity to his grief was unforgivable.

Godfrey cleared up the confusion as he continued, "Madam, will you let me finish, please? Dakota's father was a Scottish trapper by the name of Angus MacDonald, and his mother, a Sioux Indian named White Dove. Seventeen years ago, they found Sam severely wounded and they nursed him back to health. The next year, when Angus and White Dove were killed, Sam took their boy, Dakota, and raised him as his own."

Dakota remained unflinching as he listened to Godfrey's explanation. Despite the inscrutable expression on the half-breed's face, Maggie sensed Dakota's scorn for these people who cared nothing about Sam's death, much less that of his parents. Sam's fortune had been their only purpose for coming to Deadwood.

Dakota's gaze seanned the room and came to rest on her. With a sickening awareness, Maggie realized his contempt included her. She shook her head in denial. *No. It's not true. I'm not like them*, she silently pleaded.

For a few breathless seconds, Dakota's gaze remained fixed on Maggie, then he turned his head away.

Godfrey called out to Dakota who had moved to depart. "Dakota, come in and sit down. Sam's will concerns you, too."

"I've got no claim on anything of Sam's," Dakota said. "I'll get my gear and clear out."

"I wholeheartedly concur with your decision, Mr. MacDonald," Katherine interjected, her face twisted in contempt.

Godfrey threw the woman an exasperated look. "Please stay, Dakota. Sam wanted it this way." He withdrew an envelope from his briefcase. "Sam instructed me to give this to you."

Reluctantly, Dakota walked over and accepted the sealed document. Maggie noticed the envelope was identical to the one she had received from Sam Harris.

Godfrey extracted another paper from his case. "Now that both heirs are present, I'll deliver the will." He cleared his throat nervously and began to read aloud.

"I, Samuel Houston Harris, being of sound mind, do hereby declare this document to be my last will and testament.

"To my daughter, Margaret Ann Harris, also known as Margaret Ann Collingswood, and to my ward, Dakota MacDonald, I leave my ranch, the Lazy H, and all possessions thereon.

"Furthermore, Margaret Harris and Dakota MacDonald are to share equally in the considerable fortune I have amassed in recent years due to a gold strike and shrewd investments. Each heir has been given one half of the map that will direct them to the site of the buried fortune. Should Maggie and Dakota seek the fortune together, I have no doubt they will experience heretofore undreamed of treasure.

"However, if one party chooses not to seek the fortune, then the entire inheritance, including the Lazy H, reverts to the other heir.

"In the event neither heir wishes to seek the fortune, then the Lazy H and all of my buried wealth reverts to my trusted colleague and executor, William Godfrey."

"Absurd. It cannot be!" Katherine screamed. Godfrey paused momentarily to glower disapprovingly over the top of the document.

Utterly astonished, Maggie looked at Dakota whose face showed no emotion. His eyes stared far off into space as if he had not heard a word. In truth, the reading of Sam's will disgusted him, and his inheritance was of no significance to him. Dakota's thoughts were concentrated solely on Sam, his father and friend gone forever.

Godfrey continued to read.

"To my beloved wife, Katherine Harris, and former commanding officer, Taylor Collingswood, I leave my forgiveness—

along with two return tickets to Washington D.C.

"Any interference on the part of Katherine or Taylor to prevent my heirs from receiving their inheritance will result in the release of a document which will be politically and socially damaging to Mrs. Harris and Mr. Collingswood.

"And now, having disposed of my earthly possessions, I shall muse from aloft on angels, coyotes and 'just desserts.' Samuel Houston Harris."

"Why, that's blackmail," Taylor blustered.

"How dare that hypocritical reprobate threaten us," Katherine added, her face pinched with anger. "Insanity! Just the sort of thing I'd expect from Sam Harris. He always had a flair for the dramatic," Katherine ranted. "Taylor, we'll hire a lawyer from the East to have this ridiculous document declared invalid."

The banker ignored her outburst and peered across the desk at Maggie and Dakota. "Are the conditions of the will clear to both of you? If either of you refuses to honor Sam's first request, the ranch reverts to the other. If both of you refuse the last request, the fortune reverts to me."

Dakota leaned back and grinned. "Sam must have been high on coyote juice when he concocted this one."

"He was as sober as a judge," Godfrey denied. "The will is legal and cannot be nullified."

By this time, Taylor Collingswood had regained his composure. "I'm inclined to agree with my wife, Mr. Godfrey. The will is too bizarre to be taken seriously."

Katherine rose to her feet and began to pace the floor. "I was the wife of Sam Harris at the time of his death. Legally, his wealth should revert to me."

Diane, who had uttered barely a word since their arrival, spoke out to contradict her mother. "How could you have been Mr. Harris's wife when you're married to my father?"

Irritated, Katherine turned on her daughter. "Just hush, Diane. This doesn't concern you."

The young girl broke into sobs. "It does too concern me if you and Father aren't married. That makes me a bas . . . illegitimate."

Taylor rushed to embrace his daughter. "Now, now, honey, this is all a mistake. Of course, your mother and I are legally married." However, he failed to confess to the distressed girl that the remarriage had transpired the day before they had departed for the Dakota Territory.

Maggie and Dakota were forgotten in the uproar of Katherine's shouting, Diane's bawling, and Taylor's officiousness, along with William Godfrey's efforts to placate them all. The whole situation had become too overwhelming for Maggie to comprehend. She glanced at Dakota who had just opened the envelope and was studying a jagged piece of map.

She felt torn between crying and screaming. The whole affair was becoming a circus. Maggie surmised that Sam Harris must be laughing at all of them from his grave. Unable to bear the scene another moment, she dashed from the room.

Maggie raced across the yard to the corral. Breathless, she stopped by the fence and stared for several moments through unseeing eyes at the horses confined within the area.

"Are they always like that, kid?"

Startled, she looked up to discover Dakota MacDonald beside her, casually chewing on a piece of straw. Maggie, embarrassed by her family's actions, remained loyal to them and rallied to their defense. She raised her eyes with belligerent regard. "The trip has been very exhausting for my family, Mr. MacDonald. Being jostled about in a coach and threatened at gunpoint has been a shattering experience for us." Maggie purposefully included herself as one of them and lifted her head proudly. "I think we are conducting ourselves admirably, Mr. MacDonald."

Dakota hooked a booted foot over a rung of the fence. "Well, if you don't rein up, you're all gonna choke on each other's dust."

A lengthy silence ensued. Maggie stole several sideward glances at Dakota as he stared impassively at the grazing horses. She sensed he had said his piece and had put the matter out of his mind. Finally, she broached the subject foremost in her thoughts. "What do you intend to do?"

Dakota slowly straightened his tall frame.

"Ride out to the north range."

"I mean what do you intend to do about Sam Harris's will?"

Dakota tossed aside the stalk of straw he was chewing. "Do about it? I've half a mind to go on a treasure hunt." The faint glimmer in his eyes revealed a side to his nature Maggie never suspected. Dakota MacDonald had a sense of humor.

Maggie squared her shoulders, cocked her hat, and thrust up a delicate, but determined, chin. "Well, if you do, you can bet your britches, Mr. Dakota MacDonald, I'm going with you."

For several seconds Dakota stared down at Maggie, torn between putting her over his knee or shaking the pesky girl until her brain rattled. Instead, he turned and headed toward the stable.

Determined not to be put off, Maggie followed, running to keep up with his rapid strides. "Remember, Mr. MacDonald, I have the other part of the map."

Dakota stopped and glowered down at her. "You know, kid, you're a real pain in the ass."

Maggie, not easily thwarted, returned the fire. "Please stop calling me 'kid.' Kids are baby goats. And another thing, watch your language in the presence of a lady."

"Lady? That's a laugh. Get smart, kid, take

some . . . lady lessons . . . from your older sister."

Older sister! Did he actually believe simpering, whiny Diane was older than she? Maggie thought, astonished. Just because Diane was prettier and dressed herself up like a peacock out for a Sunday stroll didn't make her sister smarter. *Oh, men are so . . . dumb!* How could she have thought he would be different?

Diplomacy was not one of Margaret Collingswood's redeeming qualities. Hands on hips, her emerald eyes flashed as her temper flared. "I want you to know I happen to be eighteen years old. If you'd bother to look beyond Diane's blond hair and fluttering eyes, you'd realize I'm two years older and ten times smarter than my sister. Boy, I declare, nothing that walks or crawls on this earth is as stupid as a man."

"That why do you run around dressed like one?" Dakota strode away, leaving Maggie sputtering for a retort.

Dakota could hardly believe the kid was eighteen; he had reckoned fourteen, fifteen at the most. But then, a gal dressed as a boy with most of her face hidden under the brim of a hat, well, her age would be anybody's guess.

By the time Maggie caught up with him, Dakota had already gone into the stable and had begun to saddle a horse. "Just where are you going?" she demanded to the broad width of his shoulders.

Dakota gritted his teeth, swung the saddle

over the horse's back, and turned around. He shoved his hat back on his forehead and glared down at her. "Let's get something squared away. I ain't planning on spending the next six months picking your straw out of my hair. So just ride wide of me, kid . . . ah, *lady*."

Maggie understood the reason for his hostility. He had angered her and she had reacted as nastily as her mother. Feeling contrite, Maggie offered an apology. "I'm sorry, Dakota. I didn't mean to crowd you. I just want us to be friends." She turned and walked toward the house.

As he cinched the saddle girth, Dakota lifted his head and watched Maggie walk away. The kid looked pathetic, the picture of dejection. He could not understand why in hell he should feel guilty, but with a grimace of self-reproach, he called out to her. "Hey, kid."

Maggie stopped and turned her head.

"I'm heading up to the north range. Want to ride along?"

She grinned broadly. "Sure." Maggie ran back to the stable.

"Get me the roan mare. I'll saddle her for you."

Maggie looked helplessly at several horses in nearby stalls and wondered which one was the roan mare. Dakota eyed her quizzically. "You *can* ride?"

Unflinchingly, she answered, "Of course. I

just have trouble telling a roan mare from a . . ."—her mind groped desperately for a suitable word—". . . stallion."

Dakota grinned to himself and swallowed the obvious bawdy response. "The one in the last stall."

Maggie approached the tawny-colored horse, relieved to see the mare didn't appear as tall and formidable as the horse she had ridden in Washington. "We're going to be great friends, aren't we?" she whispered.

The mare snorted and regarded her through large black eyes. Maggie's quandary bordered on desperation. She did so want to ride with Dakota but would the horse be of the same mind?

Gingerly, she reached out to pat the animal. When the mare accepted the fondling, Maggie grew bolder. Soon she had forgotten her purpose for approaching the animal and stroked the horse with both hands while cooing affectionately in the mare's ear.

"You planning on riding that horse or just talking it to sleep?" Dakota asked, suddenly appearing beside her.

"She's so beautiful," Maggie enthused, stepping aside so Dakota could saddle the mare. "What's her name?"

"Last time I knew, she didn't have one."

"May I call her Tiger?" Maggie asked.

"Call her anything you want," Dakota said, shrugging his shoulders. "Sounds more like a cat than a horse, though," he added.

Maggie pressed her cheek against the horse. "I know, but she's the color of a big, tawny cat."

Dakota led the two horses out of the stable and handed Maggie the mare's reins. Her mind raced as she tried to recall the instructions in the textbook. Stand close to the horse . . . Face its tail . . . Gather all reins in the left hand . . . Grab a handful of withers . . . She cast her eyes heavenward and said a quick, silent prayer. With a show of bravado, she put her foot in the stirrup and swung herself onto the horse.

"Let me lengthen those stirrups," Dakota said. "Your legs are longer than I thought."

While he lowered each strap, Maggie adjusted to the feel of being in the saddle. She wished she would have had time for another riding lesson before coming to Deadwood. One lesson was not enough to give a person confidence. However, this time the ground did not appear to be so far away. When Dakota finished, Maggie grasped the reins. *Don't jerk them*, she warned herself. She planted each foot firmly in a stirrup and lightly pressed her knees into the horse.

To Maggie's immense relief, the horse stepped forward.

Fortunately, the terrain prevented any fast galloping. Within a short time, she found herself relaxing, and the thousand fluttering butterflies in her chest and stomach settled down.

Maggie became enthralled with the spectacular scenery. Even Dakota's silence did not disturb her. She felt a sense of companionship as they rode side by side.

When he finally reined up and climbed off his horse, Maggie remained in the saddle, watching intently as Dakota got down on bended knee to study the ground.

Dakota stood up and walked over to the edge of the butte. For several moments he stared down at the steep drop. "This is where it happened," he said somberly.

Maggie knew he was referring to Sam Harris's accident. She dismounted awkwardly and moved beside him. Scattered brush and trees dotted the steep sides of the declivity that ended in a dry gulch several hundred feet below.

Directly opposite and at a deceptively close distance, since the span gaped too wide for man or animal to leap, stood the face of another butte, similar in height and width. Buffeted by freezing blasts of the north wind sweeping across from Canada, the vegetation grew less dense there than on the twin slope.

Maggie stared down solemnly at the gulch between the buttes. A pall hung over the site; not a bird chirped nor a leaf stirred. The throb of her heartbeat seemed to clamor in her ears. Sadly, she turned away.

Dakota tied the horses' reins to nearby shrubs and grabbed a rope attached to his saddle.

"What are you going to do?" Maggie asked at the sight of his grim, determined face.

"I'm going down there."

"You mean climb down? Isn't there a way of approaching from below?"

Dakota shook his head. "Not from this side. We'd have to ride for hours to skirt the bluff." As he talked, Dakota tied the rope firmly to a tree. "I won't be gone long. I just have to drop about fifty feet, then I can make it to the bottom on foot."

Maggie was astonished. "You mean you've done this before?" She walked over for another look at the steep drop.

Dakota pulled his rifle out of the scabbard on his saddle. "Can you handle a rifle?"

Maggie shook her head.

He proceeded to show her how to cock the gun. "If you have a problem, point it in the air and pull the trigger to signal me."

Surprised at the weight of the gun, Maggie cocked the gun once and gave a hesitant response. "All right . . . I understand." Maggie felt uncomfortable being left alone. She had an uneasy feeling about the place, and the thousand butterflies began to flutter in her stomach again.

She held the rifle firmly as she watched Dakota climb over the side of the bluff and lower himself down the rope. When he reached the end, he grabbed a sapling and cautiously began a zigzag course from scrub to tree until he reached the bottom.

"Heck, it doesn't look hard at all," Maggie reasoned aloud. "He even went down standing up." That thought was all the incentive she needed to follow him. Laying the rifle on the ground, and without hesitation, she lowered herself over the side.